William M. (William Mumford) Baker

Carter Quarterman

A Novel

William M. (William Mumford) Baker

Carter Quarterman
A Novel

ISBN/EAN: 9783337030933

Printed in Europe, USA, Canada, Australia, Japan

Cover: Foto ©Andreas Hilbeck / pixelio.de

More available books at **www.hansebooks.com**

CARTER QUARTERMAN.

A Novel.

By WILLIAM M. BAKER,

AUTHOR OF

"INSIDE," "THE NEW TIMOTHY," "MOSE EVANS," "A GOOD YEAR," &c.

> "My boast is, not that I deduce my birth
> From loins enthroned, and rulers of the earth;
> But higher far my proud pretensions rise—
> The son of parents past into the skies."

ILLUSTRATED BY ELIAS J. WHITNEY.

NEW YORK:

HARPER & BROTHERS, PUBLISHERS,

FRANKLIN SQUARE.

1876.

TO

ANNIE E. BAKER:

YOU ARE,

MY DEAR CHILD,

SO MUCH LIKE YOUR

GRANDMOTHER, IN HER LACE

RUFF, ABOVE OUR FIRESIDE, AND SO VERY

MUCH MORE LIKE YOUR OWN MOTHER BESIDE IT,

THAT, WITH MY THREEFOLD LOVE TO ALL OF YOU IN YOUR

ONE DEAR SELF, I CAN DO NO LESS THAN DEDI-

CATE TO YOU THIS LITTLE VOLUME. IF

ANY HARM COMES TO YOU IT WILL

NOT BE FROM INDULGING

IN FICTION WHILE

READING IT.

YOUR LOVING FATHER.

ILLUSTRATIONS.

CARTER QUARTERMAN.

CHAPTER I.

MY name is Carter Quarterman. It is the story of my own life which I am going to tell. And if you should think this narrative at all slow and dull at the outset, be assured that, as it gains momentum, it will be more swift and eventful. Certainly to me, seated to-day as by the roadside and out of breath, it has been rapid and stirring enough! And as it is my *own* story, I trust you will kindly allow me to tell it in my own way.

My name is Carter Quarterman: Carter because my mother was of the old Carter family of Virginia, Quarterman being, as I will explain in a moment, the dynastic name of an equally old family of Georgia. The original Carter was the Rev. Archibald Carter, an Episcopal clergyman, who came to Virginia from England as a founder of the Established Church in America before independence in Church and State was invented, much less patented. The huge old mansion still standing in Virginia was the parsonage, and in a room held particularly sacred, once his study, you may see to-day, in a condition threadbare and dingy beyond words, the silk gown in which the Rev. Archibald used to rustle in those days beyond the Flood. There, too, is his certificate of ordination by the Bishop of London, with a seal hanging thereto almost as large as a soup-plate; while in an old and extremely long-legged red desk leaning up against the wall in the corner, tremulous with age, are heaps upon heaps of sermons. We will take out of it this yellow-parchment-bound old book, blow off the clouds of dust, and open its thick and ridgy pages. See, it is an account-book. Let us try and make out the meaning of the faded ink:

"To marrying John to Mary Green, yᵉ mayd brt per ship *Royal Lady* fr Engl'd, 10 lbs best Tobacco."

"To bury'g Henry Cardeass, yᵉ mercer, at yᵉ X roads, 8 lbs Tobacco."

"Pay'd Roger Dickyrson for Repayrs vp yᵉ manse by mak'g over this day to say'd R. Dickyrson, yᵉ African boy Aristarchus a valuation of £20."

Pages by the score of the like. That word "manse" reveals the fact that the Rev. Archibald Carter was a Scotchman; which explains, I suppose, his centrifugalism, if I may so speak, from prelacy, to be mentioned in a moment. No sensational daily, damp from the press to-day, is half so interesting to me as the autumnal mass of MSS. to which I refer. The only documents to compare with them in novelty would be, were the future as accessible as the past, those of the date, let us say, of about A.D. 2175.

He must have been a grand old soul, this Rev. Archibald Carter, so deeply in earnest in the grand old way for those souls around him, now gone with him to God. How often has my mother told me that, during certain months of the year, he would, every Saturday night as the clock struck twelve, disturb his wife by rolling and muttering in his sleep. Perfectly aware of what was coming, she would arise and light the candles and send for the older negroes, while she dressed; and then, the room filled with a wondering audience, this ancestor of mine, duly propped up in bed, in a state of somnambulism, would preach his sermon for next day, from text to application, closing with the benediction, and then sink into sweet sleep, while his congregation, often weeping, would withdraw. And the sermon was far more impressive than on Sabbath, delivered directly from the brain and the heart as it then was, whereas it was most formally read from a MS. in the pulpit, and he must have had powerful glasses to do it, the pages in the old desk being of the size of your palm and covered with almost microscopic writing; paper, I suppose, being very scarce and dear.

But those roistering younger sons, shipped over to Virginia from the Old Country to adorn the Church, must have been a hard, a very hard set. This great-great, exceedingly great, grandfather of mine could endure their ways at last no longer. Was it drinking, fox-hunting, gambling? Possibly worse. I never will know; but the Rev. Archibald Carter was compelled in conscience, and we know what that means in Scotch, to go over to the Presbyterians because of their conduct. He would tower somewhat more statue-like in the gallery of our ancestors if he could have stood it out to the end, an Episcopal divine in his surplice to the last gasp. I am sorry he did not, or could not; but I suppose he knew best.

Never mind about his son, Judge Archibald Carter. Beyond a peculiarly impressive bearing as he rode on horseback the circuits of his courts, I declare, as you will be relieved to hear, that I know little about him. There are two great paintings in the old homestead, one of three of the line of male ancestors, the other of the same number of females, all in such military rank that I did not wonder at the sabre-slashes all over them, administered by British dragoons during the Revolution. None more patriotic than the Carters in all Virginia, the old place raided upon with special hatred for that reason.

"You see, Carter," my mother would say, "your grandmother's mother had hidden all her cats in a closet under the steps when the family fled, some twenty of them in all. That closet was the only place locked, and the dragoons broke it open, sure of finding the family plate. It was partly their exasperation when the cats poured out which caused them to slash our pictures. They fired the mansion as they left, but the blacks waited until they were gone, and put out the flames. You are of good blood, my dear, and I spoke of plate; but I am obliged to tell you that, beyond the spoons and a cup or two, we had no silver. You know what an open house used to be kept in Virginia. The negroes were so wasteful, too, that, although we had plenty to eat and to wear, there was no money, or very little."

And then she would tell me, never ceasing to knit, knit, knit, as she did so, about her own father. He was a man by himself, such a person as makes an impression upon the mind forever, like a picture or a statue, very sharpened, personal, peculiar. He was away from home at Richmond, closing out his tobacco crop, in perfect health, when my mother was nine years old. One beautiful winter afternoon, as my dear mother has told me, at about the same hour of the day, I do suppose, a hundred times, she and her mother standing side by side, distinctly saw him whom they thought absent walking toward them from the front gate, as they stood in the yard admiring the setting of the sun. He had no hat on, and came up to them more slowly than was usual, with a specially grave and thoughtful manner. One or two of the negroes, in passing out to milk the cows, saw him distinctly. But, although they said, "How d'ye, Mass Archibald? Glad to see you back again," they noticed that he did not make his usual hearty reply; merely walked steadily up to his wife and daughter, and, as they exclaimed with gladness, and started forward to grasp and kiss him, he gazed lovingly, but with a peculiarly wistful expression, in their faces and vanished!

When I add that he had fallen dead at that very hour in the office of his Richmond merchant, you smile, and exclaim, "Oh, of course!" Yet my mother—and you will be satisfied before we are done with each other in reference to her—has often told me these as the simple facts of the case. She was no more certain of any thing else that ever befell her than she was of this; and it is far easier for me to believe in apparitions even than to fail of faith in her.

I shall have plenty to say about our old homestead during the temporary stay there of my mother and family when I was a boy. But so much for the present about the Carter half of my name. The Quarterman remainder thereof is soon told.

In the first part of the seventeenth century a body of men and women, of whom Richard Quarterman was a leading spirit, coming over in the good ship *John and Mary*, landed from England as a church, upon a certain specially inviting part of New England, building up thereafter, through the centuries of storms which are indispensable to oaks of all sorts, a town for that region and an influence for the whole world during all after-time. Fifty years after landing, a church was organized from among them, of picked people, which, headed again by a Richard Quarterman, son of the former, emigrated to South Carolina. Pausing there for a few years, as if merely to take breath, the same people removed, still as a church, to Central Georgia. And, really, it is wonderful how steady such blood, held true to itself within the channel of a church, is to its fountains. In 1774 this body of people, standing alone in a population of royalists, laid their determined grasp upon and lifted Georgia, as by the sheer force of superior strength, and placed it in line with the thirteen colonies against Great Britain; the State itself changing the name of their part of Georgia into Liberty County, in commemoration thereof, when the war was ended.

Within the last week I have taken a trip of two hundred and forty-four years. I began by standing among the graves of the Quartermans, sleeping, after exceedingly hard work, in regular line of gradation in the New England cemetery, every grave well weighted with rocks as a precaution against the wolves. The poetry of their tombstones is in strict keeping with the exceeding ugliness of the cherubim carved thereon. And I think no other precaution would have been needed against the wolves, had they but come in the daylight.

And yet cherubim and poetry were in harmony with the wilderness of those days, the climate, and the savage. We exclaim at the rigor of their religion. As well might their swords in such times have been lead or lath as that their faith should have been other than the iron and the blue steel it was. I began, I say, with the first Quarterman arrived in New England, and, coming down carefully from father to son, as upon the steps of their tombstones, I strode from the last of the line buried there to the first of them buried South, and so down the regular rows of my ancestors slumbering side by side in Georgia, until I reached the grave of my father's father, and sat down upon it and rested, satisfied.

No difficult matter that blood so similar as that of Carter and Quarterman should run at last into one. My father, Oglethorpe Quarterman, was at college within three miles of the Carter Homestead in Virginia; an awkward, freckled, sandy-haired, ruddy youth of the Georgia type. Nothing in the world quite so natural as that he should find out and fall desperately in love with pretty Agnes Carter at that hospitable old home; nothing more natural except that thus falling in love he should have given no rest to his soul, or to hers, until they were married. But I look up at my mother's portrait, hanging upon my wall while I write—as beautiful a woman, according to the light-built, elastic, high-spirited, Virginian type (the exact opposite of the Georgian ruddy robustness of my father), as heart could wish; and I am very far indeed from blaming him.

When I made the trip I spoke of, from the graves of New England to those in Georgia, I came back northward again by way of the Carter Homestead in Virginia. Giving myself to the work, I tried to repeople the old place with the throngs gathered to the marriage of my father and mother. All the ample yard around was crowded again with the vehicles and swarms of laughing negroes from adjacent plantations. Grave and very portly matrons, in black silks, and portentous combs projecting high above their heads, filled the parlors; their husbands, almost to a man thirty or fifty pounds less in avoirdupois than their wives, seated soberly beside them. Upon the porches, running, as all decent porches in the South do, entirely around the house, and broad enough for a highway, were bevies of girls, every soul of them in a white dress and a long bright-colored sash, and never a one of lovely bride far more composed than the radiant but exceedingly conscious groom.

Like every thing else, the service is longer and of a more substantial sort than that which is hurried through these days in time to catch the train, or the steamer leaving the wharf for Europe. As is supper also,

AMONG THE PEACHES.

them homely, or any thing like it. Standing in knots about the lawn, as near to the banisters of the porches as they dared, were pale fellow-students of the bridegroom from the neighboring college, mingled with sun-burned youths from the fields, mingled and yet separate. And, while a deep hush falls upon all, the ceremony is duly performed, the for it is a business not to be lightly completed: the partaking of the amazing supplies provided for twenty successive tables of guests—supplies, as for an army, of ham and chicken, turkey, tongue, and sausage; biscuit hot from the oven; preserves of all conceivable varieties; cake of every kind and grade and quantity, leaving fragments sufficient for the satisfaction afterward of every negro-cabin for miles around; not a black baby, nor toothless old aunty, nor bedridden old uncle, without his portion of the feast. An awful waste, possibly, yet not wholly unlike the waste complained of by some at another feast in another Southern land, which has passed away, as has the South of my father and mother's wedding-day.

I sat trying to recall the marriage, and all its music and laughter; but how utterly that, too, is passed away! My mother used to tell me of a walk she took with my father the afternoon before their wedding-day. It was in the orchard, and she would laugh and color and knit faster as she said,

"Your father was a student of theology, you know, Carter: he is as fine-looking doctor of divinity now as ever lived; then he was a tall, thin, freckled, awkward youth, although nine years older than I was. Ah me! but what a young and foolish girl I was; but oh, how happy! Would you believe it, Carter, that afternoon your father was so crazy with the idea of being actually married next day, that he insisted upon dancing a Georgia breakdown, such as he had seen the negroes dance at his home—insisted upon dancing it for me among the peaches fallen from the trees!"

She then went on to tell how old Aunt Chloe, coming to call them in to supper, had caught him at it.

"Aunt Chloe was your mammy, Carter, and she loved and cared for you a great deal more than I did," my mother said. "You know, I was back at home from Washington City when you were born, and again when you were nine years old."

2

"Yes," I replied, "I remember the last time I was there. Aunt Chloe took me with her one day when she was 'toting' their dinner to the field-hands. She plucked, in passing, a leaf from a tobacco-plant, and showed me the great green worm upon it, and—and—"

"Told you," my mother added for me, "how cruel masters made their poor slaves eat them, compelled them to live upon them. My mammy told me the same, Carter, and my mother's mammy before me. It is an old, old story, with not a word of truth in it. It is like your old story about Brother Wolf, and how he trapped Brother Rabbit with a tar baby, making him fasten himself to it by striking it with his paws—stories handed down for generations."

But let me go back once more to that wedding-day, and I will close this chapter. My mother used to tell (but not to me) how, bride and bridegroom, they knelt down side by side in their chamber the night of their wedding, and how fervently the young husband prayed for a special blessing upon them, his lips at her very ear, that she might be able to hear and join in the supplication in spite of the uproar within and without the house, of the good-byes and the laughter and the rattling of departing wheels—a fact, as we shall see, in exact keeping with the man unto the end.

There were five children of us, and born in the order in which I name them: Archibald, Habersham, the twins Virginia and Georgia, and myself, last and least, Carter Quarterman. All this is preliminary, and because I wanted you, dear reader, to know how I came by my name, of which I am very far from being ashamed.

CHAPTER II.

As I said before, you must kindly permit me to tell my own story in my own way. Allow me, then, to start with my earliest remembrance; you will find that I will journey more rapidly as I grow older.

I am not quite four years old. My father, Rev. Oglethorpe Quarterman, is pastor of a church in Washington City. Nothing very grand in that, for the capital is little more than a village, his church a new organization, his salary eight hundred dollars, six hours of every week-day spent by him writing in the Land-office, the three sermons for Sabbath prepared as he can. He does prepare them, however, for his church prospers greatly. One rainy Sabbath afternoon he replaces his sermon in his breast-pocket as he rises to preach; it is so hard to get time to write one, he will extemporize instead. Yet, hardly has he begun, before John Quincy Adams enters the door and walks down the aisle. Oh that he had kept to his elaborate preparation! As it is, he can only do the best he can. Far better, I have no doubt, than if he had used his MS.; for next day the President takes a pew, becomes thereafter a trustee of the church, and one of his warmest friends.

Allow me to place myself as if I were actually back again in that period of my life—were standing once more in my little shoes of that date. The moment I am back and only four years old again, I am seized with strong convulsions. Nothing more vivid to me than that. As I stand and watch the unpacking of a huge cedar chest, a cockroach runs up my bare flesh under my clothes. I shudder and almost scream, feeling it now. But it is over, and, still about the same age, I hold the pins in my mouth for my mother, as she arrays me in the enormous linen collar then worn by children. A pin is down my throat, and I am slapped on the back till it is out. Presto, change! And here I am in the White House, on a visit with my father to President Andrew Jackson. How vivid it all is! I dimly recall the usher as being Irish, but I actually see the old President this moment. He sits on my left, upon one side of the fire-place, my father to my right on the other, myself perched upon a chair between. The fire-place perplexes me; for I remember distinctly a particularly large and Presidential water-melon cooling in a marble basin of water on one side of the room, and my hopes all along that the General would cut it while we were there. I think the fire was because he was old; for this paper is not more perfectly before me than is that long, thin face, with the hollow temples and the hair standing up from the brow with the iron-like aspect of the whole man, worn and cold and white. I can see him take his cob-pipe from his mouth as, in answer to my father, he tells him that the story of his living upon acorns while fighting the Seminoles in Florida is as history relates.

But some one opens the door behind my father, bowing very low, my impression being that it must have been the minister pleuipotentiary from Great Britain, arrived to mediate in behalf of his master in reference to the French Claims question. And how it all vanishes like a dream!

I am still about four years of age, and a mania is raging for infant schools, and I am a victim, perched upon a bench, my weary legs dangling down, my eyes fastened upon a breastpin lying on the floor below my feet. I recall my picking it up and handing it to my teacher, as also my keen regrets thereafter that I did so.

And why is it that I can see this dark-visaged lady in black, seated in our parlor on a visit to my mother? She calls me to her, and I shrink because there is the scar of a terrible burn upon her cheek; but she beckons me to her, opening her black visiting-bag—reticule I think they called it—as I approach. I declare it hurts me to this moment, my bitter disappointment, when she merely draws out her handkerchief and wipes her nose!

I am not yet five, and still in Washington, I suppose; all I perfectly know is that a terrific thunder-storm is raging. My ears ring with peal on peal. I cover my eyes from the flashes of lightning. Nothing like it since. Not five years old yet; and now, at eight times that, I hear still the awful thunder and the Niagara of down-pouring water following thereupon. I see my mother crouched in the midst of the enormous feather-bed of the four-post bedstead, up to which you climbed in those days by carpeted and movable steps.

She puts aside the curtains, by which every breath of air was then excluded from the sleeper, who could only have slept by swooning suffocated, and calls me to climb up and escape the lightning. All my manhood is in rebellion, aroused as by the battle-drums of the tempest, and, far from terrified, I am excited, exhilarated, enraptured, by the incessant peals, the quick-following flashes, the descending torrents, as I stand at the window, and hear and see it all this moment. I suppose the tempest must have slackened, and the news must in some way have been brought to us. One does not recall the silences between thunder-peals nor the darkness between flashes. I only remember hurrying, breathless, with my mother through the pouring rain, and entering the house where the lightning struck. There the three lie before me now. The dead mother, upon her back on the hearth, a babe on either side of her bosom, which is all naked and bleeding. I can not account for the blood, unless some one had hastily tried

bleeding as a remedy. Were I a painter I could reproduce the whole, even to a faithful likeness of the woman, with her disheveled hair, and the glaring blue eyes of the twins on either side.

But I am five years old now, in a great Southern city, transported thither, for what I know, through the air. Not at all! I have not thought of it since; but here I am, with my father, in the parlor of a sea-captain, arranging for our passage to that city from Washington. The captain is an avowed infidel; and minister and captain, both large, vigorous, powerful, and impulsive men, are in hot controversy. There is a magnificent ship made of glass—masts, sails, ropes, and all—upon the hearth, and my brother and myself annoy my father so much, lest we should break it, as well as the thread of his argument, in our eagerness to see, that he stands us out on the door-step until he can finish his controversy.

How well do I remember, amidst all of my admiration for the brilliant ship, feeling, even above my intense desire to own it, a deep repugnance to the heated conversation between my parent and the red-visaged sea-going unbeliever! As I stand with my brother on the outer stoop, I tell him that I fear it will come to blows, during which the beautiful vessel will be utterly wrecked; and he makes answer that, since he can not own nor even see it, he heartily hopes it will be. Possibly the later and wiser era to which we boys belong is being born within us, for we are both entirely agreed that quarreling in regard to religion will do the captain no good; we are certain, in fact, children as we are, that it will make him worse.

But I know I am in the Southern city to which we removed now, for I am, as I speak, at the academy there, and have a medal for something or other around my neck by a bright blue ribbon, and my father is to be at home this evening after a long absence. I do not believe I have ever been quite so glad and proud since, nor quite so bitterly cast down; for this next moment I am standing in line, my toes to a chalk-mark, with other victims, and, in the convulsions of spelling a hard word, my foot slips an inch over the line. And now I am ranged around the platform with other culprits for the closing exercises (the most impressive of all) of the day. I shrink from him this moment as he begins, this dreaded Mr. White, the master, at the other end of the semicircle, with his ferrule. Here he is, I look up in his face now; black haired and eyed, his face blue-black with close shaving, sincere pleas- of the academy full of glee, I see a gray mare feeding upon the common. So clearly and perfectly do I recall stealing up to her in excess of spirits behind and seizing upon her tail, so utterly do I forget what followed immediately thereupon. It is as a later memory that I can hear my mother telling vis-

THE CONTROVERSY.

ure in his eyes as he takes off my medal and leaves my poor little palm burning from his stick. He gives me my first lesson in the science of hate. How perfectly I am taught it, as I blunder, weeping, home without my badge! I retain the hate for life, but the sorrow must have gone; for it can not be beyond a few days after, when, coming out itors for weeks after how "Carter was kicked in the stomach. We feared he could not live."

But I wonder if all I received as gospel then about Mr. White was true. That he would throw little boys up to the ceiling and catch them in descending, I know; for I saw that feat of jugglery done by him, and often.

As to his standing boys, too large to throw, upon their heads in the corner, I can testify to, for I rather enjoyed the spectacle. There were tales in reference to the punishment of the older boys of which I am not so sure. A culprit of that grade was doomed to be invited, the whisper ran, by Mr. White to dinner every day for a month, numbers of lovely young ladies being always present to see. The guests under penalty were treated with the most elaborate politeness, but were helped to rice, only and always rice, nothing but rice, and rice which they were courteously but despotically compelled to eat in enormous quantities under the eyes of the ladies.

I do not know, I am sure, nor do I care, for I am seated in a swing, this moment as then, and David, our yellow boy, is behind pushing me. I feel the rush of the air as I go to and fro: next I find myself flying to the other end of the entry and toward the brick-floor, the hateful red of which I can see this moment; and here on my forehead is the scar still. But that is a trifle to the morning that flashes upon me next, when I wake, as my mother turns down my warm cover, and proceeds to administer a whipping, richly deserved, I have no doubt; but I recall the rod, and not the sin—a peculiarly unpleasant chastisement by reason of the sudden transition from the sweetness of sleep, the morning calmness of my mother's purpose, the large amount of naked surface exposed; it was more disagreeable even than painful. And again, I am going upstairs solemnly with my mother about the same time, because I have been repeating in the kitchen certain words picked up by me at school. They were Hebrew to me, so far as their meaning is concerned; but nothing is more vivid to me than the horribly disgusting medicine, of some brown and glutinous nature, which my mother gives me to cleanse my mouth and entire system after those words. I am very thoroughly cleansed, for I recall my agony during the convulsions of vomiting, lest nothing should be left of me beyond the mere outer shell.

All this vanishes back into the past before the tolling of the bells and the rolling of drums as I go back and stand in my father's house again, that night of the negro insurrection. Nothing more certain than that the blacks have been long arranging their plans. We have assumed as granted that all along the slaves have been but as so many grains of powder under the whole fabric of society: if one rise, all rise, and Heaven above knows how small a spark may spring the explosion!

To-night they intend to rise and murder all the whites, and plunder and burn the city. Somehow, the plot is just found out, and all the city is awake and armed and awaiting the attack. Minister as he is, there stands my father that night in our bedroom, musket in hand; my mother, in her night-clothing, hastily making cartridges under his directions. The alarm is thorough and intense, but my only fear is that it may prove untrue. It will be so delightful, I think, to see some big black man breaking in at the front-door, and to meet and destroy him with the poker. I can myself slay fifty, and have keen jealousy of my father and the rest lest they will prevent. But the drums roll louder and louder, my mother casts herself, weeping, in my father's arms; he kisses us all around, somewhat awkwardly by reason of his accoutrements; and is gone. I grasp my poker, and await the onset and—the whole period is gone!

And I am at church instead. My father is the greatest minister in all the world up there in his mahogany citadel, with an awful presence by reason of his flowing black gown. I hear the low thunder of our great organ drowning the footfalls upon the tessellated border as the vast audience assembles; but why is it that I recall nothing but mere externals? It is communion Sabbath to-day, and I see the table, with its white cloth, extending down the middle aisle, six hundred feet at least, it seems to me, to the front door, lined with communicants seated on either side. But I am more interested in those sitting at the crescent table extended around the pulpit on either hand, for my black mammy is there, gorgeous to behold in her turbaned handkerchief, which rises yards in the air, with a score of people of color, white-headed, generally, and exceedingly black. The solemnity weighs me down into sleep, I dare say; for when I look again, the audience is all gone, and the portly, white-vested, florid-faced officers of the church are carefully rolling up the upper table-cloth, which reaches only to the edge of the table; and, beginning with the little piles of pennies where the negroes were seated, I see all down the long table to the very end that there lie silver and gold upon the under-cloth, slipped in under the damask by each communicant during communion, for the poor. And, ah! how early the might of money smites upon a child, minting itself upon its heart at its softest! For I stand beside my mother, a child not six as I write, and see my father putting in her lap the rolls of silver and gold he has just obtained from bank. I am not allowed to touch the sacred substance on any account, as my mother solemnly regrets that it was given her in my presence, and charges me not to whisper the fact to the servants. One paper roll has burst open on her knee; and, oh! how exceedingly desirable are the glorious coins as they sparkle in her lap with a splendor beyond that of earth!

But all the world is crumbling to dust soon after this, for there are vague whispers among the blacks down-stairs that we are going to leave. Leave? Why, only last Sabbath I sat with my mammy up in the gallery at church, and saw at least one thousand people stand up in a body, exactly a tenth of that number, as I now know, to be received into the church. Besides, the cenotaph to a previous pastor stands in ponderous marble, with a stone flame on top, on one side of the pulpit; and the church is in a one-sided condition, I always thought, looking down from the gallery, until my father has his cenotaph upon the other side. I did not dream then that the deceased predecessor of my father, so illustrious for his eloquence, had been suspended for intemperance, although afterward restored, and living during years following a long and useful life. But, then, I only knew that ours was the grandest and wealthiest church in the world, my father the greatest of clergymen, the earth itself not more reliable than the steady continuance of things with us as they were and forever. There was David, our yellow boy, for instance. We had given him his freedom, and he was periodically sailing away to Liberia, of which he had immediately become the leading man, I told my playmates, and returning again in paroxysms of gratitude, bringing back cocoanut hammocks and great African blankets adorned with splotches of blue all over, and oranges innumerable; David himself in linen and broadcloth and talking with us as if he were a gentleman, the greatest of all the wonders he brought. And now no more David! The loss was inconceivable. How was it possible for us to exist, too, without Mrs. Brown? An Englishwoman, and in worth a nugget of the purest gold, was Mrs. Brown, our housekeeper, as essential to the house as its walls or roof. How she loved me, bore with me, gave me immediate access to every jar of jam, and every tray of cakes, both before and after baking! It was Mrs. Brown who held me in her arms when they actually measured me, as I often and proudly asserted afterward to my companions, for my coffin when I was supposed to be dying with croup, but was saved therefrom by the use of hot lard and molasses. Who else shielded me from a hundred well-deserved whippings, convincing me that no child in the house was worthy of holding relationship to one so wonderfully gifted as myself? Meek, loving, silent, never rebuked by father or mother except for overworking herself, controlling the negroes under her—although they knew she was nothing but "poor white folks"—by sheer goodness, life was impossible without Mrs. Brown!

My mother—and I do not speak now as a child—was a lady of the old Virginia type, highly cultured according to the ideas of her time, but very domestic. She was beautiful, not of the apple-dumpling style, however, but intellectual and sensitive; a great reader, yet a thorough housekeeper. But, frankly, I do not think she and my father, although devotedly attached, ever understood each other perfectly. There came to her, a rustic beauty in the seclusion of her father's plantation, an adoring theological student. He is well-enough-looking; she is pious, and he is a devotedly pious youth in training for the ministry. He loves her so exceedingly that she is constrained, as by his very energy, to love him, and give him her hand. But how much does she know about his profession, its peculiar lines and shades of thought, its motives, its aims?

Exactly as much as she does of his Greek and Hebrew. Henceforth is she his wife, the mistress of his house, the mother of his children; the man is her husband, but the minister lives for her in the Arctic zone. In the tropics, I should rather say, for my father is a large, florid, powerfully built man, whose whole heart burns in that ample chest of his with devotion to his calling, living habitually as in a zone of ardent zeal, and glowing hopes, and unwearying purposes for God and man. Except that my mother was vastly superior to the lady in question, it is the story over again of John Milton and his little wife from the country; always remembering that there was no slackening of love, much less thought of divorce, in our case. How much better it would have been if Mrs. Milton could have assimilated herself to the Hebraist and immortal poet! Ninety-nine hundredths of her husband surely lay in that; and the miserable fraction of the man remaining thereafter, and for whom she could only sweep and cook and sew, was all of John Milton she had.

A doctor's wife can not enter into his cases as he does, nor a lawyer's wife into his. Just how much does a President's wife understand and sympathize with the policy, diplomacy (foreign and domestic), success, or defeat of his excellency, do you suppose? One reads of husband and wife as successful—actors together on the stage, playing Romeo and Juliet a thousand times over, and admirably because from the heart. There were Robert and Elizabeth Browning, too, keeping house together on Parnassus, filling their daily tea-kettle from the same Helicon, the more intensely one because inhaling the same inspiration. So there may be cases of wedded unity yet more perfect between the minister, as minister of the Gospel, and his wife; yet Scripture, in giving us the Apostle Paul, adds no hint as to a wife fully mated to this flaming servant of God. Why is it that the more a man devotes himself to his ministry, as in the case of John Wesley, the more apt, alas! is the wife to be a virago like Mrs. Wesley? Never were a wedded couple, I hasten to say, more devoted to each other than were my parents; and yet the fact remains the same: my mother was linked to the minister, only to the man was she mar-

ried. His life business, in which he had embarked his entire being, was in her eyes a something very important and exceedingly sacred, yet with which she had nothing approaching the feeling in reference thereto which he had.

"Yes, Mrs. Brown," I recall my mother saying to our housekeeper at this juncture, "I am attached to our friends here, to the city, to our home, I need not say, to you. I had hoped to see my children educated here, surrounding themselves with friends of their childhood, and settling down around us. It is like death to me, this breaking-up," and her eyes, red with weeping, attested her grief; "but Mr. Quarterman thinks it is best," for although my father had long been a D.D., he never was other than the Mr. to her of their marriage. "His sacred calling requires self-sacrifice, you know," and my poor mother continued to speak as if of some telescopic matter quite beyond the solar system!

An officer of our great church, who was also a rich planter, was said to have had a persistent runaway among his slave-women screwed down under his cotton-press. The greatest care was taken that she should not be hurt, and she was left there to a night of repentance. My father was shocked at the rumor, as was every other person in his church, and denounced the cruelty, if true, from the pulpit. To this hour I do not know whether the rumor about the cotton-press was true; but I do know that all the church were as much shocked at the possibility of such cruelty as is any reader to-day. This may have influenced him to leave, yet his church was prosperous, the salary ample, himself beloved, the city then, as now, one of the most delightful homes in the world. In any case, he held to his purpose of leaving like some great steamship, his household but as the little yawl which tosses upon the waves tethered behind. Nothing more clear to him than that he could do far more good elsewhere; in all the range of mathematics and metaphysics nothing more incomprehensible to my mother; the move a something to be submissively regretted, without an attempt to understand it, like the death of a child: husband and wife loving each other heartily, but she as passive as he is powerful.

CHAPTER III.

AND so we left our home in the grand old city. It was like launching the cockle-boat of our household upon the tumbling waters of an ocean without a shore. For some time my mother made her temporary home with her brother, Archibald Carter, at the old homestead in Virginia. The eyes of children have a sharpness of sight which gets blunted against the rough world as they grow older; and I can, at this moment, see this portly Uncle Archibald of mine as I can not see any person now, however striking in appearance. An unusually large man every way, always dressed in cloth of a deep blue, ashen as to face, exceedingly white as to hair, close-shaved, no more dreaming of going out without his gold-headed cane, white waistcoat, and enormous bunch of seals hanging from his fob, than of remaining at home and not being in active and absolute charge of every thing and every person within reach.

"You surely had a desirable residence, Agnes," I can hear him now saying, a day or two after we arrived, to my mother in his magisterial manner, seated with her in the dingy parlor of the old mansion, we children cleaving about our mother with the shyness of children in a new place.

"During my visit I was impressed with the high tone of society in Brother Oglethorpe's church, a gravity and dignity in the very bearing of his officers as they handed the elements down the communion-table which indicated wealth and social standing. You will pardon me, Agnes, but I feared then that the simplicity of character, the unusual fervor and earnestness of Brother Oglethorpe—"

My mother was far from being in the best spirits as she sat sewing; but her slight figure, bowed over her work, was erect on the instant. She was more than a match for her stately old brother any day—the genuine and original essence, if one may so speak, of Virginianism in her, in contrast with the more outer and empty form and manner thereof as embodied in my uncle. It was an old trouble, for her brother had utterly opposed, from the outset, the approaches of the ardent young theologian, so rustic, earnest, impulsive; had yielded to the match, as he always had to yield when this sister was in question.

"As you well know, Archibald, Mr. Quarterman left wholly of his own motion," she said. "The church had been prospered under him as under no other pastor. I did enjoy the delightful society—the wealth and leisure and luxury of our home — enjoyed it keenly, for my tastes are like your own. But Mr. Quarterman was unhappy by reason of the very grandeur and completeness of things, the fashionable congregations crowding the church as regularly as Sabbath came, the excellent choir around the organ, the beautifully dressed children at Sabbath-school—"

"Oh yes, uncle," I broke in, "you ought to have seen the cakes our superintendent sent for to Holland for our anniversary; big as a biggest dinner-plate, all covered with raised-up pictures—"

But my uncle had turned his whole person toward me in an attitude of such rebuke at my freedom of manner, that I did not need the hand of my mother on my shoulder to cause me to stop.

"Ahem!" remarked my uncle, for it was a volume of remark in the manner thereof.

"When," lifting and playing with his heavy watch-seals, "your husband resolved to remove the brandy from his dinner-table, I regretted it. A decanter of cut-glass is indispensable to the table of a gentleman. I regretted it." The regret being that of a superior being, and made immeasurable by the slow outward motion of the large hand.

"Brother Archibald," my mother added, her head thrown back as you have observed with blooded horses, and I deliberately mean the metaphor, in her tones so clear and serene, "I have told you often before, you and my husband represent wholly different classes and periods. You were born on the old place, have lived here all your life, except when you were in Congress, know and care nothing about any thing in the world except Virginia and the past and, pardon me, yourself—the case with all old bachelors, brother. My husband has broken away from his old family, as old as ours, Archibald, there in Georgia, and is entered on a new life other than ours. It is all wild and very wide to me, and I do not understand it." My dear mother faltered a little with drooping head as she added this. "All I know," she continued, "and that I *do* know, is that he is driven, against all selfish considerations of ease and family and home, to leave and to labor where he can do most for his Master."

"I would not use the expression 'master,' Agnes," my uncle remarked, rising, and without the least understanding what she said. "Master is the language of our slaves. You know how much you and your children are welcome to a home as long as you like on the old place." But we took not a bit of pleasure in his words — were glad when he was gone from the room. If my mother and the rest of us could but have yielded ourselves to be taken entirely in custody by the old autocrat! And how could he help it? He had been in sole and awful charge of the plantation, the negroes, the poor white folks around, ever since he could remember. There was not a human being on the soil of his empire but agreed in soul with the concise statement of people all around, "Major Archibald Carter is an old fool," even while each person, white and black, young and old, yields herself or himself to the keeping of the man; such power in the mere outer

manner and assumption of the major, such force upon all others in virtue of his own thorough conviction that Virginia itself walked in his boots, and swayed rightful rule in his person. Bourbonism is as thoroughly human nature as is Radicalism.

But what a happy time of it we children had those days when not actually in custody of our uncle, although it was hard to get out of it! Not a pig nor chicken could be killed, nor negro baby dosed, nor suit of jeans cut and made; not a plow could be mended, nor horse shod, nothing least or greatest could be done, but under the eye and command of this master, who never could remember the instant after that he was almost invariably wrong. Living as he did in the heaven of his own supreme self-satisfaction, how happy he was, how smoothly ran the days under his complete control! no pope more convinced of his infallible wisdom.

Yet there was a day, when, after solemn charges given to do every thing so and so, and to leave every other possible thing undone, our ever-present uncle rode off to Wrexboro', the post-office village. We were out of the jail of his presence in one eager moment—negroes, horses, children, and all. Ah, what a brilliant morning it was! the ripe wheat laid in a circle, circus-fashion, on the clean clay of the earth near the barn, a dozen of the plantation horses ridden by us around upon it, trampling out the grain. How we shouted and laughed as we whipped up our old horses and went round and round in the dust of flying chaff, the ragged little wretches of negro children the happiest of all! After just so many rounds, we would be driven off the ring, horses and all, by old Uncle Arxis, the straw raked off, the grain gathered into hogsheads, more wheat arranged, and so around and around would we go all the happy day. Delicious? It is no word for it — the ash-cake and fat pork at noon, unless it was the corn pone with heaps of honey, and the brown pitcher of buttermilk, we had at Aunt Meander's cabin at night; plenty of sweet-potatoes, roasting in the ashes, to eat with fresh butter, for whoever could find room for the same. Bless you, we did not care for old Uncle Arxis, the ebony twin-brother, so to speak, of Uncle Archibald. They had been suckled at the same time by the same black mammy, had grown up together— Stop! It may have been the master, now I think of it, who unconsciously modeled himself upon the slave —a man of really greater original vigor of character than his owner; in any case, they were twins.

Of course, Uncle Arxis was subordinate when Uncle Archibald was present, generally differing doggedly with his master, and always right. The moment the white twin was gone — no soul rejoicing in his going so much as the black—that moment Uncle Arxis was Uncle Archibald: only that he was a negro, and had no blue-cloth, watch-seals, gold-headed cane, absolute authority. He was his master over again in every tone of his voice, every wave of his magisterial hand, every dignity of his person—more fibre as of essential superiority in the better judgment of the white-headed old soul. Purely as a question of "uncle," we would have voted the white man out and the black in, and eagerly.

But I alluded to Wrexford. How the words ring like remembered squeakings of the hide-bottomed chair in which my mammy, Margaret, rocked me to sleep in her cabin—the words, "That wretched Wrexford!" "That thoroughly detestable Wrexford!"

"If I could have my way," I have heard my uncle Archibald say in those days, slowly, scores of times, "I would take Arxis and a dozen yoke of oxen, and drag every house in the town with a log-chain into the Ocoogee;" for that was the little river running by it—a stream as dirty as the town.

"What is the matter now?" my mother would say, dreamily, for she was thinking of my absent father, and puzzling over the old, old question of duty and disrupted home.

"Matter? One dozen turkeys gone last night. I counted them on the roost last night, and was out to count them before day this morning," my uncle would make slow reply. "The lock of the smoke-house is broken, too. Bunches on bunches of tobacco are missing in the cure-house. Not an egg to be had!"

"Oh yes, the negroes will sell them for liquor in Wrexford. It was always so, Archibald, ever since I can remember," my mother said. "But, you know, it is the same all over Virginia. There is not a plantation but has a Wrexford of its own near-by. In Georgia they are Corn-crackers, here you call them White Trash; but they are the same race. Those poor whites have lived down from father to son ever since the South was settled. Where did they come from?"

"What the poison-oak is to the tree, they are what fleas are to a dog," my uncle added. "Only you can never catch them, never—I have sat up night after night with Arxis."

Yes, I remember perfectly, child as I was, being in the miserable, tumble-down range of old weather-beaten wooden houses four miles from our plantation which they called Wrexford, with my uncle one day; he on his big black horse, I on a little roan pony, which I wished from morning till I fell asleep at night, with all the fervor of my soul, that my uncle would give me, but which he never did. I could paint this moment, if I had yellow ochre as well as skill enough, the cadaverous face of the clay-eating poor white who kept the chief liquor-shop in Wrexford. Did Heaven ever make—did men ever make themselves, I should say— a more despicable sort of vermin? the filmy eyes, the tobacco-juice streaming from the corners of the thin, loose lips, the furtive manner, the coolness of the awful lies! I shudder now at the stories they used to tell me of the slatternly women of the same species. On this occasion Uncle Archibald, elevated upon his horse as upon the bench, was in the enjoyment of his peculiar function of holding some one in magisterial custody; Uncle Arxis, upon his old mule a little behind his master, with demeanor still more judicial, echoing and impressing upon the "white trash" cowering in the dust before them the solemn vituperation of his white twin brother. They were, to a wonderful degree, the duplicates of each other.

"A most disreputable, disgraceful, degraded creature you are," continued my white uncle.

"A mose 'reputable, 'raceful, 'graded critter!" echoed the old negro, with admonitory shake of his white head.

"If you sell them any more liquor—"

"You jes' sell 'em any more whisky!" repeated the black, while his master paused for some doom terrible enough.

"I'll make Arxis here drag you and your den into the Ocoogee—"

"Wid oxen an' a log-chain, into Ocoogee, an' I'll bo grad to do um," the associate judge completed the old formula of wrath.

"You a white man!" added my uncle, with slow decision; "Arxis here is a gentleman in comparison with you! He would not touch gold from your hand, wouldn't drink out of your gourd if he was dying of thirst; he loathes and despises you!" And my uncle, having exhausted himself by a half-hour of steady but stately abuse, turned his horse and rode off.

"Loaves an' 'pi-ses you!" echoed his venerable coadjutor, with deepest emphasis. As I kicked my heels in my pony's sides to start him, I glanced round to see if the object of so much wrath had not sunk into the earth. It was one of the severest shocks of my childhood. I saw in the instant the poor white, with a slimy smile upon his corpse-like face, pass a black bottle from under his ragged coat to Arxis, who slipped it as quickly under his, severe indignation still upon his brow, and adding with renewed scorn, as he jerked at his mule's bridle and rode after us,

"Pi-ses an' loaves you!"

But my eyes must have betrayed me! I did not mention the matter even to my mother, whom I loved as the smartest as well as most beautiful woman in the world. Besides, I had no time for it, inasmuch' as we children were wild with the change of life from city to plantation. Have I mentioned them yet? Not since the first chapter, I fear.

There was the eldest, Archibald, by far the handsomest of us all, as well as the brightest. I see him now, as one remembers seeing some familiar tree during a storm and lighted up by a flash of lightning, standing on the top of the pile of corn one night which the negroes are shucking by the flare of pine torches. It would have been a splendid scene for a painter. The mountain of corn twenty feet high in the barn-yard; the ring of happy blacks in their shirt-sleeves of coarse gray, on and up to their waist in corn-shucks, around the base; the shadows of barn and trees and people fall-

ing this way and that as the wind flickered the flames of the torches, carefully stuck among the palings of the old fence, to one side. The painter could not paint, however, the heart-felt laughter. Ah me! what whole-hearted laughter it was! I have never heard any approaching to it since. It was just nothing at all that started the fun—a cotton-basket of shucks unexpectedly emptied upon the head of the loudest singer, suddenly smothering his voice as well as person; a sudden slide of the unhusked corn undermined from below and whelming a dozen in its avalanche; a potato hot from the ashes of a neighboring cabin-fire dropped down the back of the leader of the jubilant chorus, converting his solo into a yell, and changing the chorus, waiting to take up their refrain, into shouts of laughter which could be heard a mile. Some practical joke always on hand, generally by "dat fool nigger, Harklis," the buffoon of the plantation, despised and adored by all the hands, highly valued by Uncle Archibald, who winked at his capers, knowing how indispensable he was toward keeping "the people" in good spirits for work.

No artist could put the awful racket on paper; but he could paint my brother Archibald standing upon the very top of the Alps of corn, a boy of fourteen, slight, tall, lithe in figure like my mother, dark hair and eyes, beautifully arched eyebrows, straight nose, full of life to the very tips of his fingers, because brimful of talent so striking that I would name it genius if I thought you would believe me. I do believe Uncle Archibald, if he could possibly have thought of or been proud of any thing beyond himself, would have been proud of Archibald—genuine Virginian as the boy was in every nerve and fibre. Strange to say, he disliked him and preferred me. Standing upon the corn, the boy was as Apollo among the shepherds of Admetus. The negroes worshiped him as by an intuition of what *savants* in these days style the "religious faculty." Our stolid old uncle had his aversions to him because he knew that the boy was quite beyond, if not above, his custody. If Archy had but actually been what he would have seemed, truly portrayed on canvas! And yet—and yet! I can never forget him as he stood there then, and I have so very much to say about him hereafter!

But not more than about my brother Habersham, next in age to Archibald. If the painter could but execute that corn-shucking scene as a family piece for me! My dear mother stood beside my uncle that night on the right hand, Habersham a shrinking little red-headed boy of twelve by her side, the three coming and going like ghosts in the waving of light and shadow. I have plenty to say about little Habersham. If his maiden aunt in Georgia could have left him a fortune as completely as she had left him — herself! What I mean is, Aunt Habersham was a little old maid, very unsocial, very red as to hair as well as diminutive in stature. Yes, it must have been because she was, to speak plainly, a red-headed dwarf, that she was an old maid where old maids were rare exceptions, and so bitterly unsocial; and poor little Habersham, pale, diminutive, shrinking, was her very image. "Atavism" is what they call it when the grandfather reproduces himself in his descendant; but a mere aunt, a father's sister, had no right, unless she had been herself more valuable, to bequeath herself body and soul, as in this case, to a mere nephew!

Off on the left and beside me, Carter Quarterman, sat my two twin sisters, Virginia and Georgia, then just one year younger than Habersham, about eleven years old. And you have no idea how easy it is to tell about them, the distinctive traits being so perfectly defined. The eldest of the girls must have been named in the spirit of prophecy, or she had adjusted herself to her name, Virginia, as she grew up, the very repetition of our mother in her slight straight form, clear-cut lips and nose and chin, lovely complexion of purest white and rosiest red when well; above all, in the tensely strung nerves and inflexible persistence in her own opinion, yielding, as my mother did to my father in their removal from the city, but, like my mother, of the same opinion on any subject for ever and ever, and whatever the subject might be.

The younger of the twins had been named Agnes, but she had grown up so unlike my mother, and so exceedingly like the father, that, at first in fun, afterward because the name fitted more beautifully every day, she was called Georgia. See her as she sits or stands, incessantly in motion, by her sister in the full blaze of the pine-knots, Virginia tall for her age, and she round as a dumpling; Virginia serene and steady, and Georgia never in the same mood two hours; the elder of the twins always a lady, and greatly beloved; Georgia shocking us all every day by such forgetfulness of her sacred sex, and turning people so rapidly into enemies and friends and enemies again by her ever-varying moods and tenses, as to dizzy them into a state of great uncertainty whether to like her heartily, or dislike. Nothing pale and refined and low-spoken about her, florid and open and very cordial in the love or aversion of the moment; both sisters are very dear to us all because so amazingly like our mother and father, the regret of us boys being that Georgia was not, indeed, a boy, she was so very much like our father. Virginia listens with interest to the laughter and singing, but Georgia shucks and sings and laughs with the happiest there, until, taking sudden and mortal offense at some remark of Uncle Archibald, she withdraws in wrath to bed, and is seen no more until she breaks upon us in full and joyous peace with the world again over the waffles at breakfast next morning.

As last and least in every sense, let me add that there is nothing at all peculiar in myself, the youngest of the flock.

"I think Carter is like me," I overheard my uncle say to my mother a few days after our arrival; and shuddered to hear, "there is a gravity, a slowness of speech, a dignity of bearing, an aspect of wisdom—"

"Carter is unlike all the rest of the children," my mother made answer. "You see how broad he is in the shoulders, how sturdy upon his legs, how brown and silent. I am glad you think him like you, brother, and that you let him ride with you. We think he resembles my father; he is slowly getting to be more like him, but he is slow, if not dull, as yet in every thing. He is solid, though, as oak. Do you remember, Archibald, what a broad-shouldered, black, grave, silent girl his mammy Margaret was. Oglethorpe has laughed, and said he got more than her milk when she was nursing him. Carter actually does look like his mammy."

But at this point I doubted the morality of listening further, and slipped under the front porch, where I was reading "Sandford and Merton" while they were speaking within, and left for the negro quarters, but not before I had heard my uncle begin to say, in his slow way,

"Ahem! You do not mean it, Agnes! I was observing that the lad is more like me than the rest. I seriously hope so. Oglethorpe will be much from his family hereafter, and I am glad you will have a boy growing up upon whom you can rely. There is an aspect of dignity—"

CHAPTER IV.

"IF you suppose for a moment that my husband is not devoted to me and to our family, Brother Archibald, you are mistaken!" It was my mother who said it to my uncle across the roaring fire-place, and when she supposed me, like the rest of the children, fast asleep in the chamber adjoining. If she had said it with the least heat, it might have been the ancient story of woman's devotedness to her husband against every thing. She spoke, however, of her husband as you or I would have done of the shining of the sun at its meridian, as of a fact not needing to be stated. And she was right: no man could love wife or children more. It was assured, not only in his devotion to us when at home, or in his long and almost daily letters overflowing with affection to us when away. My father was what they called in Virginia "a good provider," that is, anticipated the wants of his family by ample supplies of all kinds, as well as by seeing to it that my mother had more than was needed of money, "that you may feel perfectly secure," as he worded it.

Supplies! People that send to the store in the city or to the grocery at the corner for every thing as they need it, do not know the meaning of the word. Not people on their plantations alone: at our home there in the city it meant a poultry-yard full of chickens, ducks, and turkeys; a smoke-house whose rafters were hidden with hanging sides and hams of bacon, and whose floor, saving a space in the centre upon which to make the smoke, was heaped with salt, flour by the sack and barrel, molasses and rice and sugar by the hogshead. And one never sees such pantries these days! They speak of the wastefulness of slavery. Oh yes, I dare say, but there was the profusion of nature, and nature at the tropics, in the open corn-cribs of the plantation, and great barns with heaps of wheat fresh from the thresher, and in which we children used to bury each other, the extremity of the nose excepted, from the very enjoyment of the fragrant plenty. But that pantry of ours! Whenever and wherever we had a home, the shelves upon shelves of preserves, for instance, each great brown jar duly labeled and overflowing with the smooth, sirupy rapture of peach and quince, orange, lemon, and, last of all, water-melon-rind cut into crosses and stars and hearts, transparent amber to the eye and entire satisfaction to the taste. Depend upon it, the glittering rows of canned fruit instead, to-day, are profoundly symbolic of our times—every thing done away from home, done by wholesale and by machinery, even to the very education of children. Last Christmas your little Charlie drew out of his stocking (the word "machinery" reminds me of it) a toy steam-engine. He is all the wiser for it, but that gift was not to your child what to me was that Christmas jar of Ocoogee limes the winter of which I am now speaking, at our old homestead in Virginia. The exquisite flavor of those limes sweetened all my sojourn there, making more endurable even our bondage to Uncle Archibald, and lingers as upon the palate of my memory to this hour.

I began this chapter by speaking of my father, but I must postpone further allusion to him for a while. Christmas has been mentioned—Christmas! and that Christmas at Uncle Archibald's breaks upon me again, as with the midnight splendors and songs once more of the angels to the shepherds. We never observed the birthday of Washington specially, though he was born South; why not, I know not. Thanksgiving-day was as utterly unknown there as were many other New England notions since introduced. Fourth of July was vulgarized by the odor of fire-crackers, and by the crowding into town of the poor whites. New-year's was by no means a holiday—the very reverse; heads of households were, as a rule, deeply in debt; and there were unpleasant circumstances incident to the new year, inseparable from a credit system almost as universal and matter-of-course in that latitude as is the system styled the solar. And so the one great holiday South was Christmas. "The negroes begin, I do believe," my uncle remarked one morning at breakfast as the season drew nigh, "the day after Christmas, to say, 'Well, it's only twelve months to Christmas, anyway!'"

And Uncle Archibald was right. We children, months before December, would be down at the negro-quarters when the hands would come in of evenings from the fields. Often it would be a day when they were specially tired out, the weather and "Mars' Archy" particularly hard that day. After all the cattle had been fed, and every "boy" and "girl" had got his or her ration of corn from the steel mill at the centre of the quarters, and of bacon from the smoke-house, and each cabin was full of black folks, grumpy and quarrelsome, a smallest angel there, black and ragged, had but to mention Christmas. The very name broke like a coming glory upon every heart, and on the instant all was joyful expectation. To this hour I do not understand why. Little sleep we children had the night before the special Christmas there of which I am now speaking. Not a black on the place pretended to go to bed. Long before day the uproar began. You spit upon a rock, laid a coal from the hearth thereon, and smote the same with a heavy axe. Let scientists explain the explosion which followed, and it was very cheap. Even Uncle Arxis superintended the loading and firing of the old anvil, the fire-arms being in exclusive use by the white boys. Even if we had not been wakened by the universal din of fiddle and laughter, the "boy" who came in to make the fire threw

his great armful of logs on the hearth with a shout which would have effectually done so. "Christmas gift, Mars' Archy! Christmas gift, Miss Agnes!" and on the instant the house swarmed with all the "house-servants" crying, "Christmas gift, Mars' Habersham! Christmas gift, Mars' Carter!" the cook putting her head into the bedroom of the girls, with "O my law! you in bed yet, and nigh on to four o'clock! Christmas gift, Miss Georgia! Christmas gift, Miss Ginia!" and as soon as we emerged from the house there were the "field hands," opening their reserved artillery in a universal "Christmas gift, massa! Christmas gift, missis!"

I do not understand it! It was not much they ever got, only a few bolts of flannel, knitted night-caps, woolen socks for the old; cheap looking-glasses, pocket-knives, beads, candy, calicoes, pipes, and the like; yet, whether they got any thing or nothing, the universal gladness was the same. I cease writing, and wonder with tears in my eyes as I recall the long-expected, long-remembered, overflowing gladness of the day, Uncle Archibald even abandoning all custody of every thing, and letting the world go from his grasp entirely. I wonder? Yes, I do know that it was the wild, blind cry of the soul for Christ; even in the realms of utter ignorance and darkness, not a syllable said about it, not a definite idea even in reference thereto, yet it was the craving of the godlike and eternal soul in the bosom of the least little slave there, as of the whitest, oldest, wisest of us all—the craving and cry of the soul after the Great Deliverer, suggested, however vaguely, by the day. Long before light, Archibald, my elder brother, had me out and among the happy black folks. The fact is, taking all the negro boys of our own age and thereabouts into conclave, for weeks before had we planned in reference to Christmas. "What us had best do?" "Molly Cotton-tail!" had been the one suggestion of every ragged counselor from the first, "an' partridges!" had always been added. Long before the late and confused breakfast was ready, we had exhausted ourselves by making all the noise possible, listening in the intervals to catch the flying sounds of like uproar from all the plantations around.

"And now for fun! Come, Carter! Come,

Habersham! You are not going to stay home Christmas, you poor little goose!"

It was Archibald who said it, as we sprung from the doors into the snow, even poor little Habersham flushed with eagerness, and striving to keep up with us. And pell-mell, white boys, black boys, curs of all grades, mingled in the perfect equality and freedom of the day, off we rushed for the fields. We would have gone had the snow been ten feet instead of that many inches deep. Sure enough, "dat ole blackberry-patch," prophesied by Arxis the younger, a very ragged negro of Archibald's age, did yield a Molly Cotton-tail, which, I should not insult you by explaining, is a rabbit punctuated behind, so to speak, with a knot of white fur, in lieu of a tail. Shouting, plunging heels over head into the snow, after it we went, yelling to each other and to the dogs, up hill and down ravine, cutting our feet upon the stalks of corn sticking up through the snow. I would give a good deal to know accurately how many rabbits we did catch and how many miles we did run that blessed day. But amidst all our eagerness, we could not but wonder at, and, with what supply of breath we had, praise little Habersham. For he was such a little, little fellow, so frail and small, his face so pale and his hair so very red, our mother would never have let him come had she known he thought of such a thing. And there he was, the toughest of us, his grip upon the rabbit crouched, frightened to death, down some old stump at the end of the race, first of all. The boy seemed frenzied with the excitement. And the rabbit, at last, was less than you could hold in your hand that night at supper; but how immeasurable the halo of glory about it! Really, its half-inch of tail was as long and as splendid to us as that of a comet.

"Now for the partridges!" It was little Habby himself who said it, after we had snatched a slight lunch of crackling corn-bread, nothing Victoria eats equal to it, down at Uncle Arxis's cabin. For here was something to take place, dignified and entirely unlike the frivolity of Molly Cotton-tails, and Uncle Arxis was to lead the expedition in person. No white boy of us dared even to touch the partridge net, a funnel-shaped affair of twine, with hoops to hold it open when set, and twenty feet long. As a great favor, Archy had one of the wings to "tote," and I the other, Uncle Arxis leading the van on his old mule, the cavalcade of boys, white and black, following on foot; every dog on the place "tolled," before we started, into an empty corn-crib with bits of rabbit, and then fastened up.

Leaving the dogs howling in a chorus of protest at our treachery, in a silence which we carefully bore like a heavy but valuable load, did we follow the hoofs of our leader, Uncle Arxis being never more solemnly like Uncle Archibald than that hour. Dismounting as we entered the edge of an old wood, and warning us back, he set the net, by the use of the wings making the opening thirty feet broad. With what ghost-like gestures did he then direct us all, so carefully instructed before, to spread out, half of us on either side, as, taking a wide sweep, he remounted his mule, the better to see and command the field, and proceeded to drive the feathered game. We could see nothing, but crept breathlessly here and there at the magisterial warnings of his hand, now directing, now checking us. We must have crept in silence for a mile or more. I had no idea where we were, when suddenly Habersham, who was just in advance of me, mouse that he was, sprung forward with a bound and threw down the open end of the net, and sat upon it!

"Oh, my law! you oughtn't to a done it, oughtn't to a done it, oughtn't to a done it!" old Arxis exclaimed and repeated, as if he never could cease, as he got off his mule. "You sha'n't come wid us nex' Christmas!"

For that was the supreme prerogative of our leader, what he came out for, to seize the critical instant to close the net upon the flock of partridges. Little Habby recked not the wrath even of so mighty a kaiser. There on the earth behind him were half a hundred plump partridges, struggling in the long convolutions of the net. Oh, the glad eagerness of the hour, each of the brown and spotted birds as big as an ostrich, in our eyes! But we were allowed only to hold the net, or the basket—a big cotton-basket—on hand for the purpose, as Uncle Arxis transferred the struggling game one by one to the same, tied them over with a fragment of canvas from a wagon-cover, had the heavy basket handed up to him on his mule, and so rode home before us all in portentous displeasure.

Dark, lowering, muttering deep discontent—could Uncle Arxis think of spoiling our coon-hunt that night? That was the awful thought of each one of us as we toiled after him home. One of us must be sacrificed to his just wrath; which of us was very evident, and the victim knew it.

"You can't go to-night, Mr. Habby," said Archy, as we discussed the point. But Habby had nothing to say, for his fire had slackened into its ashes again as he struggled to keep up with us, his poor pale face as clear to my eyes now as then.

"I certainly would not want to go, Habersham," Virginia remarked, with something of scorn, as we talked it over, supper finished, after our arrival on the front porch. "The idea of racing about the fields with little negroes all day is bad enough, catching poor weeny bits of rabbits and birds that never did you any harm in the world. But going out at night all through the plantation—I'm astonished at you!" And Virginia drew herself up in disdain, her very tones those of my mother.

"What do girls know?" we boys all broke in, and all together proceeded to tell of the glorious fun of tracking coon and possum by night with the dogs, all in a breath, until Georgia exclaimed,

"Oh, Virginia, I wish I was a boy! I would be glad to go. Here we've been shut up in the house all day. Nothing to do but eat turkey and mince-pies and make molasses candy. I'd give any thing to go. Oh, how I wish I could!"

We all knew how ardent and impulsive Georgia was in her moods, but we never could have imagined any thing equal to what followed. As an exceedingly great favor, "seeing it is Christmas," Archy and I had got the consent of our mother, in secrecy from Uncle Archibald, who would never have yielded to our going—a consent conditioned on our being sure not to do this, that, and the other. And so, in our very worst clothes, all the household having retired, Archy and I were leaving the house, when we saw a boy approaching us stealthily in the darkness.

"Hush, hush, Archy! hush, Carter! It's only me!" and, before we could take in the enormity of the act, we found that it was actually Georgia.

"Why, how on earth—?" Archibald began.

"Opened the window of our room over the back porch and slid out; covered with snow, you see; and the ground did not hurt, the snow is so deep," she replied, eagerly.

"And where on earth—?" I began.

"Oh, out of Archy's trunk," she explained. "His Sunday suit. It wasn't locked. Only this once. It's Christmas!"

How we laughed, under our breath though. She had arrayed herself as she said, even to a linen collar and black ribbon about her neck. Bundling up her abundant hair somehow, she had tied on Archy's broad-brimmed hat, and made a boy far handsomer than we had ever seen before in our lives.

"But you can't go, Georgy," I said at last. "A whole pack of dogs and negroes are going, and it is all through thickets, and—oh, it will never do! Can't go, Georgy."

"But she shall go!" exclaimed Archibald, to my astonishment. Had I said she should go, he would have been equally as prompt in determining that she should not. I speak of all these small matters so fully because they help you to understand the far greater events—ah, how much greater!—that after befell. And Georgia was not more impulsive in her varying and contradictory moods than was Archibald perverse in his way, and perversity was not a matter of mood with him; it was of the very color and iron of his blood.

We must have disputed half an hour, standing there in the snow and under the glittering stars. I suppose I am, as they say, oaken in my character, brown and stubborn; but I was right. Archibald, as being my elder brother, was that much the more resolved because he knew it was so wrong a thing to do: no pleasure in being perverse where you are right! But it was Georgia I yielded to, she was so eager; and, then, it was Christmas! So we agreed to call her George, and to pass her off with the negroes as a friend from the city, and, joining Uncle Arxis and a cavalcade of curs and field-hands impatiently awaiting us at the quarters, we plunged into the midnight woods. No need of silence now. Uncle Arxis strode on in advance, axe on shoulder, alternating:

"You hush your racket behind dar! Fuss enough to drive de coon out de country!" To his followers in his rear, with:

"Yes, hunt him, Tige! look for him, Bose! Hi, pups!" with a kick at every cur lingering behind. And so we wound and turned until I had got utterly lost, Georgia walking between Archibald and myself, the hearts of all three of us weighed down, even in the excitement, with sense of wrong-doing. I am satisfied it made Archibald more unreasonable than he would have been otherwise; for, just as we reached a rocky hill with a deep ravine "forking off" on either side, the dogs began to bark in the distance, and Uncle Arxis was sure, with the rest of us, that the coon was up the left ravine, while Archy was angrily certain it was up the right. A short and fierce dispute followed, which ended in his striking off, with a black boy or two—whom he had bought, at least so far as their hearts were concerned, that day with a box of percussion-caps—up the right fork, leaving us to go up our own way.

Because she knew I was morally right about her leaving home, Georgia kept with me, and ten minutes of headlong run, falling and getting up again, plunging into snow-banks and then stumbling over rocks, brought us to the scene of battle. But I had no heart for it. It was nothing at last but a coon up a gum-tree, surrounded with a pack of howling curs and frantic people. A few blows of the axe in the hands of Uncle Arxis, and the tree was down, and the coon fighting for life in a whirl of dogs and negroes. We did not wait even for the end, Georgia and I—for they caught eight after that, not returning until day—but turned and left, unnoticed by any.

No fear of getting lost, the night was so bright, and we had made such a track through the snow in coming. We went back as fast as we could, not a word to say, either of us, Georgia crying, with her head down and her hat over her face; not a word even as she climbed up on the shed roof by means of my shoulders, and so into her window; and, oh, how relieved I was as she shut it down softly behind her!

And whom should I meet as I stole around the dark and sleeping house but Archibald coming up?

"But who in the world—?" I began.

"Yes, it is me," said little Habersham, seeming like a mite in the deep snow and among the dark shadows; "I came on behind you."

"And I was right in striking off my way. Habby followed me, and would have died in the snow if I hadn't been there," Archibald asserted.

"As if there would have been any tracks that way for him to follow, if you had not gone," I said. But it hurt me worst that Archy, big, strong boy as he was, had let the poor little fellow walk, instead of bringing him in on his back, after all his hard work that day, too.

"Not exactly! As if I hadn't worked, too, all day!" he replied.

Perversity is only an expression of selfishness, was my thought then, though I could not have put it in those words.

"I know it all!" my mother said, when I hastened to her room next morning. "Georgia told me. She is heartily sorry and ashamed of herself. Archibald's best clothes are ruined. We will not let your uncle know. Habersham is very sick. Oh, how I wish, Carter, that your father were at home, and that we all had a home of our own! But it is all right, and God knows best!"

The fact is, my mother always talked to me as she did not even to Virginia, in many things as she did not even to my father. She seemed to lean upon me from my birth, and I loved her, resolved to do all I could.

New-year's saw little Habby, if possible, smaller and paler than ever before, but Georgia had speedily got through her agony of remorse; Aurora herself not more radiant and joyous, as she came in to breakfast that morning with a lapful of guinea-hen's eggs she had found under a hay-rick.

"Oh, Georgia, how can you?" began Virginia.

"Ahem!" remarked Uncle Archibald. "Christmas is over, and I am glad of it," and a good deal more to the general effect that the world had been going to ruin, but that he, Major Archibald Carter, had resumed the custody of the globe, and intended to hold it, and more firmly!

CHAPTER V.

OUR memorable Christmas at the old homestead in Virginia has held me for a moment; but I was speaking of my father. His loving letters were long and full and frequent. A man like Uncle Archibald has to get out of his portly body into his spirit, and out of Virginia into heaven, before he can understand such a man as my father; yet even he was glad to hear my mother read aloud from time to time one of those letters, so radiant were they with the joy of the man in his increasing and successful work. Uncle Archibald did not altogether like knowing even of a person who was so wholly outside of his keeping as my father, but he respected one who insisted upon paying so liberally and so long in advance the expenses to him of our family.

Now and then my father would break upon us in person, with a box full of presents for us children; upon that we could count with certainty. Before you would know it, there he was all over the house and the place; not a negro there but heard from him: "Well, my friend, I hope you think about your soul;" and as "Mars' Oglethorpe" certainly thought about the body in always leaving at least a picayune in the hand which held its old worn felt hat while he spoke, the advice was not forgotten. "Remember, aunty, you must die some day. Don't forget that Jesus d'ed for you: aunty, try to love and serve him," was the whole sermon; a high-colored handkerchief for the head, or, if the terrible truth must be told, a good bit of tobacco, being the benediction after sermon.

"You are exactly like a sailor home from sea," my mother would say; "besides, you spoil the people so: you ought to have asked me first. Just now you gave Maria a silver half-dollar for waiting upon me, and Brother Archibald was compelled to take the cowhide to her only yesterday!"

"But it did no good to talk to Mr. Quarterman," as my mother had said a thousand times, so genial he was, so overflowing with absolute health, so full of belief in every body.

"The only thing I do not like in my brother Archibald," I heard him say to my mother one day, "is that he never gives my children any presents." A grievous fault in the eyes of one who would not pass, if he could help it, even a dog without giving him something.

"Now, I will tell you, Agnes," he would say at breakfast, during his brief sojourns with us, to my mother, who, of course, kept house for Uncle Archibald, "what Archibald here wants for his dinner. It is apple-dumplings."

For he had that weakness, my father; but beyond a love, also, for his children, which caused him to dwell too much when from home upon their various and remarkable talents, I declare I can record no defect besides. Possibly like him in inordinate affection, but I can not help it. Only yesterday I found a soiled, exceedingly crumpled fragment of newspaper which had been taken from his pocket after his death, wretched "poetry" of mine which some editor had been foolish enough to print. I would like, or rather would not like, to know to how many persons he had read those poor lines during his travels! How many fibs in the way of polite commendation they must have caused, and on the part of the most pious people.

He insists on taking me with him in his two-wheeled gig this last time he visits us at the Hermitage. And, before I know it, I am off with him. For he wearies of "the idleness of his life" before he has been with us a week. He can not be happy unless he preaches at least once a day, physically capable of preaching, and with ease and delight, three times a day the year around; so robust he is, and in highest spirits according to the work he has to do. And what a life it is for a boy of ten! His journey as an evangelist lay this time through dense forests among the swamps of Florida, now and then running the wheel over an alligator too lazy to get out of the way, our sorrel horse remonstrating with lifted nose and ears, tail and hoof. It does not hurt the reptile, and amuses us. Once I am allowed to get out and snap my whip at the eyes of one of them, that I may see how much smarter it is than I can be with my whip in winking its eyes.

"God made it so, Carter," my father said, showing me a pitcher-plant, which he had gathered by the roadside as he spoke. "See how beautifully this lid fits upon the top, how full it is of honeyed water for the birds. It is our Father, my dear;" but there was no cant, no "religion" even, in a formal sense, in what he said. For no person was quite so natural to him and near as the One of whom he never ceased to think and speak, and yet in such a simple and joyous way as was without the least savor or suspicion of having a sermon in it; the happiest man, by far, I ever knew, and because of his religion!

"Take the reins and be very careful, Carter," he would say of an afternoon, as we drove through the close dark woods, and, leaning against the side of the gig, he would sleep like an infant while I drove. I always managed our horse more carefully than himself. When he drove, buried in deep meditation, the wheel, always on his side, would strike a stump and over we would go! And very often. We must have been passing through the Indian Reservation those days, for I remember a tall and solemn Indian finding us in such plight, dismounting from his ragged pony, hitching our horse to the tire of the upturned wheel, pulling the vehicle back, pocketing the silver dollar my father gave him, and riding on with never a word from his lips, nor a motion of his iron countenance, from first to last.

Yes, that special upset took place the very day my father had bought me my first pony, Nubbin by name—nubbin being, as the unlearned reader should know, a stunted ear of corn. Forty dollars he paid for it at a cabin where we staid that night. It was from a woman, our hostess, yellow and gaunt, that he purchased it. She persisted in putting too much molasses in our coffee, in spite of all we could do.

"Oh, you are welcome to it!" she exclaimed, adding yet another pewter table-spoonful from the mug. "It's best 'lasses, made outer ripest water-mingins. Hearty welcome. You think I've never been in the settlements, an' don't know how ter be perlite. but you're mistooken!"

And it was her politeness which made it necessary, in return, for my father to buy Nubbin after the subject had been broached. Surely Columbus, when he first stood upon the New World, was not prouder than I was upon my own, own pony! I had secret doubts but that it was only a toy pony at last, relieved when I found it could trot, even gallop. How hard he did trot! It was almost unendurable to keep up with the gig, but I would have suffered any thing rather than acknowledge it. And that squirrel leaps back through the years upon me as I write! Such a beauty, with its long gray tail and black eyes; ah, how bitterly I blamed myself when I opened the tin-bucket in which we carried our lunch, and in which I had placed it, and found it cold and stiff next morning! And that other painful morning must have been about that time, very painful! As thus:

"Carter! my love as your father makes it necessary," my father remarked, on the occasion in question, causing me to dismount, fastening both horses to a tree by the roadside, and taking me off into the woods. I wonder what it was for—wonder greatly, because it was a very severe whipping, my father was so healthful and vigorous and exceedingly earnest in all he did!

Besides, he should have remembered that the hard trotting of Nubbin, before and after, made the location of the stripes a matter to have been more fully considered!

I have not the least doubt but that I deserved it; but why is it the material part remembers so very clearly, while the moral nature has forgotten so utterly, the misdoing which caused it?

However, I never doubted my father, thank Heaven! We slept together as we traveled; and every night, about midnight, I suppose, I was aware of his getting softly out of bed, and kneeling beside it in prayer. His devotions were more to him than his meals. Always before the sun set, so as not to be too much fatigued, at midnight, at morning, at noon, I doubt if a day passed which did not find him regular as life itself in his private prayer, but never with a view to other than the One to whom he prayed.

I am but touching upon my father, and that merely to explain all that followed in reference to the rest of us. Let me not forget, however, one night in the woods. I do not know what was his idea—to please me, perhaps, possibly because his purse was running low—but he proposed, and I eagerly assented, that we should camp out one fine night.

We had the remains of our dinner, and we bought some corn and fodder for our horses, and the gig-box full of sweet-potatoes. Wheeling off to one side from the road as evening fell, we soon had our horses tethered to trees and eating, a roaring fire with the potatoes roasting in the ashes, myself not more full of boyish excitement as to our Robinson Crusoe experiment than my father. I remember how our animals would pause, their mouths full of fodder, to look at us seated upon the gig-cushions placed on the ground at the fire, as if they demanded, "Why, what do you two mean by this arrangement?" and then holding their noses together in consultation before proceeding with their supper.

"Poor Bunny dying for want of air in the bucket is avenged upon us, Carter," said my father.

I knew what he meant, for after our potatoes we were both almost perishing for water.

"I would give a silver dollar for a bucket of water from the creek we passed a mile back," my father said again. Of course I knew it was a hint that I should mount Nubbin and ride back, but I was afraid. I did not go, and it hurts me to this hour!

What interested many thousands of the best people living, and for many years then, surely ought to interest us to-day. Imagine, therefore, my father arrived at one of the many churches which had applied for his visit as an evangelist, and were eagerly expecting him; a popular lecturer in these times having no such constituency either for numbers or for fervor as his. Most frequently the field of his labor lay in some city or village, the work and its results being the same as when in the country.

I remember most vividly our arriving, one cold, drizzly day in spring, at a huge church in the pine woods. It was the cathedral church, so to speak, of all the region around. Could any thing be more disheartening than that vast edifice on that miserable day? Not more than twenty persons there, on account of the weather—the leading members who had urged my father to come—and every soul of these dismayed because of the prospect, for it is an old, old church, deep set in the well-worn grooves of many years. Besides, if my father had only known it, nine-tenths of the congregation were wearied out with their pastor—this tall, thin, white-headed, care-worn minister, who welcomes Dr. Oglethorpe Quarterman, a power in the very name of my father, as he enters the door. The pastor introduces him to the pillars of the church there assembled—grave, somewhat hard-featured men of all varieties of the planter, and hardly one of them but carries in his heart, alas! like a dagger in its sheath, some aversion or animosity of years against some other member or officer of the same church. They all shake hands heartily with the long-expected minister, and are all disappointed in him. "Can this be the great Dr. Quarterman? Impossible!" is the feeling of every man of them. They had expected a person of large build, but of grave and solemn power, too, in his whole aspect; and here is a man, instead, unassuming as a child, genial and rosy, and simple as a boy. Besides, he refuses to go in the stately pulpit at all, takes his stand on the platform below, and, instead of the powerful sermon they expected, groups them around him as near as possible, and, after brief singing and prayer, talks to them in the most natural way. Nor does he speak more than half an hour. At first they are cruelly disappointed, then interested, then deeply attentive, then really touched. He asks the pastor to give notice of the services to follow, and, after the benediction, he somehow has all present upon his own level of feeling, child-like in this, that all are entirely at home with each other, beginning to hope in regard to the future of the "protracted meeting."

It is pouring down in torrents at the next service, yet the attendance is doubled, as is the interest. All the next day there is a steady down-pour, but the congregation is fourfold.

The interest so increased that there are three services instead of two. It holds up a little next day; the huge church is filled, and by a multitude expecting to be influenced for good. And to-day the visitor ascends the pulpit, takes a text, preaches a regular sermon. It is upon a profound and fundamental doctrine. He has no paper before him, and the people wonder at the closeness and clearness of his reasoning, never imagining how often he has cast and recast the whole so as to strike the understanding most directly and forcibly. The attention is almost painful in its intensity. In twenty minutes every intellect there is as thoroughly convinced on the point as it is of any statement in the multiplication-table. Then the speaker applies himself to each individual present, and to the heart of each. His earnestness fills, but never overflows, its banks, in a rapid, affectionate, importunate appeal to every one there present to decide, and to decide then. The pastor of the church weeps and breaks down as he attempts to close with prayer, proving himself thereby the weaker man of the two; and the evangelist, always scrupulously honoring the pastor of the church in which he labors, closes the service for him, in words few and tender.

The service in the afternoon is even more solemn. Once an aged officer of the church weeps aloud, and the thrill of feeling which ensues is hushed into silence as the preacher pauses and holds up his controlling palm. Nearer the close another person, by no means officer or member of any church — a hardened old reprobate instead — can not prevent his purpose of a new life from breaking forth in words. Instantly but quietly the hand of the speaker is held up, and the audience subside into a deeper feeling under the words, "The Lord is in his holy temple; let all the earth keep silence before him!" After that, even during periods of as deep feeling as men and women ever know, not the slightest confusion or exclamation interrupts the services; the weeping is general, but very silent. The stillness is at times so profound as to be awful, and it is God!

An inquiry-meeting follows for any who may choose to remain after benediction, and not a soul stirs from his seat.

"I am a stranger among you, as you all know," my father said, coming down from the pulpit, and standing on the platform below; "nor has your pastor, any one in fact, suggested that there is need of it; but if there be any Christian man here who is alienated from any other, if he wishes a blessing on his church and himself, let him now resolve to forgive and forget his quarrel, and forever!"

He sits down. There is the silence of a great expectation; people glance furtively at the war-horse of some feud of a generation as he sits upon a front seat on the left of the rostrum, and then at his life-long antagonist, the bronze-visaged planter upon the left. Both sit with countenances cast as in iron, interested in and more ashamed and astonished at the inward relentings of their own hearts than at any thing else. Each is going over to himself the years of peculiar and undeserved wrongs he has suffered at the hands of his foe, and wondering that the other can pretend to be a Christian and not come and fall at his feet and ask his forgiveness—the foe most in the wrong being most astounded at the hard-heartedness of the other. Silence deep and pregnant ensues; for all recognize the fact that the meeting has reached its crisis. There is a movement from the rear. Can it be possible! General Peyton Rutledge, member of

Congress, infidel, open and energetic scoffer at religion in general and at Dr. Oglethorpe Quarterman in particular, as "all humbug," is the man who walks steadily down the long aisle, ascends the platform, stands very erect, for he knows that he is the Daniel Webster of all the country around, in the estimation of his own party at least, the possible President of the United States some day. He stands upright, looks slowly and carefully over the vast congregation, and says, very deliberately, as when on the floor of Congress:

"You all know me; know me well. I am not at all excited, as you see. I have attended these meetings to study the folly of men. I know men. I have not changed my opinion of them. They are all fools, consummate fools; but I have found out to-day that I am of all fools the greatest. I am not a baby, nor a woman. I do not have a particle of feeling, not one particle. But I solemnly declare to you, till to-day, I never knew there was such a person—"

The speaker stops for quite a time, and holds himself down to the calmest of statements.

"Never dreamed there was such a person as—"

He stops, compresses his lips, grows very pale, begins again:

"Of course, I know there is a God; but I declare to you I never knew that he is also a man who died to save us. I never knew there was such a person as Jesus—"

And the great, strong man breaks down, for the first time in his life, in a passion of weeping, and is compelled to sit down, the entire audience melted with him into weeping.

But there is a loud "Amen!" and people look up and smile even through their tears. The most hopeless of the life-long foes alluded to just now is on his feet.

"And I a disciple of Jesus, an officer of this church," and he holds out, unable to speak, mute hands toward his white-haired antagonist, who has also risen. Rarely is human feeling so stirred to its depths as when those two meet in mutual embrace before all the people.

At the whispered suggestion of my father, who remains completely master of himself,

the pastor of the church leads in prayer as well as he can. For there is a singular reaching-out of hands all over the vast congregation, over pews and down and across long rows of intervening people; scores of men and women are "making it up," to be the warmest of friends hereafter, each one astonished at the folly which deferred so simple and delicious a duty so long.

Another week follows of sermons twice a day to overflowing houses—doctrinal, argumentative appeals to the heart through a convinced understanding. Denominational differences are wholly forgotten, and Christians of all sects work side by side. Weak brethren make injudicious statements, but the deep feeling is uninterrupted. The crazy man of the neighborhood—and what neighborhood is without?—makes a violent harangue, yet people laugh at what he says, without halting even, in the current of their new purpose. Low characters—poor white folks, generally—set off packages of fire-crackers under the very building during sermon, bribed to do so. The preacher pauses until the frightful uproar is ended, and then proceeds, the power of the discourse deepened by such illustration of the natural opposition of the human heart.

But Sabbath, the last day of the Evangelist's labor, has come. The whole country for miles around seems to be on the ground, encircling the huge frame church in an outermost ring of horses and vehicles of all sorts, next of colored people eager to enjoy the services, the innermost circle being that of white people, filling the church and scattered all around it outside, every window and door being open; for the very blessing of God rests upon the assemblage in the mildness and brightness of a perfect summer day, although it is still early spring. The pine-trees sound through all their tops in that music, weird and soothing, which is more like silence that can be heard than anything else. There is a calm, a sobriety, a sweetness of serenity which at once exhilarates and subdues. Look at the pastor of the church; his face glows with the gladness of a new power, and the renewed love of his people. No man in this world happier than he as he receives scores into his church; for it is Communion Sabbath; an afternoon service for the slaves, at which many of them also are taken into the church. There is no feeling as of spasm or even tension on the part of any. People feel rather that they have got out of an unnatural condition, are restored to a natural, child-like, and lasting frame of mind and conduct, in which it will be the easiest thing in the world to continue—a sense at once of power and peace never known before. There is the overflowing hospitality of a "basket-dinner," ten times the food required, even by the vast multitude, for the Master is there even in the matter of the loaves and fishes.

The service is slowly closed at last, and as against the protest of all present; and as the sun sinks in cloudless beauty, the people lingeringly, and with a thousand hand-shakings, melt into the "piny woods" and are gone, bearing one Sabbath, at least, in their hearts which will be remembered forever.

Monday morning sees my father and myself on the road again, the preacher, greatly refreshed by his weeks of labor, eager to begin again in the field to be reached to-morrow night, hoping to be able to keep on forever at the same rate.

Generations will pass, but no name more fragrant than that of Dr. Oglethorpe Quarterman in the church he leaves behind. Children are named after him, pastors take a new lease of life, churches date a new era from "the spring Dr. Quarterman was here, you remember."

CHAPTER VI.

THE "protracted meeting" just spoken of is but one instance of very many during two years of increasing labor on the part of my father. Sometimes I went with him—oftener, at least, than any other of the children, for I was, undeservedly I am sure, somewhat a favorite with my father. The toils spoken of did vast good to multitudes; the benefit to our own family was less apparent, and at this time a call is pressed upon the now even more distinguished Dr. Quarterman to a church in the capital of the leading Southern State west of Virginia. It is not the importunity of the church in that city, rich and strong as it is, and of pre-eminent influence, which decides my father. My mother had felt our homeless condition, and the injury it did the children, too deeply not to have influenced her husband at last, as by the very silence of her sorrow.

"It is not our church alone, Dr. Quarterman," the leader of the committee who had come to Virginia during one of my father's brief visits to us there, remarked. "We have the intellect of the State in the Legislature which assembles annually in our city. From our pulpit you will influence the whole State, sir!" "And there is another inducement," urged Mr. Patterson, this member of the committee with whom, child as I was, I had been most struck from the moment of his arrival—a small, thin-faced, stooping, eager man, with quick eyes, thin lips, and scanty beard—thriving commission merchant, as I afterward knew. "We know your love of work, Dr. Quarterman, know the nature and success of your labors. In addition to all that has been said, we have one inducement to offer that will delight you!" and he paused in triumph, while Mr. Clemming and Colonel Archer, the other committee-men, looked with wonder at their shrewd chairman, not knowing of what he spoke.

"We have already mentioned the parsonage in addition to the salary, itself larger—" began one of the others.

"How little you brethren understand Dr. Quarterman!" interrupted their leader. "The chief inducement we can offer you is—"

"Well?" said my father, expectantly.

"Our penitentiary!" and my father's eyes brightened as the man spoke.

"Our penitentiary, sir. Our noble penitentiary! You must have heard of it, doctor; never less than a thousand convicts: just to think of it, one thousand of the most desperately depraved wretches in existence!"

"And do you think—?" my father began, with an interest in the matter which he had not shown at all before.

"That you would be allowed access to them?" replied the other; "certainly, sir, most assuredly. As we have told you, Governor Hone is a member of our church, and, I think, you might be appointed chaplain, in addition to your pastoral work."

"How many convicts did you say?" asked my father, with the eagerness of a child.

"Over one thousand, sir," replied the other, in triumph, "and fresh recruits brought in by the county sheriffs almost every day. I know your travels have extended over quite a number of States, Dr. Quarterman; but I think," added the speaker, with some pride, "that we have in our institution the very pick and choice of the rascality of half the Union! A noble field, sir! More thoroughly depraved and hopeless wretches you could not desire. I mean—"

"Oh, I understand," my father said, eagerly. "I thank you for your kind opinion, brethren, and will take your call into prayerful consideration, and let you know. Beside he added, "I must consult my wife." Con his wife? certainly! But exactly as a y g man, madly in love with a maiden, cons s his next friend. The committee knew that the matter was in all probability settled, and the whole party went in to dinner in the best of spirits.

How well I recall the remark made toward the end of the repast, by the fat and hitherto silent member of the committee of three, Mr. Clemming his name! "Pardon me, Mrs. Quarterman, but you must allow me to say it, I never tasted turkey, I never ate ham before in my life equal to this;" and I do believe there were tears in his eyes as he spoke.

"Oh, you must thank Brother Archibald for that," my mother said; "the poultry is of his raising, the ham is of his own sugar-curing."

"Ahem," said Uncle Archibald, in custody of us all from the head of his table. "Agnes is correct. I give my entire mind to my place, not neglecting an egg or a negro. But Agnes understands cooking. It is a trait of old Virginia. Wait, however, until you have tasted her sweet-potato custard. Ahem! Arxis, remove the plates!"

"I do enjoy the clabber at breakfast," said my father, who had the appetite, keen and hearty, of every man who is in perfect health and always hard at work. "You will see it in the morning, brethren, in pans two feet broad, the cream as thick as your hand. But, Agnes, Brother Clemming will take a little more of the custard."

And he did, Brother Clemming, the fat committee-man. Very far we children were from blaming him; the potato-custard in its dish of earthenware as large as the clabber-pans, browned on top, and delicious beyond expression. Fat Mr. Clemming was merely just in the sentiments he expressed next day to my mother, as he shook her hand in parting:

"We will be happy, Mrs. Quarterman, allow me to say it, if we can have a pastor who is so fortunate in his wife. You will" —and it was said with feeling—"be thoroughly appreciated among us."

My father held the promised consultation with his wife. It was like that held with her when he had resolved upon leaving their former home; the assertion from the outset of his enthusiastic certainty, in this instance, that St. Charles—for so let us call the city to which he was invited—was the very field for him, and then his entreaty that she would not hesitate to suggest any objections.

"My dear husband! I am only too eager to have a home of our own again," she replied. "Besides, you know that you have settled the whole matter already. You are as eager about it as a boy," she added, smiling.

"My way, my dear," he replied. "You say I take a rose-colored view of things. A great deal better do that than to look at all things through blue spectacles. But here are these special considerations in regard to St. Charles;" and he mentioned eagerly this, that, and the other, as wonderful advantages, not forgetting the penitentiary.

"You know we found Washington City a peculiarly difficult field, my dear," she ventured to add, as the glow of his eagerness began to slacken. "How often have you said that, of all classes of men, politicians were the very hardest to be moved by the Gospel."

"You are right, Agnes, right! no doubt of it," he took her up with fresh energy. "But St. Charles is only the capital of a State. Besides, there is a breadth of heart, a simplicity of feeling, farther South not found in Washington."

"I am willing, my dear husband," my mother added, borne down by the urgency which proved, as he went on, that it was the very fact of the city being a capital which had decided him. "You are so overflowing with hope," she continued, "that all you approach glows with the same light. I am entirely willing. But, O husband, let us go there resolved, if it please God, to make it our final home. It ruins the family, this moving about!"

How happy my father was, the matter thus settled, and how restless until it was carried out! Up at earliest dawn, in the house, out of the house, making missionary trips to the wretches of Wrexford, dropping in at the negro-cabins upon all the aged and sick he was so happy as to find there, a religious service somewhere every night in the week, he kept the whole plantation, as well as all the region around, stirred up as under the blowing of some powerful wind from a happier land. I am satisfied, however, that Uncle Archibald, the moment we were all gone, sat down in his chair, saying, if only to himself,

"Ahem! I love my sister Agnes; I respect Brother Quarterman. But I am heartily glad it is all over."

And then, gold-headed cane in hand, sallied forth to re-assert his awful supremacy, so long and seriously impaired.

With winter we arrive at our home in St. Charles. The old homestead in Virginia, Uncle Archibald, Arxis, and all, begin to melt from the memory, as the whole world will melt some day, a sort of spectral dignity as well as dimness, clothing, as it ever does, even the meanest characters of the past. We live in St. Charles, in a four-story brick-house on the principal street, and every friend there has told us, not without awe:

"I suppose you have heard that it is Governor Hercules Hone who lives in that large house over the way—our senator, you know, in Congress, before he was made Governor of the State. People all think he will one day be President. He is a member of our church."

Little my mother cares for governor or monarch, until she has secured the proper servants. As to Archibald, Habersham, Virginia, Georgia, and myself, we are as happy as mortals can well be here below, the day we arrive.

"To think we are in our own home—own, own home!" Georgia says it, so much like our father, in her overflowing enthusiasm; but all of us make chorus to her in our hearts as we go upstairs to the attic, down-stairs into the deepest labyrinths of the cellar, all over the back-yard, and so up and down, in and out of the uncarpeted house all day, happiest of all that there is no Uncle Archibald on the premises.

We sleep late the morning following our arrival, for we are very tired. I am the exception, for there is a ring at the bell about day-break, and my mother, stealing into my room on tiptoe, says,

"Carter, dear, that must be the milk. Go down; but don't wake any body else."

And I arouse from abysses of slumb ad obey, wondering why it is always I, not some other and older of the children t am called upon. I shiver with cold I open the door in the basement; but I am warm enough the next moment, for, to my speechless astonishment, I find myself in the arms of good Mrs. Brown, our blessed old housekeeper before we went to Virginia.

"Hush! not a word, Carter," she said, rapidly taking off her things. "You creep back and sleep until breakfast is ready, dear. I dare say I can find the flour and the eggs."

I do go back, but it is only to dress myself without the least noise, and come down again to find Mrs. Brown, with a good fire in the cooking-stove, stirring batter for cakes, as if our two years' separation were all a dream of last night.

"I told you when you left that I would come as soon as we had a home, dear," she replied to my eager questionings. "You all laughed at me, but, you see, here I am. I had a good place with Colonel Jackson Jones in the city, but Miss Virginia had told me in a letter all about matters—where is the butter, Carter?—and here I am. I have lived too many years with your father and mother not to love you all, and whom else do I care for in the world? Don't make a noise—where do we keep the knives and forks?"

As I opened the drawer to show her, I noticed the very same old, old black Bible

"She finds what we call her sphere in reading her Bible and doing her work," my mother used to say to us, "and she is more contented than any one I ever knew before. Ah, if we all were but as good as Mrs. Brown!"

It must have been nine o'clock before Mrs.

"YOU ALL LAUGHED AT ME, BUT, YOU SEE, HERE I AM."

lying on the kitchen-shelf, as it used to do in our other home, as long as I can remember. Besides our household and her Bible, nothing else did Mrs. Brown care for in the world. Had the walls about these been adamant, she could not have been more entirely inclosed therein, not a wish even extending without.

Brown allowed me to ring the bell, telling me all that had happened meanwhile since we had parted. At last my mother came hastily down, wondering who rang a bell, calling upon the boys, as she did so, to hurry down to make a fire. It was as good as gold to see her face as she opened the door. There sat Mrs. Brown, breakfast hot on the table in the next room, her Bible in her lap, and talking quietly to me as of old.

"Oh, Mrs. Brown!" Not a word besides, but what a volume of love in the tones, as my mother, to her own astonishment as well as to the great embarrassment of her old servant, actually fell in her arms and kissed her. You may believe I made the house ring with my long-suppressed cries up the stairs.

"Oh pa, Mrs. Brown has come! Archy, Habby, Mrs. Brown! Virginia, Georgia, Mrs. Brown! Mrs. Brown!" and the whole household were in the room in a moment, surrounding and pulling her about and kissing her. I do believe my father even contemplated something of the sort, in his first impulse, as he entered the room.

"Nothing in the world, Carter, is sweeter than loving and being loved," Mrs. Brown explained to me at her leisure afterward; and all the least matters of the family smoothly adjusted themselves around her, like the iron filings around a magnet, every thing — cooking, washing, scrubbing, ironing, and the like — happening as serenely as the processes of nature, for the word "law" is only a different way of spelling love.

I am trying to hasten toward more important matters, or I would speak at length of our settling-down at last. I was the only child who went to church with my father and mother the first Sabbath. It was a handsome church, although by no means such a cathedral, to my eyes, as was our last church in the great city. Mr. Clemming gave my mother a cordial hand in the vestibule: he could never forget his meals with us in Virginia.

"Glad to see you," he said, with unction, as he conducted us to our pew.

My father was, of course, full of his sermon, yet I know that even he could not but be proud of my mother as we walked up the aisle of the crowded edifice. Possibly Washington society, as well as that of our late city home, may have had its influence; but she had the genuine old Virginia culture of person and manner which we all laugh about so much these days. Certainly she had the most beautiful carriage of her person of any one I ever knew, besides a sort of silent fascination as by charm of blood, of ancestry —

It is just what I feared when I began these lines: that I would put too much of my idolatry of my mother in my narrative. Yet you will certainly allow me to record the fact that, as I sat beside her in our pew on the occasion in question, I glowed with satisfaction and pride in knowing how much every body must be admiring my mother; how proud they must be to have such a pastor as my father up there, so broad and fresh-colored and persuasive, but especially to have such a pastor's wife! I know that little Habersham and Virginia were entirely of my opinion; the others of the family never had as much to say on the subject.

For weeks on weeks after this, my mother was in the parlors receiving calls, in the repose of knowing that all things were moving down-stairs as smoothly as the stars, under the management of Mrs. Brown. We children had not yet started to school, and I remember we were all in the room when Governor Hercules Hone made, as our nearest neighbor as well as a member of our church, his first call. None of us were afraid of the governor after the first ten minutes. How well people, especially of Washington City and his own State, knew him! Tall, loose-jointed, angular, and awkward, except when making a speech, and then his thought made his very person eloquent. No need to be told that he was a distinguished man. Even the large mouth could not ruin the effect of his clear eye and high, fair, open brow, the whole aspect of the man being as of one always the object of regard on the part of multitudes, somewhat hollow-eyed, and worn out by it as a cliff is by the wash of unceasing seas. His wife, who accompanied him on his first call, was simply a plain, home-like, honest little body, whom he had loved and married long before he became at all known. A lady who never went to Washington, to whom her husband was "Herky" as when they first loved, and who cared very little for any thing outside of him, as not the governor but simply her husband, and for their children, a wild, spoiled set, if report was true.

A singular liking sprung up between the governor and my mother from the very first. I am satisfied he admired her more than he did my father — a sort of freemasonry as

of old Washington society between the eloquent senator of yore and this Virginia dame
—for you never would have taken my mother to be the wife of a minister, I am compelled to say, by any thing in her appearance, I mean.

"Your eldest son, Archibald, has fine talent, madam," he said, as he and his silent
bit of a wife arose to leave, for I lingered in
the drawing-room beyond, " if he can be controlled to use it as he should—fine talent.
He is only a year younger than our son Horace. I hope they will learn to like each
other. Your youngest, Carter, I think you
called him, is reliable—a noble boy. I pride
myself, Mrs. Quarterman, on reading people
at a glance, and what I wanted to say was
that your son Habersham—"

My mother must have colored, poor little
Habby was so diminutive, his hair such a
violent red in contrast with his pale face;
we often feared, too, that he was even defi-
cient; at least I imagined that my mother
must have shown mortification from something in the tones of the governor as he
added, so clear and strong:

"They are all fine children. What was
to be expected"—with a bow—"of the children of such parents? But your son Habersham, madam, is really the most talented of
them all—decidedly so. He may prove somewhat eccentric, but if he lives, you will see
that I have not studied human nature in
vain — remarkable talent! Good-morning,
Mrs. Quarterman. We live right over the
way, and will be glad, Mrs. Hone and myself, to see the doctor and yourself! Often,
I hope!"

I do not know how the governor's opinion
of Habby became known in the family, since
I never spoke of it. Archibald was greatly
amused, and twitted Habby with it in his
scornful way, until our father had to stop it
with a severe rebuke. Georgia had one of
her moods of boyish fun and frolic at the
very idea, until she saw that poor little Habby grew pale as death, instead of bursting
into tears at her treatment, upon which she
whirled over into a mood of affection and
tenderness for the boy which made him still
more angry. In some wifely way my mother told her husband of the confirmation of
her own hope, not so boldly expressed. Any

way, my father, generally too full of his ministry to give us any but scant attention,
showed a sort of respect for his dwarf of a
boy that he certainly had not manifested
before. In some motherly way, too, I dare
say, at night, after he had gone to bed, or
some morning before he was up, she had
cautiously told Habby at least enough to
awaken a new hope within his bosom. None
of us could say in what it lay, yet there was
after this a quiet self-respect in the boy, a
gleam of happiness which we had never observed before, coupled with an eagerness to
learn, which had to be firmly controlled lest
it should wreck what little there was of the
poor little mite of a body.

After all the congregation had called, my
mother entered upon the work of returning
visits as upon a business. She makes no
attempt ever to do so with her husband: he
moves too rapidly for her, for he has a vast
deal to do.

"To wait for any body and to walk slowly are two things I never could do, Agnes.
I like to have you move in slow curves and
spiral lines. It is more beautiful as well as
graceful; but we men have to go in straight
lines, direct to our object." And it is not
long before his grave yet glowing countenance, cordial yet hurried manner, step quick
and eager, are known all over the city of St.
Charles.

"Oh, if I could only remember faces and
names, but especially names!" he often said.
"I see in my congregation hundreds of persons, am introduced to scores every day, and
I can not tell who has been introduced and
who has not. I fasten my eyes upon a new
face, and study it in connection with the
name, and say, ' Now, surely I can remember
that you are Colonel Richards, and not Major
Peters — Colonel Richards! Colonel Richards!' And yet I get it all mixed up, and
am sure to say Major Peters instead next
time. I have known so many thousands of
people. They pass under my eyes like coin;
each is as like the other as are silver dollars;
it takes me months to tell them apart!"
And I do believe my father made this trouble
also a matter of especial effort and prayer.

As to my mother, who slowly and steadily
made the round of her calls, never hesitating
an instant as to face or name, remembering

accurately whether there were grandmothers and children to be asked after or not in each case; as also whether it was Mary or Augustus who had measles; I am satisfied that she made at last the most favorable impression upon the people, notwithstanding the reserve peculiar to herself.

"Would you believe it, Agnes," my father said at tea one evening, "I asked Miss Anderson the second time to-day after her children; and I am almost certain I inquired of Mrs. Parker yesterday, after her husband, whom I buried, you know, the week after my arrival!"

CHAPTER VII.

THE three officers of the church who had been to see us in Virginia—Mr. Clemming, Colonel Archer, and Mr. Patterson—were the leading men as well as officials of the church. It was impossible for you not to like Mr. Clemming. In his good-natured way he would stop any of us whom he met on the street, and give us a cordial shake with his warm and somewhat pulpy hand, always laughing; often dropping in upon us at dinner or at tea in the familiar style of the South, causing us all to linger long at the table in honor of the special ginger preserves or Ocoogee limes, produced in reference to his well-known partialities. And Colonel Archer! It is almost a pity to know such a man: you miss him, when separated from him, all the rest of your life. He was a tall, somewhat stoop-shouldered Kentuckian, in his youth the only child of wealthy parents, who had spoiled him. After being expelled from a dozen colleges, he had become a lawyer, fighting duels, editing partisan papers, running for office—his life one long and exceedingly varied "spree." In accidental attendance upon one of my father's protracted meetings, far enough away from St. Charles, he had been struck down like Paul on his famous journey, and he could never get over his unspeakable astonishment at the Christ of that first revelation. There was the simplicity and wonder of a child whenever Christ was in question; my father never being able to interest him in the least degree in any other part of religion beyond what related directly to its Founder; all his remarks and prayers in prayer-meeting being full of a freshness and force simply inimitable upon that point, his whole life being in perfect accordance therewith.

Mr. Patterson my mother never did like, nor did any of us. It was he who decided my father by casting the penitentiary into the trembling scale on his visit to us in Virginia; and he was always as shrewd, eager, incisive, and insistent in every thing. No man more eager than my father; but Mr. Patterson had the eagerness of steel—cold, glittering, exceedingly sharp as compared with the fountain-like gush of his pastor's enthusiasm, sparkling in the sunshine ever from the inmost depths of his heart, but varying this way and that with every breeze that blew; that morning of the election, for instance, not six months after we came.

"It is a matter of importance, Dr. Quarterman, that you should vote," urged Mr. Patterson, who had obtained admittance to my father's study, he having determined not to vote at all.

It seems that the special meaning of Melchizedek is the theme of the sermon for next Sabbath, and my father is unusually interested in the preparation of the same.

"A matter of vital importance, Dr. Quarterman. Your people expect it of you," continued Mr. Patterson, overruling his pastor's objections.

Now, not a soul in the church, except himself, who had some axe to grind, had ever even thought of the pastor in that connection; but people, in their eagerness, often imagine that every body else must be interested in what interests them.

"You ought to vote, you must vote, doctor!" continued Mr. Patterson, a metallic something in his tones at which my father winced. But it was so in regard to every thing; the exact hour of service, the sort of singing for exactly such an hour, the precise mode in which to conduct a funeral, what ought to be done in reference to a member under discipline, the accurate who and where and when, and what and how, were instant intuitions to Mr. Patterson—sharp, clear, final as mathematics. There were an energy and zeal and effective force about it all which delighted my father at first; but Mr. Patterson's intuitions were so very prompt in reference to matters, the largest and the least, that there was no time allowed for even consideration on the part of others. Fat Mr. Clemming laughed, and was glad to be rid of any bother about the sexton, and the organist, and all the rest. Colonel Archer would only let out his long legs a little farther, as he sat on the sofa in the vestry, and say:

"Oh, all these are small matters, gentlemen. Glad Brother Patterson here takes so much interest in them. You know this thing makes no difference, one way or the other."

And, all along, the pastor was blaming himself for a growing restiveness under this exceedingly efficient officer of the church.

"Talk of a captain sailing his ship," Mr. Patterson's clerks would often remark among themselves, in his commission warehouse; "if this concern isn't run by a captain, I'm mistaken."

Yet the chorus of the crew in question always was:

"So he does, and it's hard on us. But I'll tell you what it is, boys, that's the way he makes it pay so well. Way I'm going to do when I marry his daughter—bury the old man, and boss it over you all myself."

The point at issue is whether a church can always be run like a ship or a commission business—a question which each of us can discuss elsewhere and at his leisure.

And Mr. Patterson carried his point, as he generally did, that morning of the election, the point in this case being Dr. Quarterman, the end to which he carried him being the polls.

"Not that, not that," the layman said, in a sharp whisper, as he saw his pastor take a ticket from one of the many eager hands held out to them as they stood at the ballot-box, "this is our ticket—this, this!" urging one on him.

"Oh no, Brother Patterson, the other is the one I vote," my father made whispered reply. "I had considered it all before you came. I ought to have told you, but was so full of my sermon when you were in my study. And, now," depositing the obnoxious ticket, "if you will excuse me, I must hurry back." No child more innocent than the minister as he bows and hastens back, to blow up into fire again the sermon cooling all this time, like an ember on his table; a mere hurried whisper between the two, yet whirlwinds blow very often in the seeming zephyr of the lowest whisper! But all that my father thinks of, as he winds his eager way home again through the crowds gathering to the polls is, "Now, again, about that mystical Melchizedek; was it truly a Theophany or not? an anticipation of the Incarnation, or merely a parable?"

For my life I can not recall what all the excitement was about that day, nor, I dare say, can any body else who was there, like a spark above the roaring forge. All the whisky-shops around the polls were crowded, many temporary booths erected for the purpose, in addition to the regular establishments; not a cent to pay at any, the liquor being at the expense of Brown and Peters, the rival candidates. I had gone with my father and his friend to the polls, had been forgotten by him as he hurried home to his sermon, and there I was, a straw upon the seething swarms of men and boys, the excitement deepening as the day wore away. The negroes had no more to do with the voting than with the movements of the stars, yet all that could had come in from all the plantations around, attracted by the heat of the contest, as one is by a fire-place in winter. Every man seemed at least excited by liquor, all talking vehemently to each other as the mass was swayed hither and thither, paying scant attention to the orators, who, elevated on goods-boxes here and there above the multitude, were discussing with plentiful gesticulations the tremendous issues involved. The most attentive audience encircled a particularly low, thick-set, bald-headed, greasy old Autolycus of a peddler, who had driven his cart, emblazoned with flaming and infamous pictures, into the heart of the vast crowd, and was singing obscene songs, but in so hoarse and harsh a voice, like a loathsome frog with its mouth full of mud, that the people had to get very near to make out the details of his dirty meaning. I wish from my heart I could blot it from my memory, but the face of the blessed sun to-day is not more distinct to me, as I write, than is the wagging of that wicked old head, the rheumy leer of those lascivious old eyes, the up-and-down movement of those wrinkled old hands as the aged wretch croaked, turning, by incessant movement on his heels, from one side to the other as he did so; not selling any thing, so far as I could see—mere enjoyment of his own wickedness for the wickedness' sake!

But I was heaved away with the current first into one drinking-place and then into another, the bar-tenders in their shirt-sleeves, the perspiration running down their red faces, pouring out the free liquor to the crowd at the bar, and, over the heads of these, to the throng cursing and struggling behind. The air of my room as I write is full of the combined smell of the mint and whisky of that hour! But there is another rush, this time of boys, and I am swept, half helpless, through the outer room of a mulatto barber into his long saloon behind, all the walls covered with pictures of such a sort that I instinctively cover my eyes with my hands even as I write, and rush out again. It would have been so easy for me then to have said a word about it, say to eager Mr. Patterson, and he would have taken such peculiar pleasure in having the place despoiled, and the "free negro" who kept it whipped by the constable! What boyish sense of honor kept me from revealing it all, I can not say.

But, hustled into the centre of the outer multitude again, I find that the contest is growing hotter and hotter. It sounds like the fusilade of armies in full action. Earlier in the day there would be a shrill "Hurra for Peters!" to be answered, and with deliberation, some minutes later by "Hurra for Brown!" But the forces have closed about the polls, and the "'Ra, Brown!" "'Ra, Peters!" is unceasing and deafening. By me, on my left, is a man with a drawn bowie-knife in his hand, very cool and slow of speech, as he tells what he paid for it,

how admirable its temper, how willing he is—very deliberately—to—

"Put this hyer knife into any one of them Brown bugs, ef he comes foolin' about me. 'Ra, Peters!" this cry being thrown in with a sudden violence which strikes me like a blow. At this moment a noble Newfoundland dog halts between the man and myself, looking around in a dignified way, and sniffing inquiringly for his master. Unfortunately, the dog is black.

"You a dog, a nigger dog at that, an' hustlin' me!" is the slow remark of the man, and, with a downward plunge, the keen blade is passed through the animal! At the same moment there is, for some unknown reason, a sudden and universal yelling, the rapid report of fire-arms, a violent upheaval of the multitude, and I am lifted up and borne along by the flying mob in an agony of excitement and curiosity out of the square and down a side-alley, where, finding my own feet again, I get home as rapidly as I can; my chief motive in hurrying back being to astonish them all at home, especially Virginia and Georgia, with a part, at least, of the wonders I have seen.

Next day the excitement is utterly over, coming and going like a tropical storm. A man had his face demolished by a brick hurled by some one at the crowd on general principles, but that is all.

"I deem it my duty to say that the whole election was a disgrace to our city!" my father said next Sabbath from the pulpit, with more or less relevancy to his text. And every inhabitant of the town agreed with him, only (speaking of it as of a storm about the date of the equinox) added generally,

"Election-day, you know, and what could be expected? How little these ministers understand of human nature!"

The election is over and forgotten in a more sudden event still. Here is David, our "yellow boy" of old, on another visit from Liberia! He is accompanied by grass sacks filled with dates, oranges, cocoa-nuts, and curious fruits never heard of before. As to the sea-shells, Virginia and Georgia are in ecstasies over them! But all of us looked at David as the greatest curiosity of all. Our former slave was so short a time ago but "a very likely boy, worth at least eight hundred dollars," as many a friend told my father when he gave him to himself on condition that he went to Africa, and here he is again, clothed in broadcloth and fine linen, with mustache and pocket-handkerchief, and purse having gold therein. He has also, as he eats his meals upon the kitchen-dresser, and talks to Mrs. Brown and the rest of us while doing so, a something derived from travel and study and personal responsibility, to say nothing of his genuine love for us, which puzzled me extremely as I stood by him, trying to calculate how much he would bring in dollars now. I tell of him to all my school-mates, saying, carelessly,

"We once owned him, and he is now something or other in the Liberian Republic; president, perhaps: I never asked him!"

How strangely it happened, his standing with us one day during his stay, by the window, as the chain-gang passed! Just at that time there was a demand westward for slaves, and the route of the great slave-trade lay from the East through St. Charles, and, our house being on the principal street, sometimes hundreds a week passed along the sidewalk by our very door, always held together, like a long team of oxen, by chains. And how we hated it! I remember my mother, never out of the South in her life, turning away from the sight, her hands clasped, her eyes uplifted, saying something as if in prayer. No one spoke of it but with horror. There was a peculiar audacity, a sort of brazen effrontery, in the aspect of the blacks as they went by with a jaunty and swinging gait which had to be seen to be appreciated; it was the assumption, on the part of the slaves, of defiant indifference, not as against others so much as against the inmost self of each man of them: however blindly, every one of them protested in his own soul against the thing as utterly as any other looking on! And there stood our David at the window, stroking his mustache thoughtfully, and looking down upon them as they passed, like a sailor who has reached the summits of towering cliffs upon wrecked companions drowning in the surge below.

"It is like that disgraceful election we were just speaking of," the Hon. Hercules Hone said, the day they passed, while David, whom he had come over to talk with, was

with us. "There is no animal living for which we Southern people have a greater loathing than for a slave-trader."

"If they would not sing so, governor," my mother said. "Why do they always sing as they go by?"

"To keep up their spirits, madam. The traders give them tobacco and sugar to do it. And so you prefer Africa, Mr. David?" said the governor, and that led the conversation off upon the great topic of the day, the revolution going on in Texas.

"What I dread, Mrs. Quarterman," he said, as he rose to take his leave of my mother in the old ceremonious manner of their Washington City days, "what I most dread is lest my boys should catch this Texas fever. It would break Mrs. Hone's heart, for she cares more for her boys than she does for me. There are a great many things in this world, a great many things, my dear Mrs. Quarterman, which we deeply deplore, but can not help!"

My mother must have understood that he spoke of slavery, for she added, as she accompanied him to the door, "That is what Mr. Quarterman says, God is on the throne! Good-day, sir, and please say to Mrs. Hone how happy we will be to see her."

"And you like Mrs. President, as we call her?" the governor added, as he opened the door.

"Very much, indeed. I met her in Washington while her husband was President," my mother added. "What refined manners she has!" and in saying that my mother unconsciously defined the difference between herself and Mrs. President, for, with Governor Hone and all St. Charles, we will so style her. The peculiar charm of my mother lay in a grace and refinement as simple, natural, and entirely her own as are its bloom and fragrance to a flower. Mrs. President was a stately brunette, who wore her exquisite bearing and manner as she did her curls clustered on either side of her head, her silks and laces and diamonds. There was nothing you could object to as artificial or insincere, nor could you imagine the lady as being in her deepest seclusion other than when in society, yet "manner" expressed it all; and my mother was to her as a duchess of the oldest blood in comparison to the wife of a lord mayor; her grace, in this case, never, I am very sure, dreaming of such comparison.

"I am glad," my mother continued, sincerely, "I am glad she lives here; so glad she attends my husband's church. A more genuine lady I never knew," my mother continued, with warmth.

"I know another quite as much so," said the governor, and he bowed with old-time grace and formality, bowed with eyes and inmost soul, so to speak, as well as with his long and somewhat awkward body, and withdrew. My mother's face fairly tingled with color after he had closed the door, the subtle pleasure of the compliment consisting in the sincere respect with which it was spoken.

"And why did I not say at least something," my mother blamed herself, "as to his reaching the White House some day? I will always be but a country girl, as my mother used to tell me!" she added, sorrowfully.

As I look back I can see how my father and mother supplemented each other in the unity of their lives, like the exquisite workmanship of a skilled artificer—my father so simple, single-purposed, direct even to abruptness, headlong in his wonderful enthusiasm and devotion to his ministry; my mother so deliberate, accurate, full of all graceful care for trifles.

But Governor Hone is right in dreading the Texas fever. All the papers are full, at the date of which I speak, of the gallant struggles of the Texans for their independence; nothing else is conversed about in store and street, and at table. Young ladies wear silver stars on their bosoms, and form circles to sew for the soldiers gone or going. And, all of a sudden, there is, one bright morning, the roll of drums at the end of our street, and here comes a regiment on its march to the far-off field of glory.

How we crowded to door and windows to see them—Virginia, Georgia, Archy, Habby, and myself! Virginia has, as usual, little to say, but Georgia is overflowing.

"Oh! if I only had some roses, or at least a pot of coffee, to give them, or a flag, or a ham—something!" she exclaims, in enthusiasm. "Just to think, they are marching all

the way, ten thousand miles off on foot, and to fight and be killed, and all for freedom! Oh, how I wish I had something!"

And we all shared her feeling as the drums rolled louder and louder, and the men actually appeared in sight up street, all the boys of St. Charles thronging the street with them. But, alas for all romance, when they came to pass along the pavement by our very door! It may have been the state of their wardrobe, the total absence of funds and flags and uniforms, but Falstaff never had so woe-begone a following. Ragged, disreputable, dirty, every man of them apparently more or less drunk, they seemed to be the very sweepings and offal of the lowest dens and cellars.

"Hello, fellars, look at them two gals!" one of them shouted as they passed, carrying a leaking old tea-pot in his hand, the hot and smoking contents of which were streaming down his legs as he staggered along.

"The taller is the prettiest," called out another.

"Ah, but the short and fat one is the one for me. Won't you give a poor soldier a kiss, missy?" exclaimed a white-headed, old, red-faced reprobate, extending his ragged arms toward Georgia as he passed.

A more sudden change we never saw, even in Georgia, always liable to violent alterations of mood.

"Loathsome wretches!" was all she could say as she burst her way back into the house, pushing us all into the hall in her eagerness.

"I do hope the Mexicans will catch every one of them!" she declaimed at tea-table that evening. "The negroes singing along in chain-gangs are perfect gentlemen in comparison. Dirty wretches!" with a shudder.

"Ah, Miss Goosey, that is because they said you were fat," said Archibald; for we all knew that Georgia had a special horror of just that charge.

"No such thing, sir! Pretty soldiers, indeed! Besides, pa explained it all to us. Texas belongs to Mexico. What did people go there to live for, if they didn't want to be under the Mexicans?" And thereupon followed an eager discussion at the table, for

our parents were out taking tea that evening, upon the whole nature of the Texan
Revolution. Oh, if some one of us could but
have had the knowledge of Archibald's character which we now have! But who could
have understood him then?

Virginia, as well as Georgia, was violent
in behalf of the Mexicans. Even little Habby flashed up on the same side, as if from
his ashes. We had no idea how much the
poor little fellow had heard and read upon
the subject—far more than any of us. His
pale face lighted up, and he spoke with an
eloquence that surprised us—a subtle force
of genuine eloquence far more powerful than
the violence of Archibald, who grew more
and more excited in defense of the Texans,
his dark eyes sparkling, striking his fist
upon the table till the plates jumped, and
Virginia and Mrs. Brown had to insist upon
our carrying the controversy up into the
sitting-room.

"Horace Hone, Governor Hone's oldest
boy, told me at school yesterday that he had
half a mind to go," Archibald said, at last.

"His father and mother won't let him,"
the girls said, in chorus.

"Let him! What do you girls know of
boys? Let him! If I wanted to go and
any body tried to keep me from going, they
would soon see!" replied the excited boy.

"Bah!" exclaimed Habby, with a scorn
beyond his years; "you'd better try it!
Why, girls, you could not drive Archy to
Texas, even with a cowhide."

I was glad that our parents came in while
the strife was still raging, but I was sorry
after that they did. But who could have
understood Archy?

"Nonsense!" decided my father, when the
case had been laid before him by us all at
once. "It is nearly eleven o'clock. What

Horace Hone needs is a little peach-tree
tea," by which he meant the thorough application of a switch.

"Let any boy of mine try it! Hold your
tongue, Archibald, and go to bed instantly!
Let me never hear another word, sir, from
you on the subject!"

Astronomers say that, some day, by means
of vast crosses, circles, and triangles of fire,
we will be able, if the characters are miles
long, to communicate with the other planets.
May be so; but it is a pity any one of us is
often so utterly ignorant of what is going
on in the world of another's heart in reach
of our hand. Surely we ought to know
more of such a world when that other is
one's own child, the reproduction of one's
own self.

Archibald said nothing, and went to bed.
Nor was the subject alluded to for a week.
It must have been ten days after the Texan
soldiers passed, when Georgia burst into the
breakfast-room, exclaiming:

"Oh, pa! oh, ma! Horace Hone has run
away! Mrs. Hone's Mary was over to bor-
row some milk of Mrs. Brown, just now"—
borrowing, let it be inserted here, being of
the very essence of neighborly conduct at
the South and among the most wealthy—
"and says so. Isn't it dreadful?"

"But why isn't Archy at breakfast?" asked my father, at last, after we had talked
the matter over. "Georgia, go and call
him down. I wish to have prayers in half
an hour."

In a few minutes Georgia was down again,
weeping and exclaiming,

"Oh, pa! oh, ma! Archy is gone! He has
taken all his clothes, too! I thought I heard
somebody stealing down-stairs last night.
He is gone—gone with Horace Hone—gone
to Texas!"

CHAPTER VIII.

No need of describing the grief and confusion following in our family upon the knowledge that Archibald had fled, the utterness of our astonishment proving the utterness of our ignorance of Archibald himself all these years, as well as later days. My own feeling was one purely of deep indignation that he could treat our mother so, an indignation which, possibly, may color all I will have to say of my brother hereafter. What I hated most was that selfishness in him which forgot her in the gratification of his own perverse whims.

"To think, too, of his treating father so!" Georgia kept saying, too angry to cry until next day, when, in her changing mood, she wept and bewailed herself with even greater violence.

"What I dread most," little Habersham said, "is his coming back!"

"Why, what can you mean, Habby?" Virginia (who had been the only silent one except myself) asked, with a kind of quiet amazement.

"He went off suddenly, because he thought so much of Texas and so little of us," Habersham replied. "See if he does not take as sudden and violent a fancy to hate Texas and love home. The more he is compelled by things or people to stay in Texas, that much the more will he be determined to come back. Whatever other folks want him to do is the very thing he always won't do. Poor fellow!"

But we did not listen to him or to anybody else in the consternation of the hour. The one person not thrown out by the disaster was Mrs. Brown, who considered her duty, under the circumstances, to lie in keeping house that much the more exclusively and silently and industriously; the excitement of the hour causing her to revolve but that much the more swiftly and steadily within her own orbit. If ever individual lived wholly within an appointed circle, that woman was our Mrs. Brown.

"Be like your sister Virginia, my dear boy," she said to me, in an interval of the wild coming and going that followed. "She hasn't said hardly one word, but how thoughtful she is, trying to comfort your father and mother, and keeping her sister quiet! That is the reason we all love her so."

In the first announcement we all knew that Archibald must have gone off with Horace Hone, and my father and mother had hurried over immediately, meeting the governor on his way to our house, and turning him back that they might consult together in his library.

"I would beg of you to go to her bedroom, and try and talk to Mrs. Hone," the husband said to my mother; "but I know she is best left alone. She is crying so violently that no one can do any thing with her until she has worn herself out. She is but as the youngest of her children where they are concerned, and I am glad she is exhausting herself by weeping; it will relieve her. And now, Dr. Quarterman, what do you think we had better do about our young rascals? Don't leave the room, Mrs. Quarterman. We will need your excellent sense."

"Something should be done immediately," exclaimed my father, who was greatly agitated. "I will hire men to go. I will take the stage myself. I will write instantly to some one to supply my pulpit—"

"Will you excuse me, doctor?" the governor said, not at all thrown out by things, as cool as if nothing unusual had happened. "When we met just now in the street, I was merely stepping over to tell you not to trouble yourself about the young scamps. I am not very sorry. It shows spirit. Why, sir, I ran away when I was about Horace's age, ran away on a steamboat going down the river, and tried my luck in New Orleans as shop-boy, hotel-clerk, auctioneer, and a dozen things besides. For my part, I do not intend to do any thing whatever, beyond making believe, in order to soothe Sukey," by which prosaic name the governor always spoke of his very domestic wife. "Do them both good to see the world: let them go. I have spoiled Horace by letting him have too much money. I assure you I am not going to spoil him worse by leading him to suppose he is of enough importance to be hunted up. No, sir!" and there was a good deal of power in the matter-of-fact way the statesman said it, standing upon the rug before his library fire, rubbing his great hands together. "Let Archy go, doctor; madam, let him go! Better take to Texas than to drinking. Glad enough the young dog will be to get back!"

But neither my father nor my mother took this view of the conduct of the fugitives.

"No, sir!" exclaimed my father, with his usual energy; "I regard Archibald as if he had fallen overboard at sea. So carefully trained—"

"Then you should trust him to his training, doctor," interrupted the governor. "When the prodigal son ran away, did his father send after him? Let your boy try the swine and the husks a little. That will bring him back to himself and to you quicker than any thing else."

At this moment, however, David, who was still on his visit to us from Liberia, came into the room.

"You will excuse me, gentlemen—" he began.

"Well, David, which way did they go? Suppose we have David to go after them, governor," my father eagerly suggested.

"I would do all I could gladly," David replied; "but I am obliged to get to New York in time for our packet to Liberia, and

they would not come back for me if I caught them. Besides, I have learned something which makes me more anxious to leave. I do not know any thing about the boys. It is about a matter more important I wanted to speak."

"Bah! I think I know what you mean," said the governor, suddenly straightening himself up out of his laughing and listless manner. "Now, look here, boy," he added, as when he was speaking to a negro on his plantation; "it is just this. You make a clean breast of it! Out with it! Tell every thing you know. You had better!"

As he spoke, David drew a little nearer to his old master, the instinct to seek protection from him was so strong; but his eyes remained fastened full on those of the one who had just spoken, his yellow cheek growing whiter, and moistening his lips, grown suddenly dry, while his breath came fast and faster.

"Why, Mr. Hone!" said my father, in surprise, "there is no use of threats. If David knows about the boys, he will tell—"

"We are not speaking of them, doctor!" the governor added, impatient almost to rudeness. "Your boy here knows what I mean! Out with it, David, at once! We all know the law against free negroes—"

"I came here to tell enough to save you all, sir. I am a free man, sir, a member of the Legislature in my own country. Your threats are useless, sir. I find you know already more than I had supposed."

"I can not say we know," added the one addressed, evidently impressed by the calm and respectful bearing of the other, "but we strongly suspect. Go on, my good fellow, but tell us all."

"I will not tell how I came to know, nor will I betray any one," said David; "but I will not allow all the horrible—! horrible—! They all know how the State is drained of men gone to Texas, drained of arms, except what are in the arsenal here. How such ideas get among them God only knows. There is one man, the biggest, blackest negro in St. Charles, and the greatest fool—"

"Colonel Archer's boy, Mike. I know," interrupted the governor.

"I gave no name, but, law! Mars' Oglethorpe, you better look out!" said David, reverting in his strong excitement to the language of years ago. "I'm a-gwine away. I mean," collecting himself by a sudden effort, "that I am going to New York. You don't need me. I don't know how, don't know when, but I do know it begins here in St. Charles, an' mighty soon."

My father and mother, greatly perplexed at first, had come before this to understand without explanation what was meant.

"I have been dreading something of the kind for a month," my mother said. "We passed through it all once or twice before. I doubt whether any one has spoken about it, yet I feel sure every soul of us has had the same vague fear."

"It is like the approach of yellow fever in New Orleans, madam, or of an electric influence denoting the approach of a storm. No one has spoken to me, nor have I alluded before, in the hearing of any one, to the subject," the governor continued; "but the moment your boy began to speak, in fact before he said a word, I saw it in his face. Out with it, David. I am sure you have too much white blood in your veins to allow such horrors to take place. Besides, you are sensible enough to know how it will end!" And the governor arose as he spoke.

"Yes, sir," replied David, leaning forward upon his knuckles rested on the green cloth of the governor's table; "but please remember it is all nothing but the same yellow-fever kind of feeling with them, too—a sort of gathering thunder-storm, all at once in and among them, and without any concert of action on their part. So far as I know, they have no special plan or date settled to begin, no idea of what they will do. The field-hands are in it more than the house-servants, of course. But, you know, sir, the house-servants are always the worst when it does begin, as well as the smartest. The greatest fool of them all will make a break, and all the rest will follow it up. That is all I know, except little things. In Africa they call it fetich, voudooism, and I don't know what, and it is the same here. Only be on your guard, and it will all pass away like the fever or thunder."

But it is not necessary to detail all that followed, the thoughts of all in the room being utterly distracted for the time from the runaway youths. That afternoon David left, seriously embarrassed in his leave-taking by an enormous package of lunch, given him by Mrs. Brown, to last him to Liberia. How warm the grasp of his hands! how unspeakable the affection of his eyes in parting!

"And, at last, it is like the love of a Newfoundland dog, a very intelligent dog, of course," said Habersham, who was always saying singular things. "He is so inferior to us, you know," he added. "He loves us something in the way we love God, but I hope God don't love us with the kind of affection we have for him!"

We all agreed with our brother, although we did not say so. Now that Archibald was gone, Habersham, though much smaller than myself, who was years younger, being the latest born of all, had become the eldest brother. We all saw that he felt it, struggled to assume it. But, then, he was so very, very small, his hair so brilliantly red, his pinched face so deadly pale. There was a species, if I may so speak, of ferocity in the way with which he attacked his studies, springing upon his text-books, and clutching them to himself as with the teeth and claws of a wild cat desperate with hunger—if I may use such an illustration—far enough ahead of us all in every one of them. He read novels, poetry, history, in the intervals of study, with the same fierce zest, not so much for the pleasure of knowing.

"What you are trying to do, Habby," Archibald said to him only a few days before he fled, "is to add a cubit to your stature. No use, Habby; can't do it, no more than you can make one hair white or black!" For any thing more cruel could not have been said even by Archy, who, in a careless way, had the highest sense of his own talent as well as good looks.

"You will see," was all the poor fellow replied, but the deepening pallor of his face and the compression of his thin lips, as he spoke, meant more than the words spoken scarcely above a whisper. I recall now how I used to wake at dead midnight hearing him walk to and fro in his little room next to mine, for he always insisted upon having a room to himself, one reason, I do believe, lying in the fact that he would never have a looking-glass in his room, but always made his toilet—I know not how he managed it —without. Our mother used to say, with tears, that God only knew the agony of body as well as of mind this speckled bird, ings of Providence, would always remain a babe. To tell the whole truth, I do not think that any one of our household fully understood any other, even while we had for each other more than the affection common to families. Extremely little do we know of what is going on in Mercury, Mars,

"YES, SIR," REPLIED DAVID, LEANING FORWARD.

so to speak, of our flock endured. Affectionate as she was, I do not think even she understood her afflicted boy. As for my father, never knowing all his life any thing but exuberant health and spirits, such a powerful man in every sense, so full of occupation, I fear he never thought of Habersham except as of a baby who, in the deal- Neptune, and the rest of the planets; as much, I dare say, as the people in them do of earth; and almost as much ignorance of each member thereof on the part of every other exists in the solar system of every household. Surely He who makes each of us knows every one of us perfectly; and He loves every single strangely different one of us because He knows that one, and knows because He loves!

It could not have been a week after David left when the fever and the storm reached a crisis. The common apprehension had grown so deep and strong as to take the utterance of universal conversation, when the servants were out of hearing, about the probabilities of an insurrection. Every one said, "What nonsense!" yet no one but was influenced as by the universal infection of fear. Possibly it was a something in the atmosphere inhaled by all bosoms, black and white, for the panic culminated during a tremendous tempest.

We had sat up that Friday night of November, talking about Archibald, as usual. Letters had been written, messengers sent, every thing had been done that could be done, my father throwing all his energy into the matter, but no clue as yet. We were so worn out that we would gladly have slept if we could. The tempest was too terrible; the wind roaring with a violence more fearful than the pealing thunder or the incessant lightning, the agony of impending danger from the blacks worst of all. No appointed sound in music was ever more expected than the sudden pealing at last, about midnight, of, as if all at once, every bell in St. Charles!

They certainly had risen this time! We had so often before been wrought slowly up to the critical point and then disappointed, that I think even Virginia and Georgia were anxious, in a sense, that the negroes this time would rise, that we might see what it was like. I am satisfied our strongest feeling was a fear lest we should be disappointed again.

"Oh, I do hope not!" exclaimed Georgia, who in her hastily assumed clothing was running around as if in eager preparation for a picnic. "When will they begin, Carter? What do you think they will do, Habby? Oh, is it not splendid? Mrs. Brown won't come out of the kitchen. She intends to fight with the things she is most used to handling—her rolling-pin and irons and mop-handle. Oh, pa! I tell you what; suppose you stand on the front step and try and preach a sermon to them when they come. 'My text, dear brethren, may be found in the five hundred and fiftieth Psalm: Servants, obey your masters in the Lord.' Wouldn't it be queer! Oh no! I tell you, Virginia; you sit down at the piano, and the moment they break in, you sing, 'Flow gently, sweet Afton, disturb not our dreams.' I'll help you! Oh, pa! what is it? Please, don't let them hurt us. Oh, Carter! Oh, Habby!" and Georgia passed out of her wild mirth into a paroxysm of terror, for all the sky was suddenly bright with a great blaze.

"It is the arsenal, father," I said to him as I stood beside him at the window, hatchet in hand, for, boy-like, I knew more about St. Charles than he did.

"Do you not think it might be well, Agnes," my father said, in a low voice, as the bells rang fast and faster, to my mother standing near him in her night-clothes, "to call them all into our bedroom here and have a prayer?" But he himself spoke doubtfully.

"No, my dear," she answered, promptly, "I would not. It is only the negroes!" as if she had been speaking of an incursion of mosquitoes. Strange the degree in which utmost terror was mingled with profoundest contempt, and in us all.

"I think, pa, that their plan is to draw all the men away from home to the fire, and then attack the houses," I said; and I found that he was thinking the same thing, as, in fact, every body in St. Charles did, for the city let the arsenal burn, those living nearest contenting themselves with protecting their own homes from the flames. And so the flames ascended high and higher, the winds roaring loud and louder; the paroxysm of anxiety waiting, watching from every window, listening keenly to every sound; the heart of the whole city rolling, as with one great wave of feeling, up to a certain culminating crest; pausing there a moment, then breaking, so to speak, and passing away in foam. Up to three o'clock of the stormy morning; but, as the clock struck the time from my father's church-tower near-by, the impending clouds fell all at once in a deluge of rain. Then a dull, heavy sound, the red glow hurled by the explosion of the powder far up into the sky in a fountain of burning beams and flying cinders; Georgia, smitten by it to the floor, with her hands alternately over her eyes and ears, too terrified to exclaim or scream. For a few minutes thereafter the fiery glare down-town struggled against the rain, then swiftly faded; and as the darkness resumed its sway, I suppose there was not a soul in the city that did not feel with Georgia, as she went back to her room slowly and discontentedly, exclaiming, "Oh, isn't it a shame! To be so sure of a rising and all, and nothing at last. I never will believe in another rising as long as I live! It is too bad! If I was the negroes, I would be ashamed of myself!"

And that is all. No city or village in the South, no country neighborhood, but had, during those years, from time to time, some such panic, with one or two terrible exceptions followed by the same lack of all result. What degree of real danger was to be apprehended was in every case unknown; unknown, possibly, by the blacks as well as by the whites. As was said, the panic was more like a sudden and mysterious malaria in the air than any thing else, and as much beyond all definite science.

My father preached, on the next Sabbath, a powerful sermon on the prince of the power of the air, the application being that every one present should beware of the adversary in his own case; for, with my father, every sermon was as completely for the application as are the helve and iron of a sledge-hammer for the blow to be struck.

Some said arrows headed with flaming tow had been shot into the arsenal through a broken window; others, that the negro Mike had climbed up by the lightning-rod and fired the building through a hole broken in the roof; but to this hour St. Charles knows as much and as little of the facts of the case as the reader of this.

The next day being Saturday and holiday, all the boys in St. Charles were raking the muskets, and bayonets, and pistols, and swords out of the ashes of the arsenal, and bearing them home in triumph — Georgia, and even our serene sister Virginia, deeply interested in the quantity brought home by Habby and myself.

"It will be so nice when the next rising comes," said Georgia. "Only one is sure of being disappointed. It's always so in this world!"

Which remark was illustrated, when a committee of citizens (for St. Charles had then no police in particular) appeared in our back yard the next day, Sunday though it was, as with every house in the city, and reclaimed and bore off our rusty treasures.

Although nothing was ever done to Colonel Archer's negro Mike, universal suspicion rested upon him as the intended leader of the proposed rising. He was a black of unusual size, and of densest darkness in all senses of the word. Little children thereafter shrieked and fled when they saw him coming up the streets; the larger boys assumed a bravado as he passed, trembling under it all; while every one eyed him curiously wherever he went. And he was nervously conscious of it — not a baby girl in the city a greater coward than Mike in open day.

How singularly the heart works in the bosom, too, of one like Mike, as genuine a negro as if he had never left Africa! The Sabbath afternoon following upon the burning of the arsenal, an alarm ran through the city that a young man universally known was drowned while boating on the river. With all the boys in town I hurried down to the banks while the body was being dragged for. As I stood upon a projecting point, I noticed that Mike was standing beside me, eagerly watching the dragging for the dead, full of ejaculations at every incident. Suddenly the boat in which was seated Major Hampton, my teacher in the school I attended, grappled something in the river bottom. During the breathless expectation of all who rushed to the spot, the body was slowly drawn to the surface, the boat being some dozen feet from land in very deep water. As the sodden face was lifted to the surface, the dark hair falling away from it, Mike, standing beside me, backed himself with violence against the crowd behind him, and then, running to the edge, made the leap as of a leopard upon the drowned man, striking him loose from the grappling-irons, and having to be drawn himself from the water while drowning, as, like almost every negro living, he was unable to swim. I did not know which astonished me most, the sudden oaths of Major Hampton, whom I had supposed a devoted Christian, or the conduct of Mike. And who can tell? Was it a nervous desire to reinstate himself in the estimation of men by his zeal for the drowned man, or was it the blind impulse of mere excitement?

But all is forgotten as the drowned man was once more grappled beneath the muddy water. In a moment he is drawn ashore, stripped and rolled upon a barrel, face downward, rubbed with whisky, kneaded in the stomach and breast by Major Hampton, kneeling upon him for the purpose, with his sleeves rolled up.

"Run for your life, Carter," he said to me, "and get your parlor bellows!" and I had gone and come with it at a rate of speed which left me almost as devoid of breath as the man lying there so blue and cold. None the less, the impulsive major, having knocked out some teeth with the thole-pin of the boat and inserted the nozzle, I toiled to inflate the lungs of the poor fellow, responsive to the kneading of the major—such strange mixture of the terrible and the ludicrous in it all.

"If it but please God," said the major, his emotion now taking the form of frequent and fervent ejaculations. Up to my father's arrival the major had been profane beyond description, as well as lewd and intemperate; and now that he had joined the church, we all, my father especially, lived in an agony of fear and of hope as to the result. The drowned man never breathed again, and it is Major Hampton chiefly I have reference to in mentioning this incident at all.

"What kind of a prayer-meeting did you have, my dear?" I have often heard my mother ask my father Wednesday evenings, on his return from that service, and as they were disrobing in their room next my own for bed, upon the nights of her absence from meeting.

"Well, Agnes, the attendance was large; there seemed to be much feeling; but then —" Here followed something like a groan.

"Major Hampton! Ah yes, I suppose so." My mother would be sure to complete the sentence. "What a singular providence he is!"

CHAPTER IX.

THE church had made good to their pastor the promise of shrewd Mr. Patterson that he should be chaplain of the penitentiary of the State, located in the suburbs of St. Charles, and I am satisfied that Governor Hercules Hone did not attach to his certificate of election as Governor of the State a hundredth part of the value my father did to the document by which he was put in complete spiritual charge of the thousand criminals, more or less, composing his prison parish. Whenever I possibly could, I accompanied my father on his visits to the penitentiary. He took great pleasure in his morning and evening ministrations at his own church, but the happiness of his life lay in that Sabbath-afternoon service at the penitentiary: the institution was more to him, in some senses, than his own household.

One reason I liked to go was that I was sure to meet Colonel Tom Maxwell. It was only on occasions of state that the colonel part of the name was ever employed, the vernacular usage being "Tom Maxwell," "Colonel Tom," "Old Tom." In fact, had you known the person, you never could have used the word "Tom," even in calling by that name your son or your horse, your dog or your black boy, without awakening in the mind of— it would almost seem—even an animal so addressed as well as your own, the idea of the tremendous Tom of whom I speak—to me, until I die, the typical and representative Tom of the race!

"How are you, doctor?" and "Halloo, Carter! that you?" would be his greeting at the inner door of the penitentiary, as my father and myself arrived at half-past two, to the minute, of a Sabbath afternoon. "Glad to see you. Come in." And he would give us each the grip of a big hand as we entered, for the colonel was of the huge Kentucky mold, near seven feet high, and overbroad in the shoulders even for that, his wide, warm face beaming upon you like the sun risen above the mountain range. You may have seen a seaman in command of a steamship, or a commander-in-chief in full uniform on horseback at the head of his army, possibly an autocrat upon his throne in imperial robes; but never did these men or any other seem more adapted to their summits of power than did the warden to his, the only question being, was the penitentiary made on purpose for the man, or the man for the penitentiary? Certainly you could not conceive of them apart.

"All ready and waiting, doctor!" the burly host of the occasion would say, and it was as if you had ascended the deck of a great steamer, had entered the lines of an army, had stepped beneath the sceptre of an emperor, so completely did the vast institution of towering walls and stone buildings seem, with its dense and peculiar population, under the complete mastery of that one will, no monarch quite so proud of his realm as Colonel Tom of his. For artistic purposes, I can imagine a very small warden ruling as vigorously, and by very quiet means; but I am compelled to speak of this Napoleon Bonaparte of my youth as he actually was; and I was always glad to get under him of a Sabbath afternoon, as one is glad to get out into a fine day, or under the blowing at sea of a good strong wind.

"You have your way of work," he would say to my father, resting from his rapid walk in the chapel while the turnkeys were mustering the prisoners, "and I have mine! No, I thank you, doctor; I make it a rule never to sit down while a prisoner can see me: being on my feet is part of my system. I have told you before, every rascal you will see in this room this afternoon is here by force of circumstances. His father was a thief, his mother a harlot, his home a hell—that's what's the matter with him. Or his father and mother were fools, and let him have too much money. Worse, perhaps, they were overstrict, and disgusted him into doing what he did; force of some sort. Or it was whisky, or woman, or starvation, or some other bad companion stronger than the man himself. Every soul of us is a straw, and goes as the wind happens to blow: force, doctor—all the difference is in the degree and direction of force. The lawyers are such knaves, the juries are such fools, the judges such soft-hearted old women all over the State, that none but the very worst scoundrels get sentenced here. Chain and stone wall and strong will are what hold them here. All a matter of force, and of what happens to be the strongest force."

"You have been reading books about force, colonel," my father began, a strong resemblance in certain points of build and breadth and florid healthfulness between the two men, with the mutual liking which belongs thereto.

"Not a bit of it, doctor," replied the warden; "people don't write about the kick of a mule. It's the sheer power of a man on men, like a rider on a mustang that bucks—strength, or—down you go! Just imagine Major Hampton, will you? warden of this institution!" Colonel Tom continued, with exceeding contempt. "Before the major joined the church, I understood him well. Since then I do not. He comes here and wants to talk to the old convicts, as if they were not the gray rats of the place, the hardest cases of all; wants to talk to the sick, when, in ninety-nine cases out of a hundred, they are shamming sick; wants to be with the dying, when it's because they are all racked and worn out with wickedness, in the delirium tremens of all manner of cursedness, that they are dying. Oh, he's in earnest. One day we were putting Jock

Harket into the dark cell—hell we all call it, no light, and not enough air for one man, let alone two—and the major, who happened here, wanted to be shut up in the cell with the man twenty-four hours, you know, to talk to him—talk!"

"Major Hampton is not the only one of my church who comes here to try and do good?" asked my father, who believed in that person with all his heart, yet with his brain did not believe in him at all.

"Oh yes, doctor, Mr. Patterson comes," the warden said, with some sarcasm in his emphasis on the name. "And a sharp, shrewd one he is, sharp as a steel trap, and the convicts have enough of trap here without him. We are good friends, Patterson and I; but, doctor, do you think you know Mr. Patterson?" And the warden looked, as it were, down from a height, and with the manner of a father toward a child, in relation to the chaplain as he spoke.

"What do you mean? Certainly I do," my father replied, with that kind of apprehension in the very marrow of his bones, as he spoke, which creeps through the mercury, if one may say so, when a storm is coming.

"You do? then all right!" said the warden. "Yes, Colonel Archer comes; he is a gentleman. It reminds me of the way some men believe in Andrew Jackson—the way, excuse me, parson, Colonel Archer believes in Christ. To people in general," the colonel continued, "religion is a set of rules and regulations, a kind of beautiful system of things, you know," with a wave of his hand as if speaking of the weather; "but to Colonel Archer religion is nothing whatever but one person, Jesus Christ, and the loving and minding him. Singular idea! He believes in Jesus Christ, and in nothing else. If the colonel could only get these rascals to see it in that light! They don't believe in woman, doctor! That's the last thing, so far as this world goes, that gives from under them, like the plank from under a man's feet when he is hung. It's not this woman nor that woman, and a terrible time most of them have had in that; but when a man comes to feel sincerely as well as speak about the sex as you would about a heap of rotten apples, it's all up with that man. He has lost his faith in every thing, hasn't the faculty of faith; it's gone, like his losing his pocket-book, like losing his legs in battle—gone, and gone for good!"

All this took place in the chapel while we waited for the prisoners to be unlocked from their hundreds of cells and marched in, my father and myself resting on one of the hard benches, the warden standing beside us, no more needing to be seated or even capable of sitting down, apparently, than a bronze Washington on its pedestal.

"Oh, as to Major Hampton," continued he, "the man is wild and freaky, and full of twists and turns, and jerks and jumps. He's pitched into religion exactly as I have known him to pitch into politics. He's too fast and too hot. He talks to the men, argues, pleads, weeps with them when he has a chance, but they look at him without understanding him at all; the more eager he is, the less they understand it, you know; like a fellow standing on the shore and watching the surf all in a foam of noise and froth. 'Think of your mother,' he said to Jock Harket, in for rape and murder; 'you remember your mother, Jock?' 'Yes,' said Jock, his head all brass, like the top of an old-fashioned andiron, 'I ought to remember her, always drunk and lamming me over the head with her wash-board.' The major don't get at the men, doctor! Colonel Archer believes in Christ, but the major believes in you, doctor! It's Dr. Quarterman, Dr. Quarterman all the time;" and there is a broad laugh over the warden's face. But he has not an idea how the chaplain suffers from Major Hampton: it is the major that ruins every prayer-meeting, until Wednesday night is like a quartan ague to my robust father, so healthy a man too; but the major is a sort of suffering which eludes all remedy.

At this moment the convicts began entering the doors of the chapel, each so much like the other in his striped clothing, cropped head, pallor of face, and furtiveness of eye peculiar to prisoners, that it seemed impossible to tell them apart; merely a mass of crime, the individual atoms as indistinguishable as are the molecules of malaria.

"Slower, men!" says the warden, standing his full height, broad and strong and wholesome to see, with his clear, healthy countenance, three revolvers on each side under his blue army overcoat. "Lock-step, if it is Sunday!"

"The law catches them, doctor," he proceeds aloud, the convicts no more to him than the flowing beside him of a very muddy Mississippi, "and puts them in here like steam in a boiler. I earn my salt, as I am a force big enough, without starting a rivet, to hold them. One hour, doctor. Muskets, men!" and he takes his stand by the door, a turnkey, musket in hand, at the end of each of the long rows of men waiting in front of their benches. The burly warden looks carefully over the heads of his subjects, in grave enjoyment of his empire. I am satisfied that shrewd Mr. Patterson had caught from the warden, with whom he had extensive dealings in business, the gratification he had expressed to my father at the amount of rascality in the penitentiary. Here were convicts of all shades and grades of crime and character. As their terms expire, their keeper is compelled to let them go, it is true; but, then, he is always getting new subjects in their place, every county in the State steadily sending in its tribute, new and peculiar types of wickedness added every week. Frederick of Prussia took pleasure in his regiment of giants picked from the population of the world; but Colonel Tom Maxwell has a higher satisfaction, something more than mere stature, in this case. Here are standing in rank, under his eye, the very grenadiers of crime. He has the joy with which one handles dualine or nitro-glycerine, the deep delight of strength in grapple with strength, one man a match for a thousand. The warden impresses his powerful person upon the assembled mass, glancing at him with furtive eyes and hands closing into fists with the instinct of wild cats within the leap of a lion, as he coolly and steadily surveys the congregation. He is very deliberate about it, unwilling to cease from it. He has quite a clear estimate of the might of the rascality in the room; knows of the plans for escape hatching at the instant in the brains of the more cunning of the criminals; conjectures schemes possibly more subtle and dangerous, of which his spies will tell him to-morrow.

As a general computes an enemy contrasted with himself, so does Colonel Tom form accurate measurement of the terrible force present, and of the counter-force in himself. To him it is purely an affair of tons, pounds, ounces; so much scoundrelism upon one side, just so much power on the other side to counteract; to the chamber of a revolver, to a grain of powder upon his side, does he balance force with force. He can and does estimate, too, as one does the hidden steam of a boiler, the exact amount and desperation of will upon the side of the convicts and of opposing will with him. All this he understands, as of any matter of long experience with slate and pencil. The force Dr. Quarterman can possibly bring to bear he dimly acknowledges, but can not for the life of him fully appreciate. He is in the position of every philosopher before Newton discovered gravitation. Colonel Tom knows that there is a power indefinitely wider, higher, mightier, sublimer than he either uses or understands.

"I'll be hanged," he says to himself, as he slowly surveys his flock of exceedingly black sheep, "if I can come at this Gospel business any more than a baby. But it's the law to have a chaplain. And there *is* a something in every scoundrel here which I can't get at with a revolver any more than with a shower-bath. And it may be the parson's Gospel is a sort of something which may lay hold on the part of a fellow which lives after he dies, and raises him beyond the stars *for* what I know or care. But it doesn't hold him here worth a cent. The instant a convict begins shamming pious I see his game through and through; trying to get a pardon, more likely leading a plot to break out. But service lasts only an hour, sharp. Besides, I'm here on the spot, and on my feet." And so he thunders,

" Seats!"

The congregation subsides into a sitting posture, Puritans to a man so far as their closely cropped heads are concerned. Their Napoleon abdicates to his Elba for an hour of watchful repose, still standing on his feet, and the sermon begins.

Now, a minister wholly unlike Colonel Tom Maxwell would have made a pitiable failure as chaplain, from very contrast with the colonel. However vigorous in bone and brain, a merely bookish man would have seemed a visionary one, in comparison with a warden so practical and sensible; would have seemed so, not to all others there, but—and that would be the worst of all—to himself, too, a mere dealer in vaporous sentiment; would have felt so even while indignantly resisting the unworthy influence. Yet such a chaplain would have fared better, in the estimation of convicts and turnkeys, than one who was timid, dyspeptic, nervous, liable to undue exaltations and depressions from temperament, or small salary, or years of being snubbed by vestry and choir. The broad and vigorous health of the warden, the absolute confidence in himself, and habitual assertion of himself, on the part of Colonel Tom, would have had the effect upon such a minister as the shining of the sun upon an ember on the hearth, making it ashy, even if it did not put it out. But the excellence of this father of mine lay in the fact that he was no more bookish than the colonel, and as much accustomed as the other to mingle among men, although not quite so closely nor with the same exceptional class.

What was better still, not even Colonel Tom had a heartier digestion for beef in any shape than did this chaplain for the tripe which, if it must be said, was his favorite article of breakfast fare. The colonel was not half so fond of his pipe and whisky in the seclusion of his home of an evening as was this parson of his cigar and tumbler of brown stout, from both of which, however, he had rigidly abstained for years.

The warden laughed more loudly at a good joke, but the other laughed more easily and heartily. I was full of the glories of Greece in those days, especially of the Olympic games, and I used, when I ought to have been listening to the sermon in the prison chapel, to be matching my father, mixing up the dates of things, as a Christian martyr in the arena against the colonel as a ferocious gladiator of pagan proclivities; and I am as confident this hour as I was then that, running, or boxing, or wrestling, or fighting with the spear or sword, my father would have made a finish of the warden in no time; my reason being that, as a Christian, my father had open connection with the inexhaustible reserves of power outside himself, while this big pagan had nothing to go upon beyond the supply in his broad but speedily exhausted breast.

Yet, no man beyond the limits of our family I liked quite so much as I did Colonel Tom. I had such a passion for him that, at times, I wished I was a convict — an innocent one, of course — to be under his sway, it seemed so positive and wholesome. Pagan as he was, I liked him vastly better than I did Major Hampton, although he was my teacher; hated Mr. Patterson in comparison.

I said that the prison service began, but I do not intend to preach here and over again the sermon that followed. I do not recall one syllable nor one specific thought of my father's uttered on that or any other occasion there. I doubt if any one else present does, in comparison to the final effect, at least.

First, there was a very familiar hymn, led by my father, joined in by all the convicts, in all the versions of the tune known by them in their diversified localities in other days. Very little Colonel Tom knew about church music, but he disliked the singing; there were the accents in it of revolt and riot, a breaking over, vocally, of all wards and walls, that resembled lack of discipline. It was very bad when my father began his chaplaincy, but by lifting his strong voice and asserting himself more vigorously he came more thoroughly up to the colonel's idea of a warden, in this part of the service, than any one had supposed possible; but it was all male voices, harsh thunder at best, the Gospel assurances in the words of the hymns seeming to be rather from Sinai than Calvary.

Next, a prayer. It must have been the result of his own close and continual habit of prayer, for surely there is the mastership of habit here as in all else; but from the moment the chaplain said, "Let us pray," there was, at least, profound attention to the end. When, on the stage, Hamlet believes with all his heart that it is his father whom he sees, all the audience believe it too, and thrill in unison with him. Certainly no one could hear this minister pray without feeling that the speaker was addressing a Person present, whom he believed in, feared, and loved far more than he did any other person living. I used to glance at Colonel Tom through the fingers over my eyes, during the deep urgency of my father with his Father, toward the close of a prayer, but there stood the warden, erect and white-eyed as a statue, conscious only of the bearded rows, so to speak, of cropped heads before him.

Then followed the sermon. The general effect was as if, with his elbow upon the stand before him and leaning forward, in a casual conversation he had said, "As you are aware, my friend, two ones are two. As you also know, twice two are four. Now, we are all agreed that two fours make eight, and consequently that two eights are sixteen. That two sixteens make thirty-two, that twice thirty-two are sixty-four, no man of us denies. Hence is it that we are cordially agreed that twice sixty-four are one hundred and twenty-eight, and that twice that are two hundred and fifty-six. Who of us, then, pretends to deny the five hundred and twelve following as multiplying that by two? nor dare you doubt the one thousand and twenty-four following upon the same process carried out in reference to the five hundred and twelve." Only that his statements were religious, and not mathematical, they were so perfectly brief, clear, consecutive, and undeniable as to compel the dullest as well as the worst there to go with him up and up and into tremendous consequences, yet consequences not less surely certain than the hundreds, thousands, millions toward which the arithmetical path would lead. The summit upon which the speaker placed at last the vilest wretch there was, and as upon rock, that the case of every man of us is not how we stand with men, but with our Maker, a sinful and undying creation with an eternal and holy God! Not until the preacher had got every one present to feel, if but for the instant, as certain of this as the preacher himself felt, did he say a word of the one way to be at peace with God by Jesus Christ. The certainty of what they heard was the hold he had upon them, a purely intellectual certainty; but the double certainty, urged afterward and last, of salvation by Christ, lay in its being made a heart certainty; the feeling upon that awful height being as of an Alpine traveler grasping upon the very edge of abyssmal destruction after the one Saviour in clear sight and easy reach before him. Then came rapid, beseeching entreaty, as though the speaker were on his knees at the feet of every convict, the urgent appeal upon every man to lay hold upon Christ there and then, and at peril of his life, without one instant's delay! The breathless intensity of interest in every man there, Colonel Tom included, lay in the fact that every one was compelled to think more than ever before in his whole life of himself. And so, with a short prayer and a benediction, accepted by all as from the very heart of the chaplain, the service was over within the hour.

Colonel Tom was too healthy a man to lie about it, as well as too perceptive and practical: there was a power exerted upon the men by every sermon which was but a variation upon that, though in ever-fresh variety of thought and illustration, a power wholly for good, a power immeasurably beyond any thing lodged in chain, cartridge, muscle, or even will. But the colonel had no conscious intention of yielding himself a prisoner thereto, when, at his request, we took tea with him on one occasion after service, in his very comfortably furnished rooms within the walls.

"This is Mrs. Maxwell, my wife," he said, introducing us to a diminutive little lady in ringlets, "and these are our babies. Make yourself at home. If you will excuse me"—and he lies down at full length on the floor of his parlor—"I feel tired of standing; always relax a little with these young rascals of an evening."

Although my father was eager for a talk on personal religion with the colonel, like a sensible man he gave it up for the time. A sturdy and dreadfully spoiled little Tom of four years old was astride his father's breast, two little maidens still younger accommodating themselves on his long legs, feeling in his pockets as he lay, the girls as much the image of their mother as Tom was of his father. As to Mrs. Maxwell, all ringlets and smiles and feminine affectations, any body could know the colonel thought her a beauty, by the number of pictures of her in all attitudes on the table and over the walls. My father made himself at home, as he always did, although it was evident, having his sermon for the night upon his mind, that he was in a hurry to get away, his special object in coming being defeated. We did not stay long, and what struck me most was this: the colonel lay at his length upon the carpet so very comfortable, his children so happy with him and he with them, when—

"Tom, get up! Supper!" said his kitten of a wife, with a touch of her foot in his side. What surprised me as a boy was the promptness with which he got up. Had I been so big, I would have done nothing of the kind until I had got ready.

"I suppose I must, Carrie!" he said, but arose instantly as he said it.

"Yes, Mr. Tom, you'd better!" exclaimed the boy, clinging, crab-like, to his father's breast as he arose. There was something in the accents of little Tom, and in the instant obedience of his big father, which clashed, I knew not why, with my conception of the Napoleon of the penitentiary. But we soon after went home, and I forgot for the time all about it.

CHAPTER X.

ONE day I opened the door of my father's house and admitted Professor Dinsmore, and not into our home alone, but into my entire existence thereafter.

"Is Dr. Quarterman at home?" he asked, and it was characteristic of him that he laid his hand upon my head—for it was I who answered his ring—as he spoke, but as coldly and mechanically as if it were the handle of a pump. I receded, and looked at him as I said, "Yes, sir." Tall, lean, ashen as to face, iron-gray as to hair, clad in black, with a white neckcloth, I knew at a glance that he was a minister, and yet he was nothing of the kind; knew so surely that I would have sworn to it that he was poor, whereas he was a wealthy, and a very wealthy, man. I showed him upstairs into my father's study, and he made his home, highly honored by my father, with us for several days. Cold as he was, austere, never smiling, thoroughly conscientious, that grave professor infatuated my father as I am confident a man of his own glowing and impulsive temperament never could have done. I heard him sum up his entire mission to my father—he never addressed himself to my mother, much less to any of the rest of us—at the tea-table the night before. Having accomplished his mission, he left.

"I have studied the subject for many years, sir, upon all sides. There can be no flaw or defect, I am confident;" and he spoke in short, cold sentences. "I have visited every section of the State purposely. The plantation, of which I have informed you, I have bought. The necessary buildings are now being erected of logs. The future structures will be frame. I have myself spent one month in Paris purchasing the philosophical apparatus. After due consideration, I have selected Dr. Harrison, with whose reputation you are familiar, as principal. The enterprise begins next June, the first Monday."

"What a noble enjoyment you must have in being able not only to plan, but to carry out, such a scheme! My dear sir, I almost envy you the happiness," exclaimed my father, who was, I think, the more outspoken in his enthusiasm in that he had not been able to interest my mother in Professor Dinsmore and his hobby, as he had hoped.

"No; I deserve neither praise nor envy," Professor Dinsmore made grave reply. "I am getting to be an old man. I must soon die. Providence has blessed me with large means. I have no child or near relative. The school in question has been the thought and purpose of my life. I am glad you consent to give that which you have toward it. I am glad, young sirs, that you will be enrolled among the earliest alumni of the Archimedean Institute."

This last remark was slowly addressed to my brother Habersham and myself, seated on the opposite side of the tea-table, and we looked up with a wonder not unmixed with terror, first at our father and then at our mother.

"Yes, yes, Agnes, it will be the very thing for the boys; the very thing to make men of them—strong men, men in body as well as in mind, for that is the glory of the system. Carter here," continued my father, filling up the chasm, so to speak, of astonishment which followed upon the professor's announcement, with his enthusiasm—

"Carter will be a Samson, and Habersham will thrive and tower into a son of Anak!" and he added a good deal more. But my mother sat silent, merely asking the professor if his cup was out. We boys knew that the thing was decided; but, somehow, the silence of our mother was more impress-

he continued. "Labor will make study a delightful rest, and study will lend peculiar zest to labor; hearty appetite will wait on both. The very thing, my dear, the very thing!" But my mother was silent. Not ungraciously so; no lady at the head of her table could be more pleasant to a guest; but

I HEARD HIM SUM UP HIS ENTIRE MISSION TO MY FATHER.

ive than all the glowing descriptions our father was giving of the life we boys would lead at the Archimedean Institute, half indoors in diligent study, half out in the sunshine, and fresh air, and invigorating labor of the field.

"I was raised in the rice-fields and cotton-patches of Georgia, and I know what I say,"

her own ideas in regard to the matter were innate ideas, her instincts and intuitions as inseparable a part of herself as her hands and her heart, while my father's views had been poured into his receptive nature out of the professor as physic is poured into a generous goblet out of a phial.

"Mrs. Quarterman and myself have conversed upon the subject," added my father at last. "As is natural to a mother, she hesitates at parting with her boys. The more she thinks of it, the more she will become reconciled."

And that was his mistake. Always good, and impetuous only in varied modes of well-doing, it was his very nature to change and vary; but my mother never changed—from the outset she had her own idea. This proposition of Professor Dinsmore came upon her, rebelling and protesting against it from, as it were, before its first mention, and no amount of explanation or argument had influence the slightest against the steady flow of her intuition in opposition. It was part of her beautiful nature, the soul of its steadiness and serenity. To all reasoning she had in this, as in every affair coming up, never a logical refutation to suggest, but simply knew that she was right, as she invariably was, and held unswerving on her way; but without a particle of collision with her husband, even in word or gesture, always yielding to his wishes, but never changing from her original opinion.

"I declare, Agnes," I overheard my father say to her that night after they had gone into their own room, "I am astonished at you! After all that the professor and myself have made so perfectly clear to you, too. You are as steady upon your axis as is the globe, and all our arguments are no more to you than the winds are to the revolving earth, or the shadows of the clouds upon it as it turns;" for my father was very full of Dr. Chalmers's astronomical discourses just then, at home as well as in the pulpit; but he spoke playfully, the thing being settled in his own mind.

"But I can not help it, my dear," she answered, quietly; "I am as silent, too, as the earth, if you please, on its axis. I can not explain why I do not like it. I do not know, except that I do dislike it heartily. I may be all wrong. We will see!" This was, of course, a mere sentence or two of the long conversations they doubtless had on the subject before and after.

So, when Mrs. President drove up in her carriage a day or two after, and the subject of the Archimedean Institute came up in the parlor between herself and my mother: "If

you will kindly allow for my ignorance, my dear Mrs. Quarterman," the visitor said, in her pleasantest manner—for, like all the world besides, she sincerely liked my mother—"but I can not say I approve Professor Dinsmore's ideas. He called on me, and explained. I have not contributed," and she arranged certain lace frills around her chin, which, as a silent sort of boy, I used to think were as essential to her existence as its gills to a fish. The fact is, in view of the enormous salary enjoyed by her husband when alive and President, all agents seeking aid made a point, when in St. Charles, of calling upon her, "to pay my respects," each generally styled it.

"Dr. Quarterman has gone over the plan with Professor Dinsmore," my mother replied, "and is delighted. He thinks it will be the very thing for our boys!" But, as she went on to say why, it was clear that, however gracefully worn, she had clothed herself in her husband's conclusions as she did in her silks, she herself remaining the same under all.

"And you have not heard—" Mrs. President began as she arose to leave, "pardon me—"

"From Archibald? Not since his letter saying he had reached Texas, and was determined not to stay. Governor Hone told you of it; our boys were together. You may imagine, madam"—and my mother's eyes filled with tears as she took her visitor's hand, no child simpler in her grief.

"I do, my dear Mrs. Quarterman, I do! How sincerely I assure you I do!" her guest made answer. And yet, why was it that all her manner was a something apart from herself, the very tears rising responsive to my mother's in her eyes, as artificial as her pearls? She rolled away in her carriage; but to me, as, I dare say, a singular sort of boy, she never seemed to alight upon the earth; forever in some sort of carriage, in parlor, or church, or wherever I, at least, ever met her. And yet her manner fitted her exquisitely, and no one could say that she was affected.

But I am thinking and speaking just now of Professor Dinsmore. So far as I know, a better man never lived. A more unselfish philanthropist never gave himself to the last energy of his nature, to the last cent of his property, and all into the air, and for nothing at all! There was a deep and glowing heart in the cold and formal exterior of the man, bursting from him in the Archimedean Institute like a geyser from its Iceland snow, to accomplish about as much good as does that spasmodic gush of boiling water, and to subside almost as suddenly. Would that no miserable child, if the figure may be pressed, had been scalded to death by the overflow of that generous but mistaken professor!

If Job was right in his maledictions, then will I also curse the day when Habersham and myself were born into the Archimedean Institute, that dire event taking place some months after the visit of the professor to us there in St. Charles, Habersham being about sixteen and I some three years younger, but at least six years larger than he. As Professor Dinsmore had said, a plantation had been bought by him for his grand experiment. To fit it for his purposes, two additional stories had been heaped upon a large wooden building in the centre of the estate which had been the home of the former owner, a number of frame cottages erected en échelon around it, and a dozen double log-cabins as students' rooms, with a chimney common to both "pens," added to the negro quarters several hundred yards from the central building of all, upon the summit of which swung the bell. When Habby and I arrived — it was in October, the Institute having opened in June—we found two hundred boys on the ground, for the idea of the school was new, and its author had been as efficient in making it known as he had been liberal with his means, the sole purpose of his heart being to do good in the best way he could imagine, only that the way he imagined had been so erected by him in his very soul, so adorned with silver and gold, and so steadily contemplated, that it had grown into an idol excluding all besides. I do believe the professor would gladly have given at last his life to it, as he already had all besides.

It was a week or two before my brother and myself settled down into the special "pen" of the double log-cabins assigned us, a room sixteen feet square, so "chinked and daubed," i. e., filled in with blocks of wood and mortar between the cracks of the post oak logs, as to be very comfortable. We had each a cot in his own corner, a looking-glass on my side of the room, our trunks in place of wardrobes pushed under each cot, a tin pan for washing, with a coarse towel hanging thereby, a closet on either side the ample stone fire-place for our wood, and—that was all. The curse of the South, according to Professor Dinsmore, was that its boys were raised in idleness, and he and we were to revolutionize the South, and possibly Christendom, by initiating a Spartan system of simple living — three hours of work afield in the afternoon, and three hours devoted in the morning to study.

We liked it at first amazingly, Habby and I, there being a faint flavor of Robinson Crusoe about rising at the sound, if not of a parrot, at least of the great bell every morning at daylight, making our own fires from the pine knots in our closets, huddling on our clothes, and hurrying through the grass all wet with dew to the hall in the centre, in the great lecture-room of which, upon hard benches around the bare walls, we sat during prayers. And surely the world has rolled nearer to God since then, for the professor, Herman Clark, is, it is to be hoped, a Christian impossible to these days. "Hanky" was his name among all the students, from the fact that he never was seen without a handkerchief in his hand—a white-faced, flaxen-haired, stoop-shouldered, easily blushing, gentle-voiced bachelor of forty-five years, who knew Greek and Latin as well, I dare say, as Aristotle and Cicero, and who was as profoundly ignorant as they of the century or people of the place in which he lived.

It was he who hurried with us of a frosty dawn into the hall, handkerchief in hand. Mounted on the platform at the end of the room, he called the roll, read a chapter from the Bible by a flickering candle, and offered a prayer. It was so dark down the long room that, even if he had not been so near-sighted, he could hardly have detected the fact of near half the students being absent, room-mates alternating in attendance to answer for each other, any ambiguous friend answering for both when both were away, and I think that this regular lying was the beginning of all the disastrous immorality which followed.

But how a man so enthusiastic in regard to Greek and Latin as to inspire his classes with positive energy and ambition could be so utterly without a spark of soul in the religious services, I can account for not otherwise than by supposing him to have lived so exclusively in Greece and Rome as to regard their very gods also as more genuine than any other. A shivering, false-hearted, miserable business was that morning service, and the chapter and prayer, from the lips of "Hanky," were the coldest, falsest, most wretched part of it all. No one, unless it was Habby and myself, made even the show of listening to either, shivering, whispering, glad to get through the corpse-like form, and be done.

But, ostrich-stomached as boys generally are, I do not think we went to our refectory to breakfast afterward, except from animal instinct for food. Not in the Archimedean Institute alone have heads of colleges been altogether too much occupied with sublimer matters to give a thought to the daily food of their pupils. A coarse-grained, shock-headed ex-overseer, Joab Fish by name, had undertaken the boarding of the students per contract and per capita, and it must have been exceedingly low, his price. If anybody said grace, I do not recall it; nothing more vivid, however, to memory than the dishes of fat bacon, "big hominy," cups of coffee, hot and black and strong, "corn dodgers," plates of dark dough, smoking from the oven and known as biscuits; plenty of molasses in sticky pots up and down the table; enormous dishes of meat and vegetables being the variation upon all this which constituted dinner. I was built, as they used to tell me at home, of oak, and could stand it. But how poor little Habby survived is still a mystery to me; for we had to go with the multitude in the rush, also, of their eating, every soul eager to be done and out of the long, low shed-room which constituted our refectory, if only to be from under the presence of our purveyor, who walked down the long table, around the farther end up the other side, and so down and around again in slow procession until the meal was eaten.

An hour after breakfast was given to sweeping up the rooms and making up the beds by such of the students as were compelled or bribed to do so by their respective room-mates, or who alternated with them in the work, those free from this duty playing ball or "shinny" until the nine-o'clock bell sent all to their rooms for study. Eleven o'clock saw every student rung into his recitation-room in the main building, the higher classes under the instruction of Professor Harrison, of whom the originator of the school had told us. No man living whom I respect more than I did Professor Harrison. How could I help it, when I saw him, the handsomest and most gentlemanly man in face, carriage, bearing, in the very tones of his voice, I ever knew? Possibly his portrait is so framed in the coarse surroundings of his situation as to exaggerate its contour and coloring. There was a grace about him, also, an affability, a feminine refinement, which made the rudest student involuntarily lift his hat from his head when the professor approached.

It had been, I believe, the fashionable whim of the hour in the Southern sea-port city from which he had come to us, to take the batter-cakes at breakfast from the plate with the fingers, and, from being once or twice at his table, his hand was so beautifully formed, the thing was done so gracefully, that a fork for the purpose seemed barbarous to me. With his gold-headed cane in his hand, his perfectly polished boots, his white handkerchief, twenty years in advance of his age in that, his natural yet cultured manner and all, Professor Harrison was the most stupendously ignorant individual I ever knew.

Not of belles-lettres, moral philosophy, natural science, the languages, the usages of society, nor of religion, he being a sincere Christian. Perfectly adept in all besides, it was of his students that he was inconceivably ignorant. Had he been stone-deaf and born blind, I do not know how he could have been more unacquainted with them than he was. I am speaking but the sober fact when I say that had the Archimedean Institute been located in the moon, for all practical ends he would have known as much of its pupils as he actually did, being their principal. I have watched him presiding at examinations and commencements in his silk gown, have dined in company with a score of the students on set occasions at his hospitable table, have heard him deliver lectures full of eloquence and poetry as well as sterling information, have seen him in his recitation-room in arms-length of eager and deeply interested students as he expounded some beauty of Homer or Virgil, or performed, with deft and dainty fingers, some curious experiment in chemistry, and all the time as absolutely ignorant of the students clustered about him as if they had been dead and—you will justify me directly— damned centuries before. And if his were not, possibly, but a specimen — the same thing true in many another instance — I would say no more upon the subject.

When I looked over the students in my slow, deliberate, silent, I fear ox-like, fashion, after Habby and I first came, I was most struck with the fair, laughing, almost beautiful face of a boy of fourteen or so. The brown hair clustered about the broad brow and soft blue eyes of the little fellow in a way I had seen before in the case of girls alone. There were a plumpness and agility about him, too; but all was forgotten in his audacious mastery of almost all; a sort of magnetic assurance, as of one who had seen more of the world than all of us put together, though so young.

"Did you notice that boy with the hair all about his forehead?" Habersham asked me, as we were going to bed a few nights after our arrival.

"Yes. His name," I eagerly replied, "is Alonzo M'Callum. I found out all about him. His father was—I think he is to-day —a missionary to India. He was born there. His father has sent him to America to be educated. I want to become well acquainted with him. We will be friends, I know. Did you ever see a boy—" and I launched out into warmest praise of his person. "They tell me," I added, "that he is the smartest boy here—knows every thing, is a splendid speaker, writes poetry!"

It was not until I had got through that Habby replied at last, and thoughtfully:

"Carter, do you remember that picture in pa's big Bible Dictionary which he gave us—abandoned it to destruction, as he called it — the picture of the hooded snake of India?"

"The cobra de capello," I said, for my memory is all the talent I have.

"Yes; that's it, so venomous and beautiful that no cure has ever been found—" Habby continued, very seriously.

"But what in the world—" I interrupted.

"I suppose I am like my mother," my diminutive brother went on, "but I get an idea of a person from the moment I see him, a clear, fixed idea. And I never change it, because it is always true. And I tell you, Carter, that Alonzo M'Callum, if that is his name, is like that snake from India; and" Habby looked up at me with his small, sorrowful eyes, and added, "He is a bad boy. I don't know how, but he's the worst boy here, and I am going to have nothing to do with him. Nor am I going to let you, Carter." Habby said this with his most serious air, as my elder brother. Had any of the strange boys been present, they would have stared and laughed out at the idea of the authority over me of a brother whose head hardly reached my lower shirt-stud, and whom I could have picked up and tossed over the roof of our log-cabin almost; but if any boy had laughed, I would have been very apt to have "boxed his chops," as my teacher in our former city home continually styled that operation. I always deferred to Habby, and, if possible, yielded to his very decided views. Not so much because he was my elder; to Archy, oldest of all of us, I would not have submitted for half a second; but my deference helped Habby to believe, you see, that he was not so very small at last.

"Nonsense, Habby," I replied, however. "What notions you do get into your wise head! As father says, you are always too intense. The boy's father is a missionary, and you will find that he is as good as he is good-looking. He has such an influence over all because he is so good!"

Habby said nothing, and after our prayer together, as we had promised our mother, we went to bed. My brother's cot kept creaking so all night, that I knew, which was very often the case, that he was not sleeping well. "It's because those fellows have been staring and laughing at him so," I said to myself, lying as still as I could, that he might not be disturbed by thinking I was awake. "He feels badly. That's what made him talk so about Alonzo M'Callum;" but a wakeful night I had of it. The fact is, our coming to the institute had been like storming a battery, my poor brother knowing from bitter experience the ridicule he would excite, and I in my stolid way sympathizing with him in the prospect; he had endured such agonies of weeping over it in his room of nights before we left St. Charles, that I had feared there would be nothing left of him to go to school with me. Had it not been for Archy's flight, the increased interest our parents had in our education on that account, especially Professor Dinsmore's visit, my father would not have persisted against the protest of his sensitive son and our mother. But, then, my father always went with all his soul into whatever it was; he cherished, too, some vague hope for Habby, because of what Governor Hone was often saying of the boy's talent. It may have been our contractor's hot biscuits also, but I was fighting for my brother the night long. Toward morning, I had in my dreams arranged for him to go upon a pair of stilts I made for him. But, somehow, he had got his stilts curiously entangled among the folds of a snake with Alonzo M'Callum's head to it; and hastening to help him, the bell for morning prayers clashed upon my visions, and I woke up.

CHAPTER XI.

THERE was a charm to Habersham and myself, as to all the students at the Archimedean Institute, in the manual-labor part of the system, for a while at least. There was a subtle savor in it of stories we had all read about shipwrecked sailors making the desert island upon which they were cast into a paradise by dint of hard work. We missed the cocoa-nut-trees, the monkeys, wild goats, and unexpected caverns, as well as incursions of painted savages, dreadfully and from the first. Besides, it was impossible to imagine Joab Fisk as the gallant captain of our wrecked crew. By no vigor, even of boyish fancy, could we conceive of that very coarse and shock-haired commander saying to us cheerily, "Now, my lads, here we are on this island. Avast there! lend a hand! Heave away, and let us make every thing ship-shape until a vessel comes to rescue us!"

The contractor for our food, this Joab Fisk, had contracted also for our labor; terribly perplexed he was as the days glided by, with the wholly unexpected measure of the former, even more so of the latter. A member of the Pariah Order of Poor Whites, Joab Fisk's doom had been hitherto that of an overseer in the South, for some unexplained but invariable cause the most despised of all occupations—a species of being not black enough to be a negro, but far from being, so to speak, white enough to be a master. As with all his class, the one aspiration of his soul was to save money enough to buy a negro. To own if it were but one negro boy, to call him "Mars' Joab," was the aim of his existence. But if it was to be a "likely boy," one thousand dollars or thereabouts was essential, and, throwing him out of all his calculations, he could neither feed nor work us as he had the negroes of his former experiences. The blacks he could compel; but if he tried compulsion with us, there would be an explosion ruining all his hopes of gain. Almost all of us, too, belonged to the master class to whom he had been used to submitting all his life. He could not conceive even of treating us as other than his superiors, and how was he to make us work? It was all devolved on him. Neither Dr. Harrison nor Hanky ever entered our cotton-patch or had any thing whatever to do with it. With our mornings devoted to study, their duty began and ended; they never even alluded to the matter except in certain phrases of chapel prayer, which meant, to us, as little as the rest of the supplication, which was less than nothing at all.

At two o'clock in the afternoon the bell rang to work. There were penalties if a student did not go afield; but no one wanted to stay away; it was fun alive to go. Being in the fall, it was the cotton-picking season when Habby and I arrived. A special exemption had been made for him because of his infirmity; but go he would, and it was just like him. It is easy to imagine some two hundred boys, hardly a soul of us who had ever before regarded such work as other than for negroes to do, going to the cotton-house, about a mile from our rooms, and, in the centre of the cotton-patch of several hundred acres, yelling, tripping each other up, snatching off and throwing caps and hats away as we went. At the cotton-house stood Joab Fisk, in an agony of dull and helpless impatience for us to begin, dealing out cotton baskets, made of white-oak splints, each basket about two feet broad, and two feet or so deep. Negro fashion, we would put the empty baskets over our heads, the rims resting upon our foreheads, and, so, troop-laughing and blundering against each other to the field fence. I couldn't blame the fellows for yelling with laughter at Habby, for with his basket over his head—he would not let me carry it—he was quite extinguished, poor fellow, all basket, and mice-like feet beneath.

Beginning at the worm-fence, each boy took two rows of cotton, about four feet apart, working down the centre and picking right and left as he went. I declare, there is a downright craving in my hands, as I write, to grasp once more the soft, pulpy abundance of the cotton bursting from the brown pods all down the long, long rows. The worst of it was lifting and placing the basket down and still down before you as it got heavier and heavier; whether he was older brother or not, that I insisted on doing for Habby, who worked between the rows next to me as his basket filled. This soon left us behind our companions, for which I was far from being sorry, although I did, from beginning to end of our stay there at school, and for Habby's sake, all that I could, to be as popular as possible.

What nonsense it all was! Some of us worked from love of the exercise; the fathers of some had promised to give them all they made; but very soon the clods of dirt began to fly—now and then an unripe cotton-boll, green and hard as a walnut—shouting and singing going on the whole time. And the imbecile agony of Joab Fisk—now perched on the rider of the worm-fence to overlook us, now walking across the field and down the rows, the object, wherever he went, of clods and accurately aimed cotton-bolls—was too great for words, had he dared attempt them. He was like the celebrated lawyer whose habit it was to handle a ruler while addressing his jury, and who broke down and lost his case when his wily opponent had removed that implement from his reach. Without his usual cowhide, Joab Fisk was indeed a king without a sceptre; forever picking up and dropping again every chance stick that lay in his way. But I never knew him to remonstrate; the boys knew too well—and, more, he knew—that he was an—overseer! overseer!

"Why, M'Callum, what are you doing?" I asked, during the first week of our work, when, to my great pleasure, the missionary's son happened to be picking cotton in the row next me; for, after gathering enough cotton to make a layer, he was putting lumps of black and waxy earth in, with about every tenth handful of cotton.

"Don't you call this rich soil?" he asked, in his innocent way, opening his blue eyes, looking at me through his tangle of curls, archly and full of fun.

"Yes, as cream—river bottom, you know," I replied; "but what then?"

"Then I'm enriching the cotton. That's the way I've seen the ryots do it in India, when no one was watching. Old Fisk won't find it out, you know;" and there was a cool ignorance of the existence even of any other reason in the matter which astounded me. His deceit seemed to be as much a part of his nature as its coils and venom are to a snake; and he was so simple, child-like, even fascinating, in the softness of his eyes and tones.

I am satisfied it was he who introduced the first idea of such a thing among boys generally too high-minded for that peculiar sort of deception. Partly for the fun's sake,

partly to outwit "old Fisk," chiefly from
the malarious contagion which lives in evil,
the custom became almost universal. After
three hours' picking, the moment announced
by a horn blown by the overseer at the cotton-house, we shouldered our baskets and
marched to that point to be weighed. Some
of us made an honest effort to "tote" our
heavy baskets on our heads as did all negroes in the land; but that we couldn't
stand, their inherent or acquired thickness
of skull giving them the advantage. Very
rapidly did Joab Fisk hook each basket to
the steelyard, weigh and enter the same on
his greasy old book, for he had years of practice with the negroes. As each basket was
weighed it was emptied out in a yawning
chasm opening into the floor beneath, ready
for the gin; too much in a hurry to detect
the amount of the field which had gone
with the cotton. In the end, the balance
of weight must have been, after ginning, the
grand astonishment of Joab Fisk's existence.

"I do believe, Carter," said Habersham to
me one day as we walked home from the
cotton-house, "that, except you and me,
every fellow on the field puts clods in his
pick!"

"Oh, well, that makes our baskets the
lighter to carry," I said, for in addition to
the full weight of my own upon one shoulder, I held the handle of Habby's on one side
as he walked beside me. I was so stout and
strong that he never knew how tough a job
it was, for I was careful to whistle or talk
as we walked, that he might see what a trifle the additional burden was to me. And
it was not brotherly love alone, the greater for his infirmity. In fact, at home, Virginia, Georgia, Mrs. Brown, all of us, had a
growing sense of there being something in
little Habby beyond what was possessed by
any of the rest of us—a marked superiority
which would assert itself yet some day.

"It is like small-pox," Habby added,
gravely. "The way it spreads among the
fellows. I insist upon it, Carter, that you
never do any thing of the kind. It's a lie!
And it's mean!" he continued, with an intensity of tone and of manner peculiar to him.
My brother was like a large man, body and
soul, crushed down by an inexplicable providence into a dwarf. An unexplainable

providence, because the fact of his inherit-
ing his infirmity from his maiden aunt in-
forms one merely of the process by which he
was so diminutive, and nothing beyond that.
Yes, Habby—and the fact became more
striking every day—held and condensed
and concentrated in his small self the heart
and soul of a giant. Therefore, "intensity"
is the word which describes my brother—
intensity.

"Small-pox!" I exclaimed, "you are right.
But if the putting dirt into our pick of cotton was all the small-pox here, I would be
glad."

"Why, what do you mean?" my brother
said, looking sharply up at me with his pale
and—there is no other word for it—"peak-
ed" face. But, as he spoke, he blushed as
red as his own hair, and then became more
ashen than before. He did not press the
question, and I made no explanation. Although secluded to ourselves by our own
thorough religious training, as well as by
Habby's infirmity, we were slowly coming
to know enough to fill us both with horror
and dismay.

And so the weeks and months rolled
round. The work gave us exercise enough,
and we gave ourselves to our studies in a
way which awakened the contempt of many
of our fellow-students, as well as the appro-
bation of our teachers. Owing to his weak
health, my brother had been before so detained from study that, although much older than myself, we began at the Institute
together in our studies. But you might as
well have harnessed a dray-horse beside a
full-blooded racer. Habby caught the precise idea of the study, whatever it was, from
the outset, and as if with our mother's instant intuition, while I was puzzling without getting into other than deeper puzzle
the more I strove to understand.

"It is amazing, Carter," Habby would say,
when we were together in our cabin over
our books; "nothing can be clearer! I have
gone over it with you so often. It is as
plain as day. Let us try it again. Look
here," and Habby towered beside me like a
giant while he explained the Latin, Greek,
algebra—whatever it was.

"My skull feels six inches thick!" I would
say at last. "I want to understand. I got

up before day, drenched myself all over with the coldest water I could find, and have gone at it like mauling rails. The harder I work, the less I know. It is the old story!"

"What's the old story?" demanded Habby. It was the old story of the adventures of Jack the Giant-killer among ogres of mighty stature. The dwarf was a genius, and the giant always a blunder-headed fool; but I did not tell Habby so, and I merely replied:

"A rabbit runs so fast while a greyhound runs so much faster. Then, if the rabbit has so much start, and the course is so many feet, when will the dog catch the rabbit? The more I think of it, the less I understand! The very trying to work the sum gives me, it is a solemn fact, a curious crawling pain—"

"In your head, Carter?" Habby asked, with anxiety.

"No, I wish it did. A queer sort of spasm in the pit of my stomach!" And I was glad I said it, Habby laughed so, a thing he very rarely did; but it was a fact. What is more, the same feeling comes back whenever I try to grapple, to this day, with mathematics or metaphysics. Natural science I like, apart from its calculations; languages, too; but those twin children of the sphinx I respectfully decline.

It is of my brother I am speaking, however. The class used to nudge each other, at first, and laugh when Hanky would pass his handkerchief from one hand to the other at Latin recitation, and say,

"Mr. Habersham Quarterman will read," and all my blood tingled with Habby's as he would stand up beside me amidst the titters of all and begin. After a month or so there was nothing of the kind. There was, instead, a peculiar intonation in the professor's voice when he came to call my brother up, as if it had been a pleasure long expected, a movement of respectful and even flattering interest among the boys, a thrill of pride in my own bosom when my brother was called. Had the Greek or Latin been, instead, the easy English of a First Reader, Habby could not have read it more smoothly. What bothered the rest to death was so simple to him, that he did not seem to be proud at all of mastering it. All the time he read, Hanky would continually pass his handkerchief from one hand to the other, a smile upon his somewhat moon-like face, enjoying it, in relief from the stupidity of the rest of us, as only a scholar like our professor could. The laugh now was when I got up to construe, the contrast was so very great; but I was glad from my soul I was so stupid, since it helped to make my brother and the rest forget all about his size.

It was better still when, after some months, we came to recite in mathematics to Doctor Harrison. Upon the rostrum on which he sat was the dreaded blackboard, to which the doctor would invite us in turn to demonstrate those preposterous riddles, at least so I think, in algebra and trigonometry. The best of it all was when a dozen or so had gone to the board, had chalked and wiped out and entangled themselves until the spectators were as glad to have them sit down as they were to get to their seats.

"Mr. H. Quarterman!" said the doctor, and every soul there shared in the pride I felt as Habby went, like a lion rather than the mouse he was in body, up to the board, and wiping it clean as high as he could reach on tiptoe, drew and demonstrated without pause or mistake, as if it were merely a question of two and two making four. As I said, it seemed so easy to him that he had no conceit in the matter; and being so very small, he was a sort of pet among the students. Not that he had the least familiarity from or with them, but that he was always pointed out, when strangers visited us, as the genius of the Archimedean Institute.

"Hanky or Harrison? That little red-headed mite has more in him than wagonloads of them!" was generally the summing-up of matters.

Only upon one other occasion did they have a laugh at my brother. We had been at the Institute about a year when the first public examination took place. Nobody had any deep faith in the success of a school resting half its weight and structure upon manual labor, but all the country around was at the speaking with which the exercises closed. Our chapel was cavernous in size at prayers of dark, cold mornings; but every thing in the way of decoration had been done with flags and flowers and mottoes, and, with every seat crowded by the *élite* of the region under the plentiful lamps, and all of us exhilarated by the music of a brass band from the nearest city, the effect astonished the most sanguine among us. Professor-Hauky was there, if I may be allowed an impertinence which had almost driven from every mind his true name, in a new suit, handkerchief and all. Our principal, Doctor Harrison, towered aloft, gorgeous to behold, in his academic robes; wonderfully becoming them, too; fully conscious, as we wished he should be, of his high estate.

As I glanced over the array of gentlemanly planters, with their swarms of wives and daughters, every woman there beautiful to us, who had been so long secluded from female society, my heart beat high with pride in our institution, until I looked over the ranks of boys of the institution, seated, dressed up to the last degree, upon their ranges of side-seats, and then—almost a sense of nausea, as of one at sea, at the horrible falsehood of things. The sudden contrast of female beauty and purity smote me like a blow. I noticed the mothers and daughters looking at the students, and whispering and smiling among themselves, admiring us, we all felt, as being such talented and learned youth, the hope and pride of our State for the future; and, knowing what I did—

But the speaking begins, for the band has worn itself out on "Hail Columbia." Ordinary school-boy declamation by the first eight or ten youths, and the audience had begun to tire, especially as it had good-naturedly lavished its applause somewhat wastefully from the first. At last, and there is quite a flutter among the ladies, "Alonzo M'Callum" is called by the principal. I can see the boy now as he stands, so modest, apparently, and smiling, and positively charming upon the stage, with blue eyes, and clustering hair, and voice low and sweet, as with the luscious ripeness of tropical suns.

That he was the son of a missionary sent back around half the globe for his education, added greatly to the interest. But how well I understand the peculiar glancing of the boys, among whom I sat, at each other, as the speaker began, in a soft tone, some poetry descriptive of the peace and purity of a Christian home! Nothing could be more beautiful than the uplifting of his eyes, the spreading-out, in appeal to heaven, of his hands, the modulation of his child-like accents. We were prepared for his self-possession. Singularly familiar, for one of his age, in things of this world — even more familiar, if possible, from his peculiar education, with the affairs of heaven—there was nothing on earth or in heaven for which he had the smallest reverence. That we boys all knew of him, and long before this hour.

Not a mother there but, as he finished, could have clasped him to her bosom with tears of pride and affection. And yet, not a woman there, had she but known, in the instant of embrace, exactly who and what the boy was, but would have plucked him from her bosom, and have hurled him with all the fury of her woman's strength from her with loathing beyond language. The horror to me was, and is, that purity and vilest impurity should be so close to each other with impunity; that foulest impurity could cloak itself so perfectly in the garb of the most artless and child-like innocence.

There were tears as well as applause when the boy came down from the stage, smiling and bowing, every girl there, I dare say, in love with him. I was greatly exercised, just then, about my brother. The principal had, quite cheerfully, excused me from speaking. He had offered to excuse Habby. Such was the respect he had for him, from his standing as a scholar, that he concealed his amazement when my brother declined being excused.

"You have taken one hundred, my boy," Dr. Harrison said at the time. "You stand perfect in our reports, the only student approaching it. You need not speak. You are nervous; never spoke before, you tell me. I would not—"

But Habby spoke. We all knew there would be a titter as he ascended the stage, and it was so loud, the audience being taken by surprise, that I blushed and shrunk down into my boots till I felt much smaller than the one erect and facing the crowd upon the stage. The silence following the first movement continued so long that I glanced fearfully up. I do not understand it. There is a magnetism in sheer power, resident in the eye, commanding and controlling others before a word is spoken. Possibly the people had heard something about his talent in other directions; but there was silence in some measure, possibly again of pity also, for one so diminutive.

Having no eloquence myself, I do not comprehend the matter. But my brother was too thoroughly conscious of his own power to doubt it, any more than when before the blackboard or when reading Greek. The speech of Antony over the body of Cæsar had been assigned him, and I wondered if the Hand, without which not even a sparrow falls, had not ordered it that, on the right of Habby, there happened to lie on the stage a heap of overcoats, marvelously like a human body. At any rate, the orator availed himself of it, pointing to it, as he proceeded, as to murdered Cæsar, dead and draped from sight at his feet. For the first time in the lives of many there, they heard eloquence in the truest sense of the word. The profound silence from the first deliberate word, the breathless attention, the thrill as evident through the audience as the ripple running over a lake, the riveted eyes and parted lips of all as they listened, the perfect mastery of himself and of them on the part of the speaker, all proved the despised dwarf an orator in the highest sense of the term.

Dwarf! My brother towered into a son of Anak as he stood. From that day my love for him transformed itself into pride. Thereafter, whenever he and I were thrown together among strangers, in the cars, or at hotels, and along the streets, the glances and smiles of people seeing Habby never disturbed me. "Oh, if you only knew," I said to myself, with pity for their ignorance.

There was not much applause as he took his seat; people were too much surprised at themselves and their own emotions, too. No one present, however, but took for matter of course, as they did the date of the day, that the speech they heard was the event of the day, the speaker the pride and glory of the institution, his very infirmity, curiously enough, becoming part of the pride and glory of the thing. I hardly said a word about the matter to Habby; he never alluded to it to me. We both understood it all too perfectly to use words. I exhausted and satisfied myself by writing home.

Habby and I were hurrying away after the speaking was over, when we saw a cripple hobbling toward us from the departing crowd.

"It's Purity Baxter. Hold on, Habby," I said, as the poor fellow so named came to our side with hand timidly stretched out. I do not think either my brother or myself was particularly pleased, although the homely face of the boy was radiant as he simply shook us both by the hand and turned away without a word.

With the exception of Habersham and myself, he was the one student who, so far as we knew, stood firm amidst the freshet of filth and all demoralization which was sweeping the Institute to its doom. His name was Baxter, and he stood fast in virtue of standing, like Habby and myself, apart from and as upon the banks of a foaming torrent, which was bearing to ruin the wreck and riffraff upon it. He was an orphan, very poor, exceedingly homely, who had been cast into the Institute by an uncle impatient to be rid of him, as one casts an old shoe into a gutter: not that his uncle knew of matters at our school as they really were any more than did our own parents. From the outset of his arrival, the boy had been struck by the existing state of things with an astonishment from which he never recovered, having, it seems, been carefully instructed till the time of her death by his mother, in their log-cabin, somewhere among the post oaks and sandy bottoms of the State far away from the abodes of men. You will see that I have not the smallest intention of making a hero of this poor yellow-haired, sallow-visaged youth, since I tell you that he was of the class of poor whites; his copperas clothes, large hands, and depreciating demeanor, left that out of all question. "Old Jeremiah Baxter," "Parson Baxter," "Saint Jerry," and, as the most sarcastic of all, "Pure Baxter," were some of the names by which the students called him, having for him a contempt a good deal heartier than if he had been a dog of blood and breeding.

As no one would room with him, the poor

fellow occupied a cabin all to himself. I am heartily ashamed of it to-day, but I suppose we were like all boys, Habby and I, in having almost as little to do as the rest with one who was so thoroughly and unanimously despised, for boys are as destitute of sentiment as are crocodiles. It is beyond human power to convince them that any other boy pretending to such a feeling is other than very ill or a hypocrite. At least, heartily as Habby and I loathed the conduct of the students in other respects, it never occurred to us to blame them for the contempt in which they held poor Baxter—"Piety Baxter." It may have been a shame, but it was a fact, that although we never were unkind to "the parson," we never at all relished, my brother and myself, his humble attempts to cling a little to us, and repulsed him, I am sure, as effectually as the rest, even while we respected and pitied him in comparison.

I remember one midsummer afternoon. Instead of being at work, as it should have been, pulling fodder in the corn-field, the entire Institute was bathing in a creek which ran through a corner of its grounds. The place in question was the one place in which any body could bathe, the water having hollowed out a basin for itself there broad and deep, being, before entering and after leaving this hole, a wide but very shallow stream. That afternoon, "Pure Baxter," for that was his most common nickname, had pulled and bound his fodder up and down the dusty rows as near to my brother and myself as he dared, keeping up with us as well as his lame leg would allow, until his work was done. Noticing that he then climbed the rail-fence, and stole away through the wood, along the banks of the creek, Habby and I had the meanness to follow and see what he was about, more because we had nothing to do than any thing

else, for the idea of bathing among the obscene and uproarious multitude, shouting and plunging about in the water, ducking and being ducked, was out of the question. To say nothing else, we were certain to have our clothes hidden while we were in the water, and to be compelled to steal to our room after dark naked if we tried it. Creeping cautiously along, we saw the poor fellow trying to wash off the dust of his hard and hot work as well as he could in a group of brushes, where the creek was too shallow almost for the bathing of a bird. One of his legs was as straight and as stiff as a post, from white swelling, as he had told us, and we laughed at his desperate efforts to draw on his stocking upon the foot of the rigid leg after he was done. As soon as he had dressed and carefully combed out his yellow hair, we saw him kneel, as well as he could for his stiff leg, against a post oak. The shouts and oaths and laughter of the mob of boys above may have caused him to do so; but it was pitiful to see his round, dull, freckled face uplifted, praying aloud, but in a low voice, while the tears flowed down his cheeks.

"I thought he was always reading those times," Habersham said to me as we stole away, heartily ashamed of ourselves. "So did I," was my reply, for "Pure Baxter," like all of his grade everywhere, could not read at all unless he read aloud, any more than he could write without putting his tongue out as he did so, moving it with every motion of his laborious pen; and we had often heard the dull monotone of his voice in passing his cabin of nights, and laughed to each other about his diligence in study; so far, especially, as algebra was concerned, a useless diligence; for if I could never work out those perplexing equations, it was a kind of miserable satisfaction to me that I did far better, at least, than "Pure Baxter."

CHAPTER XII.

My brother and myself had been away from home at the Archimedean Institute about six months when Archibald, prodigal-like, came back from Texas. And very hard of digestion, indeed, had he found the husks of that far country, in return for which he had made himself so indigestible to his associates there that they had willingly yielded to the influences brought to bear by Governor Houe, and sent him back. As to Horace Houe escaping with him, my brother had quarreled and parted with him on the way to Texas. Somehow, Horace had taken an heroic part in the fifteen minutes' charge upon the Mexicans which swept Santa Anna from the field at San Jacinto and secured the independence of Mexico, by which means the boy, for he was but a year older than Archy, had secured to himself the grant of lands, the glory, and the assurance of whatever office he might wish from a grateful people as long as he lived, all of which my brother had managed to miss. But little he or our family cared for that, since he was safe at home once more, Horace Houe still remaining, with his father's hearty consent, and against the weeping remonstrance of his mother, in the new republic.

Yes, Archibald was at home again. For some weeks he remained indoors, until his weariness as well as general raggedness could be repaired. Georgia had gone into raptures over him from the hour he entered abruptly at the back door, startling Mrs. Brown from her perennial calm into a kind of silent fury, in the preparation of the fatted calf for the prodigal, which, in her estimation and Archy's, meant rice batter-cakes, tender and brown beyond the dream of cook or eater, before or since.

"Oh, isn't Archy a hero!" Georgia said to her sister that night, when the new arrival had been duly escorted to his bedroom, petted, and kissed, and consoled, and forgiven to the utmost of his desire. "He is bronzed like a veteran, straight as an Indian, so determined and independent. Of course, I pity poor little Habby, and we all believe in Carter in his way, you know, but Archy is my hero. See how all the girls at school will be making up to us, so that he may be good friends with them. Oh, hasn't he grown handsome, Jenny?"

"I suppose so, Georgia," Virginia replied, more quietly, "and, of course, I'm glad he has come back. But, somehow, I wish he had staid, like Horace Houe. When he had gone into a thing, he ought to have stuck to it!"

"Why, Virginia!" Georgia exclaims, "after you heard him tell last night how obstinate Horace Houe was, and how his captain wanted to make him do things! I'm glad he had a will of his own—glad he had the spirit to leave them when they treated him so."

"Mother doesn't say any thing, but I know, in her heart, she thinks as I do," Virginia said.

"Well, and pa and I think alike—we always do," replied her impulsive sister. And she was right. Archy had found his father somewhat cold at first, but, as the son grew eloquent in describing his sufferings, and how right he had been in his plans against the ignorance and mistake of every body else in Texas, the father slowly relented, and then became enthusiastic in reference to one so promising in every respect as this his eldest-born. After allowing Archy a month or two of rest, my father, a hard worker himself, went eagerly into the matter of settling his son at some business for life. The Archimedean Institute was rejected by Archy with scorn; prompt and positive, he would be a merchant. For special reasons my father shrunk from getting him in with Mr. Patterson, commission merchant, but, on second thoughts, it occurred to him that Archy might be the very providence needed to bring about a more perfect understanding with that officer of his church than had existed for some time; and so with shrewd Mr. Patterson was Archy placed.

"It is the very thing, Agnes," my father said to my mother, with energy; "Mr. Patterson is a strict business man—is doing a fine business. Archibald has more talent than any son I have. Depend upon it, he will succeed nobly. He has to make a beginning, of course; but I would not be surprised if Mr. Patterson took a strong fancy to him. I do not mean become attached to him; Mr. Patterson, you know, is not a person of that sort; but you grow to like Archibald on account of his business value. It will draw Mr. Patterson and our family closer together; and, mark my words, Agnes, I would not be surprised if, in five years, Archibald were taken into partnership with him!"

Alas! in less than five months my brother had left his employer in disgust. I never knew the details, but it threw the relations between pastor and officer into a worse attitude than before.

"Mr. Patterson says that Archibald is admirably adapted to business," my father explained, somewhat sadly, to my mother, "that he is swift and accurate at figures, writes a copper-plate hand; but, but—"

"That Archibald is perverse," my mother added for him: "perverse!"

"You know that Mr. Patterson, a most excellent man in many respects, is himself very opinionative. You can not tell, Agnes," continued my father, "what pain and trouble he gives us in church matters, he is so set in his ideas about every thing, even the least—so inflexible and unyielding."

"I know it, my dear, when he visited us

at my brother's there in Virginia," my mother replied, "and you will remember my telling you of it. Those slight, wiry, dark-visaged men, with thin lips, narrow foreheads, hollow-chested, head bent forward, quick yet cold manner, all belong to one class. Let Mr. Patterson have his way in every thing, and a more faithful friend unto death you could not have; cross him in the least matter, and—"

"Then you do think the fault is with him, not Archibald?" my father added, hastily, for the topic was specially disagreeable to him.

"Not wholly. I do not think either you or I understand Archibald," my mother replied. "You always tell me that he takes his prejudices and inflexible ideas from me. Perhaps he does, but he takes his warmth of imagination, his ardor, and impulsiveness from you. He is a strange medley, my dear husband. I fear he will give us great trouble. Perverse! It is the only word I can think of. And he is our first-born. I do not know what our little Habby may turn out to be, but Archibald has a hundred times the talent of dear, good, plodding Carter. My brother Archibald was right," and my mother could not help laughing as she said it; "put his uncle's blue coat and gray trousers on Carter, his gold-headed stick in his hand, a plantation in his sole charge, and, in many respects, the boy is the man over again. I do not know where my brother got his queer ways; I do believe he copies old Uncle Arxis, unconsciously, of course, instead of the old negro copying him." My mother laughed again. It was curious, but whenever she spoke about her old home in Virginia, she seemed ten years younger, and laughed like the happy girl she used to be there. To the rest of us it was comparatively a dull old place; to her it was as paradise was to Eve, looking back to it from later years.

And that was but the beginning of trouble with my brother Archibald. After leaving Mr. Patterson, he was thrown into a chance connection with an artist making his temporary home in the place. I do not know whether it was the slouched hat and long hair of this painter of portraits, or his desultory life as a wandering genius; possibly there was the love of art, as there certainly was the inspiration, in Archy's case. Such things were wholly out of my father's line; but when he did come to understand it, he was as full of enthusiasm as ever.

"Would you have ever imagined it of Archibald, Agnes?" he said to my mother. "I ists in Washington. I showed them to the artist himself, and he spoke of them in the highest terms. He has consented to instruct Archibald, and told me frankly that he regarded him as having a much greater talent than himself."

Very few pastoral visits did my father

ARCHIBALD TURNS ARTIST.

do not pretend to be a judge of such things, but his drawings are something wonderful; I could no more draw, for instance, that figure of the Goddess of Liberty than I could fly through the air. I showed them to Governor Hone, and he was as astonished as myself. Mrs. President told me she never saw more promise among any of the young art- pay, during which he did not produce, before leaving, some one of his son's drawings, and show it to his friends, full of ardor and fatherly pride. But—and the One who constructed the heart can alone understand its working—in proportion as his father grew warm upon the subject, the son grew cold; his interest in the matter steadily lessening as his father's increased. When he had reached the climax of hope and confidence as to the brilliant and lucrative future of his eldest-born, that eldest-born had reached the lowest depth of disgust about it, and utterly and forever gave up the whole thing.

I am not certain whether it was the law or the navy which came next, being away from home—only this, that at one time Archy had secured, through my father's old acquaintances in Washington, an opening of some kind at Annapolis, and had actually entered, at another time, the office of Governor Hone, who kindly assured my parents:

"If your son will but stick to it, he will make a splendid lawyer. Of course," the governor said, laughing, "there are the obstacles of his moral and religious training to be gotten over; but we lawyers soon conquer all scruples. As to talent, no young man has more. If he is fool enough to go into politics as I have done, no telling what a distinguished rascal he may become. Thousands of talent; but it requires that a man should stick. That is it, stick!"

But as soon as nothing stood in the way of the navy, the nausea of my brother in reference to it was deeper mentally than it would have been physically had he actually sailed. As to the law, he had told my mother that "its home was the bosom of God, and its voice was the harmony of the universe," even quoted, also from Blackstone, he believed it was, that "the law was a stern mistress, her right hand overflowing, nevertheless, with wealth and honor to those who won her"—but, whichever of the two, navy or law, came first, the end was the same. It was a cruel pity, but in exact proportion as the eagerness infused into the family from my father increased in reference to any project, it as surely decreased with Archibald. Just as they had rejoiced in the thing as settled, he had, for innumerable excellent reasons, finally determined to abandon it. Once arrived at that point—

"You might as well reason," my mother said, "with one stone-deaf. He is my child, but I can not understand him. It must be some terrible defect in our training; possibly our unsettled life when his character was being formed. It is not that he is inflexible—"

"But that," my father finished for her, "any wish of ours has the singular effect of determining him in precisely the opposite direction. If it were not deceptive, it might be well for us to pretend to a violent dislike of the next plan."

"What would be the use, my dear?" said my mother. "Even when he has resolved, the very fact that he himself has taken a fancy for any course itself disgusts him with it. I am his own mother, but God alone understands and can deal with him!"

I am glad Habby and I were off at school and did not know fully concerning all this. Georgia passed through a score of moods about it, now petting and being so proud of her handsome brother, with his regular features and dark hair and eyes, and wonderful intentions for the future, and then scorning and despising and refusing to speak to him, the transition period being one of genuine sisterly weeping; for the briny water of her tears always, if I may so speak one I love dearly, separated from each of er the islands of her manifold moods. I ¿ afraid all this had an influence upon V ginia; but, no, I can not say a hardenil influence. Her clear, seemingly cold manne had, in some wonderful way, not even a sug gestion of other than tender womanliness under it all.

"What a lovely creature Miss Virginia is growing!" Mrs. President said to my mother, during one of her calls, as she wrote us boys at school. "I never saw a young person who seemed more unaffected. She has so much natural grace, the sweetness and freshness almost of a babe. How she is beloved! She has, pardon me, my dear Mrs. Quarterman, the singular faculty of fascination which you will remember in ——;" and Mrs. President named a certain celebrated belle who queened it in Washington years before.

"I thank you!" my mother replied, warmly. "Virginia is unselfish. Indeed, she never seems to think of herself."

"And that explains why she is so unaffected, so purely a child," Mrs. President added, adjusting bracelet and ribbon as she spoke, herself a species of social Minerva, very agreeable and gracious, yet mailed from touch, if not in the helmet and cuirass of that deity, certainly in a costume, of manner as much as dress, which rendered her unapproachable even when she seemed nearest.

"Georgia is a dear girl, but is different," she said, in leaving. "And to think that they are twins!"

"Oh yes; Georgia is an English milkmaid, rosy and full of her impulses. Virginia would seem a lady in a hovel, and Georgia would look countrified even"—my mother bowed as she said it—"in the White House."

"But such a milk-maid as the English poets sing with rapture," Mrs. President repaid my mother. "Dear Mrs. Quarterman, do come and see me!" But why should my mother draw such a sigh of relief after her visitor had stepped into her carriage? And it was the same with Governor Houe over the way, when, as he told my mother, he had enjoyed the pleasure of Mrs. President's society.

All this time my father had given his soul to his work in St. Charles. Every Sabbath morning and evening he preached in his own pulpit; but every Sabbath afternoon was given, and with zest as well as zeal, to his service in the penitentiary. To all outward appearance he had been at home with Colonel Tom Maxwell, and the colonel's complete collection of the varied and desperate wickedness of the State from the first; but it took him really some weeks to adjust himself thoroughly to his convict congregation, as well as for them to adapt themselves to him.

"The way of it was this" (Colonel Tom was accustomed to speak of it afterward): "there is an amazing variety among the convicts, although they do all look exactly alike in striped clothes and cropped heads; some young, some old, some in for rape and murder, others in for stealing; some for forgery and counterfeiting, and they are the smartest. Others for defalcation, and they are the greatest fools. Some were convicted of setting houses on fire, and they are the sneaking sort. Others for highway robbery (rough gambling they call it), and they are the desperate kind. Half of them swear they are innocent, and about a tenth or so are innocent, or are the dupes of scoundrels who put them up to crime, got the proceeds, and left them in the lurch. Whoever and

whatever they are, as I told the doctor, one thing grips and holds them all alike, and that is—force. It don't matter what kind of force, showering, or the dark cell, or being chained up or worked down, always death if necessary, and a strong will in the warden to do whatever needs to be done—force, you understand. And credits for good behavior, percentage on work done, and the like, are a weaker kind of force, but in some shape force grips and holds them all. It's a kind of hobby of mine, and when I told the doctor that, he said, 'Certainly, colonel; but there is a higher force which will close upon and hold what nothing you have got will touch, and that is the heart.' And the Gospel is that force, I suppose you mean, I said; all right—go ahead. The law allows it; you have one hour a week to try it on them, and I have the rest of the hundred and sixty-eight hours for my kind. I was always present, too, and on my feet, while the doctor preached. Nothing could be simpler, plainer, quieter, than the way the doctor went to work. I thought he was going to talk to them about their mothers and wives and children, about dying—work on their feelings, you know, and so he did, but not until afterward. He talked to them in such a way first as made them understand and believe, as certain sure as they existed, about the One that made them, and how they had wronged Him, and then came down upon their feelings. See! That is the way the revival began. But when it was under full way, he never allowed any exclaiming or crying-out; all he had to say he said in his hour, and then sent them to their Bibles in their cells to think and read and pray it all over, each man by himself. Of course, there were a few extra meetings for special conversation, and taking the communion, and the like; but the work and the discipline never relaxed one hour. I saw to that, and that is all."

It was all, except that my father got into the habit of resting himself twenty minutes or so in the rooms of Colonel Tom after service, by talking a very little with the colonel, as that giant lay stretched out on the floor, his children seated astride of him, obedient beyond either of them to the least wish of his small wife. The two men were singularly like each other as well as unlike, and a strong attachment of a wholesome, manly kind sprang up between them. But Colonel Tom never relaxed an ounce of his weight nor a hair-breadth of his commanding height, much less a particle of the pressure of his will, upon his prisoners or turnkeys, for all that. Something to me, as a boy, always exceedingly refreshing in Colonel Tom; not a bit of the uncertainty and feebleness and sickly sentiment seen but too often in many a man who never entered a penitentiary, or who, so to speak, never left a church. Your feeling, the longer you knew him, was a species of—hurra for Colonel Tom! and a general idea that Tom was the best of names for a boy-baby, if you wished him to grow up to be the manliest of men!

As the months rolled on, the work in the penitentiary under the new chaplain became the talk of the State. Had not my father urged upon the colonel a wiser course, the services would have been crowded by visitors from abroad; as it was, every thing was kept as evenly as possible in the tenor of its way, quietness being with my father, ardent as he was, but another name, under such circumstances, for depth and permanence of religious life.

"All that I do in the penitentiary," he said to Governor Hone, over of an evening for a little conversation, "is delightful to me as, if I may so style it, a recreation. But my heart is in my work as pastor of my church."

"We have increased, you know," the governor would say, consolingly, for he knew my father's grief. "We are the largest and strongest church in town."

"Ah, you do not understand, governor," his pastor would reply. "I merely talk to the convicts; but you have no idea the care and labor I expend upon my sermons for my church. Not a discourse but is rewritten, often more than once. You would not think so, since I never take the manuscript into the pulpit. I know that, especially when the Legislature is in session, I have the choicest intellect of the State, in part at least, present to hear: and what an influence these politicians would have, the editors quarreling so furiously and all, if they were but to become Christian men in good earnest! And yet—"

"We are a hard set, doctor," Governor Hone replied. "I do feel for you, trying so earnestly to get at us from the pulpit. Nothing can be more self-evident," with his senate-chamber wave of his long arm and large hand as he spoke, "than your arguments, more striking than your illustrations, more affecting than your appeals; yet, I acknowledge—"

"And I do try very hard not to be vehement, not to be so earnest as to defeat my own object," said my father, who had the bad habit of interrupting another in conversation, with his eyes absent from what the other was saying even before his tongue confirmed the fact of the persistence of his mind along his own path of thought. "I give ten times the study and toil and prayer to my own people, especially to my pulpit preparations, than to any thing I do for the convicts, and yet I might as well dart straws against icebergs. Look at the scant attendance at our prayer-meetings! I confess I am becoming thoroughly discouraged."

"You remember, it was the same with the politicians at Washington, my dear," my mother, who was sewing beside him, suggested. "You often said, of all people on earth they were the hardest to influence for good. Excuse me, governor!"

"You are right, madam, right," said Governor Hone, lifting his loose-jointed body from his chair, with a smile upon his genial face, worn as it was by the long and steady wash, so to speak, of seas of people approving and disapproving. "We are a hard, hard set, madam—the hardest set going. That was an excellent sermon of the doctor's, 'Beware of the leaven of Herod!' Yet I could feel it glancing off even while it hit me full. And when did you hear from Archibald?" continued the governor, slipping, as he did every ten minutes, to the fire-place to spit, for he was an incessant tobacco-chewer, unconsciously illustrating, by the manner, also, of the question, the slight interest he took in what so profoundly interested his pastor. Of course my father was concerned for Archibald, but not at all as he was for his preaching, even although his first-born had again disappeared, this time leaving no clue as to his intentions.

"Not since he left, governor," my mother replied. "We are greatly distressed."

"So is Sukey—Mrs. Hone, I mean—for Horace there in Texas. If she were not so plump," added the governor, "I tell her she would cry herself away. Never fear, Mrs. Quarterman; he will be all right in the end. You know what a domestic woman Sukey is; never leaves the house. Come over and see her."

"I would rather," Governor Hone said to himself, as he crossed over to his house, "have my Horace in Texas, swearing and fighting—yes, gambling, drinking, and worse than that—than have him at home and be a fellow like that scamp of theirs. If a boy is bad, it is better to be bad straight out, and without so many curly-cues!" For the governor was but a Western governor, and owed his popularity to his open-heartedness even more than to his broad-brainedness, if such a word may be coined.

CHAPTER XIII.

My brother Habersham and myself were two years at the Archimedean Institute together. During all this time we did not visit St. Charles once, the simple fact being that we could not afford to do so, as it was in virtue of the most stringent economy alone that our parents could pay our expenses there, small, comparatively, as they were. For the same reason they could not visit us, the more especially as my father was in such demand in reference to protracted meetings in all the region in which he lived, that, while he sincerely loved us, his duties at home and abroad took up every hour of his life. Even our letters were few and far between, because of the postage—twenty-five cents in silver on each letter—there being then no such tendency of friends toward each other, no such strong current of loving intercourse as exists, now that all obstructions are removed from the channels of the same, our very hearts beating, it seems to me, more rapidly and fully—the mountains being tunneled, the plains being covered with railways, the oceans underlaid with wires—in the quickened circulation of these days. I suppose this intercourse of affection, deepened, hastened, uninterrupted between us all now, in comparison to former times, is part of our progress toward the absolutely perfect communion without barrier, of the good to whom God's entire universe will be thrown open eternally. Even if we had enjoyed hourly intercourse with our parents, I am far from sure that we boys would or could have told them every thing. Terrible as it was, neither Habby nor I could

have entered upon such matters; the vileness was too vile, we could not have spoken about it; and I do believe that part of the quickened current of mutual love, round and round the world, now shows itself in the fact that in these days it rises mightily against, breaks over and sweeps away barriers, seemingly as natural and impassable as mountains and seas, which once existed in such matters as these also between even parent and child.

To the mingled delight and dismay of my brother and myself, Virginia and Georgia broke suddenly upon us in our cabins at the Institute one Saturday morning. It was all through Professor Dinsmore, the founder of the Institute. As a peculiarity of the coldness or the modesty of his very benevolence, he had never visited the Archimedean idol of his soul since it went into operation. So excessively interested was he in a scheme in which he had invested all his heart, as well as almost every cent he possessed, that I do believe he shrunk from watching it too closely, as one does from opening a letter which contains a matter of the last importance. While hovering around it at a distance with unsleeping solicitude, he happened to be at my father's, and, in sudden response on his part, which amazed him more than any one else, to a vehemently expressed wish to that effect on the part of Georgia, he promptly consented to take the girls with him in his carriage, and spend a Sabbath with us, it being not more than a three days' journey from St. Charles.

"It is perfectly splendid!" Georgia exclaimed, that Saturday, when she had kissed us, and before she had told us the news from home. "I would give any thing if Virginia and I could be at such a school. What a funny little log-cabin! Look at those queer little cots! Do you keep your clean things in those trunks under them? Here's where they keep their wood, Jenny; I thought it was their wardrobe. See, they've got their blacking-brushes on the shelf where they wash! Did you ever see such dirty towels? And you make up your beds yourself? Robinson Crusoe over again. What do you keep in this desk? ears of corn, as I live!"

"To pop of nights when we are too hungry to stand it any longer," I exclaimed; "but don't speak so loud, Georgia. The fellows in the next room to this hear every word you say."

"Who lives there?" asked Virginia, in her low tones.

"Oh, a fellow named Alonzo M'Callum. His father is a missionary in India or China," I replied, in the hurry of promiscuous talk which follows upon sudden meeting with one's kin.

"Please fix so that we can see him. Dear little fellow," Georgia exclaimed, "how lonely he must be! And so good, too, dear little missionary! I'm glad he is so near you. The idea of hanging that ridiculous bit of a looking-glass where the light shines full on it!"

Habersham glanced at me, his ashen face covered with a glow, and then more ashen than before. Here was Georgia, plump as a partridge, all overflow of life and health and happiness, and Virginia, so quiet and sweet and lady-like, both as beautiful to us as angels dropped down from God, but like angels alighted (not knowing it) in the slimiest and most malarious of swamps.

"If one of those scoundrels dares to speak to either of them, I'll kill him!" Habby managed to whisper to me. "I can't bear they should be touched, even with the eyes of those—"

"Hush!" I said, seizing Habby by the sleeve.

"What is it? What is it? Mustn't have any secrets from me. Oh, Jenny," Georgia continued, "we forgot to tell them about the big cake in our trunk, and ever so many things besides! Professor Dinsmore's carriage stopped at the gate. He is the kindest, dryest, best man I ever knew, only as solemn as an owl. We are going right on directly, to stay all night at Dr. Harrison's —only a mile away, you know—and come back to church here to-morrow. Have to leave Monday. I'm so glad you are so nicely fixed, and are getting to be so learned. You don't know what a trouble Archy has been to us." And so she went on to tell us every thing, having to be continually warned about the occupants of the next room, who, we well knew, were listening in their wood-closet next the dividing logs of the two cabins, and eagerly, to every word they could catch.

"And you have grown so much, dear Habby—are looking so well," Virginia managed to say as soon as possible. "I would hardly have known you."

"Do you sincerely think so?" said Habby, with the delight of a child; and after both sisters had as eagerly assured him of it—fibbing frightfully, I feared—his spirits rose, and his tongue ran as if he had been drinking wine. I confess I could not see that he had grown taller; but that might have been by reason of my being so closely with him. Anyhow, I was glad they thought so, or thought they thought so.

"We are so proud of you—and of Carter," Virginia added the last words out of respect for my feelings. "Why, papa carries your teacher's letters in his breast-pocket, shows them to all his sick folks when he visits them. Mamma says she had to beg him not to forget and give notice of your high standing from the pulpit; he did speak of you in prayer-meeting. We all laughed at him," continued Georgia; "it was just like Major Hampton, we told papa, when the major tells people at meeting what a splendid sermon papa preached the Sunday before. Oh, you can't tell how papa hates to hear him; sits there and looks down and looks up, and begs somebody to sing or to lead in prayer as soon as he can!"

"Colonel Archer never does," Virginia added; "he thinks more of—of—Christ," she added, gravely, "than any person I ever knew. He never speaks in meeting about any body but him. Colonel Archer is the best man I ever met," she said, earnestly. "He was very bad once—used to fight duels and edit papers, and all sorts of wicked things—and now he is as gentle and loving as an angel. I've heard papa tell mamma that he loves Colonel Archer more than any man he ever knew."

"But oh, you can't think what trouble Mr. Patterson is giving the church!" Georgia bursts in; "he is so sharp and set and determined, but it is Archy—"

"Hush, Georgia! Papa hopes," Virginia interrupted, "that Colonel Tom—his real name is Maxwell, you know—the large, ruddy warden at the penitentiary, is becoming a good Christian—"

"Has the funniest little bit of a wife you ever saw," Georgia breaks in, "and minds her like a spaniel; but he's a splendid man. We've needles and thread with us; bring out your things, boys, and let Jenny and me sew the buttons on while we talk. Mamma told us to be sure and remember!"

"Please don't be offended," Virginia suggested, "if we sweep your floor a little first. It is not dirty, you know, but, then, it is not clean—that is, if you have a broom anywhere." And I remember thinking her cuffs, as she took hold of the broom, the whitest and neatest things I ever saw; and she was so much like my mother, too.

It was the happiest time we had known since we came to the Institute; but we were glad when we helped the girls into the carriage at last, as soon as Professor Dinsmore had got through looking around with Professor Hanky pointing out this and that, handkerchief in hand, and they had driven off to Dr. Harrison's to stay till morning.

"I wonder if angels float about over us knowing as little," Habby said, moodily enough, as we sat together in our room, suddenly grown so dirty and mean, after supper. "It's too bad!" This was added with reference to a song which was being sung by Alonzo M'Callum in the next room just then, followed by peals of laughter on the part of his chums, himself, and the roomful of students gathered in there, as usual of evenings; and whenever you hear just that peculiar sort of laughter, you can make sure of the dirty nature of the fun which causes it.

Let me say here that I am perplexed as to how what I have to say at this point shall be said.

Perhaps I can be shortest about it by being plainest—that is, as plain as I dare be. Boys as we were, and having had a home training, it was some time after we got to the Institute before my brother and myself understood matters. As we did come to comprehend the loathsome lewdness which was rotting the school throughout, I think the very excess thereof helped to drive Habby and myself into our position of horror and disgust. The very robustness, too, of my health may have had the same effect on me that the feebleness of my brother's constitution had on him; but mortal hatred of the vileness which seemed to be the universal usage inspired us both, and, from whatever cause, islanded us as amidst a morass absolutely indescribable.

"It seems to me, Carter," Habby would say to me of evenings in our room, "as if they read, thought, spoke of nothing else in the world. It is the very dialect of devils, as papa used to say of swearing, only this is all that and worse. It is the last thing we hear at night, the first thing that is shouted to us from the other room in the dawn of the pure fresh morning."

"Perhaps boys are so at other schools and colleges," I would say; "and it may be we are queer and peculiar old maids, as they tell us all the time; but it is horrible. At the table, going to and from prayers, at play, out in the fields at work! We are getting hardened to it."

"Alonzo M'Callum," Habby added, "has packages of abominable books and pictures, I don't know from where. To think of what ruin one bad boy can make! He puts me in mind of the genius of Shelley, the poet, when he was a boy, although his heart seems to be as full of filth as it is of blasphemy. You know the poetry he slipped under our door; what a woman's hand he writes, and the poetry of it, horrible as it was, was really beautiful. I never imagined," groaned poor Habby, "that such a boy could exist. He must be a great deal older than he looks. He is always telling about India and how the natives do there. It's a thousand times worse than if he had come from a region of small-pox!"

There was an energy in the very putrescence of the rotting soul of the abandoned boy, an eagerness to spread the leprosy of his lewdness, which I now recognize as a zeal inherited from his devoted father, only how terribly reversed!

"Don't let's talk about it any more," I answered. "I'm glad I'm so stupid, and that you have to work so hard with me over our books. We have to pitch in, you know, that much the harder to keep from hearing and thinking. And I suppose we ought to tell Dr. Harrison to write home, do something; but you know all the trouble they have at home about Archy already. Where's the lexicon? What do you think those Latin fellows put things so far apart for, Habby? The very word that ought, in common sense, to be next is put off a mile down, at the very end of the sentence. You'd be welcome to my big bones if I only had your brains. How'll you swap?"

But I am sure neither my brother nor myself felt it all quite as badly as we did that Sabbath the girls were with us. We had not seen any ladies for a long time, and they were such a sensation as that bare and dreary chapel had never known since the evening of the speaking. We met them as they stepped out of Professor Dinsmore's carriage that cool, bright day, and if Habby and myself could have been but as oblivious to the actual condition of things as were Professor Hauky, Professor Dinsmore, and Dr. Harrison, our enjoyment would have been unalloyed. Virginia and Georgia had improved so much beyond all we had hoped, were so very good-looking, in fact, that we could not help telling them so, which, of course, made them look, blushing and smiling, that much the more so. If I were a milliner, I could make this hour the very frills and mutton-leg sleeves they wore, according to the style then prevailing, so well do I remember how they were dressed; something so pure and flower-like, and charmingly feminine in them, after months on months of the dry wilderness we had lived in of Latin and Greek and mathematics, and the society of such associates therein.

Nothing could have been more elaborately prepared or eloquently delivered than the sermon Dr. Harrison gave us. He was as handsome and graceful a preacher as ever delighted a fashionable audience with the melodious modulations of voice and gesture, and, in honor of Professor Dinsmore, the sermon was one of his very best, full of classic quotation and striking thought. The very culture and purity of the man separated him that much the more hopelessly from his congregation. To him they were merely a body of gentlemen—young, possibly too heedless, and lacking in serious thought, yet full of all high and noble purpose. Near a hundred sermons of the kind we had heard from the doctor, with about as much effect upon the current of human passion flowing downward beneath them as the rainbows which overarch it have upon Niagara. If the doctor had but known his audience!

"What a fine-looking set of students they are!" Georgia said to me as we were assisting the girls into the carriage after service, all in a flutter and glow from a sense of being universally admired. "I hope you know them all, boys. You mustn't be queer, and keep yourself aloof. When vacation comes and you can visit us, you must be sure and bring one or two with you, for you must have some very dear friends among them."

"Who," asked Virginia, in her lowest tones, as a pair of the students passed us respectfully, "are these two? I never saw a more beautiful face for a girl, even, than that one with the hair curling about his forehead; but the tall, spirited one with him is studying for the ministry, I know. Who are they, Carter?"

"Well," I replied, "the curly-headed chap is the Alonzo M'Callum I told you about. The other is his room-mate, Charley Marston; but he is not studying for the ministry, not studying at all!" And my faith in woman's intuition has suffered by that remark of my sister ever since.

As usual with him, Habby had been as silent and as grave as an owl so far; but now he suddenly exclaimed, as Dr. Harrison and Professor Dinsmore seated themselves, and were about to drive off,

"Dr. Harrison, if I come up to your house to-night, could I see you and Professor Dinsmore a little while?" looking up with eager face.

"Certainly, Habersham," the doctor replied.

"Of course, Mr. Quarterman," Professor Dinsmore added, with a tremor of nervous surprise upon his cold, gray, set face at the earnestness of my brother. "Dr. Harrison has told me so much of your high standing, that I will be glad to see one who is doing so much credit to my—to the Archimedean Institute."

But Habby did not go. "I said it suddenly to commit myself," he explained to me as we went to our cabin. "I would go if I could, but I can not. I can't tell on them. Besides, it's too abominably bad to talk about!"

"Then I will," I announced, when he declined going with me to supper. As I came back from Joab Fisk's hot biscuits and molasses that night, Charley Marston, seeing me walking alone, lounged in his gentlemanly style along by me, and made, in a casual way, the most flattering remark in regard to my sisters. Of course, I was sorry for it the next moment; but I turned, hit him between the eyes square, all my soul in the blow, with my fist, and walked on and over to Dr. Harrison's, a mile or two away, leaving who would to pick him up. And, let me confess it here, it was very far from the first time or the last in which I had done about the same thing. Generally it was with reference to Habby, or in return for some dirty joke, and this is the first time I have spoken upon the subject to a soul; but I can not help feeling now, as I did then, that it was a hearty and wholesome sort of thing to have done. Habby vented the intensity of his feeling in words, and in lying awake all night; but I was stolid as an ox, and as strong. The only way I could sufficiently express myself was to strike.

"You did not say one word at last," Habby said, from his sleepless bed, after I had got back that night, and was undressing, as silent as could be, in hopes he was asleep.

"No, Habby, I couldn't," I said, and went on to repeat all the nonsense Georgia had been telling me at Dr. Harrison's about an apothecary, Clarkson, in St. Charles, in connection with Virginia, and so turned it off as I crept into my creaking cot.

We walked over to breakfast to Dr. Har-

rison's and told our sisters good-bye, they kissing us rather than we them, and felt relieved as they drove off with Professor Dinsmore. Habby was intense enough, and I was stout enough for almost any thing; but our united energies were not sufficient for the task with the professors we had proposed, and we walked back to the Institute with a hatred of it heartier than ever before. But then they had trouble enough at home with Archy already.

And it all came to end at last with the Institute as naturally as mortification closes with death. I never did know fully how. I think it must have been the actual downfall, at last, through Joab Fisk, the ex-overseer, who held the contract for our board and work. His fatal mistake was in his estimate of how much the boys would work and how little they would eat. The idea that a lot of wild youth, turned loose (after a morning of confinement to study) in the field, would do any thing resembling serious work, was preposterous. The fancy that, in the absence of any one who could compel them, they would make a pretense even of labor, was amazing in the case of one as destitute of imagination as Joab Fisk. He understood negroes, and, with them to feed and to work, would have made money; but these he did not understand, and his mistake broke him all to pieces.

However, the ruin of the school would have taken place under any one, in consequence of the demoralization, more utter and universal than I dare describe here. Dr. Harrison and Professor Hanky and the tutors never entered field or workshop, really despising that part of the system, the fundamental idea of the whole upon the part of Professor Dinsmore, as heartily as the students themselves. The dry-rot, or, rather, the deadly disease introduced by that one fair-faced leper from India, struck day by day through and through the whole Institute. There was an almost entire cessation from study. Upon the same principle on which clods of dirt were put into the cotton, "keys" were universally used in the mathematics, as well as "translations" for the languages actually pasted between the leaves of every Horace or Virgil.

What struck Habby and myself greatly

was an almost total discontinuance, as matters grew worse, of the usual games. "Cat," "shinny," "town-ball," "prisoner's base," "follow my leader," and the like, plays requiring exercise in the open air, gave place to the spinning of little wooden teetotums with numbers on them, cards, and all other gambling sports, the students shrinking as by diseased instinct from open day and hearty exertion, into dark corners and utter idleness.

There was no longer even pretense of work in corn-field and cotton-patch, nothing but riot and turbulent idleness, until Joab Fisk abandoned the mockery of overseeing us in despair. Habby and I clung closer and closer to each other over textbook as well as cotton-basket, doing the best we could, wondering at the stone-blindness of Dr. Harrison, Hanky, and the rest of the teachers. In one thing alone we had any comfort in those dreary days, the ghastliest hours of which were at morning prayers and Sunday services, and that was that it could not last. We knew that the universe itself would soon tumble to dust and dissolution if matters were everywhere else as they were with us.

CHAPTER XIV.

I HAVE alluded to "Pure Baxter" in a previous chapter, and his uncouth congratulations of my brother the night of the speaking.

I think Habby and I were more conscientious in regard to him after, but not so very much, I fear, as you would suppose. Enough so, however, to go into his cabin one afternoon, when he had missed him for some days from Joab Fisk's table. As we had supposed, the poor fellow was in bed, sick with some of his many ailments. It was the first time we had been in his room, which was very bare, but cleaner and neater in some ways than our own. On one side of the room was the old hair-trunk which held all his wardrobe; a round looking-glass hung in its pewter frame of the size of a box of blacking, to a nail on one side of it; a hide-bottomed chair or two and a wash-stand completing the furniture, with the exception of the cot on which he lay, and a swinging shelf containing his handful of books.

"Halloo, Baxter, what's the matter?" I demanded, as he scrambled back into his rickety cot, after unfastening his door, upon learning who we were.

"Nothing at all; only sick," he replied, looking up at us, more frightened than anything else, with his large eyes of the kind called—I know not for what reason beyond that they were of a light blue—"buttermilk eyes."

"Any body been to see you?" I asked.

"Only Dr. Harrison. He was in for a minute when he missed me from recitation so long," he said.

"Give you any physic?" I asked.

"Box of pills and a bottle of something. It's on the floor here under my bed, so's I can get it without getting up. Please let it alone," for the one idea of the poor fellow was that we had come in to play him some trick.

"But what about your eating?" asked Habby.

"Oh, Mrs. Fisk is very good," the poor wretch replied, nothing but his round, sorrowful face, set in its yellow hair, to be seen among the blue coverlets of his bed, drawn to his chin and held tight there in case we should try to drag it off for fun. "She sends me something every other day; says she'd come herself to see me if she weren't driven to death. I put it in my trunk to keep the flies off. Welcome to it, if you want it," he said; for Habby had lifted the lid of the trunk, and, sure enough, there it was, a blue-edged plate heaped with pones of cold corn-bread and fat bacon, varied with heaps of cabbage and turnips.

"Why, you poor chap, your food would kill a rhinoceros!" said Habby. "Much sick?"

"I wasn't much sick; but Lonny M'Callum and some fellows broke in here one night," the boy replied. "It was only their fun, but they said they would try the water-cure; they didn't leave me any water, drenched me with it all, lying in bed. It's summer, but I don't think lying in these wet things is good: I've been as hot as fire, and then as cold as you please, ever since. My leg hurts me like sixty, and I can't get a wink of sleep. Oh, I'll be up in a day or two."

"All right; we'll be in to see you again," was all Habby or I could think of adding as we left. The fact is, Dr. Harrison never once came into our heads. He taught us in the recitation-room, and he preached to us, alternating with Professor Hanky, of Sundays, and a kinder-hearted man never lived. The trouble was that neither he nor Professor Hanky, outside of recitation-room and chapel, had any thing more to do with us than with Joab Fisk's pigs or chickens; knew, for any practical purpose, no more about us than if we had spent the intervals of recitation and prayers in the centre of Hindostan, which with most of us, by reason of Alonzo M'Callum, was really the case.

"What's the use?" Habby said, when at a later day I suggested letting the doctor know. "That poor soul has been sick all his life; he's used to it. He'll be up again in a few days."

We made a point, however, to get at least fresh food for him from Joab Fisk, carrying it to him every night when it was too dark for the fellows to see us, as well as replenishing his brown pitcher with water, and other like services, which he received with many thanks, but also with a continual lookout as to the sort of joke we were certain to play him, sooner or later.

There was not a particle of sentimentality in Habby or myself, as I have said, in the whole matter. The room was too miserably mean for it. The poor fellow was too utterly unromantic for any thing of the sort, even if he had not been a "low-down" chap, suffering from we knew not what degraded vices, personal or hereditary; and then Habby was absorbed in his morbid moods and hard studies, while I was nothing but a boy, and a very ordinary boy, of the common run of the species. Yet we could not but become interested in one who

was so utterly dependent upon us. Besides, he got to telling us, when the fever was hottest upon him, about his mother. We knew what sort of woman she must have been—tall, gaunt, haggard-faced, with her cheap calico hanging around her as if around a post, sandy-haired, sickly, sorrowful, and poor to the last degree: you could tell what the mother was from seeing her child. Yet with that poor fellow, rolling and groaning, and as homely as a boy ever gets to be on earth, it was "Manmer, manmer, manmer!" all the time of his fever, mingled with half verses from the Bible, and old-fashioned snatches of hymns and queerly worded prayers. I suppose her child and her religion were literally all the woman had in her cabin in the woods. When he was free from fever and pain, we got him at last to tell us a good deal about his "raising," but he was very shy of speaking about his "manmer," always on the lookout for some mischief we would do him, at the very least the fun we would make of him and of her. We saw that he took his pills and other physic according to the directions written on the boxes and phials, and told Dr. Harrison and Professor Hanky so when they came to the door of the cabin every few days to ask about him. Why disguise it? Up at least to a certain point, the sick boy was very little, very little indeed, more to us than a sick puppy! A negro-child would have had its mother and its mistress to nurse it, and carefully; but, you observe, "Parson Baxter" was a gawky, poor white-trash boy, ugly and sickly, more unfortunate than a negro in having no one to own him in any sense. It was a mistake, his living in an institute at all.

Yes, boys are but a species of crocodile. We pass, the sarants tell us, through all the animal types previous to the hour of birth; but we are twenty before we become human beings in good earnest. Habby and I became very tired of our poor charge; we were almost sorry that we had taken the duty of caring for him upon us. But, then, having done so, we were as faithful as we knew how, and did have a growing interest in him in virtue of his religion, rude and crude as it seemed to be, never dreaming for a moment of how sick he really was.

One sultry night about ten o'clock, Alonzo M'Callum, Marston, his room-mate, with one or two others, broke into Baxter's cabin as Habby and I were seated therein working together over Virgil, helping the sick boy, as he seemed to need it, to his medicine or his water.

"Halloo, parson, sick ?" M'Callum exclaimed, standing over the shrinking boy. "I'm a doctor, and know what's the matter with you; playing possum's the matter. I thought the water-cure had made you well. Come, hop up, and give us a sermon !"

"You let the boy alone," I said.

"What business is it of yours, Parson Strong ?" M'Callum said, giving me the nickname by which I generally went. "I suppose I've just as much right here as you. Shut up! Come, get up, Mr. Purity! preach us a sermon, sing us a psalm, or dance us a breakdown," laying hold of the bedclothes.

"Please, please, don't," moaned the miserable boy. "I never did you any harm in my life. I am so weak and sick—I haven't had any thing to eat for nigh a week, nothing but physic."

"Why, here's plenty, you fool !" said M'Callum, taking from the wash-stand a horrid mess of stale bread cooked in molasses, which Mrs. Fisk called pudding, and, standing with the soap-dish full of it beside the boy, he endeavored to force upon his compressed lips a pewter spoon loaded with the loathsome fare.

"Please don't, sir! I'm so sick you can't tell !" said his victim. "For Jesus' sake !" he cried, as if in desperation—"your pauper" (papa he meant) "was a preacher ; he believed in Jesus—please let me be !" And the boy seemed driven wild, his face so large and white, so hollow-eyed in its tangle of yellow hair.

"What do you know about my pauper, as you call him ?" the other said, with a sort of cold rage. "And—Jesus !" There was that in the tones in which it was uttered, tones of contempt and hate, which I can not describe. "You poor, mean, clay-eating, low-down cur, listen; I'll sing you a religious hymn !" And with one of the sweetest voices I ever heard, Alonzo M'Callum began to sing, to a familiar hymn-tune, something I had often half heard from him before—

beastly words which he must have caught from some educated Hindoo or apostate Christian before coming to America.

I am generally slow, and was planning the campaign when Habby precipitated matters. Climbing upon the old hair-trunk, he had hurled himself like a wild cat therefrom full at the face of M'Callum, and, livid with fury, he was striking, scratching, kicking, as they rolled over and over on the floor ; to my horror, but not so much as to his own when I told him of it afterward, cursing his antagonist, too, more like a crazy person. There was a general scrimmage, of course ; but the venomous fury of poor little Habersham had more effect than any thing I could do, and in a few minutes we had the invading crowd driven out, the stout door well barred with a board wrenched from the position it had filled as mantel-piece over the fire-place, and were picking up the torn books, and scattered pudding, and broken chairs.

"We are in for it," I remarked, as soon as I could get breath enough to speak coolly.

"No objection," said Habby, who was trying to stop the bleeding of his nose. "They didn't do it," my brother added ; " you know it always bleeds when I exert myself violently. Of course."

This exclamation was in reply to the smashing of the glass from without. But it is not necessary to describe the assault upon our castle for the next hour or two. Logs thrown on the roof, stones hurled down the chimney, desperate thumps upon the door, accompanied by yells and oaths. But what astonished Habby and myself amidst all the uproar was the change in the sick boy. Instead of cowering under the bedclothes in terror, he had so doubled his bolster under his head, and piled up the pillows upon that, as to lift himself almost into a sitting position ; and there he was, so calm and bright and happy, that we failed to understand what was to follow, only by reason of being as ignorant as boys generally are.

"Never mind, Jerry," I said to him, "all this row will make you well. They'll soon get tired out, for they can't get in your old cabin, and it's after midnight now ;" and as I spoke the crowd outside did depart, with many a promise of the vengeance to be inflicted next day.

"I'm so much obliged to you, am so sorry," the boy said; "and I have got real well all at once. Oh yes, I'll get up in the morning. All along I couldn't stand it, you know, their dirty ways and all that. I was so very lonely, too, since my mammer died. If ever a fellow tried to get as near to Christ as he

"Hush, Carter—look!" Habersham, who was standing by the bed, interrupted me. "Did you ever see?"

The poor boy had undergone a change which we could not understand. The sallow hue had left his face, leaving it as white as snow; the yellow hair seemed no longer

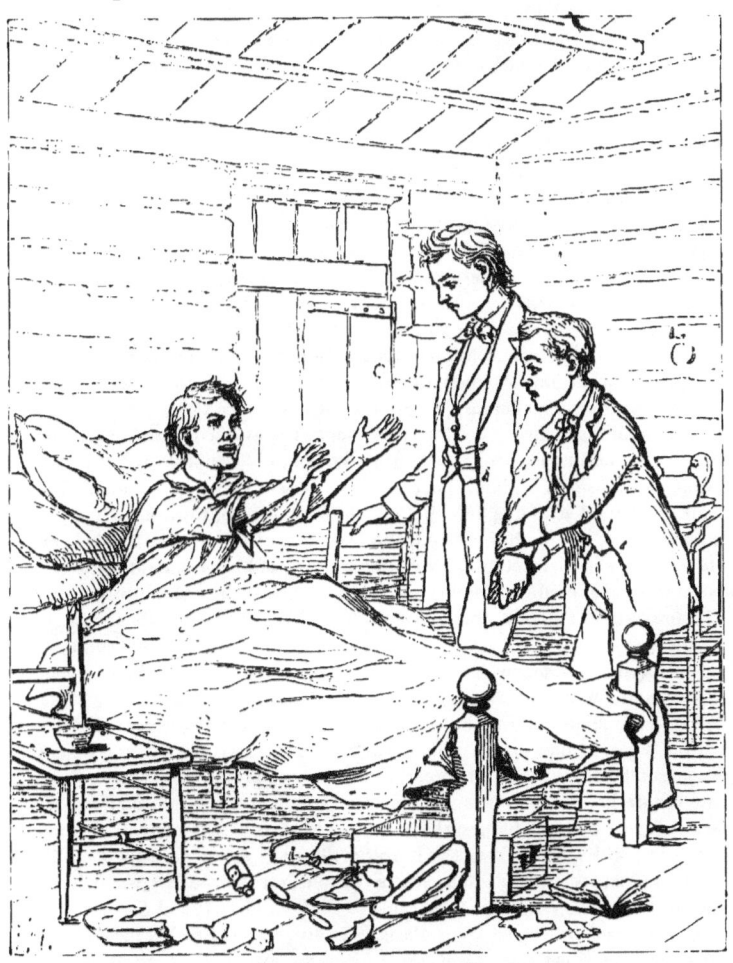

"HUSH, CARTER—LOOK!"

could—she talked to me about it, you know —I did. All of a sudden, I ain't afraid a bit."

"Very well, Baxter," I said; "you are all right. Lie down. Habby and I will stay till breakfast. To-morrow we will tell Dr. Harrison all about it. He will fix their flints for them—"

coarse; the eyes were wide open, and full of soul; the hands were lifted as with that joyous grace seen nowhere but in those of a babe crowing, with arms extended toward its mother—an uplift, an eagerness, a transforming rapture of expectation.

"Run, Carter, for Professor Hanky, for Dr. Harrison, for somebody! Run, stupid!" said

Habby, almost beside himself, as I dashed around the room in search of my hat.

"Oh, maumer! Jesus, too! Maumer, maumer!" from the sick boy. "Yes, sir," with ecstasy wholly indescribable of wonder and gladness. "Maumer told me about you. I knew you, sir, at once. Oh, maum—!" And the uplifted hands trembled and fell, the light was gone from the ashes, so to speak, of the eyes, and the body slowly sunk down. To our unspeakable surprise, Baxter was dead.

And why detail all that followed? With poor Baxter the last pretense of life departed from the Institute. For months before midnight hands had been writing on every available house-side and board-fence blasphemous words and obscene pictures with chalk or charcoal, the marks re-appearing as fast as they were erased, reminding me since then of the abominable inscriptions upon the walls of Herculaneum and Pompeii, drawn there who can say how soon before the storm of fire and ingulfing ashes. So far as I know, all the mortal disease originated with that one leper, Alonzo M'Callum, the worst boy of all. No need of going into details of that destruction, the studies ceasing, the students leaving, the instructors taking situations elsewhere, the creditors coming down upon the property—all, as it were, in one week.

While we waited for money to go home upon, Habby and I went one evening of the early fall into the main building in hopeless search after some of our books, which we thought might be in the laboratory. The Venetian blinds had been left unfastened and were swinging on their hinges, the window-sash being still left up from the heats of summer; the damp wind was blowing in upon the costly philosophical apparatus imported by Professor Dinsmore from Paris. What had been polished rose-wood, brass, and steel, was already become an array of cracked and rusted ruin. The maps were flapping in rags from the walls, the curtains torn into rotting strings by the wind. The floor was littered with torn books and fallen plaster. The odor of acids and fetid gases upon the air, a fitting emblem of the expiring smell, so to speak, that lingers in that region to this day; and it is all that is left

of it, of Professor Dinsmore's expensive experiment—all that was left, the evening we stood there, of the Archimedean Institute, except the professor himself.

Near-by the Institute lived a farmer who supplied us with excellent milk, the one wholesome article upon Joab Fisk's wretched table. The professor had made this house his home in his last efforts to save something from the wreck of the doomed Institute. It seemed a pity that this farmer's wife should have wearied the old and dying professor with the stories just then of her pig-sties and hen-roosts, as well as melon-patches, stripped by the students in a decadence of their school as desperate as that of Rome or Corinth. Yet it did not much matter, for he was dying as it was—very old all of a sudden, friendless, denounced by the wrangling creditors, utterly broken in heart as in health. So far as I ever knew, he had never entered upon the scheme except from a sincere desire to try an experiment which he was convinced would work wonders for the youth of his State and the whole South, and, possibly, the entire land. In any case, without hope of reward, he had given to the experiment every pulse of his heart and every cent of his once ample means. Nothing had resulted but absolute failure. He lay upon his mattress of shucks in the narrow shed-room of the farmer's cabin, very white of hair, very gray and cold of countenance, silent and quiet. I suppose the one word "bewilderment" expresses his feeling, for he had little to say beyond a few simple directions as to his funeral, and the disposal of the wrecks of the Institute, as far as they would go, for the satisfaction of its importunate creditors. A colder man, a chillier man I should have phrased it, never lived; but he had given himself and all he possessed with his utmost force to his idea of doing good, like an avalanche, even if it be of snow. Having spent himself and been utterly spent, and all for worse than nothing, there was nothing left him but to die. For days before his death he lay on his poor bed at the cabin of the impatient farmer, stern and silent. Habby was getting in from the wash and packing up our clothes at our old room in the abandoned Institute before we left for home; and I had grave doubts as to how we were to get there, having paid most of the money sent us by my father to the fretful wife of the farmer as board, while I watched, unasked, by the bed of the dying man. He never imagined I was there for that purpose; but there was no one else to do it; and I had my pallet of a quilt or two on the floor of his room almost unobserved.

"Yes, Lord, yes," I heard him say that last night, for I had been so often awakened by the restlessness of Habby during his miserable nights that I woke readily. "Yes, Lord, yes," in a low, clear whisper of one unconscious that he was uttering his one unceasing thought even in a whisper, and, as I was dropping over the edge of sleep again after a long silence, "Yes, yes, yes, yes, Lord; our little Luly was the first, Willie next; it was very hard when Mary—yes, yes. Then our wifie—Lord, such pain, pain! Oh, Christ of Gethsem— I loved her so, so, so! The little ones, too. Yes, Lord, yes, yes." Long silence, during which I would have crawled out in the darkness, but I knew he would hear me and know that I had heard him. "Now, this," he added in lower accents, "I thought, I hoped! Yes, dear Lord. Take the will, the wish! Even so, Father, for so it seemeth, seemeth—" And I pressed my hands steadily to my ears that I might hear no more, conscious, however, all the weary night through, of the almost incessant monotone—"Yes, yes, yes, Lord!"—of the dying man.

I was at the turning-point just then, when, in ceasing to be a boy and becoming a young man, youth has a season of unbelief, as at other periods it has whooping-cough or measles; and, soon after getting home with Habersham, I told my father the whole story of Professor Dinsmore's effort and failure, in the study one afternoon, as a perfectly unanswerable argument against Christianity, getting quite heated while I spoke as from the fuel and fervor of my own words.

"My dear Carter," said my father at last, with a patient smile, after I had talked myself out, "Professor Dinsmore is but one of ten thousand cases;" and he told me at length the story of William of Orange, assassinated after near half a century of struggle against Spain, leaving every thing seemingly to go to ruin. "Yet Protestantism results, my boy, from what seemed," he added, "that agony of failure. How do you think I feel, Carter," he continued, after a little, "when, after years of my most importunate effort these politicians, under my preaching, harden like sand before the surf into granite?" For my father used what was considered as an extraordinary degree of illustration in his preaching for those days.

"Christ on Calvary seemed the most disastrous failure," said Habersham, who was with us, "and yet all Christianity is from that!" And he said it, and a good deal more to that effect, with a sort of electric energy, his face glowing suddenly through its habitual paleness like a living coal through its film of ashes. My father looked at his infirm boy with surprise, and then said,

"God bless you, my son!" the tears rising to his eyes as he spoke. The fact is, my father, hale and strong and sensible as he was, had a good deal to try him just then, besides the chronic pressure for money, that malady hereditary to the apostolic succession of ministers.

CHAPTER XV.

"It is because we have reached a dead-centre," my brother Habersham said to me, in explanation of our somewhat doleful circumstances, a few weeks after our return from the Archimedean Institute.

"A dead-centre?" I asked, more like a little boy of his grandfather than one would have expected of a stalwart youth of sixteen in conversation with a brother, who, if several years older, was so many sizes smaller than myself. The fact, however, was, that somehow my father himself, so fresh and joyous in virtue of his perfect health and quenchless enthusiasm, seemed younger than Habby; my mother too, merely a little girl in contrast with him, in virtue of a certain refined simplicity of bearing and charm of complexion, which she had retained from her Virginia country home, as she had its peculiar idioms and inflections of language. As to Habersham, he had run, so to speak, all to head. I do not believe he was an inch larger than when ten years of age; but by reason of hard study, sleepless nights, frequent sickness, and strain of thought, tense and never relaxed, his pale and care-worn face was as that of a patriarch, as was all his conversation.

"You forget, Carter," he said, somewhat impatiently, "that time I explained it to you, when Colonel Tom showed us the engine at the penitentiary. The dead-centre is the point at which the crank pauses a moment at the highest and at the lowest turn in its revolution. We all have been smoothly and steadily active, and, after a while, we will be again; but as a household we are motionless just now. At any instant we go on again, but whether it will be up or down, who can tell?"

"Yes," I said, but not at all moodily. I left that to him and, in her way, to Georgia. "Archibald is gone, and never writes; father is hopeless of influencing his church as he does his penitentiary; you and I are unemployed, and do not know what to do; good Mrs. Brown, down-stairs, is the only one who lives as serenely round and round in her circle as the kitchen clock."

"It is a miserable weakness," exclaimed my brother in his intense way, getting up impatiently, putting his hands in his pockets, and walking up and down the parlor, in which we were waiting for we knew not what, that dreary afternoon, "to feel, like a fool, that one has got to the end of every thing, the darkness before you as solid as a stone-wall, your nose grinding against it, no more future forever. If I do have a contempt for a fool, it is when he feels in that way!"

And it was of himself that Habby was speaking. He had the greatest capability of contempt of any one I ever knew, and the very gall of its bitterness he reserved, alas! for himself.

"I'm very busy studying men," I tried to divert his attention by saying cheerily; "somebody says, 'The proper study of mankind is man—'"

"It was Pope said it, and," my poor brother interrupted me, "if there is one man above another for whom I have a special contempt, it is for Alexander Pope."

The two were so much alike in infirmity and genius that the feeling was but part of his self-contempt. Insanity is merely diseased self-consciousness; and, strange to say, without an atom of selfishness in his nature, Habby's whole life was an unceasing action and reaction between excessive self-appreciation and depreciation as excessive and morbid.

"Now, there is Major Hampton," I went on. "He is sincere. There never was a man more ardently a Christian. His whole heart—"

"Not one grain of sense," Habby snapped me up, savagely. "One would suppose he would know by this time that people don't want to hear him. The warmer he is at prayer-meeting, the colder everybody else gets. And not to know that the deepest emotion is expressed by lowering, not lifting, the voice!"

"Ah, well," I said, "from being an abandoned sot he has become a consistent Christian. Not a horse or carriage goes out of his livery-stable on Sunday, even for a funeral, if he can help it, and Sunday the very day on which he might make most money;" for the major had changed from teacher to livery-stable keeper since we had been away at school. "Why, Habby!" I added, "he won't let a race-horse enter his stable. And there is General Hugh M'Neil settled here since we left. He is a gentleman of the grand, old-fashioned, stately type of South Carolina—"

"But not of Virginia," Habby broke in. "Uncle Archibald had his faults, but he never said, as General M'Neil did that day he dined here, 'If you will allow me, my dear madam, I will reply in the affirmative. Your preparation of that turkey causes it to be so succulent, that I may not deny myself the gratification of again partaking;' his very words, and you know it!" And my brother had given the pompous manner of the chivalrous old soul so admirably that I laughed heartily. Yet no one felt like smiling, even when in the general's company: there was such a genuine loftiness in the man that smaller words than he habitually used would have been out of keeping with his slow and sonorous tones.

"Well," I said at last, "there is Mr. Apothecary Clarkson, that we tease Virginia so much about."

"Except that he is not tall and thin and starved, he is the very man Shakspeare meant by his apothecary in 'Romeo and Juliet,'" my brother replied.

"I like him," I argued; "he is so round,

and soft, and neat, and modest. He is only as a mouse to a mammoth in comparison with General M'Neil, but he is as true a gentleman in his way; although I wish he did not send Jenny so much perfumery. I'm sure," I continued, since Habby did not think enough of Mr. Clarkson, even to add his usual "humph!" of scorn, "you can not object that Dr. Grex is a mouse. There is a—I will not say gentleman, but an out-and-out man for you; yes, a sterling man!" But I was sorry that I said it, for Dr. Grex was the reverse of my brother. Tall already, the doctor made himself more so by a military bearing, which gave him a defiant appearance, bronze-visaged, black-eyed, and bearded as he was, prompt and peremptory of speech. However, as I said already, Habby despised people only so far as they resembled himself.

"Yes, he is rough, uncouth—a sort of King of the Cannibal Islands," he replied; "but I like him because he is himself, just as I have a thorough liking for Colonel Tom at the penitentiary. Next to God, human nature is the grandest thing in creation—that is when it is as God made it." And I could see that he fell to brooding over his infirmity: all paths led, alas! to that.

"Well, and there is Cosma," I continued; and as I said it, Habby, who was facing me, wheeled suddenly and walked to the window, and never turned from looking out as I continued: "How kind it was in Governor Hone!—Cosma Adams is her name, isn't it? I don't believe one word about her being their relative; at least the relationship is very distant. I tell you, Habby, it was because she was dead poor, had no relative or friend living, that they took her. Did you ever see such a bread-and-butter girl in all your life? Her face is as round and as full and as rosy as a harvest-moon. As good a creature, as pure and good-natured as you could wish; but she is just like those Circassian slaves—white and soft and ignorant. I don't wonder the Turks say they have no souls."

"Yonder is Mrs. President getting out of her carriage, at Governor Hone's door," said my brother. "Why can't she do it in a natural way? Now she has turned to give directions to Bob, her negro coachman, modulating her tones, selecting her words, accentuating her syllables, even with Bob. Look how she lifts the hem of her dress to cross the sidewalk, as if it were a pedestal. She got so used to being the focus of all eyes, when she was in the White House at Washington, that she thinks the gaze of the world is on her always. How different from mother!"—for, as we had grown up, "ma" and "pa" had given place, in speaking to and of them, to "mother" and "father"—"who no more thinks of herself as being looked at than a dove does or a deer. What I hate," Habby added, "is the unnatural—nature, pure, sweet nature, is my idea. It is God's. He said 'very good' over it. He abominates any thing not according to nature, and so do I."

"Well, then, there is Cosma Adams," I persisted; "she is nature with a vengeance. No wonder, poor thing! she lived in a log-cabin among the post-oaks, on a little scrap of an acre or two with her old father, fifty miles from any body else. They taught her to read at home; and Mrs. Brown told me she had told her that she did not see any body but her father, after her mother's death when she was eight years old, sometimes for months together. She said they would welcome a peddler who chanced along as if he were a king. I dare say his pack of ribbons and beads was more to her than a Broadway store to a girl on her first visit to New York. You know Mabel Patterson, what a dark, smart, sharp girl she is; pretty as you please; but what a contrast to Cosma Adams! Neither of us like Mabel, eah!"—the exclamation being as much like that as can be put into print—"not one bit! But Cosma has no more smartness or shape than a lump of sugar."

"They ought to send her," I continued, "to live at Mrs. President's. I looked over at her last Sunday: she is in mother's class at Sunday-school. There she sat, so plump, and soft, and white, and silent, gazing at mother with her lips apart, and her great round eyes—they look just like a stag's—wide open as if they never would shut again. Mrs. Hone told mother that she is good-natured as can be, loves their children dearly, but is so—I think it was stupid she said—that they hardly knew what to do with her."

"I never heard you chatter so before, Carter," said my brother, with irritation; "gossiping like Miss Praxley. There's another woman I can't endure," he added: "if she had married twenty years ago, when she ought, now! It is unnatural not to be married."

"I'm sure you ought to sympathize with her," I hastened to say, blundering, as I generally did, because of the very haste of my good intentions. "If there is a smart, talented, sharp woman in this town, it is Miss Praxley. One gets afraid of her fun, as she calls it; but a more talented—"

"Talented! Yes," added Habby, "because she never married. And fun? Yes, she has more wit, even, than any body else, but it's her only escape from her desperate wretchedness!" For my brother was an old man in language as well as thoughts and feelings. He had told me that he seemed to himself to do centuries of thinking and feeling during the long and miserable nights he lay awake, not sleeping a wink from dusk to dawn. Now, I slept like a log. Even when Habby's restless tossing and talking to himself wakened me, I knew I could do nothing for him, and that he would hate to have me know that he lay awake, and so I would roll deliberately and deliciously over the edge of the precipice again into unfathomable abysses of the sweetest sleep. I awoke every morning at Habby's call, thoroughly refreshed, and strong as an ox. Therefore I made matters as pleasant as possible for the household, and Habersham in particular, during this dead-centre of our fortunes, as he called it.

And it was pretty trying, especially at breakfast. Our father sat at the head of the table in his usual health, and without a shadow of gloom about him, yet full of the sermon he intended to write the moment he got through. He never took his MS. into the pulpit, and, on that very account, wrote and rewrote every page of all he preached with painful accuracy, as the great trunkfuls of the documents testify to this day. Whatever was his theme, into that he went with his whole soul. On one occasion his reading, since settling in St. Charles, lay in the line of Romanism, and it took a series of discourses to express his growing horror of the enormities of the Man of Sin; nothing quite so clear as the unscriptural wickedness of popery! His temperament swept him along like the Gulf Stream, until good Colonel Archer ventured to remonstrate as to whether the Master would use quite such language, for, with Colonel Archer, Jesus was the instant and invariable test by which every thing and every body was tried. As to Mr. Patterson, saturnine and bitter, he closed his conversation on the same subject with his pastor by saying, "One or two more such sermons against popery, Dr. Quarterman, and you will have every sensible man in your church eager to subscribe toward building a Romish chapel. Who cared for the pope? and you are creating an actual sympathy for him." So far as fat Mr. Clemming was concerned, no one could assent more cordially, when in conversation with his pastor, to the enormous wickedness of Jesuits, Inquisition, Alexander the Sixth, confessionals, and the like, and to the importance of putting Protestants on their guard against the same; but, then, in conversation ten minutes after with others, he would heartily assent to the opinion very generally expressed, adding himself, "Oh, yes, certainly, I agree with you; what is the use of attacking people who are not here to defend themselves? Controversy never did any good, anyhow!"

As to all other evangelical churches, my father so heartily agreed with them that it was often urged against him that Dr. Quarterman was, in fact, more of this, that, and the other denomination than of his own. Yet, when compelled to it by what he considered his duty, beginning in a quiet way the statement and defense of the views of his own denomination, the Gulf Stream, once turned thitherward, would rise and roll and pour warm, strong, and with ever-increasing volume in that direction.

"It is the man," Governor Hone would say to my mother, dropping over of an evening. "He goes into nothing into which he does not put his whole heart. Look at our penitentiary. Colonel Tom Maxwell tells me the doctor has made such sheep of the convicts that any force there is a sort of farce; little more use for revolvers and chains, bolts, bars, and the like, than if they were toys

and the officers were playing at keeping jail. Of course, Colonel Tom exaggerates, but he says he wasn't built to be a shepherd over sheep; and if the prisoners do not get up a revolt soon, do something or other requiring discipline, he intends resigning. He is joking, of course, for the colonel thinks there is no man in the world like your husband."

"I am glad, Governor Hone," said my mother, "that Dr. Quarterman has had the penitentiary to keep him occupied, as well as sincerely glad of the good he has done there. He is restless when he has not enough to do—is not evidently accomplishing something. I wish he could feel more satisfied—"

"By his success inside our church," Governor Hone added for her, as she hesitated. "No pastor could be more beloved and honored; but, beyond a certain point—" the governor completed his meaning with a wave of his hand, as when in the Senate-chamber at Washington. What he meant was, beyond a certain point human nature not only will not be coerced, but human nature will rise against the compulsion—will resent and resist any coercion to be and to do what it acknowledges is right.

"These convicts," the governor added. "are boxed up by four stone walls; they have to stand and hear and reflect. They can't slip away from themselves any more than they can from their chaplain. Almost every man in our church is a politician, or dependent upon politicians, and we are, as a class, the worst men living—yes, madam, the toughest, intellectually the most corrupt and hopeless class, and getting worse and worse every year. If I had my way, madam," added the statesman, gathering up his loose limbs and standing up, as he always did when he grew interested in what he was saying, "I would collect every politician in the land into one vast penitentiary, walls a hundred feet thick and a thousand feet high, Colonel Tom as warden, and turn them over till they died, every man of them, to Dr. Quarterman. America would be the happiest land on earth then, and your husband the right man in the right place. Good-evening, my dear madam. Do come over and see Sukey; she never goes out, you know."

7

I have often heard my father say that he never had cause in his life to regret a syllable my mother ever said, much less any thing she ever did.

"It was on my tongue, Carter" (this explains why I mention it), she remarked after the governor had gone, "but I try to be so prudent; it was on my very lips to tell the governor—he is so fond of a good joke—what a thermometer Major Hampton is to your dear father—a something, I mean, to show him when he is getting too warm. When the series of sermons on the prophecies was going on, the major became so violent at prayer-meetings in vindication of the prophecies it almost turned the whole into ridicule. It was frightful the way he spoke of the Catholics there during your father's sermons about them. It puzzles the officers of the church to know what to do with the man. He was so very wicked and is now so good, is so heartily in earnest, so eager to benefit every body, so fervent in prayer, and visiting the sick, and he gives almost all he has to the various causes."

"Why do the officers not have a kind talk with him?" I asked, for I had been so long away at school I did not fully understand.

"All of them have talked with him," said my mother, "and your father has even prayed with the major in his study over it. But he says it is his duty to speak in meeting, and he dare not disobey. It distresses your father. He says it is like the damsel that followed Paul at Philippi, praising him at the top of her voice along the streets, except that it is impossible to believe that it is a bad spirit possessing the major. Your father never was so puzzled in his life," my mother said, laughing. And it was such a relief to her to have me to talk to about things she never mentioned to any other person in the family. It is the solid satisfaction of my life, that as long as I can remember she relied and rested upon me.

"It is not genius or talent I like," Virginia had once said, in her quiet way, "but strong common sense."

"They are so fussy, the talented people, Miss Praxley and Habby there," Georgia concurred, herself the fussiest of mortals, "that I can't endure them! Habby is so cross, and Miss Praxley is so very smart, it is

like mustard and pepper. Now, Carter, and Mrs. Brown, and myself—oh yes, and Cosma Adams—we are the bread and the beef. Yes, and Squashy here—you darling!—is like the sugar!"—Squashy being the name of Mrs. Hone's last baby, generally brought over by Georgia, when in that mood, of an afternoon, to be cuddled and kissed and then got very tired of and carried back. Mrs. Hone was a very domestic woman, with a swarm of children, and, especially toward the advent of yet another, the mother was very willing Georgia should, provided she promised to take wonderful care of it, be a mother to Squashy as much as she wished. It was a shame so to style the infant of the governor of a sovereign State, but the little lump of flesh and blood was so yellow as to its abundant hair, and so superabundant as to cheeks, and shoulders, and body, and dots of legs, that the name came to it as naturally as the lumps of sugar from the dish, or the kisses and spasmodic huggings from Georgia, and the petting from all the rest.

But I was intending to say how doleful a time it was to us all just then. My father had the largest salary of any pastor in St. Charles, and my mother was versed in economy as some persons are in poetry, and good Mrs. Brown was as methodic, as to the supplies passing through her hands, as was the coffee-mill of its morning grains, to the grinding of which I awakened every day. But we kept open house, and it was not often we did not have some friend to supper, if not to dinner: some agent for something or other in the guest chamber all the time. My father said, too, that a pastor must be an example to his flock in liberality. The presents made him by his people were frequent and munificent; but they would not risk wounding his feelings by giving him money or, in fact, any article of substantial value toward housekeeping; it was a gold-headed cane, a splendid inkstand, a silk dressing-gown, a superb London edition of some cyclopedia or other, a set of costly silver or china, or something of the kind. My father never used the very magnificent arm-chair which obstructed his little study; it was generally heaped with religious papers and uncut Sailors' Magazines; but what a rest it would have been could the money paid by his friends for the same have gone to remove certain pressing debts instead!

The solemn fact is, the family were greatly in need of money at the juncture of which I am now speaking. What could my mother do? As to Virginia and Georgia, the idea of their doing any thing to help never entered their dreams; and such a thing would, if carried out, have shocked the community, destroyed the standing of church and pastor. The wind, which makes vessels move all the faster the harder it blows, but smote upon them as upon flowers rooted to the spot, and having nothing else in the world they could do but bloom and breathe their fragrance upon the air. Habby and I felt it worst of all.

"It was all very well," Habby said to me at last, growing more irritable every day, "very well for a month or so after we came back from school. We had been gone a good while, and a little rest and talk and being petted was well enough. But now, what? Here we are, Carter, great, bulking fellows, dependent on our father. And there is Archibald, the smartest as he is the oldest. Humph! Look at the girls, whom you and I ought to be providing for."

"Did you know that Apothecary Clarkson is actually addressing Virginia?" I replied, for I felt so deeply our situation that I would not talk upon the subject.

"Bah!" scoffed my brother, "I'd as lief she married a mouse. Talent! What am I good for? I tell you, Carter, I'm getting so I can't stand it. I hate to sit down to table. I can't bear to have father help me to the beef. I'm so ashamed of helping myself to butter! To think how old I am, and never did any thing all my life but live upon my father! Reading, and reading, and reading, for what?" and my brother, who had not slept at all, I felt sure, the night before, walked up and down the room, his pale face becoming more ashen, making his hair seem of a brighter red. "I tell you, Carter," he said, "I'm getting desperate. I feel within me the fire and the force of a giant and—look at me, and see how my Maker treats me. He manages to find bones and body enough for every ass that brays, and yet"—and there was a wild gleam of insanity, almost, as he ground his teeth and stood in front of our little looking-glass gazing steadily at himself—I never knew him to do it before—with scorn and contempt. "You rat!" he said with rage, at last, "you miserable abortion! you, you—" and, not intending to strike the glass, hitting, as ever, only at himself, at one furious blow the mirror rattled to atoms at his feet. Having thus reached its climax, the storm broke and rolled away in peals of laughter. That is, on my part, I can not say that I altogether felt like laughing, but I did it as the best thing I could think of just then. Some of us have heads inches thick and natures slow to move beyond measurement, but this burst of feeling on the part of my brother was enough to decide even me. I went to bed and slept sweetly all night, whatever he did, for, from that moment, my course in life was transparently plain.

CHAPTER XVI.

MY most intimate friends will open their eyes wide with wonder and then have a good laugh over it, because this is the first time I have ever breathed a hint to that effect, yet I can not remember the day when it was not a thing already decided upon by me, that I, Carter Quarterman, would be a minister. There were personal experiences of mine in reference to religion, concerning which it is impossible for me to say a syllable, now or at any other time; but I suppose, next to that, it was because from my birth I thought my father was, as a minister, the happiest as well as the most respected and influential of men.

I was a silent sort of body, particularly in reference to myself; and, although no son and mother were ever more confidential than we two, I know that even my dear mother never dreamed of such a thing. I never became a minister, as the reader will be relieved to know. Had Archibald settled down to business, I might have at least tried to carry out the supreme wish of my heart. Or, if my next elder brother, Habersham, had been of a vigorous constitution, it would have been otherwise with me. But that night he shivered our looking-glass, my life-long aspiration perished as by the same blow. I am of a robust and healthy nature, have grown accustomed to a wholly different life, yet the One who made me knows that death itself could hardly have been so bitter as was this disappointment. Even death looks forward to resurrection; but this loss was to me eternal. To this hour I have more pain in thinking of it than I care to confess; and I write these lines as an epitaph upon myself as I heartily hoped I might have been, and will never refer to the subject again.

Habby said that the dreary time at home after we came back from school was like the point at which the machinery pauses. With me it was but the pause of a month or so, and I do not recall any since.

"Now, look here, Carter," I said to myself, as I dressed the morning after the conversation with my brother just recorded; "there is not the slightest use of bothering any body at home about this matter in the way of talk. Nor is there any use in running around. I dare say Mr. Clarkson would give me a situation in his drug-store, but I could not bear the confinement. Besides, the idea of a great broad-shouldered chap like myself rolling out pills and measuring prescriptions is absurd; my fingers are not delicate enough. I could grab at, and I believe stop, if it was running away, the strongest horse Major Hampton has in his stable; and I know that the major would put me in charge at a round salary, but I know, too, that mother and Virginia wouldn't like it. I am coarse enough now, and horses would make me coarser. There is Colonel Archer, he would have me in his law-office, but it would take years before I could get to the bar; and if you think, old fellow, I intend to let you live upon your father in that way, you are thick-headed with a vengeance. Then, what about Dr. Grex? Ha! let's hold on a moment. What a splendid fellow he is, so tall and straight and vigorous—doesn't care a cent for any body. I do wish he would comb that tangled hair of his occasionally, and not walk with his head thrown quite so far back. But there is no affectation about him. He saws a leg off as if it were a log, except that he has more pleasure in it. I do like Dr. Grex, as I like Colonel Tom Maxwell, as one likes a clear, cold morning.

"What a pity it is he is such an abominable infidel, such a deliberate and desperate heathen! Halloo, Colonel Tom—I had not thought of that! I wonder how much he would give me; and I'm strong enough with my fists in case there should be a row, and the colonel is pining for one among the convicts. But Virginia and mother will never hear of that; and as to Doctor Grex, he might strike me full in the face with a 'No' if I asked him, and even if he said 'Yes,' it would take years before I could be paid for even holding people while he cuts them to pieces.

"General M'Neil, as clerk of the Supreme Court, would receive me like an embassador from an emperor. I can hear him this moment: 'I am able to reply in the affirmative, it gives me considerable pleasure to state. The emoluments offered you for copying opinions under my superintendence will not be commensurate with your qualifications; yet, for the sake of your esteemed parent—' stuff and nonsense! Yet the general's words became him as Mrs. President's dress and manner do her. What's the use? It's Mr. Patterson, of course! Hold on—Miss Praxley! She would do it! I declare solemnly," and I actually stopped in the act of tying my neckcloth, "I've half a mind to try it. She would do it, if it were only for the fun of the thing! Not more than ten years older than I am. Run away? Wouldn't St. Charles have an electric shock? And what a lovely pair we would make walking down the aisle! What a fool!" I recalled myself to myself with indignation. "And you were not going to talk about it. You knew from the first it was Mr. Patterson." But I stopped as I went down-stairs to look in at Habby. All the sleep he seemed to get was in the morning, and I had to step lightly. I could tell what sort of a night he had passed, by the state of his bed, all tumbled and tossed by his restless rolling, and I leaned over him, as he lay literally exhausted, with such a worn-out look upon his plain, pinched face, so old, old, the red hair all drawn, like that of a drowned man, over his broad, high forehead. I loved my poor brother: I dare say because he was so talented, but I had grown to have the affection, in my dull way, of a woman for him. To speak frankly, neither the girls nor my mother understood Habby; my father, because he was so busy and so vigorous, least of all. And Habby was so sarcastic, bitter, moody. There at the Archimedean Institute we two were thrown so completely upon each other also. He had helped me so much in my studies, and I had helped him so far as a strong arm was needed; ours was a sort of union of body and soul. I ought to be ashamed of it, but there were tears in my eyes as I leaned over him that morning. I am sure a mouse could not have been more velvet-footed than I was, but as I looked upon him his eyes were suddenly wide open and looking full in mine. I hated so to have disturbed him, blundering as I eternally am, that I slipped away and down to Mrs. Brown without a word; but, somehow, there was a wholly new and closer relation between us from that hour.

I went to Mr. Patterson's commission-house direct from prayers, which followed upon breakfast. I would a good deal rather have asked a favor of Scotchy Strange, who kept the leading billiard-saloon of St. Charles, gambler, drunkard, bully—notoriously the worst man in the city. Satan is, we all know, so bad because he was once an angel and fell, and Scotchy Strange was pre-eminently bad, in virtue, in vice I should rather word it, of having apostatized from his training as the son of an eminent minister in Scotland; upon the whole, he was avowedly the worst man I remember. Mr. Patterson had been thoroughly disgusted with Archibald's course when with him, and was far from being the zealous friend to my father he used to be; was, I had reason to believe, really an enemy instead; which, however, was but another reason why I was resolved to try him; but oh, how I hated to do so! I walked as rapidly as I could, like one on his path to the dentist, and who fears that his night-long resolve to have a tooth out will fail before he can get there. Reaching his imposing establishment near the post-office and at the very centre of business, I hurried by a clerk or two who were sprinkling and sweeping out within, and found Mr. Patterson in the little partitioned-off room at the back, just arrived and unlocking his iron safe.

"Good-morning, Mr. Patterson," I said, and then added, not seeing a particle of recognition in his eyes, " it is Carter Quarterman."

"Good-morning, sir," he answered, with a sort of sour surprise; and I saw by the change in his swart, sallow face from surprise to dislike, that he knew on the instant why I had come, and had his refusal ready. The disadvantage with men of his strong and bitter prejudice is that the deep aversion they may feel will show itself; the skin as well as the lip is too thin to hide the measure of dislike they entertain. And, even at that critical point in my fortunes, I asked myself if this could be the same man who was so eagerly and energetically my father's friend when we first came, his face then so brilliant with smiles, his long hands so cordial in their grasp!

"Well, what is it?" he asked, turning from his safe to his tall red desk, and arranging his ledgers for the day's work. They used to say at home that I am something of a Spartan in conciseness: on that occasion, at least, in as few words as I could, I related very respectfully my situation, and my purpose to go, if I could, into business.

"Well, but what is that to me?" Now, if he had faced me looking full in my eyes as he said it, I would have made an excuse for troubling him and walked out; but he stood with his back to me as he spoke, opening and shutting his books, his small, projecting head low down between his shoulders, his hollowed-out temples making his head seem still narrower to my side-view. "You have blundered as usual, Carter," I said to myself. "Why didn't you go to him at his house? And don't you know people are always at their worst so early in the morning? You know enough not to have come to him at all. Yet this is your best chance in St. Charles, your only one: go ahead!" And I continued aloud,

"I am very strong, as you see, sir. Your business is the out-of-door, active sort of work I would like better than any other, and your house stands the highest in the town. I thought if you had an opening—"

"Do you happen to know," he said, still with his back to me, "that a brother of yours—Alexander, Archibald, something of the sort—was once with me?"

"Yes, sir," I said promptly, "and that is one reason why I called." He was too shrewd not to understand what I really meant, and I felt that as an advantage on my part when, as if he did not understand, he replied:

"You should have said you were cool as well as strong. If your father thinks"— sorting the papers upon his desk with a nervous haste — "that because he happens for the present to be pastor of the church I attend, and which I helped to organize before he was heard of, he can use me as a convenience, he is mistaken. You did not know me!" And I wondered, as he said it, whether a man with so malignant a face could get to be a saint, singing some day before God in heaven, by reason, notwithstanding all that, of being so exceedingly energetic, as well as free with his money, as a church officer here.

The manner of Mr. Patterson was worse than his words, and all my blood was boiling; but my love for all at home, and my purpose to try it out to the end, having no other way open to me, held me as steady as a vise. I was glad, too, that I had not known before coming how bitter he was.

"No one but yourself, Mr. Patterson," I said, respectfully, "knows, or ever will know, any thing at all about my coming. I knew that you were a severe master, but I wanted to learn your business more than any other, and I wanted to know it thoroughly. I ought not to have troubled you, sir. I am sorry I did," which I most sincerely was. "Good-morning, Mr. Patterson."

As I said it, he turned from his desk to go to his safe again, and for a second or two we looked each other in the face as I bowed and left. No man in St. Charles quite so sharp, shrewd, and experienced in men as he. Scotchy Strange was a blasphemer, black and bitter and bad, but no man could be quite so intense in his displeasure as Mr.

Patterson, his not so much the lesser bitterness of gall, the metallic bitterness rather, inflexible and unchanging, of quinine. Scotchy never entered a church, of course, and Mr. Patterson never failed of a service on Sunday or of prayer-meeting. His delight was to be on the spot when it rained tioned the Church; Mr. Patterson always spoke of the Church, never of Christ. Such was Mr. Patterson, and I was only Carter Quarterman. He made no reply to my respectful good-morning, but I felt, as I walked out, that by reason of his keen knowledge of people he must know me thorough-

FOR A SECOND OR TWO WE LOOKED EACH OTHER IN THE FACE.

so hard that no one else, besides my father and the sexton, was present. His prayers were concise statements of want, clear and urgent rather than supplicatory; but no man could do more, or give more, or endure more for the Church than he. Colonel Archer had exclusive reference to Christ, never mentioned ly, and that, knowing me, he had no ground for disliking me that I could see.

From Mr. Patterson's store I walked steadily out of the city, and a good four miles into the country. I knew of no other place in St. Charles at which I could apply for a situation, and when I found myself at last

in a barren old field, abandoned, with broken fences, to blackberries and stray stock,
I had "worked off my steam," as they say
on river boats, to such a degree that I sat
down upon the edge of an old gully, my
weary legs dangling down over its edge, to
rest a little before going back.

The city was built upon a series of rolling
hills, soon melting away from brick houses
closely clustered together into broad plantations, each having its large mansion near
the various highways, with negro-quarters,
cotton-gin, and press away off in the fields
behind them. It was summer, sultry, and
slow, and dull, the dead-centre of the year
as well as of the family.

And now a little matter took place which
I almost resolved to leave out, it looks so
like fiction, whereas it is, like every line I
write, simple fact. As I sat down, a whole
herd of hogs, which were reposing in the
mud at the bottom of the gully, half arose
in loud protest against the intrusion. I hate
a hog, and, boy-like, always threw something
at one on sight; but nothing was handy, and
I was tired out, and so we all settled down
together into a sociable idleness. By merest
accident I noticed, as I sat, that the hogs
had wallowed out one side of the gully, leaving it perfectly black in contrast with the
red earth. Very slowly, indeed, I grew interested enough in the fact, as I got rested,
to root out the swine, that was half my motive, and to examine the matter. With my
knife I dug out a lump of the black substance, put it in my pocket, and walked
home. For many a long day I forgot all
about it, but I think you will agree it is well
worth while my putting the fact on record
in its place, for the sake of what came of
it afterward.

Dinner was over when I got home, and I
eat so heartily of good Mrs. Brown's cakes
and pies, that she was constrained to remark, as she dried her hands and arms of
the soap-suds from a washing-tub:

"I'm glad to see you eat so, Carter; but I
didn't intend to bake until day after to-morrow; and now I must go at it right away.
You are growing bigger every day — will
be as large as your father, if you'll only be
half as good."

When I came down-stairs after brushing
up a little, I found that Miss Praxley and
Cosma Adams were in the parlor.

"Good-day, Mr. Sunburn," said the former,
as I came in; "you are more brown than
beautiful. What mischief have you been up
to?" for Miss Praxley "detested old folks,"
although herself beyond I don't know what
age, and took special pleasure in the society, and, I fear, slang, of young people. She
was rich and good-looking, very full of her
fun, and people said she was "peculiar," and
laughed with her as well as at her. "Of
course, I don't care as much for you as Cosma here; but I'm a little tired of Miss Virginia. My dear Miss Propriety," she added,
to the last, "did you ever do any thing at
all out of the way? You are as proper as
Mrs. President."

My sister Virginia was a little languid,
and Miss Praxley wearied her, and we were
all glad when Georgia came in from school,
and entered, on the other side of the room,
into a sort of romp of words with Miss Praxley, whom we all really liked, for she was
energetic and generous beyond all of "our
members," a kind of Mr. Patterson in petti-
coats, all the bitterness and obstinacy left
out. My mother came in, after a while, and,
somewhat to my dismay, Cosma Adams, seated between Habby and myself, had to be
entertained. I wondered that Habersham
did not slip out to his everlasting books upstairs, for he never went into society, seemed to be shrinking into himself from it more
and more. But he had been obliged to come
down into the parlor when the ladies called,
no one else being then at home, and he staid,
relying upon me to relieve him of Cosma.
And if ever a person tried hard to interest
her, I did, if only to drive Mr. Patterson out
of my mind. She had improved since I saw
her last, and seemed to be a modest, silent
somewhat freckled country girl; nothing remarkable in her plump face, beyond her beautiful teeth and large and wondering eyes.
She had come with Miss Praxley, and that
lady was full of some project—for tableaux,
I think it was—among the family, on the
other side of the parlor. I tried to entertain her, as against time, Habby showing a
sort of indolent comfort in being near her,
but never opening his lips.

"I was out in the country this morning.

You lived there before you came, Miss Cosma?" I said at last, and in despair.

"Yes, sir," she said, and brightened so much about the eyes and lips that I added:

"Please don't say 'sir;' I'm only Carter. Tell a fellow something about it—your country, I mean."

"There was nothing about it," she said, gravely. "There were only father and I; my mother died when I was eight years old. We lived there together, that is all."

"Yes, I know," I said, solemnly; "your house was a good deal larger than the State-house down town. From the upper windows you saw great fields of cotton, and corn, and negroes. A wide river rolled by."

"No," she said, relaxing a little; "there was nothing but a creek. In winter it had places full of minnows and mud-turtles. In summer I would sit on a log, and dabble with my feet; but it would go dry."

"And the house?" I asked, trying to make her feel at home. She answered:

"Oh, it was but a two-story log-cabin, not as big as this room. We cooked and eat down-stairs; two little rooms up stairs, one for father, and one for me. I lived there ever since I can remember. I love it dearly."

"How glad you must have been when the stage stopped at the door to leave papers! So many people, too, coming and going," I said.

"Oh, that is your fun," she replied, beginning to enter into the spirit of the thing under cover of the rattle of talk across the room. "There was no stage. We didn't live near any road. It was only when people got lost that they stopped at our house. It was nothing but a cabin on the hill-side, big walnut-trees growing around it, with a well on one side. Why, the field where father worked was only two or three acres, full of stones and stumps and blazed trees. We were off so to ourselves that I started rabbits every morning when I went to the well after water. I've seen deer run across our field often and often. And there were ever so many snakes. We had a cow."

"I knew her," I said, gravely; "she looked exactly like Miss Praxley: her name was Mrs. Grundy, and she hooked."

"She didn't," my companion said, with energy, "for I milked her. She did not look a bit like any body, and her name was Pink. That was her color. I loved her dearly, and she always—"

"When you went out, said, 'Good-morning, Cosma,'" I ventured. "She told me so herself."

"Oh, she never!" said the girl, like a girl. "Moo was all I ever heard her say. We had a dog. Bran was his name. Rabbits were so common, he would only look at them and wag his tail. A buck hurt him with his horns: Bran jumped on the buck drinking from the hen-trough at the well. We buried Bran in a corner of the fence under a walnut-tree, and piled up stones over him. I thought I never would stop crying. But I had a cat, and I was glad they would not fight so any longer. You would call it dull; but I loved it. After all the work was done, I would take my doll, and sit under the trees by the well, and sing and sing. That was when I was a little thing. Father taught me to read; would take me in our little wood-wagon to the cross-roads to get my things for me, and things for the house. Our horse had only one eye; he used to plow. His name was Zeus."

"Deuce?" I asked.

"No, Z-e-u-s," my companion spelled it for me. "Father said it was Greek. Most of his books were. I read the Bible over and over again. I skipped a good deal, but I know all the stories and parables by heart. How I used to read and read! Of summer under the trees; not much of winters: we had no gas, you know. But how I used to love to sleep, right under the clapboards of the roof, you see. I could touch them with my hand as I lay, and the rain falling on them made it seem so snug. But father sent to Governor Hone—we are related—before he died, and they took me away. It was a happy, happy time we had there—so happy!"

"Cosma!"—Miss Praxley called to her across the room—"how you rattle on! I'm astonished at you. But don't let Mr. Broadboy humbug you. That silent brother of his, the Rev. Mr. Wise, is the one you should listen to!" For one of Miss Praxley's peculiarities was that she had a hundred names for her friends.

"Don't mind Miss Praxley, Miss Cosma," I said; "and I'm as fond of Pink and Bran and Zeus, just from hearing about them, as you are. And don't you remember those three solemn frogs. I almost saw your father the day he dug out that hen-trough—out of a walnut log, you remember, and when you moved it there were those three frogs in a row."

"Why, how did you know it, Mr. Quarterman?" the girl said, opening her eyes; "but so they were. I've upset the log trough hundreds of times to see them."

"I wonder you didn't read," ventured Habby, who seemed to be interested; "something besides the Bible, I mean. Don't you love to read?"

"Read? No, I don't. If there is one thing I hate to do, it is to read. I never would again," the girl said, with entire candor, "would never open a book again as long as I live, if I could help it. Mrs. Hone never does. What's the use?"

Mr. Patterson had hurt me badly, worse than I had thought at first, and the girl was a relief. Besides, I wanted to amuse Habby.

"But what do you like," I continued, gravely, "besides me? Of course you like me most."

"No!" she said; "I don't know any thing about you. Like? I like to milk. I didn't like to churn; but I like to drink fresh buttermilk."

"So do I," I said, sincerely, "when it's out of a big, clean, yellow gourd—the little bubbles upon it are so cool to the tip of your nose, and then the little lumps of fresh butter in it, too. With fresh hot-corn pone, and plenty of butter and honey—" And I smacked my lips sincerely, for Mrs. Brown is not the only member of the household that remarked pretty often on my appetite.

"So do I," Cosma said, simply and sympathetically; "I like to knit, but not to sew; and to ride Zeus, not bareback, you know, but with a blanket thrown over him. And I love sunflowers and hollyhocks, and to drink out of the well-bucket when I'm hot; and I do love to sleep. You can't think how I can sleep, sleep!"

Habby seemed to take a sort of satisfaction in sitting there, and, with her face

brightened by the topics, the young girl and I became good friends, and were sorry when Miss Praxley said, at last:

"Well, Mr. Chatter, I do hope you and Miss Butter are satisfied. The Princess here, and Miss Bounceabout could hardly bear a word I said. Good-day, Mr. Solemn"—to Habby—"I see you are composing a sermon, and we will come and hear it when it is done. Come, Cosma; at least fifteen of Mrs. Hone's babies are crying for you, and that blessed little Squashy leads the chorus—come."

The same night—and it must have been near midnight—I was aroused by my brother out of my usual deep slumber. He had evidently not slept a wink, and I saw in an instant, sleepy as I was, that something beyond any thing I had ever known before had befallen him.

"Carter," he said, "I am suffering great pain. Please dress and go down to Clarkson's, and get me a phial of laudanum."

"Toothache?" I asked, grumblingly, yet I knew at once. "Don't stop to talk," he said, not impatiently. "I do not want to disturb you or any one else. But I have suffered so long and so terribly that I will not endure it any longer. Go, and as quick as you can!" Now, I do not think that the smartest people have all the sense there is in the world. An ox may be neither a nightingale nor an eagle, and have, none the less, an instinct as strong, if not as refined. Had Habby been merely pale, I would not have noticed it; but he was livid instead. Besides, he was too calm and set in his manner. Once or twice he lifted his hand to his cheek, but instantly let it fall again, for it was impossible for him to lie. There was a certain tone of kindness to me, too, which was suspicious. I got up, however, and went down without a word, and as I felt my way down-stairs, I slowly knew what to do. In fact, the moment he left my room I had slipped into my pocket a phial of red ink with which I had been at work trying to teach myself book-keeping, in case I got into business, aided by an old treatise I had bought. Shutting all the doors after me as I went down, I stirred up the fire in the kitchen well enough to see; next I washed off the label of my phial, poured out almost all of its contents, filled it up with water, and shook it well, leaving it quite near the color of landanum. Strange to say, I had no specially sentimental thoughts about it. Archibald would never have done such a thing as Habby proposed, would never have dreamed of it; but I was afraid of this dwarfish genius, so unlike us all. I remember it even flashed upon me that it was another evidence of his genius, recalling what he had so often told me about Chatterton. After waiting by the kitchen-fire long enough to make him think I had gone to the apothecary's and got back, I crept upstairs, and gave him the phial, saying, "There it is, Habby; I hope it will relieve you."

"Thank you, Carter; I am sure it will," he said, in tones which convinced me that my instincts were right. "Good-night; and," he added, "don't light your candle."

I suppose my wits were sharpened; but I understood even that. So that when I felt for and found a letter upon my table I knew perfectly well what that meant, and was careful to put it down exactly as I found it the same instant. Then I went to bed, and to sleep. It seemed but a moment when I was awake. But it was late, and the sun was streaming into my room. Habby was standing beside me. To my astonishment, he was radiant with joyful excitement. I glanced at the table; the letter was gone; and I slowly understood it all as I dressed.

"I slept like a log," my brother said, "and you can't tell how much better I feel to-day. I'm so grateful to God that I am — that I am—I mean, I am so glad I am well. You have no idea, Carter," he added, "what an unprincipled scoundrel I am — in a good many ways. But I am going to try and not be such a miserable mite any more. What a glorious day it is! Oh, you never mind; things will come right some day!" And he fairly rattled on in the happiest mood I ever knew him to be in before or since. Of course, I never opened my lips to a soul, much less to him; but I do know that, having touched that night the lowest point of his dead-centre, he has risen ever since. I prefer to speak about it thus in the fewest words possible.

CHAPTER XVII

It was just one week to a day, after my conversation with Mr. Patterson, that I happened to be passing his business-place in the centre of St. Charles. Although I thought of nothing else during the interval, I had said nothing to any one in regard to securing employment, because there was, after going over all of them in my mind, not a soul to whom I could speak. I am satisfied that every member of the family, with more or less intensity, was suppressing a good deal of thought upon the same general subject, unless it was Georgia, who took life very much as a rosy cloud of morning takes whatever breezes happen to blow, most of her breezes, however, springing up within herself: often freshening into gales, and blowing in any other than a right direction. Habersham had grown moodier, more sleepless and savage, as the days wore by; but I had no fear now that he would do any thing desperate. I no more suggested my matter to him than I would have suggested a spark to powder. As to my mother and father, their very silence was more to me than any words, for ours was a large family, expenses were heavy, money very scarce.

As I said, I chanced to be passing the broad double doors of Mr. Patterson's establishment. It was on my way to the post-office, and I noticed, as I drew near on the same side of the street, that Mabel Patterson was standing, her face from the street, conversing with her father, who stood just within his doors. I also observed that a dray had backed up to the sidewalk, laden with three hogsheads of sugar, to judge from their dirty appearance, and—it was all done in a flash! The driver must have been either a born fool or drunk, or, which is much the most probable, so exasperated at some of the sharp words which Mr. Patterson was quite wont to use to those under him, that either without noticing or caring where the girl stood, he pulled out the last of the two iron standards in the tail of the dray by which the hogsheads were held. One moment more and the girl would have been struck from behind with the full force of the hogsheads. In the act of lifting my hand to my hat, in case she should see me with a sidelong glance, and, seeing, should conclude to recognize me, I saw the descending cask, rushed in between, was knocked down, and lay at full length on my side, actually "chocking" the hogshead as well as the two others behind it, the tons of sugar not actually rolling over and crushing me to death upon the pavement, because they had not got the momentum they would have had by the time they would otherwise have struck the lady.

We are queerly constituted. My chief feeling, as I fell, and then endured the enormous pressure upon my person, was one of supreme pleasure, a sense of solid satisfaction. I was worn out with want of occupation just before, and now I was doing something! Then came a flash, as of a magic lantern upon a screen, of the astonished face of the girl turning round, and of the sallow countenance of Mr. Patterson, his hat off and a pen behind his ear. It is absurd, but I thought, "Won't that drayman catch it from him for this!" and then I had fallen over the edge of a precipitous cliff, deep, deep down into utter unconsciousness. I am fain to tell all the facts, and must add that the first time I saw the drayman, long, long afterward, even before apologizing to me for his carelessness, he remarked,

"It's glad to see you I am, Mr. Quarter Carterman, by reason uv wanting to ask you a question."

"What question, Mike?" I demanded.

"'Tis this, sir; what in the name of the saints did Mr. Patterson mane by tearing out, and as soon as he saw you under the sugar, yelling at me, 'This is a plot between you, ye villains!' Holy Mary! what plot did the old man mane? It bothers me intirely. If iver a cross-grained, supicious, malignant man iver drew breath, it's him: mighty free with his soft words, and his hard money when he likes; but a thousand times worse nor a tiger where he don't like. Plot between us! It bates me intirely. Can you tell a man what he meant, Mr. Carterman?" But all that was long afterward.

On coming slowly to consciousness, although one mass of pain from head to foot, I brought back with me from the depths the same sense of supreme satisfaction. Yes, solid, positive satisfaction, underlying all my bruised body and broken bones like the very bed upon which I lay, the enjoyment of a sudden duty as suddenly and fully done; and I believe I would have carried it with me into heaven, had I gone on into that world instead of returning to this.

I awoke, to know, through the mist and meshes of bewilderment and pain, that I was not at home. Had I not become insensible, I am sure that I would have resisted to my utmost the disposition that was made of me; would have insisted, with the ox-like obstinacy with which I am charged by my friends, upon being carried to Dr. Grex's office, anywhere rather than directly home to shock my mother, or to Mr. Patterson's to distress myself, as the result proved. For so it was. I came gropingly to consciousness again, to find myself as if I had exchanged my body for a sort of wooden box paining me at every point, and in a room which I had never entered before. For some moments I lay still, looking slowly around from the mantel to the engravings on the wall, to the figures of the paper-

ing, and the furniture, trying to find out; but all was new and strange. I had taken for granted that the lady seated by my bed was my mother, or Virginia, or Georgia, or good Mrs. Brown; and, now, looking full at her, I saw to my horror that it was Mabel Patterson.

"I beg a thousand pardons," I tried to say; "excuse me for lying here; I was not aware—" And I tried to get up, only to rack myself as against a box which was all points and sharp edges. Mabel Patterson!

"Not one word, sir," she said. "Please lie still. They will be here in a moment." Yes, of all persons in the world, it was Mabel Patterson, and I wondered if she did not know why I grew suddenly so hot in the face; for I remembered it was a stealthy kiss upon my forehead which had completed my slow awakening a little before from my stupor.

"Mabel Patterson! Here is a pretty kettle of fish!" was my coarse statement of the case to myself, as I lay with my eyes closed, for before I went to the Archimedean Institute, I had met Mabel at Sabbath-school, and had fancied that, as is the way of boys and girls, she had taken a liking to me. The more she did what I supposed was intended to show her liking, that much the more, boy-like, I receded. She was dark, with an abundance of black hair, and quick, keen eyes—a girl of decided character, prompt, impulsive, liable, like her father, to prejudices, either for or against any one, sudden and strong. Although three years younger than myself, what I imagined to be her marked school-girl liking for me simply alarmed me. About six weeks before Habby and I left for the Archimedean Institute, she said to me in a low tone, as we stood together at the library of the Sabbath-school one Sunday afternoon, waiting for the librarian to give us our books,

"Wasn't it you, Carter?"

"Me? What?" I replied, greatly put out.

"Ah, never mind, you know what; never mind. You are the only boy I know who would have done it."

Nothing more was said. And really it is not worth narrating, but the Sabbath night before she was walking rapidly home by herself from church, her father being detained, as he often was, to a meeting of the officers of the church. I was some yards behind her, also alone, when I saw a half-drunken man, who was leaning against a lamp-post, put his arm around her waist as she passed, and try to kiss her. It took but a moment for me to run up, plant one foot behind him on the curb-stone, and, with a firm hold upon his collar, whirl him backward over my knee into the mud of the street. He was quite stout, very top-heavy already, and made a tremendous splash. The girl fled homeward with a little shriek, as I did to our house as well as I could for laughing; but, because it was Mabel Patterson, I never told any one about it. The liking of the girl for me after this, at least what I fancied, like a conceited young fool, was her liking, became so marked, as I imagined, that I was rude in avoiding her. The fact is, I made such blundering business of it that Mabel at last took a violent dislike to me, and seemed glad of an opportunity to show it. I had not seen her all the years since, had not once thought of her, I am afraid; and now, here I was in her father's house helpless—my nurse, Mabel Patterson.

"Eternally blundering, as usual!" was all I said, closing my eyes, and then shuddered to feel another kiss, a fervent one, upon my forehead.

"Box or no box, I'll get up and run," I said to myself, and opened my eyes to see that it was my mother this time, Mabel having disappeared.

"My dear Carter," was all she said, so quietly, such music in all her face and manner and tones; no, there never was before or since such a perfect lady as my mother. Virginia is like her, but the perfection, the quaint excellence, so to speak, of my dear mother belonged to a sunny something in the region in which she grew up.

"Your father left for a meeting in the country this morning," she went on to say; "Virginia and Habersham will be here directly. We won't venture to let Georgia come just yet," she added, with a smile, her hand on my brow.

"Is she making any to-do over it at home?" I asked.

"Georgia loves you dearly, Carter, and is

making a terrible time of it," my mother said, laughing. "It is all Mrs. Brown can do to manage her. For we all do love you, Carter, more than any one else in all the world, I'm afraid." Ah, the sweetness of her way of saying it!

"Love me?" I began with genuine surprise. "I had not thought—"

"No, sir; not a bit of it," said another voice, loud, harsh, decisive. "If I'm called in, Mrs. Quarterman, you must be called out. You must let me have my way. You can not stay, madam; should not have come in. Please go at once. Charles!" and I knew, as she left, that it was Dr. Grex.

"What on earth did you try to chock a hogshead for with your body? I did think even a boy would have had more sense," he added, turning down the bedcover, and running his hands over me as if I were a sick negro instead. Yes, Dr. Grex, tall, rough in face and manner, as well as in his exceedingly plentiful and disordered hair.

The doctor had been an active, a very active, surgeon all through the Crimean war, going over there from his medical college from pure love of cutting off legs, reveling in the blood and agony of the battles from devotion to his calling. The devotion of a sculptor to his art best represents the enthusiasm with which Dr. Grex went at his patient with, so to speak, mallet and chisel. But people dislike to be treated as so much marble, and only the reputation of the doctor, as by far the best as well as the roughest and most independent of surgeons, would have given him the practice he had—the chief practice of St. Charles and all the region around.

Nothing was more common those days at that political centre than "difficulties" which resulted in leaving somebody killed or badly wounded, Dr. Grex being as invariably called in at the concluding stages of the affair as bowie-knives and pistols at the point going before. But the most noted peculiarity of the surgeon was that he was an infidel. People can hardly understand now what a weight went with the word in those days and in that latitude. Even Dr. Grex dared not speak upon the subject. Any avowal of infidelity would have ruined him, had he been ten times the surgeon that he was.

But he never entered a church, and was full of sarcastic remark in reference to Christians. As it was, people classed him with Scotchy Strange, the bad billiard-saloon keeper, his roughness being regarded as part of his intellectual wickedness.

He had given me a thorough examination while I was still unconscious, Mr. Patterson being so fortunate as to catch him in his office, and had now returned with his negro boy Charles, as strong of limb as he was jet-black of face, and who had been trained to do what his master ordered with the stupid precision of a blacksmith's vise.

"I intend hurting you like thunder. Will you take chloroform?" he asked, as he spread out his surgical articles upon the table beside my bed, Charles laying off his coat, rolling up his sleeves, adjusting himself, from long habit, to the case with as little emotion as a pair of tongs.

"No, sir, I won't," I replied, promptly. "I'm curious to see the operation."

"Very good. Don't get to whining like a sick puppy. Charles!"

And as he said it, the doctor disarrayed me from head to foot with a rapid hand.

"You are a stout fellow, Carter, my boy; brown and tough as oak; wooden all over, head too, I dare say," he continued, contemplating my naked person with somewhat of a cannibal-like satisfaction as he passed his swift palms over me from head to foot, asking as he went, "Hurt here? hurt now?" and, when he had completed a thorough examination, "Ha, not as bad as I had hoped," with a laugh; "but," encouragingly to himself, "pretty bad, pretty bad," and, between the doctor and his grim assistant, it did hurt as they went to work with a will upon a broken shoulder and fractured ribs.

It seemed singular to me at the time, the curious kind of solid satisfaction underneath and quite beyond reach of all the pain. An actual satisfaction, not this time as of duty done, but now of duty begun again; a positive pleasure in it as, with teeth set and breath drawn with the regularity of an engine driving a boat up stream, I endured greater pain than I had before supposed possible to be endured by any one. Deep down in my soul I felt, and as if I were intrenched there and apart from, independent, and master of, my body that I had reserves of endurance in me for ten times that measure of suffering, for infinite and unending pain, if need be—a species of triumph in confronting and defying the worst that agony could do.

"Regular Spartan, heh?" Dr. Grex remarked, pausing to throw up his heavy hair from his forehead with his left hand while he wiped the moisture from my brow with the other. "The sweat is the only way you let out your pain; sweat away, Carter, my boy. But what an ass you were to lay yourself like a log before a rolling hogshead! If you had checked it with your head instead, it wouldn't have hurt you. Charles!"

And at it this inquisitor and his black familiar went once more. At least I suppose so, for somehow I slid the next moment, as over the rounded edge of some Niagara, into utter unconsciousness; and when I woke again, it was to find Dr. Grex and Charles gone, their work done, and my mother and Virginia and Habersham bending over me, with tears and kisses, so far as the ladies were concerned. Habby, however, was cynical to the last degree.

"You were at least doing something," he said to me when he got the opportunity; "and I am the older. I wish it had been me, though it had crushed me dead!"

"I am sorry to bother you all so," I said; and was about to add, "Oh, how I wish I could be at home instead!" But I knew that remark would add to the trouble, and I kept it to myself. I smiled to think that good Mrs. Brown would go instinctively to making rice batter-cakes, as she invariably did when any body was taken sick, whether I was there to get them or not.

"What does Georgia think of things?" I ventured.

"Georgia? Oh, she has gone off into a gust of new aversion to Mabel Patterson," my mother said, in lowered tones and with a smile. "She says if you had hurt yourself for her, now, or Cosma Adams, she wouldn't have cared; but she is out with you, Carter, for having done it for Mabel. She says you ought to be heartily ashamed of yourself."

"We told her," Virginia added, "that Mabel is an only child, and has had no mother

since she was a baby to keep her from standing on her father's sidewalk while things
were rolling about. Dr. Clarkson sent it,"
Jenny added as I held her hand, in the act
of bathing my brow with cologne, by a look
of inquiry at the huge cut-glass bottle; but
I knew it before she spoke.

"Yes, he caught up with us on the street;
came up panting behind us with it," my
mother said, with a mischievous look at Virginia. "He had heard of the accident. It
will be in all the papers, Carter; they will
agree about something for once, I suppose."

"Jenny treats him so coolly, I wonder he
doesn't pine away," I said. "You should be
ashamed of yourself, Jenny, he is such a good
man, so round and smooth and soft-spoken.
I like Dr. Clarkson!" For I did not want
to speak about myself.

"So do I," said Virginia. "The parlor
seems unfurnished when he is not seated on
the sofa by the piano. Georgia laughed so at
supper the last time he was with us, when the
Sally Lunn gave out, you know, she got into
such hysterics over it, I was sure he would
never come back. Georgia can not endure
him. She flounces out of the room the moment he comes in. If he were not so good,
he never would come. Oh yes, I love him
dearly!" The fact is, we had talked over
the whole accident, and how much I was
hurt when they first came in, and, now, by
mutual consent, rattled on, to hide anxiety,
about any thing and every thing else. Habby is not the only morbid member of our
household; I, for instance, always have had
a dislike to being the topic of conversation,
always changed the subject when I was, oft-
en abruptly, I fear; not being the polished
and highly cultured individual you would
naturally have expected in the son and brother of such persons, had you ever known them,
as my mother and Virginia.

"I like Dr. Grex," I said, "just as I like
Colonel Tom Maxwell; something so wholesome about them. You know I never fancied Mrs. President much, because I am so
'uncivilized;'" and I went on to tell about
some of Dr. Grex's remarks, especially how
peremptory he had been in turning my
mother out of the room.

"Did you ever notice, Jenny," I said, for
my mother was out somewhere to make

matters smooth and convenient with Mabel
Patterson and the servants, "the preposterous fur cap the doctor wears? He killed
the animal, whatever it was, himself upon
one of his hunting excursions. What a tall,
splendid-looking fellow he is!"

"I can not endure him," said Virginia, with
a flush; "a coarse, rough, disagreeable person
is bad enough, but for a man to affect roughness as he does is contemptible. If you must
go and get your bones broken, Carter, it is
a great pity you could not get a gentleman
to—"

"Oh, come, come, come, this will never do,
never!" And, without taking off his queer
cap, the person spoken of came, the third time
that day, into the room. You must go out,
madam—miss, is it? This foolish chap must
be kept perfectly quiet. I left express or-
ders with the fool that answers the bell. If
he were my Charles, I'd tan his hide for him.
Come, miss, I can't have it!"

Virginia was standing beside me, bathing
my brown face with cologne, when he br.
in upon us. It was by reason of the refl
tion thereof, so to speak, upon Dr. Gre
face during the silence following on
rude tones which caused me to turn
head, with considerable pain, too, and I s
that my sister had deliberately taken b
seat, and was looking steadily at the doct
with a face of serene amazement. There
was a something in her attitude and bearing which could never be put on paper. We
have always had an absurd feeling in our
blood as if we were of royal lineage, and
Virginia looked at the surgeon as Elizabeth would have looked at Raleigh or any
of the rest if they had attempted such language.

"I was saying, Carter," she went quietly
on, "that it is so much better that a man
should also be a gentleman. I have brought
my tatting with me, see;" and she held up
her ivory sticks, or whatever they call them,
"and I am going to work by you while you
doze or sleep. You mustn't talk, Carter."

I dare say my sister's beauty and her own
unconscious consciousness of it had their effect, for I never saw her looking quite so
pure and fresh and lovely as with the loveliness, somehow, of her soul in her eyes and
face, as she did then. How wonderfully she

was growing to be like my mother! It may have been a magic charm in her style of dress, the rare combination of its colors that day with her complexion; or it may have been some peculiar grouping and draping of curtains behind her; possibly her sympathy with me, by reason of the peculiar nature of the accident, may have brought the charm of her beauty to her outer self, I'm sure I do not know why. But I do know that, for once, Dr. Grex had met, and most unexpectedly to him, his full match. As I had turned to Jenny before to understand what was reflected in his face, the next moment I had to turn my eyes to his rough and bearded countenance to comprehend the deep color that suddenly suffused my sister's cheeks and brow and neck, and I understood it in the astonishment of admiration which the doctor was too blunt and outspoken a man to prevent expressing itself, at least in his eyes and manner. It was all so sudden and embarrassing to all of us, that we were glad my mother came in on the instant.

"My dear, we must go," she said, with an inclination to the surgeon, that indescribable curve of the head which she had learned in the old, old times. "Good-bye, Carter; come, Virginia;" but my sister was slow in wrapping up her work and rising from her chair and bidding me good-bye; very slow and collected about it, indeed. I fancied that Dr. Grex was a little louder and rougher with me after they were gone than before; but, somehow, his rudeness did not seem to me as natural and unaffected as it had been.

CHAPTER XVIII.

FROM the first hour of my accident I felt that the whole thing must be unpleasant to Mr. Patterson. If I must get myself crushed in the act of saving his only child, it did seem hard on him that I should be laid, a perpetual reminder thereof, under his very roof.

"How are you this morning?" he would say to me, coming to my bedside after breakfast, and drawing on his gloves as he spoke, to go to his business. "How did you sleep? Are you suffering much pain? Can I do any thing for you down-town?" But he said it in such a hurried way, was evidently so little at his ease, that I could not but sympathize with the sallow-visaged, nervous, and keen-set man, so capable of hearty devotion of purse and person whenever he could have his own way, and so bitterly set in his hostility when he was crossed. I understood matters perfectly. My father had thwarted him, and for years now he had brooded over some way of asserting himself against a pastor so popular, but in vain. And here was I crossing him also; yet in such a way that it was impossible for him to resent it in the least degree. I had no feeling but of thorough liking for the many practical and admirable traits of a man who was universally conceded to be the best business man in St. Charles, fully capable of managing any and every thing in the way of a bank or a railway, an insurance company or a manufactory; no better trustee of a fund or executor of an estate living. I would have preferred to be under my father's roof; but, being where I was, I adjusted myself to the house as I did to my slowly mending bones; and in virtue of my temperament, I was entirely at my ease, at least in a moral sense, and was completely at home with Mr. Patterson even when he was ill at ease with me.

"I can imagine how he must be troubled all day with questions as to my hurt," I said to myself one morning, after he had bid me an uneasy and awkward good-day, and had departed. "Let me see if I can not fix things;" and so, in my slow and steady fashion, I applied myself, as I lay, to thinking it out. My father had got back, and was in to see me every afternoon. Had I been dying, I hardly think he could have given me one of his mornings, so sacred were they to his study and his sermons. My mother and Virginia came and went continually. Georgia

8

made a point, even to the derangement of her own school-hours, to call when she knew Mabel would be at school; for even I shrank from any concussion between the two impetuous young ladies—Mabel deep and determined like her father, and Georgia ardent and open like hers. Mrs. Brown did really and truly love me, or she never would have got out of her orbit as she did, bringing me crumpets and cakes, which I am satisfied had been hitherto mere poetic aspirations in her own mind, realized for the first time under the pressure of affection for me and profound distrust of Mr. Patterson's cook. But I consulted with no one; it is not my way. I did think of doing so with Habersham, he was so moody and miserable, purely to give him that much employment; but concluded I would not.

"Mr. Patterson," I said at last, "there is one thing, if you will pardon me, I would like to ask—"

"Certainly, certainly," he said, shifting his safe-key from hand to hand, for he was just starting that day, breakfast over, for his store, "oh, certainly."

"Please, what has become of Mike?"

"The scoundrel who hurt you? Discharged. He was in a temper about something I said to him. I believe he did it on purpose to hurt Mabel. Why do you ask?"

"He has a large family of his own," I said, as if merely thinking it over, "and his superannuated parents are living with him. Excuse me, I only asked;" but I had too much sense to say any more. My host understood me on the instant. When I got out again I found that Mike was in Mr. Patterson's employ again, ten times the man for work he was before, and, however Mr. Patterson managed it, I am sure it was a relief to him to do that much for me, although it was all that ever passed between us on the subject.

"How are you this morning, Carter?" he asked me the week following upon this, coming in just after my own people had gone. "I hope Mabel has not neglected you. If there is any thing I can do—"

"Will you please hand me my pantaloons, Mr. Patterson?" I replied. "They are hanging in that wardrobe." And when he had got them, "Please take out a little paper package from the right-hand pocket."

I think Mr. Patterson must have thought me out of my wits as he placed the parcel in my left hand.

"Chewing-gum, I suppose," he said, "or tobacco."

"No, sir," I replied, "none of us use either;" but I knew already how suspiciously he would regard that reply, for—and he was the only person in St. Charles holding such an idea—a hatred of tobacco was one of his bitterest opinions. I think he made it the more of a hobby on that account, for such a notion as that was laughed at as a fanaticism unworthy even of contempt. If there was a man or boy, white or black, in all that region who did not use the weed, I never heard of such a person, apart, I mean, from Mr. Patterson and our family.

But I was speaking of the parcel in my hand.

"It is something I have never spoken of to any one," I said to Mr. Patterson; "I wish to consult you about it. Will you please sit down a moment. The morning I got hurt," I continued, as my host took a seat near my head as I lay, "I had dropped in at the rooms of the State geologist, on my way to the post-office. They know me there, and I wandered about among the specimens of ores and fossils. I wanted to find out what that is;" and I shook out of the paper a lump half the size of my fist on the bed-cover. "Can you tell me what it is, Mr. Patterson?"

My host took the object suspiciously between his finger and thumb. I remember how long and nervous his hand seemed as he did so. He looked at it, smelled it, tasted it, weighed it in the palm of his hand. I watched his face closely as he did so. What an amazingly sharp, smart, swift-minded person a business man gets to be when of the temperament of Mr. Patterson, and under stress of the unceasing strain on him that he endured and enjoyed! The trouble with him was that his skin was too thin for the sudden vigor of his inner conclusions; the very thinness of the lips, also, making them too lithe and flexible to be under the complete control of one whose very success must lie, not more in thinking and feeling clearly and instantly and vigorously, than in concealing his thought and feeling from any with whom he might be bargaining at the time. He could not help it. He understood the whole affair at once, and perfectly. Without saying a word, he went to the chamber-door, opened it, looked up and down the hall outside, and carefully closed it behind him. When he came back to my side he had recovered himself, and seemed as cold and indifferent as a man could be, but it was too late.

"What do you think it is, sir?" I asked, as he laid the lump carelessly on the little stand beside my bed, resting his hand beside it.

"I am no mineralogist," he said, composedly. "Is it a specimen from the shelves of the State geologist?"

"Dr. Zwenky thought it was when I showed it to him that day," I replied. "When I asked him what it was, he said, 'You must put dat back, mine leetle big boy. Leetle boys must look and learn, but dey must not meddle, nor big boys eider.' Then I asked, 'But what is it, Dr. Zwenky?'"

"And what did he say?" added Mr. Patterson, trying to hide his eagerness under a smile at my mimicry of the German, for I attempted to imitate the doctor because I myself was greatly excited by the excitement of Mr. Patterson.

"Oh, nothing, sir," I replied, "except, he said as he looked at the lump all around and around through his owl spectacles: 'Ah, mine young friend, if we could only find one leetle bit of dis in dis State! Dat is from England or Ohio—de label is off—I forget which. Ah, if we had one goot ap-propriation from de State to make one grand survey, but dey want de gelt for bolitics.' I am keeping you too long, Mr. Patterson," for, weak as I was, I felt that I was master of the situation, felt physically stronger every moment, and oh, how exceedingly glad for Habby and the rest no tongue can tell! And my original purpose in speaking upon the subject, in part at least, was to put my host more perfectly at ease with me. It is so much easier and better to be manly and be done with it; and so, "He said," I went on, "that it was coal, the best article of bituminous coal. The doctor became more and more interested as he examined it, still supposing it was a specimen of coal from his collection, and told me that the stratum must be from four to six feet thick, and a great deal else that I could not understand, half German, half Latin."

"And it was from his shelves?" Mr. Patterson asked, with suppressed eagerness, rising to his feet.

"Oh no, sir," I said, simply; "I could not have had it in my pocket to-day if it was. I did not tell Dr. Zwenky. You are the only person I have mentioned it to. If you will go into it with me, I will be glad; I am anxious to give my brother Habersham a complete education. Why, Mr. Patterson, my brother, such a little body as he looks, so weak and small, is the most talented boy you ever knew in your life." And in the pride of my heart I launched out into a glowing account of the success and standing of Habby at the Archimedean Institute. It had become the habit of my life by this time to defend Habby, even when no one had alluded to him, from the false inferences I knew they would foolishly draw from his appearance. I was so full of Habby and his wonderful genius that I hardly noticed it, but I fancied even then that there was a softening in the rigid countenance of the dogged and severe old man who stood listening patiently to me, his fingers mechanically closing and unclosing around the fragment of coal upon the little stand, placed there for my medicine and meals.

"But what do you want me to do, Carter? Of course I knew all about your brother; your father told us all about him, and often enough, long ago."

"Please sit down, Mr. Patterson, for a moment," I said. "I don't intend asking it of you as a favor—that is, not only as a favor—but as a matter of business. I have seventy-three dollars and sixty-two and a half cents in bank that I made picking cotton at the Institute; but you understand things so much better than I do. Now, if you will go in with me, you see. The land is not worth ten dollars an acre. We ought, I suppose, to make compensation to the owners afterward in addition, but if you would go ahead and buy up the land meanwhile—"

"Where is it—near St. Charles?" he asked.

"I am so desirous as to Habby, and—

and— You will be true to me, Mr. Patterson?" I stammered.

"Yes," he said; and although I could have wished that he had taken my hand as he said it, I saw that he meant yes entirely, and no two school-boys could have been more heartily at ease and at home with one another as I proceeded.

"You remember that day I called on you about a situation?" blundering, as I always did, in asking such a question.

"Certainly, Carter," he said, "and I have been wanting to say to you how greatly—"

I interrupted him, "What I was going to say was that it was such a providence you refused me—that is the way my father would look at it!" Then I told him in full about my walk into the country, my discovery of the coal in the gully wallowed out by the hogs—the whole story, in fact, the exact location of the land and all—and I know by his keen attention how deeply interested he was.

"And now, Carter," he said, rising at last, "if Dr. Grex came in and saw your excitement, he would take a stick to us both. Let matters rest. Do not speak of it to a soul. I will keep this coal, if you have no objection. Your business is to be as quiet as you can, and get well and strong. I will attend to things right away. But you must not be so sure; there's many a disappointment. No coal has ever been suspected in the State. Besides, it may be a very small quantity, not enough to create a market. All that is to be done I will do. Go to sleep."

Strange to say, I took his advice, and rolled over the edge, as usual, into the depths of slumber, and I do think I can sleep as hard, sleep as tremendously, as anybody. I seemed to have all of Habby's share of sleep, poor fellow, as well as my own.

"Won't you take my order for my money in bank?" I demanded of him, as he put his head in for a moment next morning on his way to business.

"No, not to-day; but I may want it soon. I will want it if we buy. When you are ready for her, and she has washed up the breakfast-things, Mabel will come in and give you a game of chess. Morning!" I must say here that, in washing up the cups and saucers, glass and silver, after breakfast,

Mabel did what every lady in the South, however many negroes she owned, always did. At home, before we arose from the table, Mrs. Brown sent up from the kitchen an enormous pan of hot water. Placing this in the tea-tray before her, my mother, with a crash towel, three yards long, over her left arm, always washed up the things. Whoever happened to be there made no difference, and, as she washed, and elaborately wiped cups and saucers and spoons, we had a thoroughly social talk together as we idled around the board, rolling the napkin-rings across the table or trying to land a milk goblet with a spoon balanced on its edge around the circle without letting it fall. People in our day would be horror-smitten at such conduct; but we were idler and happier then.

Mabel Patterson came in after finishing her duties that morning, solely, I suppose, because Cosma Adams had "put on her sun-bonnet and run over," as she and all the rest phrased it among the ladies in St. Charles, to see how I was.

"I'm almost glad you got hurt, Mr. Quarterman," Cosma said, in her simplicity, after our first salutations, dangling her sun-bonnet by its long calico strings as she stood by my bed flushed from her walk; "I hardly knew Mabel before. Now we have got ever so well acquainted!"

I did not want to look at Mabel after that, and therefore asked,

"When did you hear from Pink, Miss Cosma?"

"Pink? Our cow?" she exclaimed, with wide eyes. "Why, what?"

"Miss Cosma Adams," I said, gravely, "didn't you tell me Pink had a pen of her own?"

"Did I? Yes, she did, at the house-end of the pasture lot," she replied, looking at me with the child's face of her country innocence.

"Well," I added, "she wrote with her pen to your Uncle Hone, to complain to him as governor of the State about the way you used to ride on her calf."

"Oh, what a story! she never!" exclaimed the girl. "And I never tried to ride it but once, and then it ran from under me, and I fell on the grass."

"Anyhow, Bran saw it. Old Zeus said 'Neigh, neigh,' when the governor sent to find out. It was he who told a story, because he liked you for scratching his ears. Please get the chess-men, Miss Mabel," I continued; "I want Miss Cosma to see what a splendid game you play, and how stupid she and I are."

Our visitor stood upon one side, holding her sun-bonnet in her hand, with doubting eyes as Mabel arranged the chess-board, removing the things from the little stand at my head to do so.

"Oh, it is gambling; it is a sin!" she said at last, with anxiety. "If you tell stories so, and gamble, too, where, Mr. Carter," she added, with grave sincerity, "do you think you will go?"

"Nonsense!" Mabel Patterson began, with tones and manner very much like those of her father. "I beg your pardon, Cosma," she corrected herself immediately; "a story is wicked only when we deceive or try to deceive, and that about Pink was his fun. Gambling is when things go by chance, and chess hasn't a bit of chance in it, has it, Carter? Mr. Carter, I mean."

"No, no chance, all smartness or stupidity. Now, this horse-headed thing," I explained to Cosma, looking on askance, "is the knight. See what a stumbling sort of move it has, always bouncing about in every body's way. Just like me. That white piece on her side and this black one on mine are the two queens; they are the ones that do most in the game; all the rest are men, you see, and can not stand against the women. Two of them, you see:" I rattled on, to hide a good deal of pain just then in sides and shoulder; "one of them is Miss Mabel, and the other is Miss Cosma."

"Then I will be the white one," said Cosma, eagerly.

"Very well, and I will be the black one," Mabel said, not looking up, but setting herself steadily to her game. What with the matter of the coal, the pain, and the presence of two such young ladies, to one long secluded from female society, or society of any kind, I felt sharpened up like a razor fresh from the hone. Yes; Cosma, with her milk-maid fairness, plumpness, rustic simplicity, was the white queen. But Mabel Patterson was something more than a brunette, in comparison with this blonde. She knew that I was watching her face as she sat, her hand hovering over her queen, meditating her next move, and knew, oh, how much more of all that was depending than did her companion, whose conscience would not allow her as yet to assent so far to our playing as to sit down.

"Beautiful black hair," I said to myself, of Mabel; "forehead low, but well rounded; eyebrows perfectly arched; straight nose; lips red and flexible, but not full, unless it is of purpose."

"Miss Mabel," I added aloud, and, as she looked up, "eyes," I continued to myself. "so black and deep and determined;" but I merely added, "Please do your best this time. I want to see if I can not beat you."

"I will," she said, her eyes lingering in mine, and then falling upon the board. Nothing more. It may have been my quickened sensitiveness, owing to the pain I had endured and was then concealing, but her full, steady eyes were to me, during the flash of that instant, as the gates through which I saw my future for ever and ever. Allow me to keep my history perfectly straight and clear and true by saying that I had never been in the least, nor was I then, at all in love with Miss Mabel Patterson. I am compelled to say that aversion was my deepest feeling; the prettier she was, the stronger the aversion, and she had too much of the quickness of her father not to know it. I have a lumbering way of philosophizing, and it came to my mind on the moment, surely our eyes are nearer to the texture of what our bodies will be in heaven than any other part of us. Suppose a fellow were clad to-day in frame and flesh as crystal as is the eye, how ethereal he would be, how translucent to light, imparted or received. Yes, and how very awkward it would be in my case if it were so with me this instant.

When I looked up at Cosma Adams, I saw that she knew something was in progress that she could not understand, a game deeper than chess. Her full, round cheeks were paler, her blue eyes larger, her full lips opened as if about starting upon a run.

"Miss Mabel is beating me, Miss Cosma,"

I said, plaintively at last, as my adversary deliberately placed her queen in my back lines, castle, bishop, knight, and every thing else of hers threatening my king from the front.

"What do you let her do it for?" Cosma said, with energy. "She shouldn't beat me!"

and, as a matter of course, smiling and putting the men in the box. "He doesn't try hard enough."

"Yes, that's the bother, as it was with me in algebra," I said. "Habersham did it as easy as breathing, and I am willing enough; the trying is as hard as I can drive, but it

"MISS MABEL IS BEATING ME."

"Yes," I said, "perhaps so. But Miss Mabel always beats me. It's the way God made us. I am as powerful against her as a mouse with — no, you are not a cat — as an ox against a leopardess, Miss Mabel."

"That is only his fun, Cosma," my adversary said, as she checkmated me — serenely

is all against a stone wall, somehow. I'm afraid it's the same way with you, Miss Cosma," I added; "I don't believe you could ever learn—excuse me—to play chess to save your life; there is a pair of us, you see."

"Good-morning, Mr. Brokenbones," Miss Praxley exclaimed, breaking in upon us as

I spoke. "And here is Miss Buttercups. Good-morning, Miss Patterson."

I was glad to see Miss Praxley just then, but I knew she did not like Mabel because she called her by her right name.

"Nice thing for you to be calling upon a young man," she added to Cosma, whom I knew she was very fond of. "I was so shocked when Mrs. Hone told me about it, that I came after you right away: this poor fellow has had mischief enough done him already."

"Why, Miss Praxley," Cosma exclaimed, taking it all with the simplicity of a child. "Mabel invited me to come. Mrs. Hone said she would if she were in my place; and when I went over and asked Mrs. Quarterman, she said, 'Do, Cosma; Carter will be glad to see you.'" And she said it so innocently, her eyes so wide, that I could not help laughing with the rest, even if I was racked with pain. But I was glad Miss Praxley came.

CHAPTER XIX.

My eldest brother Archibald had suddenly returned home about two weeks after my accident. Heaven alone knows where he had been, and what he had been doing, for he was very silent in reference to the details of his adventures. The one thing which he endeavored to impress as deeply upon our minds as it was upon his own, was the cruelly unjust way in which he had been treated by every body everywhere. As a book-keeper in a wholesale boot and shoe establishment in some city, he had been grossly insulted by the clerks; as an assistant in some art-rooms somewhere else, he had been so misused by the visitors that he would not stand it; as one of the crew of a vessel to New York, he had a Nero for a captain; as the teacher of a country school, scholars and parents had conspired against him. I do not suppose he himself could remember each event of his career since leaving home; but one thing was very clear, that in every situation he had been forced to leave almost immediately after entering upon it by the conduct of the parties with whom he was thrown.

"Neither your father nor myself has ever understood Archibald," my mother said to me, on her first visit to my bedside after his return. "He is our first-born, the handsomest, as he is, Habersham perhaps excepted, the most talented of you all. Did you ever see a more striking youth in your life, Carter? What a forehead, what a form, what energy and force! He draws beautifully, writes what they call a copper-plate hand; is familiar with all literature, quoting, when he is in the mood, passage after passage from orators and poets. For his own amusement, he has written essays, dialogues, poetry, which would distinguish any one; but you know how it was when Colonel Archer secured him a situation in the Seminary; and it is the same of every thing: the moment any one of his many talents is named, a disgust for that particular talent seizes upon him, a distaste and aversion only less decided than his disgust for the person who endeavors to persuade him to use it. You do not know, Carter, how your father and myself have prayed over him, for we have seen long ago that the sure way to drive him from any thing is to try and argue or persuade him to do it. We have tried indulgence and severity—"

"He told me all his wrongs," I replied, "when he was here yesterday. I have been studying it over, as the negroes say, and I have got a plan. You will laugh at it."

"Well?" my mother added, for she placed a vast deal more reliance upon my slow-coming ideas than they were worth; but with little hope in her tones: too many plans had been tried and failed.

"Good Mr. Clarkson dropped in to see me a moment after Archy left yesterday. He brought me a bottle of bay-rum, which he said was excellent for—"

"The beard," my mother added for me with a laugh, although I was beginning to have really a very respectable growth upon my face.

"Spare your blushes," my mother continued. "Never mind, Carter; broad shoulders and solid opinions and dogged energy are often accompanied by very thick hair, and—"

"Please," I interrupted, "I spoke to Mr. Clarkson, and he consented on the spot to have Archibald come into his apothecary shop for a while. It will be impossible for Archy to take offense with him."

"It is a shame," my mother broke in, "the way Georgia acts toward Mr. Clarkson! He is no more to Virginia than one of his perfumed puff-balls; and Georgia ridicules him to his very face. She was in such a gust of fun at something he said or did in our parlor the other evening, carried on so with Miss Praxley who was there, about it, that I told her afterward I would certainly send her from the room if she was so rude again. When she gets into a gale, Carter, she frightens me: she has all her father's enthusiasm about every thing; and yet, when she is in the mood, she is far better than her sister at housekeeping, at her music, at every thing."

"I have seen her entertain a roomful of company," I added, "when you were not at home, and she astonished me as well as charmed every one by her grace and genial courtesy; actually threw Jenny into the shade for the time! But Mr. Clarkson said he would see Archy to-day, and I told him if he represented to Archy that the arrangement was merely for a time, and especially, if nothing was said about our desiring it, he would be more apt to consent."

"Well, perhaps so," my mother said, with very little hope in her tones.

"But that is the least part of my plan," I continued, after my mother had helped turn me more toward her as I lay, for I was terribly bandaged still, lying there more like a log than a young man who had all his future to earn. "Now I know you will laugh at me," I said; "but I tell you it is a splendid idea! All that Archy needs is some one who can grasp and manage him, somebody who can take him completely and forever out of his own hands."

"I do not know who can do it unless it is the Being that made him," my mother added, with such utter hopelessness upon her dear face! "Your father and myself have done our best in vain. He has been a puzzle to us from his cradle. The harder we try, the worse the result. We feel as if it was our only course to leave him utterly alone. And to think of it! Our first-born, and all that he is so capable of being!" The tears rose in her eyes as she spoke, for you can not imagine how superior Archibald was to Habersham and myself in every thing except that astounding perversity of character.

"Don't laugh when I tell you," I said, seriously. "And the great thing will be for Archy never to dream for a moment that we have any such an idea. Our plan is to be as dull and stupid about it as posts, not to stir a finger or a hair; but to leave it all to her!"

"To her?" my mother asked, in astonishment.

"Yes, to her!" I said, with the desperation of Columbus, Daguerre, Jenner, Harvey, Fulton, or any other great discoverer or inventor, in the first announcement of his apparently ridiculous notion. "Stoop down, mother, lower still;" and when her ear was at my lips, I whispered a name in triumph. My mother repeated the name in accents of astonishment, adding, indignantly,

"You must have received some injury in your head, Carter. The idea!"

"Very well," I added, composedly, "we will see. All I ask is that you will never speak of it to a soul."

"Absurd! I wonder if you suppose I would!" my mother replied, with energy; and I am constrained to record here that the divine intuitions of the most gifted woman are duller than the dullest dullness of men— when some other of her own sex is concerned. An acid has no influence upon an acid, nor an alkali upon alkali, and so through the whole domain of nature as of chemistry; an object is sensitive only to its opposite. I had no desire to discuss the matter further even with myself, and was glad that Virginia came in at this juncture to relieve my mother, who looked gravely at me as she bid me good-bye. I am satisfied she feared that my brain was injured.

"There is one thing I wanted to say, Carter," my sister remarked, after we had talked over Archy's return and all the lesser news of the day. "Mother wanted to speak to you about it, perhaps she has spoken. It is about Cosma Adams and Mabel Patterson," my sister continued, with the air of a grandmother, as she took out her sewing. "I speak of it now before anybody comes in. They are very unlike, but they are both very nice-looking girls—each in her way. Now, Carter!"

"Blaze away, Jenny!" I said, somewhat coarsely. "You see how helpless I am. Go on. Beautiful and charming and dangerously fascinating girls, you were saying—"

"I said nothing of the sort," my sister replied, "and you say it only to hide things. Cosma is going to be really beautiful. In her way, of course, I mean. She is a pure, good country-girl, but very ignorant. It is true," my sister added, "that Governor Hone is to give her the best of educations, and Miss Praxley is taking her into society, and giving her a thousand hints. And she has wonderfully improved. But she is nothing at last but a country-girl. Now, Carter, be on your guard!"

"I will," I said, with something like a smirk, I fear, upon my face. "Go on, grandma!"

"Of course, I have no fears about *her*," Virginia added, with her Queen Elizabeth air; "but I did want to speak to you about Mabel Patterson."

"Because you *do* have fears about her?" I asked.

"The circumstances of your case are so singular, your getting yourself so badly hurt in her defense—that is all. And then," my sister added, "you are here in her care. It is all perfectly natural."

"What is natural?" I demanded, with the blood heating my cheeks as I asked.

"I see that you understand, Carter. You know the attitude of her father to us: how he overwhelmed papa and all of us with civilities and costly presents, until he found that he could not have us, like wax-dolls, to do exactly as he wished in every thing and all! It would never, never do, Carter; never. He is a soured man; harsh, set in his way, bitter, prejudiced! Officer of the church as he is, he would hardly stop at any thing to crush any one he hated. I never knew a man who was so much like those ground rattlesnakes we used to see, you remember,

at Uncle Archibald's, stealthy and swarthy and venomous. It is wrong to say it under his roof, but—" and Virginia spoke in lowered tones, "look at his narrow, projecting forehead, the next time you see him, at his small keen eyes, at his peculiar jaws: he is exactly like a viper. And Mabel is his own, own daughter, Carter. Take care!"

"Take care?" But I contradicted my exclamation by my redness of face.

"I see," my sister said, mournfully. "We all relied on your strong sense, Carter. And one would have supposed you would have been disgusted. It is the gentleman that ought to fall in love first, and not the lady. Mamma has said so a thousand times. Oh, it is too bad!" continued my afflicted sister, dropping her sewing in her lap. "Archy is so perverse; there is no telling what Georgia will do in some of her wild moods; Habersham is so small and weakly; you are all we have to rely on; and, oh, Carter, she is such a hateful, hateful girl!"

To my amazement, Virginia was actually crying, serene and gentle as she always was. "You can not think," she sobbed, "how we dread it at home! Georgia got into a fury about it last night, and said she could wring Mabel's neck for her with her own hands, and I wish she would!" said, to my profound astonishment, this lady-like sister of mine, and with energy.

There was but one thing to do. Putting the clean handkerchief she had just brought me to my eyes with my one uninjured hand, I proceeded to weep as violently as I could without being heard out of the room!

"Why, what do you mean, you provoking boy?" began Virginia, laughing in spite of herself.

"That you should be Mrs. Apothecary Clarkson," I sobbed, with energy, "it bub-bubble-breaks my heart! My sis-sister Virgin-ginia, of whom I was so proud;" and I indulged in a suppressed howl of anguish.

"The idea!" exclaimed Virginia, with scorn.

"Yes, yes, bub-bub-but I know he will, because he loves you so!" and as her face cleared, I added, "Oh no, Miss Jenny, let's be sensible! I love nobody in the world, not a picayune's worth, except my mother first and before all the world, then poor little

Habby, then you and Georgia and the rest. Bah!" I added, with wholesome emphasis, "I've too much work to do for you all, please God, to indulge any such nonsense. Besides, I haven't any such inclination. Exactly the reverse," I said, looking fully in Virginia's clear eyes as I spoke; but there came upon me, as I said it, that singular glimpse of mine into the far future through those dark, deep, determined eyes! No man could be clearer in purpose or more honest in all he said than I; but I was glad that, at this instant, Dr. Grex broke into my room without knocking, as was the custom of that rough practitioner. And how very beautiful Virginia looked just then, flushed from our conversation as well as radiant with joy at the assurance I had given her! We Quartermans all estimated each other immensely beyond our sober, market value. I may say it on paper, although I do not believe in my heart that my estimation, at least, of the rest of our family is too high. On this occasion I would have made oath that Dr. Grex agreed with me so far as Virginia was concerned. He seemed actually dazzled by her appearance into a sort of confused bow as he strode to my side, his queer cap upon his head, his excess of very black hair all awry, his linen far from as pure as it might have been, his entire manner about as rough as a dozen years or so of associations such as medical colleges, hospitals, dueling parties, and mobs of murdering roughs in general could make it.

"You lying here still!" he exclaimed, as he stood by my bed; and seizing upon the bedclothing tucked about my chin, he began to turn it down, regardless of the presence of Virginia, who arose with astonishment in her face. I held to the bed-covering as well as I could with my well hand.

"Hold on, Dr. Grex," I said with a gesture, so to speak, of my eyes toward my sister; "you forget!"

"Oh, she will not mind," he said; "Florence Nightingale was with us at Scutari, and she didn't. Charles!" with an oath at his black shadow, "what are you bowing and scraping there for?" The fact being that, with a negro's habitual respect for a white lady, his boy Charles had assumed an attitude of respect to the one present. In the act of uttering the oath the eye of Dr. Grex rested, because he could not help it, upon the astonished face of Virginia, and he saw that the oath had struck my sister almost as full in the face as if it had been his fist instead. On the instant the surprise was gone—nothing but scorn for him and profound contempt—for it is wonderful how much of her soul she could show in her face, the feeling there being the more vivid as against the background, if such an expression may be allowed, of her usually quiet manner. My surgeon was to her nothing but a very brutal dog which had suddenly burst into the room, and every line of her face and tone of her voice gave that meaning as she paused a while, her contemptuous glance full in his, and then remarked, slowly and quietly, "Good-bye, my poor Carter; you are doubly unfortunate!" With a light kiss upon my forehead, and a gracious "Morning, boy," to Charles as she passed him, she had left the room with no more acknowledgment of Dr. Grex than if he had been indeed a dog, and a very disagreeable one at that. The whole thing was over in a moment, but it hit and hurt the doctor so severely that he forgot even to try to hide how badly he was struck. Virginia ought to have known it, but the extra violence of the man on entering the room was a sudden affectation to conceal his pleasure at meeting her; for a man of deeper and stronger emotions I never met.

Only the day before Colonel Tom Maxwell had dropped in to see me, exhilarating me with his burly stature and hearty tones, and when I had told him of the skill of Dr. Grex, he had replied:

"What a fellow he is! He is always called in at the penitentiary after a scrimmage with the prisoners, or when one of them tries to cut his own throat with broken glass, or any thing of the kind. They don't do it now, but they used to do it before your father came to be chaplain. He has turned what used to be as flourishing a State-prison on as a man would wish to see into a big church."

"Dr. Grex has?" I asked.

"Oh no, your father. Dr. Grex? I should think not! But, under all, Dr. Grex has just as big a heart as your father; only your father takes it out in preaching, and the other doctor in cutting and cursing. In this way: A prisoner severs, say, the artery of his thigh—tries to bleed himself to death. While Dr. Grex is patching up the pieces, the fellow tells him, in the reaction which is sure to come, how well off he was once, how he was led astray, how desperate he is at the disgrace, and so on, and Dr. Grex will listen in his off-hand way that shows how heartily he sympathizes with the poor scamp. He told me, the last case of the kind, in the presence of the man too, that if I let the affair get into the St. Charles papers he would break every bone in my body, and then set them again all wrong. I'd like to see him try it!" added Colonel Tom. "Why, I've known him," he continued, "when some miserable woman came about the penitentiary with her draggle-tailed children, seeing about her husband, to empty his pocket, gold too—for he charges people that can pay tremendously—put it in her apron, and send her away with benedictions that sounded mighty like profanity. I'm far from excusing him, you mind," Colonel Tom added, who had himself been exceedingly profane before his intimacy with my father; "yet Grex is a splendid surgeon—as kind inside as he is rough without!"

But I mention all this to explain why I did not resent more warmly his roughness when my sister was present. To return to Dr. Grex. I would have been a greater blockhead than Habby says I am not to see that my surgeon had fallen desperately in love with my sister. As I came to know afterward, it was his first experience of the kind; and, when his rough, tough nature had given way, the whole man came down with a crash, as is always the case with people of his sort. How he rattled on, when she had left, to hide it! I had asked him many questions during his previous visits upon the subject of physiology, in which I took special interest, and to which Habersham had one of his most intense aversions, and the talk turned naturally in that direction. I dare say it was because I was her brother, because he did not want to leave the room in which she had been; but he entered on an argument, his palm upon my brow where she had left her kiss, to prove to me that there was no difference between man and any other animal beyond a higher organization. As he talked, I came to understand that he was not merely a materialist, but that worst form of a materialist, an automatist. That is, he held that men were nothing but matter, and matter organized and working under laws, precisely like an eight-day clock of more exquisite workmanship, and with, on the average, a longer time of running; at best merely an automaton. It was all new to me then, and I grew to be deeply interested as he told me how and wherein the human machinery was constructed, with but slight variations, upon that of any lower mammal. He had also a store of anecdotes from his reading or observation in hospitals of men whose degree of talent or whose habits as good men were suddenly changed into bad, or the reverse, merely as the result of a broken head. What he told me of the mental as well as bodily actions, automatic, of course, of persons during sleep-walking, seemed, with many other things mentioned by him, to prove that we were only machines at best. Had I not been the brother of Virginia, he would not have wasted his time upon me; but he grew eloquent as he talked. I think he wanted in some measure, and unconsciously to himself, to redeem himself through my report in her eyes; and no telling how long he would have gone on had not a messenger come to the house-door in breathless haste to tell him of a "shooting scrape" down-town.

"At Scotchy Strange's billiard-saloon, of course," he said, not at all in a hurry.

"Dey say de man is all cut up, too, an' bleedin' to death," urged Charles, who had gone to the door.

"Let him bleed," was all the doctor said, as he slowly arose, and continued the particular incident he was relating, not in the least hurried.

"Do man says, please make haste," Charles, who had gone out, returned to say: "de man was almost dun dead when he started on a run for you—dis man, I mean!"

"Look here, you black scoundrel," the doctor replied, deliberately, "if you say another word, I'll knock your head off! Do you hear?" slowly putting on his cap.

"Yes, sah!" said the negro, as coolly as his master.

CHAPTER XX.

IF I may use such a figure of speech, I would say that the seed of the Quarterman plantation, seed in all the varieties thereof, was now thoroughly got in, and there ensued a time of comparative repose upon the part of all, while the germination went on with a force from God, as imperceptible and yet as irresistible as that of the globe upon its axis.

There was, for instance, that discovery of mine, the hogs being the pioneers thereof, in relation to the coal. It was precisely in the line of Mr. Patterson's inclination and business training, and while I was slowly getting mended as to my broken bones, he had made full investigation as to dip, quality, quantity, cost of mining, demand for coal, cost as compared with the supply of wood, and all the rest of it. After such investigation, at every step of which he had informed me after we were alone together of evenings, he had drawn my little deposit from the bank, and, with additional funds of his own, had purchased the whole tract of otherwise worthless land for ten dollars an acre. I was far from being at ease in thus defrauding, as I feared, the ignorant owners.

"It is owing to your nervous condition," he said; "you have suffered much pain, have taken no exercise. Business is business. When I give money, I give. When I do business, I make the best bargain I can. That's the way I get something to give. Pure nervousness and nonsense. Make haste, man, and get well!"

In what splendid spirits he was! I could not have believed that the lank, sallow, stoop-shouldered, prejudiced man could have been so illuminated from within, at other times like a lantern whose light had gone out. He was positively handsome and eloquent as he talked over our prospects at night, after Mabel had gone to bed. There seemed to me so much of the fierceness of a tiger at the scent of blood in the keen eagerness of the man after the money to be made in our speculation, that I disliked his occasional allusions to the providence of God in the matter exceedingly. The smell, in his case, of distant money was so accurate and strong, that I wondered he had not himself discovered the coal long before. Both Heaven and myself, it seemed to me, were very subordinate parties in the matter.

But one thing troubled me greatly. What I wanted with the coal was to send Habersham off to college. I knew the poor fellow was fretting out his soul at home, lying awake of nights, morbid, miserable. The only solace he had was in teaching Cosma Adams Latin, Governor Hone making that arrangement, as I well knew, more as a mode of giving Habersham employment and money, than for the sake of Cosma, whom he classed with his wife, Sukey, and his babe, Squashy. As was often the case with men of talent and distinction in the South at that date, Governor Hone had a whimsical horror of any thing like marked talent among women, especially among those of his own household. Well do I remember the hearty aversion he used to express in our parlor for literary women: "They may do caged up in their books, madam," he would say, "but actually living in your home! I would as lief have a squalling parrot in mine. There was Madame de

Staël; how sincerely I sympathize in the aversion for her which Coleridge, Byron, and Goethe express, after personal acquaintance!" In fact, the vacuous softness of the members of the governor's family was as essential to him as is a feather-bed to the weary; a repose indispensable after the sharpnesses and severities of politics.

"How does Cosma come on in her studies?" I asked of Habersham one day, merely to start him, as he sat, moody as usual, and miserable, beside my bed.

"Fully as well as you used to do, Carter," he snapped me up. "I wondered, when we were at the Archimedean Institute, at the amazing talent you showed in blundering at your Latin and mathematics, hitting out ways of going wrong beyond the imagination of other people, a perfect genius for mistaking what was as plain as a pikestaff; besides, there is some excuse for her: she is a woman."

"I hope you are not as impatient with her," I ventured, "as you were with me."

"I never was impatient with you," Habby replied; "Job himself would have been astounded at such preternatural persistence in making mistakes. I suppose I do express myself sometimes when she does worse than usual."

"I can just see you at your lessons," I laughed, "Cosma sitting there, and you here. She trying to run through a conjugation, you scolding her; and you have no idea how venomous you are, Habby. I can see her this moment, her lips parted a little as you scold, her eyes opening and opening in astonishment, filling with tears, I wouldn't wonder. I say, Professor Quarterman, have you got as far as *Amo, Amare, Amari, Amatum*?"

I only meant it in fun, and was surprised to see my brother's face grow as red as his hair, then paler than its usual ashen hue.

Exclaiming "Stuff and nonsense!" he put on his cap with a jerk, and was gone before I could stop him. But I was even more surprised at a sudden and singular pain in my heart at my own joke, as well as his way of taking it. I detected, too, a meanness in the additional desire I now had to send him off to college, even if I had to beg, which I hated more than I can say, some

advance from Mr. Patterson upon our coal speculation for the purpose. I would almost rather have broken all my bones over again; but, when an unpleasant thing has to be done, the sooner it is done, the better, and I spoke of it to Mr. Patterson that very night.

"Mr. Carter," he said, with the old sourness coming back into his face, giving its sallowness a green tinge, "I do not see how I can do it. Business is business. You know the whole thing may be a dead loss at last. I am sorry, but I do not see my way clear to make an advance; just now money is very tight."

"Very well, Mr. Patterson," I said; "all I care about the coal is that I may send my brother to college. He can not wait. I will get somebody to call on Colonel Archer, and beg him to come and see me. I may be able to sell out my interest to him;" but I feared it as I spoke, for Colonel Archer never had any money. When he was duelist, partisan editor, popular politician, and all that, his money was spent long in advance of his income. True, he had become a humble and sincere a Christian as is often met. But he had carried his loose habits in reference to money into his religion; there was something savoring almost of dissipation, if I may say so, in the way in which he gave, not to the cause of Christ, so much as to Christ himself, an absence of judicious calculation even in that.

"Colonel Archer!" Mr. Patterson exclaimed; but even he dared not express contempt for the colonel's impecunious condition. When he gave, it was to a cause, a definite, visible, business-like operation of some sort, even if it was spiritual; and he gave deliberately, systematically, and precisely so much, according as he liked, and especially as he had himself the management of the cause in question. "Colonel Archer!" he exclaimed. "Yes! Perhaps so!"

"I can at least try," I said. "Then there are General Hugh M'Neil, Mr. Clemming. Dr. Grex is as rich as he is rough. There's Governor Hone. I'll try Mrs. President. If I can't do any better, I will try Scotchy Strange, bad as he is. Miss Praxley has money. Colonel Tom Maxwell would go into the coal with a rush. Major Hampton would help me, if he had to sell out his livery-stable. I'll get the money," I said, in my slow way, "if I have to hobble up and down every street in St. Charles on crutches!"

"I never said I would not make a small advance," Mr. Patterson replied. "Your brother will need enough merely to take him to college; small payments all along after will keep him there. I'll think of it. Meanwhile don't speak to any one about it."

The next morning Mr. Patterson heaped my bed with all sorts of legal documents to sign, binding me to repayment.

"I know these have no legal force, you being a minor," he said; "but it will ruin all if we talk about that coal before we are ready, and I can trust your father and you." Upon which he proceeded to name a sum, but I had observed that blanks had been left in the papers as to the amounts, and, if I never could manage Latin or mathematics, I was steadily coming to know how to manage Mr. Patterson. It delighted me like coming into sudden possession of an unexpected gift, a certain sense arising on the instant within me of business capacity.

"If you will double that amount," I said to Mr. Patterson, "I will sign; if not, I won't."

I spoke confidently because I was master of the situation. If I had the intuition in regard to poetry or eloquence that I have in a trade, I do believe I would be a poet or an orator; I heartily wish I had any thing like the same sense of certainty where love and religion are concerned! Anyhow, when Georgia was leaving, after a visit to me next day, I begged her to send Habersham down to see me.

"I do wish he would come and live with you," Georgia said; "he is perfectly insufferable. Mother says that he groans, and tosses about all night. He certainly does all day. He is moody and miserable. Every few days Cosma comes over. Habby can't stand the babies at Governor Hone's, so they have their lessons in the back parlor. It's all dus, da, do, dum! I bang away at the piano in the front parlor. The moment I stop they throw me out, so that I make false notes all the time. I'll send him, if you'll keep him. There's no peace in the house with him; he is a perfect nuisance!

But, Carter," said Georgia, "it is so funny about General M'Neil and Virginia. You know he printed a book on elocution once, in real earnest, he did. Ever since he talks according to the rules of oratory. They say he writes out and rehearses before his glass at home all he says in company. You ought to hear him deliver his oration to Jenny. Jenny sits there as sober—— But it is the funniest sight! Jenny says—to say something, you know—'What kind of weather do you think we will have, General M'Neil?' and he will answer, 'Weather more salubrious soul could not desire, Miss Virginia. Breezes more beneficently balmy I have never inhaled. Were woman but as sweetly compliant as was Eve, surely paradise would be our possession;' and whole hours of such nonsense, Jenny listening like a queen to an embassador. Let me show you how," and Georgia struck an attitude and imitated the stately general and his elocution, until, hearing the front door open and shut, and, not risking a meeting with Mabel, she said, "Oh yes, I'll send Habersham!" and was gone.

But my brother did not come for several days. When he did, I was touched to the heart by his woe-begone appearance.

"Well, Carter, what is it?" he abruptly demanded, as he stood by my bed. I got him to prop me up with pillows, and then I began at the beginning, and told him the whole story, unknown up to that instant to any body but Mr. Patterson, of my finding the coal, and all my partnership with Mr. Patterson. Then, while he listened with intensity of interest in his poor dim eyes, I took from under my pillow the shot-bag of specie, and poured it out on the bed-quilt, and told him how eager I had been to help him to go to college, and how very glad I was that he could now start whenever he pleased. But I was alarmed for my brother's wits as I finished. He had been turning paler and paler as I proceeded, until his wan, pinched countenance was positively livid. He hardly allowed me to finish, when he broke into a passion, by no means of tears, much less of gratitude, but of bitter wrath at and upon himself.

"You miserable fool!" he said, in low and bitter tones, setting his teeth and clutching at his hair, "you wretched insect!"

"Why, what on earth, Habby?" I began, in unfeigned surprise; but he had whirled himself away from my bed, grinding his teeth, tugging savagely at his hair, and saying, as if to himself, unconscious of my presence, "You most miserable mouse! You detestable molecule, atom, animalcule!"

ly selfish—and, great heavens, what have I got to be selfish about?—as deformed and despicable inside as I am out. A poor, pitiful, sneaking, contemptible—"

"I am ashamed of you!" I said, with authority, for I understood him by this time. "You are a man. You are a man of splen-

SETTING HIS TEETH, AND CLUTCHING AT HIS HAIR.

"For Heaven's sake, Habersham, what do you mean?" I demanded.

"Don't be a blockhead and pretend you don't know," he said, impatiently, standing at the window, his back to me. "As if you don't see! If there is an animal I do detest and despise, it is a mean, miserable, intense-

did talent. Don't tell me a falsehood, Habersham, and make believe you do not know it. Governor Hone knows it. The whole Archimedean Institute knew it, as you know very well. God knows it, and that is the whole reason he led me—ask father if I'm not right—into finding that coal, so that you might finish your education and serve him so! You are—"

"Can't you understand?" he interrupted me. "Who's talking about talent? That dirty M'Callum was talented. It's the unspeakable moral meanness! Thinking eternally and exclusively of myself. You caring all the time for me, and I never caring one cent for you. You most miserable louse!" with a fresh clutch upon his hair, and I heard a suppressed anathema from between his teeth.

Upon which I laughed so heartily that Mabel Patterson knocked and put her head in to see if I had called for any thing. But I thought it my duty, and read Habby a good lecture upon his impatience and distrust, and utter want of faith toward God. I don't know whether he listened to me or not, for he said no more, still standing at the window and looking out. When I had said all I could think of, he merely said, "Good-bye, Carter," and was going when I called him back. I had set my heart upon telling them at home all about the coal-mine; but I knew what a pleasure it would be to him to do so, and I begged him to do it.

"But be sure, Habby," I said, "not to exaggerate our prospects. It is only a speculation as yet. We are confident, but not certain. And it must not be mentioned out of the house. That's all. Good-bye."

I confess I was most sincerely gratified at Habersham's thoughtfulness. Instead of telling them, he almost frightened my mother to death, by saying to her, on his return, hurrying past her to his room with a pale face, that I wanted to see her and my father immediately.

What good it did me to tell them when they came in, so eager and anxious about me! My dear mother heard me all through, her hand upon my forehead, saying all she had to say in her bright tears and her silent kisses. My father had been plucked away, somewhat abruptly, from the middle of a sermon he was writing, and, while he was very glad indeed, I confess I was disappointed a little. He never did, somehow he never could, attach its natural value to money. A more enthusiastic man in regard to a mission-school, a reforming drunkard, an in-

quiring skeptic, a series of sermons, and the like, it is impossible to imagine, full of ardor and hope as a boy. But about money, unless it was to give to some society or destitute individual or other, it was hopeless, the idea of arousing in him any enthusiasm whatever. I had thought that he would rub his hands together, as he used to do in talking about his work in the penitentiary, or about some protracted meeting, and walk up and down the room, glowing and smiling, and full of hopeful suggestion; but he did nothing of the sort on this occasion. He was happy, of course; that he was always.

"I am glad, Carter, very glad, my dear boy," he said at last. "It is very noble in you. But if Habersham is not going into the ministry, he has education enough. If . it please God to turn his heart that way, I will be as glad as the rest of you. I would joyfully make any sacrifice to enable him to do that. We will see, will see." And he was gone to rekindle, if possible, the cinde of his sermon, which he had left cooling ɛ this time upon his study-table.

But it did not matter. As soon as he wɛ gone my mother settled herself down besi⟨ me, and we had a good, long, joyful, tho. oughly sensible talk over our plans. H⟨ dear face was clouded but once. It wa when I said, in the haphazard mention of fifty other things,

"You think I am wild in what I said to you about putting Archy in her hands. You just wait."

In her judgment that was too absurd a matter for discussion, and she left me, with a kiss, to send Virginia. My sister was but a later edition, so to speak, of my mother, and took, when she came, as quietly as did my mother, all my glowing declarations of the home I hoped soon to buy for the family, the watches and dresses for Georgia and herself. I do not know how it happened that I got to talking, in the headway of my happiness, about Dr. Grex. I told her what a sterling, sensible man he was, notwithstanding his profanity, infidelity, and boorishness in general. I had just done describing to my sister his ideas about our being nothing but matter, mere walking clocks, admirably constructed automata, when in came the man himself. If it had not been that the way from my father's house to Mr. Patterson's lay past his office, I would have wondered at his knowing so well when Virginia happened to be visiting me. Somehow, of late, as surely as she came he was certain to drop in too. On this occasion he had left his queer cap in the hall, knocked before he came in, had left Charles behind him, and did not swear, although fully as bold and independent in his manner as ever. I knew I could depend upon his discretion, and in as few words as possible I told him, too, about our coal discoveries. I think he had taken a sort of off-hand liking to me before, and we were soon at home with each other, especially as he had made a half apology to Virginia when he first came in for his unintentioned discourtesy during their previous meetings. He seemed somewhat annoyed when I told him that I had just been telling my sister about his materialism. One thing, however, led to another until, in defense of '·'s views, he grew warm and warmer, and ·· became downright rude and violent in s earnestness.

"You have been educated to believe in ·od and the soul," he said at last. "You ·ever reason or experiment at all. It is all ·ure prejudice and bigotry." And there·pon he launched out into ridicule and de·nunciation of the idea of future punishment, which was, by-the-bye, wholly irrelevant to his argument.

I never saw Virginia to such advantage before. She was standing when he came in, and remained standing, although Dr. Grex had seated himself on the other side of my bed. She was as calm as a May morning, and as bright; half the force of what she said, and she said little in comparison with him, lying in the modest yet serene confidence of her manner and tones.

I can not even attempt to give an outline of the conversation, which must have lasted for hours, growing more and more earnest. At last my sister had to go.

"What do we know of God?" she said. "Look at the six thousand years of suffering by reason of sin in this world, and who can say it will not be so in the next if sin is there too? All we know is that God loves us so well, he gave his Son to suffer and die with and for us. Our business is

to love and serve our Saviour now. When we get into the other world, he will explain every thing to us."

"Do you know what the judgment-day is for? I will tell you," Dr. Grex said, without waiting for a reply. "It is not we who will be on trial then. It is God himself, granting there is a God. That is the day he has appointed to apologize to his wretched creatures for the horrible way in which he has treated them, heh?"

"One thing is very plain," Virginia added, as she drew on her gloves composedly, "which is, that you have no clear or settled idea about it whatever. You say in the same breath that we will be at the judgment, and that we are nothing but machines, have no souls; that all there is of God is force and law, and then that God will be on trial and apologize. I'm glad I heard you, Dr. Grex," she added, smiling; "before this I thought infidelity was something to be feared. I thought it could advance some strong and terrible arguments. I never dreamed it was as wild and unsettled and foolish as it was wicked. You will excuse me, sir," Virginia said, with a smile, "but I am astonished. It is not the head, Dr. Grex, it is the heart that is foolish, because it is wicked. You really despise your own arguments as much as I do. Excuse my plainness; and—good-morning."

It was Queen Elizabeth treading like a queen upon the velvet cloak of Sir Walter, spread upon the mire before her, with the exception that, in this instance, it was Sir Walter himself upon whom the dainty foot was placed as she walked out of the room.

"I only did it, you know," Dr. Grex said to me, his whole person as rumpled and discomposed, so to speak, as was his abundance of black hair, "to see how she would look and speak when aroused. She may be right, for all I know. But what," he added, with a startling contempt for me in his manner, "do *you* know about it?"

Habersham was off to college before we had fully realized that he really and truly was to go. He had set a time to come and tell me good-bye, but he never came. Instead of doing so, he wrote to me as soon as he could after leaving, and a very curt note it was, that I would know why he had rath-

9

er not. So he went, it did not matter to me. As to our coal speculation, let me say here, that the first joyous surprise about it over, there was small romance connected with it.

Of course, the papers made a great to-do over the matter, Mr. Patterson and myself becoming the heroes of the hour. But there was a world of slow, hard, discouraging, expensive work to be done before the least returns could be come at. In fact, every tinge of romance was soon gone out of it, and our mine became nothing but a business in which the only thing to be done was to toil away steadily and patiently.

CHAPTER XXI.

As soon as I was able to leave my bed—and, in fact, a good deal before — for I had become exceedingly impatient thereof—I got Major Hampton to remove me in one of his hacks to my father's house. Archibald had taken possession of Habersham's room, which, for the sake of poor Habby, was by far the sunniest of the two allotted to us boys; and I was once more in that which I occupied before Habby went to college. But ages seemed to have rolled away since I was last there.

"What a little bit of a boy I was when I was here last!" I said to my mother in that first good long talk we had together on the evening of my return, after, I remember, she had got back from prayer-meeting with my father; for it was Wednesday night.

"You were always like a grown man, Carter," my mother replied. "You have more than your share of age. Virginia, Georgia, Archibald, each in a very different way, inherit your father's perpetual youth. You know there is not a person who is freer from levity than he is. The last man any one of his most intimate friends would think of taking a liberty with, yet he is as playful now as he was that afternoon he danced the breakdown for me in the old orchard, just before we were married."

"I doubt whether he ever passed," I said, "one of the children in his life without pulling us by the ear or pinching us. I am sure I never happened near him, when he was shaving, without getting a touch of the lathering-brush upon my face!"

"Do you know," my mother added, with a blush and a laugh, "for a dozen years after we were married, your father pinched me so that it was almost a martyrdom. It is his eager, restless, overflowing energy. But his purity and glowing hopefulness and habitual refusal to look upon any other than the bright side—all his child-likeness is because the chief and most constant feeling he has is of companionship with God, as a child with its father. He is full of hope, now that Archibald has settled down with Mr. Clarkson at last, to become an apothecary who will astonish St. Charles. I do hope," my mother added, as I smiled in spite of myself, because she looked so steadily at me—"I do sincerely hope, Carter, that you have forgotten that absurd notion of yours in connection with Archibald. The very idea!" she added, indignantly.

"And how do Virginia and Mr. Clarkson come on?" I asked; for I had my reasons for not wishing to speak further in regard to my oldest brother.

"It is positively ridiculous," my mother said, laughing. "What a good, patient, much-enduring man he is! Two or three nights in the week he is sure to be in the parlor, silent, smiling, devoted. Virginia comes and goes in and out, hardly excuses herself, plays and sings at the piano, converses with other company, does her sewing, embroidering, whatever it is, as if he were a sofa-cushion or a fleecy poodle. If she can but think of something for Mr. Clarkson to do for her down-town next day, or if it is merely to hold a skein of silk for her to wind while he sits, it is all he cares for. But it is disgraceful," said my mother, with energy, "the manner in which Georgia conducts herself toward him. She is positively rude. You have heard us say, Carter, that when she undresses for the night she always throws her pins on the floor. I have never been able to break her of it, and she treats poor, patient Mr. Clarkson in the same way. She makes fun of him to his face, ridicules Jenny for his devotion to her in his presence. I had actually to threaten her, when he was in the room, to send her out of the parlor!"

"And what about General M'Neil?" I asked.

"It is *too* absurd!" my mother laughed, having a mother's pleasure, too, in what she was about to add. "He gave his first attentions to Virginia, but seems to have transferred them to Georgia. What a grand old soul he is, Carter! He reminds me so of the dear old days long, long ago; he is such a stately, yet simple cavalier. The general is a great admirer of Sir Philip Sidney, but as true a gentleman, under all his affectations, as Mrs. President is a lady under all her mannerisms. I used to think that it must take him hours to dress before he comes to our house. I wondered if he did not write out and memorize what he says there. Governor Hone tells me, however, that he is just as grave and oratorical in all he says to people around him in the court-house; that he is far more solemn and stately than all three of the judges rolled into one. It is his nature; and he is so generous and noble, and above all suspicion of meanness, that it is impossible not to esteem him. It is steadying Georgia. The mere fact that, despairing of Virginia, he is laying siege to her—it frightens her, for the first time in her life; and I am glad of it.

"And how is Cosma Adams doing in her studies?" I ask of my mother, with some hesitation, as she rises to go; for more than once my father has called to her from their room, "My dear Agnes, it is later than you think."

"In a moment, my dear," my mother replied to my father, and something very like a groan was heard in answer to that; for well did my father know what a moment meant when my mother and myself were talking together at that hour.

"Wonderfully well," she continued to me. "Miss Praxley is making a hobby of her, teaching her every thing in regard to dress and society. It happens very well for the poor child, for Mrs. Governor Hone is a moth-er to her family, and nothing else. The governor is proud of the fact that his Sukey, as he calls her, is exactly like the mother he had in the old log-cabin. They were the first settlers here, you know. 'There were about a dozen of us,' he told me, 'white-headed boys and girls. My mother,' he said, 'was a good, sensible Christian woman. No woman's rights about her. She clothed her husband and children, managed the negro women, whipped us boys soundly when we needed it, saw that we had plenty of milk and mush and molasses; and that,' he said, 'was all I wanted Sukey to be.' I am vexed," my mother added, suddenly, "that Habersham has begun writing to Cosma Adams. The first letter after he left was to her. It is just like those talented people, so utterly ignorant of the world. Cosma is a simple country-girl, improving very fast, I dare say. But look at her round, full face, and at her unsophisticated blue eyes, opening so wide. She is a dear, good child, and who knows what nonsense Habby has in his head, and may put in hers? She brought me his letter. It was full of high-flown sentiment about the pleasures of travel. She could understand it little more than her Pink could, the cow you are always teasing her about, Carter."

The truth is, my mother enjoyed her talks with me as much as I did. She seemed glad to lay aside her parlor caution, so to speak, her perpetual prudence and watchfulness upon herself, and to be, as it were, a girl again. My father was so full of his sermons and parish plans, and, in some way, she felt more at home with me than with her girls even; certainly she never looked quite so young and beautiful in parlor or church as sitting upon the edge of my bed, talking to me, while she "did up" her hair for the night.

"My dear child, you do not know how *very* late it is," came from my father's room. "I have a sermon to write to-morrow, and I want to go to sleep."

"In one moment more, my dear," my mother called back. "I wanted to say to you, Carter," she said, as she kissed me, "be very guarded about Mabel Patterson, my dear boy. She loves you devotedly. Hush, hush! Unless you can love her in return, you must be very careful not to lead her to think so. She is very pretty, of a very deep and determined character. Her father has acted so that I have not seen much of her for years, but I fear she is too much like her father, Carter. Good-night. It makes matters worse your being in business with him. God bless you, my dear boy," coming back to kiss me again. "Remember, Carter, you are our reliance," and I could hear through the closed doors the murmured remonstrance of her husband at her keeping him awake so long. That was one peculiarity of my father. He was very fond of porter and brown stout at dinner, but gave it up cheerfully and utterly, as he had given up the decanter of brandy from his table at an earlier stage of the temperance reformation. No man could like a smoke in his study, to compose his mind before going into the pulpit, more than he did; but he had given that up just before coming to St. Charles, for the Master's sake. On his evangelistic tours among the rougher portions of the country, he gave up a looking-glass to shave by, since it was often not to be had. It required a rigid watch upon the part of my mother, or he would have parted with all his next-best clothing to needy applicants, as he did his money; and most gladly would he have given his life at the stake, had there been any Diocletian to demand it, for the Master. But the one thing he could not do without was sleep. No man ever had guests more habitually at his board, and a more genial host you could not desire; yet, the wants of every child at table first seen to by him, there was a certain quick eagerness of his hands with knife and fork, even in the pauses of the use thereof, while he told some anecdote, which was as peculiar to the man as is its tremulousness to the aspen-leaf. Like every man in full work and perfect health, my father thoroughly enjoyed his meals; yet he could and did live, when circumstances required it, on the coarsest fare—a "corn johnny-cake" as much enjoyed by him as the sugar-cured ham or the browned turkey; but he could not live without his full supply of sleep, which he arose from in the morning as one arises from a banquet. I do know that a holier man never lived, nor a man less like an anchorite. He possessed the fullest and

rosiest vigor of bodily enjoyment, in harmonious keeping with a spiritual life as steady and strong. Especially in public prayer he would rise to heaven in adoring communion, at times so seraphic as to bear up with him the intellect, if not the heart, of every hearer, and it was his splendid bodily as well as spiritual health which enabled him to do so, as with the unwearying ease of a child at play.

"We will have bodies as well as souls," he used to say, "in heaven, and we will enjoy God and heaven, which will be simply the entire universe of the Creator thrown open to us forever, with body as well as soul. And why not now? We will do without sleep there; but," he would add, "that is one of my great weaknesses: I must have plenty of sleep here. I can do without every thing but that."

I was entirely mended as to my bones by the time Habby had settled to his studies in college. Mr. Patterson said it happened that one of his clerks was leaving about that time; but I think he helped it to happen. We had from our Southern dealers, for sale on commission, cotton, hemp, a little sugar, hides, corn from up the river in flat-boats; tobacco, which Mr. Patterson denounced incessantly and bitterly, yet made excellent commissions upon; flour, wheat in bulk, and the like. From our Northern correspondents we had iron and steel, all sorts of farm and plantation implements; shoes (especially brogans for the negroes), cotton cloth in all its varieties; and "notions," which we accepted with a sneer, and sold, when we could, with a scoff. Whisky came to us from both sides, and was a staple, in a sense, superior to that of corn or wheat. We did not do a regular business in negroes, for the negro-trader was almost as heartily despised with us as he was at the North; contempt with us being the leading flavor of our regard for such, as hatred was, I suppose, the chief feeling in reference to them at the North. If, however, a "likely boy" could be worked in by way of exchange, say, for a good threshing-machine, well, why not? A correspondent of a dozen years' standing got to be an old friend. Suppose such a planter had a stout boy of thirty years old, who would run away, a distiller, you know, could see what *he* could do with him by letting his master have through us so many barrels of whisky in barter.

"A stout negro is worth a thousand of such," I remember saying one day of a patent steel grist-mill we had just received from the North.

"Why?" demanded Mr. Patterson, somewhat sourly.

"God made the one." I thought myself quite sharp in adding, promptly, "and a Yankee made the other!"

"Bah! nonsense!" he said, in his abrupt manner, turning away. There was something in his air then, which I had observed whenever negroes were the topic, that thrilled me with a deadly, sickening suspicion, that he might be inclined in his secret heart to Abolitionism! But no; such a suspicion was too horrible, and I cast it out of my mind precisely as I would have done an idea that he had murdered some one. Nor do I think I could have imagined such a thing, if it had not been for his absurd hatred of tobacco.

I knew from the first that my work would be hard and unceasing, poorly paid, and with very slow promotion; and it was worse in every sense than I had supposed. Holidays for clerks were no more dreamed of then than were sewing-machines, or the abolition of slavery; and, Sunday excepted, it was as steady a strain upon me as is its boat to a canal-horse—all uphill, and neither halt nor downhill; which did not matter, however, for I possessed perfect health, and enjoyed hard work. But, in comparison with all this, the moment I came to the matter of my association with Cosma and Mabel, it was as if I stepped off a cliff of rock into the realm of rolling clouds.

I can continue my narrative much more easily and clearly by saying, as I have said before, that, while I could not but respect and admire, and very highly esteem, Mabel Patterson, I did not, and could not, love her. By reason of my long confinement under her roof, as well as having often to call there in the course of business after I got well, I had become intimately acquainted with her; and, the more I saw of her, it was more and more impossible but that I should esteem and appreciate a girl of her growing and

strengthening character. It was not that her father had given her the best education St. Charles afforded, nor that she had slowly developed from a crude, violent, ill-regulated, because motherless, girl into a silent, quiet young lady who impressed you with the belief that her purposes were as deep and as determined, if not as dark, as her eyes. What hurt me most was a certain fearful silence and shrinking from me which I never observed in her toward others. During the sessions of the Legislature her house was thronged, and with some of the most desirable men in the State, for Mr. Patterson was as rich as she was beautiful. In fact, as I could not help observing, she had plenty of offers.

"Lawyers," I would say to myself, in my room, of an evening, "doctors, merchants in business for themselves, young politicians sure to go to Congress, men a thousand times handsomer, more educated, richer, more refined, more desirable every way. And all because she happened to take a foolish liking to you when she was too young to know better, and because you upset that drunken legislator in the mud, and afterward got hurt for her by that detestable hogshead of sugar. You scoundrel!" (I would fall for an instant into Habby's way of thinking), and say to and of myself, making a clutch for my hair. But I would end it all by going off into a peal of laughter, and that would be as suddenly halted by my being ashamed of myself, with burning cheeks, that I was such a conceited ass as to suppose Mabel really liked me, when the probability was she cared nothing for me at all. In the midst of it all, I would drop off suddenly and soundly to sleep; for we worked very hard in her father's store.

I was madly and miserably in love with Cosma Adams, that's a fact! What is more, I was more wretchedly in love with her every time I saw her, and she never would understand me as she ought, because I had joked, and teased her so about Pink and Zeus and Bran. Then there were those long, rhetorical letters coming to her from Habersham, full of the glories and the grandeurs of he himself did not know what. He was everlastingly recommending this book and that, and there were pages on pages of his own poetry, glowing with his aspirations and all the rest! She did not care to see me, I do believe, except to talk to me about what he had written. "Oh, Mr. Carter," she told me one day, "just to think! He says I am the first to know it, but his letter yesterday was all about his having finally resolved to be a minister. He has such splendid talents, and he says it is such a glorious calling. I wonder you are content to sell sugar and tobacco and things; but, then—" And Cosma checked herself, and looked at me with a kind of divine pity in her eyes, the clear eyes of an infant.

"You have none of his talent," she meant. Of course, I understood. How incessantly the words about Paul rang in my ears while she talked! "His bodily presence is weak, and his speech contemptible; but his letters are weighty and powerful." I hope I may be forgiven, I could almost have laid hold upon her and shaken her! No, but I could have taken that miserable mite of a Habby, and dropped him down the mouth of our coal-mine! Not at all; it was myself that I was enraged with.

I am relating all this in a very confused manner; but the truth is, I was amazed at Habersham, and may have (not intending it the moment before) said something to Cosma the evening she told me about my brother becoming a minister, to undo any

effect Habby was producing upon her. It was mean in me to do it in his absence, very mean. I suppose I was so much in earnest that I did not hear a ring at the door; but I heard Mrs. Brown tell my mother afterward that Mabel Patterson was in the hall at the time waiting to see Virginia, but had come softly down into the kitchen to beg Mrs. Brown to excuse her to Virginia, and had gone home out of the side-door. "She looked so pale from her walk," said Mrs. Brown, "that I begged her to rest till I got some cake; but she wouldn't, and went." The next day Mr. Patterson remarked at the store, incidentally, that Mabel had gone to spend a month with relatives in the adjoining State. Candor constrains me to add that I was at this time exceedingly disagreeable in my bearing in business. I am generally downright in manner, and apt to enforce upon other people my own convictions, and pretty vigorously, since they are, right or wrong, very clear and decided. A good deal of a bear I am, I fear, as hirsute folk often are; but I must have been so to an extraordinary degree at that time.

"Wuss nor the old man iver dared to be," was the way in which Mike phrased it. But I left all that at the store. I never carried it home. Not that I was more amiable there, but, in part, at least, because I knew how well my mother and sisters would guess why I was so cross.

CHAPTER XXII.

I SAID, a chapter or two ago, that there was with us a brief period during which the planting of the manifold seeds of things was done eagerly, energetically, and all at once. Following upon this there was a long period of comparative inaction, during which the varied germs developed and grew as of themselves. When, however, the crop ripened, it was as if in a tremendous hurry again, and all at once.

There was, for instance, that affair of Archibald's. For a wonder, he had made himself, so far, contented behind the scales in Mr. Clarkson's drug-store. And no man could have gone into the establishment and not have been struck with the appearance of my brother. Had you bought an alleviative of him, in the agonies of the toothache while you did so, you could not but have said to yourself of my brother, "What on earth are *you* doing here?" Tall, with very black hair and beard, his eyes brilliant, erect and graceful in bearing, power and meaning in every motion, the man was utterly out of place: the bar or the pulpit seemed his true sphere. We all knew it could not last long. If Mr. Clarkson had not been the roundest, smoothest, easiest of good-humored employers, Archibald, tired out although he was for the present with the perversity of the world toward him, would not have remained so long. I had thought of obtaining settled work for him as manager of our coal-works, which were slowly but steadily becoming a valuable property; but Mr. Patterson would not listen to it for an instant. An intensely practical man himself, his aversion to my talented but impracticable brother was very great. So far it had taken every dollar of my share of the profits to repay Mr. Patterson's advance when Habersham left, and it was all I could do to get money enough to keep Habby supplied, expenses at college being so much greater than we had supposed. So morbid was he, that he "could not endure to be hustled about by the mob," as he termed it, at the college libraries, and we had, therefore, to supply him with means to buy every book he used. I was glad to do all I could for Habby. It was very rarely he wrote to anybody unless it was to Cosma Adams; but we knew in many ways that he was regarded as a genius.

"No man has ever taken," a professor of the institution wrote to my father, "one hundred in grade since Aaron Burr graduated. Unless his health gives way, your son may do this. Certainly, we regard him as the most decided genius we have had since Burr. What a pity he is of such an unsocial and morbid nature!"

I winced sometimes at the shabbiness of my best suit, especially when calling upon Cosma Adams, in regard to whose opinion I was growing wonderfully sensitive; but when I thought what a man my brother was to be, I had a pleasure in making any sacrifice for him beyond all that my money could otherwise have brought me. I am afraid Mr. Patterson told Mabel; but no one else, in my father's house even, knew how much it took to keep Habby comfortable. It gave a new sacredness, however, to the matter that, in reply to an urgent correspondence upon the part of my father, Habersham had intimated of late, as to Cosma, that he might become a minister.

I have wandered from Archy. My mother scoffed at a certain plan of mine in reference to him to such a degree that I never spoke again about it to her, and she thought I had abandoned the, to her, absurd idea; but I thought then, as I think now, that the one thing to do with Archibald was to— I declare that I intended, up to writing that last word, to have said frankly what my plan was. I believe I will wait. I will say merely this, that my scheme was a thoroughly sensible one, if it was startling. Certainly, no human being knew of it except the three most vitally interested. But, oh, the hard work it took! Sincerely, I do not believe any poet toiled harder at an epic, such delicacy of treatment as well as energy of imagination was required. I know you say, "Why not tell us the whole thing, and be done with it?" It would be best; but I can not, unless it be to say that Metternich himself never had diplomacy more difficult upon his hands. Metternich was, so to speak, Austria itself when in act of treating with, we will say, France. In this case the diplomate represented nobody but himself, and I had to treat with an Austria on the one side, and a France on the other, each far more willful and unreliable than any Austria or France that ever existed. Let us say no more about it just now. I will simply add that, hard as we worked down at the store, that work was not a circumstance compared to that which the matter I am speaking of required at my hands.

Events were rapidly ripening as the months rolled away. Yes, and as the swift years passed on. It is out of the question trying to give the dates or seasons of the year. As to recording here the conversations, that, also, is impracticable; I could not begin to do so with any accuracy; besides, one is too impatient to tarry long enough. Moreover, all the various threads of our family matters were so unceasingly crossing and recrossing while the weaving of the family history was going on, that you can not detach the one from the other for a moment.

There was, for instance, the singular affair of Dr. Grex and Virginia. I have told how he was struck down at my bedside by Virginia's beauty. Not that it was so extraordinary. She did not equal my mother, in my eyes, but she was to Dr. Grex the most wonderful young lady he had ever met, in virtue of being, I dare say, unlike those with whom he had been associated before —a type of loveliness wholly new to him. The love of Mr. Clarkson for Virginia was an ardent but (and because she was what she was) an absurd and laughable affair. The more devoted it was, that much the more ridiculous it seemed.

Dr. Grex was to Mr. Clarkson as Don Quixote was to Sancho Panza, strong, angular, determined, violent : the doctor, I am fain to add, with none of the knight's exquisite courtesy. He confined his insanity, like the Don, to one mania. With the Don it was the delusion of believing that he belonged to a past age of chivalry, which never existed. On the other hand, Dr. Grex believed in himself as the cavalier of a future chivalry—the chivalry of an age when Christianity will have descended into the tombs of all the dead religions, and the positive, actual, material will be the only thing in which men will believe or for which they will care. Glorying in being in advance of his times, Christianity was the caitiff giant at which the surgeon was forever riding. It was part of the rough independence of his character; for, in the South in those days, infidelity and abolitionism were one, and those who held such opinions were usually too prudent to express them. To be an infidel was to be all that was low, coarse, vulgar; there was the smell of whisky in it, the rattle of dice, the scandal and wrangle of divorce, and all uncleanness. Nothing but the extraordinary reputation of Dr. Grex as a surgeon enabled him to survive the odium belonging to the word, people classifying his unbelief as part of his roughness and eccentricity. Nothing less than his desperate affection for Virginia would have driven him to visit at our house over all the barriers which he knew to exist.

"You say that Christians are dogmatic," I remember Virginia saying to him one evening after he had become a frequent visitor, "as if any body could be as dogmatic as you are, in the opposite direction. You say we are bigoted. Dr. Grex, you are the most bigoted person in your unbelief that I ever knew. We read about the

Chinese, and their conviction that every body else is a barbarian; and all you lack, sir, of being as foolish—excuse me—is a pair of white shoes, and a cue of hair down your back. I have read of the pope regarding himself as infallible; and there you sit and speak about Christians as if you were talking about insects, as serenely infallible as if *you* were a pope!" My sister never said any thing violently, for her charm lay in her serenity; but I am satisfied the doctor often broached the subject, in order to see the color come into her cheeks, and her soul into her eyes. I wondered at it, for, tough as he was, he could not but wince under the scorn; or, still harder to bear, her womanly pity as for a man who was deformed. But, then, the doctor's deformity was in her view a something of his own wicked doing, and the pity was very like anger. Virginia could not remember the day when our religion was not the chief, as it was the most certain, thing of our lives — the one cause of all that was good and loving in her father and mother, and all of us. It was to her as if Dr. Grex had asserted that the sun had no existence, or was but a lump of mud thrown into the air, for the instant, from the wheel of a passing carriage. Oh, the power of that serene and sweet and absolute certainty!

"I dare say you sincerely think so," Dr. Grex would reply, passing his long fingers through his already thoroughly rumpled hair; "but I am a man of plain common sense. I have taken to pieces every square inch of the human body. I find men are only more finely organized cats and dogs. I never found any more soul in a man than you find in a frog. So of the earth under you, it is made up of so much soil, metal, rock; and all the stars of heaven are only varieties of this globe. There are all sorts of laws and forces at work here, in the same way, for ever and ever. It's the same, so far as the microscope or the telescope shows, everywhere. If there is any soul or any God, I never met them. All humbug!" added Dr. Grex, with violence. "Heh?"

"Do you look me in the face?" my sister replied, standing by the piano at which she had been playing, and looking down upon the surgeon who was seated on the music-

stool, whirling himself upon its screw, now to this side, now to that, with his long legs spread out, restless and uncouth. "Do you dare to sit there and tell me that I am only a kind of cat?" It was not the lovely color in her face as she said it, nor the modulations of her quiet tones, nor the exquisite carriage of her person which she had inherited from our mother; it was the soul in the woman asserting itself. The doctor ceased unconsciously from his restlessness, and gazed full in her face. It was indescribable. For the first time in his life the possibility of there being, indeed, an immortal soul, at least in her case—an imperial something in the body, but wholly superior to its mechanism of bones and muscles— the fact, and the certainty of the fact, broke upon him. All his association with people had been of a merely bodily kind before, nothing beyond the smart and sharp, often desperate, exhibition of mere humor or good-fellowship, greed or cunning, ambition or anger; things common to animals of all grades; things of which the mere mechanism and ganglia of the nerves common to all were adequate cause. But in the face of this woman was a sudden revelation of a something separated by a bridgeless chasm from all that — a soul which his own soul recognized as with a sudden bound.

"And do you tell me," Virginia continued, in her eagerness not even flushing under the intensity of his gaze, "that any other than God could make *me!*" And then, as her excitement sobered down, and the blushes began to come, "Dr. Grex," she said, "please do not think me rude, but I can not endure to talk with you any more this evening. Excuse me, please," and she had left the room. There was nothing for the doctor to do but to get his queer cap in the hall, go home, and comfort himself by finding the negation and denial of all he had seen in Virginia in the contemplation of Charles, his boy, as stolid as he was black.

"If men," he muttered to himself, however, as he went to his office, "have, as the Bible says, been convinced that there is another world after this, and a God, by the appearing to them of an angel, I don't see why it may not be so in my case. Of course, I don't pretend that I know for certain every thing in the universe. I don't believe it; but, for what I know, there *may* be a soul and a God. People always have thought so, and everywhere. Heh? Oh, hang it, never mind!"

And this was but one of many interviews between Dr. Grex and Jenny. There would determined than himself. Virginia regarded the doctor as being, in some senses, the manliest of men; yet, when the everlasting theme came up, as it always did, she felt herself, and instantly, to be immeasurably his superior. What confirmed her therein was that she was aware that he knew it also.

"DO YOU LOOK ME IN THE FACE?"

be a firm resolve upon the part of both that religion should not be mentioned; but, almost without exception, it would come up every time, and in every case the visit was hurried thereby to a rapid and premature ending; for the surgeon, for the first time in his experience, had found a person more

"What I know," she would say to him, "I know partly, as you yourself do, from the instinct of my immortal nature; more clearly and certainly still, I am confident of it from a revelation assuring me even if I doubted. The actual fact, Dr. Grex, is that you shrink as much, in this matter, from yielding to your own nature, as you do from yielding to revelation. And you know it!" her eyes full in his.

"May I be shot," Dr. Grex would anathematize himself as he left the house, "if I talk upon the subject with her again! It always ends in making her seem an angel and me a cur. The fact is, I never will enter that house again, unless somebody there breaks his neck and sends for me!" Which resolve was always sealed with an oath; but within the month he was sure to be there again, and there was a repetition of the same old story.

It was about this time that there raged in St. Charles a singular epidemic for giving parties; such a mania as has made the very mention of a party a mockery there to this day. The beginning was with Governor Hone. For many weeks an ever-deepening gloom seemed to be settling down upon the city, and especially upon our church. Without any apparent cause, people said, "How miserably dull and disagreeable every thing is!" No one took his usual interest in his business or his children, or cared to call the one upon the other. Never were matters quite so uninteresting in Sunday-school and church. All the week my father looked forward to his Sabbath-afternoon service in the penitentiary as the oasis of the world to him just then.

"It is dreadful, governor," Miss Praxley said, one evening to his excellency; "it is a sort of social ague. You can positively see the green scum of our stagnation in the faces of the people. Look at Cosma, if you doubt it. Was ever any pond as stupid? If it goes on, people will be committing suicide or something. Come, Governor Glorious—" for Miss Praxley had a new name for every body—"you are the man to stop it. What is the use of your being governor if you don't do something?"

"Very true, Miss Praxley," said the governor, gallantly. "I create you secretary of state. Write out a proclamation that people must stop being so dull, and must be as bright as Miss Praxley, or go to the penitentiary. I'll sign it. Or it shall be a proclamation for a fast-day or a thanksgiving, as you please."

"Like the Yankees. No, sir," replied Miss Praxley, who was singularly full of restless liveliness these last few weeks, her eyes and little curls about her forehead in as incessant motion as her tongue and fingers. "I tell you! This is the very idea. Make Mrs. Motherly here—for they were at the table —give a party."

"Exactly," the governor hastened to reply. "Sukey, I do wish you would. Georgia Quarterman will take Squashy and a dozen or two of the other children out of the way. Cosma, what do you say? If you will roll up your sleeves, Miss Praxley, and help."

"It will aid him to go to Washington again," Miss Praxley urged upon Mrs. Hone. "Come, madame la mère, do consent!" And Mrs. Hone, startled at being styled a mare, did consent. But it was not until after the governor had kissed her, and called her, in the strict privacy of their nursery, his "dear old Sukey" a good many times; for, polished gentleman as he was in Washington and in company, no plainer old planter ever lived than he when in the bosom of his household. That was the way the parties began. But, once begun, it seemed as if they never would cease. Pulpy Mr. Clemming had one. Major Hampton had one, and insisted upon my father remaining to the end, and closing with prayer. Mrs. Colonel Archer gave one, although we all knew that the colonel could not afford it "just then." The largest was that at Mr. Patterson's, and Mabel astonished us all by the dignity of her demeanor as hostess. There must have been fifty of them, great and small, before the epidemic ceased. But the whole season culminated at the house of Mrs. President; after hers, the wave, so to speak, steadily rolled down and out, although a wearisomely long time it was in doing so.

"I do wish, Mr. Broadshoulders," Miss Praxley said to me, at the opening of Mrs. President's party, and as part of "breaking the ice" of the same—"do wish you would tell me which it is."

"Which what is?" I asked, although I knew so well what she meant.

"Look at her," Miss Praxley said, with a motion of her chin in that direction. I had been looking that way before. It was Miss Mabel Patterson to whom she alluded. I suppose it was some skillful combination of the colors of her dress, but a more brilliant and beautiful brunette it was hard to imagine. Quite a knot of gentlemen, friends of Mrs. President's, from Washington, were grouped about her, and what a contempt I had for the brass buttons of certain military youth among them!"

"I do not like Mabel," Miss Praxley said; "she is too set in her ways, too prejudiced and desperately determined; but how can she help being like her father, especially as her poor mother was, they say, snubbed to death by him when she was a child? But it gives her that perfect ease of manner. Those Washington people never met a more charming belle. You had better look out, Mr. Booby."

"Miss Mabel is a most estimable and beautiful girl," I said, in a dignified way, for I did not like Miss Praxley's freedom. "I rarely see her, however. She is absent from the city most of her time, off among her relatives. Her father is very little company for her—"

"Carter Quarterman," Miss Praxley said, laying her gloved hand on mine, "there is one thing you are dying to have me do for you. Perhaps. And I will hunt him up if I can find him here to-night. But you attend to your own business. Quarterman, indeed! You are not a tenth of a man. Knowing all that you do," she added, with her eyes upon my face, which began to burn; "your name ought to begin with a big F, and have two o's and an l for the rest of it! I'm going to look for him," she added, as she left me.

Little I cared, for at the moment Cosma Adams passed in the thickening crowd, and I rose and joined her. Cosma Adams! Of course, I know that a skilled artisan can take a handful of clay, and mold and make it into a vase which shall be as exquisite in its beauty as a poem. Yes, and I know that our Master can pick out of the filth of the hovel the vilest beggar's brat, and make it into the purest of Christians on earth, to be the loveliest, at last, of saints in heaven. But you can not understand the change in Cosma, dear reader, not having known her when she came to St. Charles from her log-cabin, in a linsey-woolsey dress, with hair browned

by the sun and tangled by the winds; face freckled and vacant; eyes as empty of meaning as eyes could be, without being those of an idiot! It was a pity we lived so close to Governor Hone's; we could not help knowing the poor child well. Good Mrs. Brown took a fancy to her, and Mrs. Brown's cakes down-stairs were to Cosma like the delicacies of paradise; but the idea of Cosma ever becoming an associate for any of us —for any other than Squashy, in fact—never occurred to any one. Yet, out of that material had emerged this Cosma Adams! Of course, the statue was in the marble at first, or all the chopping-away of Phidias would not have formed it; but what reminder of the child she had been was there in this charming girl, in the full bloom of her fair face, in the beauty of her great blue eyes? And yet there was such reminder in the child-like simplicity wherein lay her greatest beauty at last. Yes, I was in love with her, madly and miserably in love with her, and, as usual, either she could not, or would not, understand me—always treating my advances as part of my teasing and jesting when I first knew her, so that I was glad to get away from her to Miss Mabel Patterson. She received me as quietly as she always did, but had so very little to say to me that I was again at a loss.

"I met a friend of yours while I was absent," she said, at last, and, as if to say something, "a remarkably pleasant and talented gentleman. His father was a distinguished missionary — Mr. Alonzo M'Callum—"

"Oh, Carter," my sister Georgia interrupted us at this moment. "Excuse me, Mabel, but yonder is General M'Neil. He is coming this way, and I will scream if somebody doesn't come to my relief. Go and tell Mr. Clarkson over yonder behind Virginia, or that Dr. Grex, to come and stay with me and talk to me all the evening, or I will wring his neck." In fact, Georgia was in the full gust of one of her moods, and I knew the pertinacity as well as appalling sincerity of General M'Neil's chivalrous ways, and I did as she desired. No sentinel at his post more inflexible than the general in his position by the side of Georgia; a large, square-faced, solemn-visaged man, with a portentous neck-tie, and the aspect of serious business in all his bearing, yet true and pure and good as a little child.

"My dear Miss Quarterman," I heard the stately general say to her when I passed, "as I before observed, not dryad among its oaks, nor naiad dripping from its fountains, is as much so as yourself. How vain and meretricious would be the illusions of poesy were they not made real to us, in rare intervals, by those who image forth in their own person a loveliness beyond futile imagination! As I said previously—" But I lost what followed, laughing as I went, to see how convulsively Georgia clung to good Mr. Clarkson, her whole person turned toward him, and away from the general as much as she dared. For General M'Neil stood so high, there was so much of genuine chivalry in the ceremonious soul of the man, that even Georgia was afraid of him. Every body thought him the most terrible of bores, but nobody ever said so, every one ashamed of himself, or of herself even, for thinking so.

"Alonzo M'Callum!" I said to myself that night, and steadily thereafter. "And so you are the handsome and charming student they have been talking about so long in connection with Mabel! You are, are you? Humph! This is a new feature of the case with a vengeance."

CHAPTER XXIII.

The epidemic for giving parties ran its course in our city, and the violence thereof brought with it a reaction which expressed itself in the very unanimous remark, "Well, deliver me from hearing of parties again!" With the reaction, the former apathetic condition of things returned, and in an intensified degree.

"What is the matter with every body, Mr. Wisehead?" Miss Praxley demanded of me one day, interrupting me dreadfully at my work among boxes and hogsheads in Mr. Patterson's store, while she lingered and talked. "The faces of people are like the ponds near your coal-works," she said— "yes, they are actually green with the scum of stagnation. Can't you induce Mike there to roll a hogshead upon me?"

"I would if he were here to try and chock it," I replied; and Miss Praxley's comely face grew radiant as I said it. I know she was eccentric, but she was too rich to have any work into which she was compelled to pour her energies. Besides, she had not remained unmarried but by reason of some shock which—and no one knew exactly what it was—had arrested her life from its natural channel as wife and mother to overflow, from sheer force and abundance, in a hundred unusual directions. Apart from her trenchant and unwearying spirits, we all liked her very much. True, one would tire a little of her exuberant life occasionally; but, then, when you had time to rest a while, you were glad to hear her quick, light step, and to see once more her bright face with its profusion of little curls and its sparkle of beady black eyes. Except Mabel Patterson and Cosma Adams, Miss Praxley was the person, in connection with another, who kept my hands very full those days; for we are always more anxious about other people's matters when we think they are placed in our hands than we are about our own.

As sure as you live, the malarious stagnation in St. Charles, as well as the trial and failure of party-giving to do more than make it worse, was preparation indispensable to what followed. First came Mrs. Brown's sickness. Good Mrs. Brown! From my earliest memory she had lived, except during our brief sojourn with Uncle Archibald, in our family. Even bearing my father and mother in mind, Mrs. Brown was the most faultless person I ever knew. She arose, to a minute, at five o'clock the year around, and breakfast was on the table when we came down at seven by a process as steady as placed the hand of the clock to that numeral. More so, for we often forgot to wind up the clock, or it got out of repair; and good Mrs. Brown needed, in her unbroken regularity, no help from outside. The Bible and hymn-book were her exclusive reading, attending church and prayer-meetings her sole recreation. She always insisted, in her mild way, upon having a flower-plot in the back yard for nasturtiums, mignonnette, and parsley, and the care of these was her one dissipation. Had you known her slightly you might have called her stupid, but my mother thought her a wonderful woman, a perfect treasure.

"It is because," Georgia explained one day, "she never is sick, you know. I don't think she is so wonderfully good."

"You are never sick, Miss Georgia," I ventured, "and yet you are as uncertain as the four winds. Last week you insisted on having poor little Squashy here, cuddling and hugging and kissing it all day, rocking it to sleep, tossing it about until it was like a big bubble in a whirlwind, and then you suddenly got tired, said it was an odious little wretch, with no more sense than a pat of butter— And now it's Mr. Clarkson—"

"Hush, Carter," my mother said; "we are talking about Mrs. Brown. She is as regular as the automata we read about, yet we all respect and love her for a hidden something in her which none of us understand. Your father says that there is a secret in her silent, methodical, invariable goodness beyond his comprehension. We have come to take her as we do the Sabbath, as a matter of course. Some day we will appreciate her more than we do now." My mother had said about the same thing every time Mrs. Brown was mentioned from my earliest recollection. When the mania for party-giving was dying out, Mrs. Brown's sudden and dangerous illness brought this prophecy clearly to our minds.

Had the spring or summer failed in its coming, it could not have surprised us much more than Mrs. Brown's failure in her orbit. Yes, there she lay in her little room at the head of the top stairs, so very ill that Dr. Grex had been hurried to her at midnight. And only for a few days, alas! What the result was to be soon became but too evident, and Georgia devoted her time to weeping over her own selfishness.

"If I had read to her more," she said:

"she never asked me to; but I know she liked it. And I might have sat with her of nights, oh, so much more than I did, helping her darn socks and mending things. I am so, so sorry!" Then Georgia would make another visit to Mrs. Brown's little room to cry over and kiss her there, and come downstairs again in a stronger remorse; while my mother and Virginia, and the perfectly stupid black girl, Creecy, did all together not half the work which our sick housekeeper had done so quietly and thoroughly. But it was not in Mrs. Brown's nature to lie still, and be waited upon by us. If she could not move, as for so many years, in the even round of her life in this world, there was another in which she could.

Such a change had taken place in Dr. Grex during the last year—for many months had fled since my accident—that it was as much a desire to be with Mrs. Brown as to be with Virginia that caused him to take his turn in watching, generally with Jenny, I am free to say; for the moment Georgia ceased working with the patient, and seated herself at her side at night—she fell fast asleep. "Every thing or nothing" seemed to be a motto rooted into her very nature.

"I never met exactly such a case," Dr. Grex said to Virginia, Georgia sleeping sweetly in the arm-chair between them, during one of those nights. It was said in answer to the story Jenny had told him of the years of devotion, and the yet more singular evenness of temper in the life of our housekeeper.

"It looks very much as if all I've told you of automatism is true. By nature and habit this good woman had become a mere machine. There is nothing of soul in that, heh?" said the doctor.

"I am weary, Dr. Grex, and so are you, of such nonsense," my sister replied. "As if I had not already told you how devotedly she loved us, how deeply we respect and love her. What is there in a clock that loves and is loved? Is there any thing you will have, dear Mrs. Brown?" Virginia added, for the patient at this moment opened her eyes.

"Thank you, Miss Jenny, nothing," she replied; "but I heard you, and I can not sleep."

"Dr. Grex was saying how interested he was in your case," my sister said, after several other matters had been spoken of, to break the long silence which followed.

"Mrs. Quarterman tells me you have found out my ailment, doctor," the sick woman said. The cheek-bones were too high, the features too coarse, the forehead too furrowed, for her to be any thing other than homely; but it was a good, honest face now turned to the physician.

"Of course," he replied. "That is why I can not help you, and why all medicine is more of a humbug even than usual in your case. Cancer of the stomach, heh? You never let any body know? You are a remarkable woman to have hidden it so long. I honor you," he said, with a gentler tone, as she colored, painfully.

"My mother died of it when I was a great girl," she said, slowly, after a while, "in the hospital. Dr. Quarterman took me out of the hospital to his house. All my life since I supposed I would die in the same way. I never spoke of it, but I knew it."

"And that is why you hid your suffering, and why you didn't care to lead any other life?" asked the surgeon; but the woman said nothing.

"Dear Mrs. Brown, papa says you know you can not live," Virginia said, drawing nearer, "and that you are not afraid to die. You are not afraid, are you?"

A smile upon the face of the dying woman was the only reply; a sufficient reply, it was so bright.

"You think about heaven, I suppose," Dr. Grex said, "about its being a splendid place —thrones and harps, and golden apples on the trees, and all that, heh?"

"No, sir," Mrs. Brown answered, with a dignity that rebuked the questioner. "I know I am going to heaven. I believe that I will soon be there, and will live there forever. But it is not often I think about that."

"Well, what is it, then?" asked Dr. Grex. "You are as composed as we are. I never met a happier person, and I know you have had terrible pain, heh?"

"You can not understand me, sir," replied the woman, "nor will you understand it yet, Miss Jenny; not even your father and mother perfectly. It can not be said in words." And then, after a long pause, looking Dr. Grex steadily in the eyes, and as if stating

some fact in regard to household matters, "My Saviour was with me all these years. More and more every year. Never as much as now. I suppose that is why I didn't care for company. Jesus is with me. I will be with him forever. He is all I want." The force of what she said lay, however, in the manner. It was simple statement of fact, and the eyes of the surgeon read in hers the undoubted existence and character of the Person of whom the woman spoke, as one reads of Cæsar or Washington upon the printed page, and, reading, must believe.

"Miss Jenny," the dying woman added, "I've known you from the day you were born. Never marry any man that does not believe in Christ. If he doesn't believe in him, he can not believe in you. No man can love you and laugh at your Saviour."

"I never will," Virginia replied, as quietly.

"No man," the dying woman said, after quite a silence, "can pretend he cares for you when he knows the whole story of who Jesus is, and what Jesus has done for us, and does not love him." And how profound the silence that followed upon these words! It was so deep that it seemed to have power to wake Georgia.

"Oh, you dear, darling Mrs. Brown!" she said, in a gust of affection, in the very act of waking. Kneeling by her side, and putting her arms over her—"I am sorry, sorry you are so sick. I am so ashamed of how cross I have been with you. And I might have staid down in the kitchen with you much more than I did. Perhaps you would have enjoyed having me teach you how to do crochet-work, or something. Please forgive me, and get well. And when I would make such a fuss, you never said any thing but 'Oh, Miss Georgia, please don't;' and you in such pain all the time." And Georgia exhausted herself, and the others too, with alternate caresses and self-reproaches. But it was all over very soon, our good housekeeper dying, one Saturday afternoon, as quietly as she had done every thing else.

It is strange how similar events will come at once, but it was the very week of her funeral that Colonel Archer was shot. It was Scotchy Strange, the billiard-saloon man, who did it. Nothing could be simpler. Colonel Archer was prosecuting attorney; Scotchy had been indicted by the grand jury for keeping a disorderly house. The grand jury had done the same thing at every term for years past, but the man was regarded as a "dangerous customer," and the prosecution had been very languid. Possibly Colonel Archer would not have been so zealous had not a promising youth from his Bible-class been led astray at Scotchy's billiard-hall to the breaking of his mother's heart. In any case, Colonel Archer threw himself at the man along the lines of the law with the terrible energy of the old days when he wrote editorials and made political speeches, of which a fight, more or less according to the code, was the invariable peroration. It was an old story those days, the result. Scotchy Strange posted himself near the door of the post-office one morning; and when Colonel Archer came for his mail, shot him down with a revolver.

No man was more astonished, in all the excited crowd that ran together, than Scotchy Strange, at least, seemed to be.

"Why, gentlemen," he exclaimed, with oath heaped upon oath, "I never dreamed but that the man would *fight!* You see, I challenged him all square and regular. He said he wouldn't go out with me; told my second so; said he had given all that sort of thing up. But, then, that wouldn't prevent his having it out on the street, you know!" The surging crowd cut short the indignant assertions of the murderer, as it hustled him before the nearest justice of the peace.

"Of course, I know," he continued, when he was before that magistrate, and could get his breath, "that the colonel had joined the church. He couldn't fight in the regular way. But who ever supposed he wouldn't have his revolver in case I met him on the streets? He's done it a hundred times, you all know. He wrote me he wouldn't, I know; but the moment I saw his umbrella in his hand, as he came, I knew, or, at least, I supposed for certain, there was a revolver down in it; umbrella shut up, you know. And he *saw* me! Well, may I be—" and no form of oath was left out of the emphasis—"if I ever knew a man, an honorable man like Colonel Archer, do such a trick as that! A high-toned man like him, and have nary a

revolver, not even a Derringer. Cheat a fellow like that!" The man was a huge, grizzle-bearded scoundrel; but somehow his words did not carry conviction with them. The more violent his language, the less force it had. The colonel did not have any weapon, and the man knew it, that was plain.

It was into Dr. Grex's office the dying man was carried. The doctor was off somewhere, as usual; but hard riding upon the part of every man who had a horse convenient, toward all points of the compass at which he was known to have patients, soon brought him. His first surgery on his arrival, so to speak, was to hurry every one out of his office. It was a dense crowd, and it was determined to see or die. The process of ejecting it, on the part of Dr. Grex, was an operation in itself resembling amputation. A dozen voices informed him, as he did so, that the colonel's wife was on a visit out of the State. "I am glad of it," the surgeon said, as the door being shut with the help of his bla Charles, he cut open the clothes of t' wounded man. It required only a look the location of the wound, a little blue s of the size of a pea, and he stepped to t door, unlocked it, held it open only an in or two by force against the pressure of t heaving mass of curiosity without, and sa..., as if he were alluding merely to the probability of rain or not, "Halloo! somebody tell Dr. Quarterman I'd like to see him a moment, if convenient. And Mrs. Quarterman, or some lady. Yes, and one of you look out at the post-office till Colonel Tom Maxwell comes for his mail, and tell him to step in here. No, not one soul of you to save your lives!" he added, as he shut to the door with his shoulder to it, locked it, and turned to his patient.

"Well, doctor, what is it?" Colonel Archer asked, as he lay upon the peculiar bed in the doctor's office, which had held, ah, how many a like result of "a difficulty" before. Dr. Grex passed his hand through his hair, smoothed away his heavy mustache to right and left from his mouth, and said, looking at the colonel, "Yes." Only that. It was in the tone and manner. The questioning eyes of the wounded man closed, his hands made a motion as if they would come together, the lips stirred as if in prayer. It was supplication, but it was all put into a word, a name. Then the eyes opened again as if from refreshing sleep, clear, calm, happy.

"I am so glad I didn't," said the dying man. "Old times were so strong in me, I had them out and loaded. But I left them behind. One of Scotchy's clan was passing; I called him in and showed him. He went ahead, and told the man. Murder, doctor, deliberate murder."

At this moment a score of voices outside informed Dr. Grex, with many a thump upon the door, that Colonel Tom was there. Unlocking the door, the doctor allowed that portly and panting individual to come in, and then shut it to again and locked it, only to unlock it and say, as he confronted the excited crowd:

"What are you men crushing and crowding so here *for?* Heh? The colonel is done for, and Strange did it, because he knew his man hadn't a thing about him. Not one thing. The colonel had sent him full word not ten minutes before. He wouldn't have dared do it, if he had not known there was no risk. What are you fellows doing *here*, heh? A fool might know *this* isn't the place. Bah! And when you all know that scoundrel as well as I do. Heh?" It was said with exceeding contempt.

"You've done it, Doc," the warden of the penitentiary said, as the other shut and locked the door. "Can't say that I object. I wouldn't have him as a boarder, anyway. Lawyers are too smart for that. They would wait till the excitement ran down, then clear him. Of course that is always the way. All right."

"What do you mean? I wanted you to help keep these people out. Stay as long as you can. Charles!" And the surgeon proceeded, with the help of his black boy, to perform his functions.

"After what you have said, they won't trouble *us*," Colonel Maxwell coolly replied. "And you did right." Sure enough, there was a sudden lull in the noise outside. The crowd seemed to have lost on the instant all interest in the wounded man. Gathered in knots, they were talking apart in low but not excited tones. After a while all of them, as by a common impulse, sauntered slowly away, but with their hands in their

pockets, and with a sudden affectation of utter unconcern, which would have astonished any one who did not comprehend American institutions as established in that latitude.

"The jail is strong, you see; at least I suppose so—ain't it? Heh? Besides, the crowd was growing too big to keep out," Dr. Grex replied to a questioning look of his patient, and then added, coldly, "The jail ought to be strong enough to hold them out as well as him in. It *is*, now isn't it?" Colonel Tom, the warden, looked at the surgeon with an inquiring glance, his head a little on one side, merely remarking,

"You think so? He'd be safer down at my place; but all right, I'm willing. Halloo, who is that? Go away, you can't come in here;" this last remark in answer to a tap on the door, and a low request to be let in. With one hand full of instruments, the doctor stepped promptly to the door, unlocked it, and let in a veiled lady.

"Oh, doctor, I am so sorry to hear it," Virginia said; for it was none other than my sister. "My mother has gone with my father to a basket-meeting fifty miles away. Carter has got Mr. Patterson's horse, and has gone for them. Mrs. Archer is away; so is Miss Praxley and Mrs. Houe. I thought I would come—" But she said no more. At a glance from the doctor she laid aside her bonnet, got a basin of water and a sponge, and came and went as if by intuition of what was needed.

"And the very fellows that will head the thing," Colonel Tom meditated aloud, and in continuance, as he leaned against the door, "are men that have done as bad as this often — fellows that have a grudge against Strange; the best of them are loafers who are dying to do something to work off their steam."

"Tom," said the wounded man, in a whisper, "if you have any regard for me, stop it. You can. As you are a Christian, Tom;" then the finger of the surgeon was on his lips.

"Plenty of time, colonel," the warden replied. "They'll not try to do any thing until night. Oh yes, certainly, of course;" and the speaker nodded his head too many times up and down in affirmation to convey the idea of much purpose on his part.

"In about how long, doctor?" whispered the wounded man. Dr. Grex paused, and looked curiously at the questioner. He had seen many a man die. Some had tried to mask themselves, in dying, with brag and bravado which deceived nobody. Some had died game; that is, very much, indeed, as a rat terrier, a bull-dog, or a game chicken would have met its end, in grim defiance. Some had gone from the world whimpering or blaspheming, as the case might be, with miserable fear. Most had died so stupefied with drugs, racked with pain, distracted about their worldly matters, or exasperated with rage, as not really to have faced death at all until after death. He had seen Mrs. Brown die, a few days before, exactly as if she had put on her bonnet and was going to church. But Colonel Archer, as sensible a man and lawyer as we had in St. Charles, was asking about death as your boy asks about Christmas; about its dinner; about that gift you have brought it according to promise in your pocket. The child-like sincerity of his gladness was as striking as its depth and eagerness. In a few words, and as if to have it out of the way, he announced, while Virginia wrote it rapidly down, the disposition of his property, and his last words and wishes about his wife. I have carefully kept from saying a syllable about Mrs. Archer, for there were no children, and I intend saying nothing here. All in the room understood matters about her; all St. Charles did. Notwithstanding this, no husband in his situation could have said much more. His three friends winced a little at some loving words from him in regard to her, as if a dying man should have had stricter reference, even in the midst of his forgiving love, to the truth; and there was a relief upon their part, as upon his, when the colonel had got through with all his arrangements of that kind. Then there was a brotherly warning or two sent to Mr. Patterson by this his fellow-officer in the church. I am afraid Colonel Tom delivered the message a little too concisely, for I am quite sure Mr. Patterson did not like it at all. In fact, he said so at the time; was that much the more perverse in the matters specified afterward to show that, knowing so well that he was right, he was not influenced by

any man, dead any more than living. Next, Colonel Archer sent cordial words to his pastor.

"But remember, now, Miss Virginia," he said, lifting his finger as when addressing a witness in court, and smiling. "Don't forget; remember to tell your father that I would have been glad to have seen him here, but I didn't need him. *He* is with me." He said it with an outer motion of the palms of both hands lying upon his breast, as if to one who filled the room. "He is sufficient. I never knew who He was before!" But the gladness of a child whose mother has just come, after a long absence, can alone express the aspect of the man as he spoke.

"You are going to heaven, you know," Colonel Tom endeavored to phrase it, as if to make up what his friend had left unsaid.

"Why, so I am!" said the dying man, who had not thought of it before. "But it is not that. Just to think—Jesus! I may see him in ten minutes! Jesus himself, Tom! You know how John and the rest were with him in a boat together, walking, and talking at table with each other. To think, Tom, that I will be with him in the same way—with Jesus himself, and forever!" And the slackening palms moved upward.

Had the one spoken of been visibly there, the face of the colonel could not have expressed sincerer gladness. But how account for the awe which fell upon all present? It was a sudden something there at once thrilling and calming, a light that could be felt. Or did his absolute and intense certainty do it all? Even Dr. Grex would, on the instant, have denied that this accounted for it.

"God is the Unknown and the Unknowable, doctor. You materialists are right there," the colonel continued, in a whisper. "But," a pause, during which the gladness of that perfect certainty suffused all the ashy face again, fairly sparkling in the happy eyes, "the Lord Jesus Christ hath brought life and immortality to light. No man, Dr. Grex, no man knoweth the Father, save the Son, and he to whomsoever the Son will reveal him."

A long pause here, no one daring to stir as the wounded man lay, with cheeks growing whiter, eyes dimmer, breath more difficult to draw every moment. Then life comes back to the glazing eyes, he reserves breath and strength for an instant to say it, and—not Thomas more assured than he of the Person to whom he addresses himself— he exclaims, with lifting hands, "My Lord and my God." As with the eagerness of Peter casting himself overboard to get to Christ, the man is gone.

If Colonel Archer had not been so absorbed, he might have urged the rescue of the murderer upon Colonel Tom Maxwell more at length, possibly more effectively. It is to be regretted that the warden should have forgotten it.

"Do you know, Tom, that the mob broke into the jail last night—they took Strange out, and hung him?" Mrs. Tom mentions to her husband at breakfast next morning. "The milk-cart brought the news just now."

"Did?" her husband replies, hardly looking at his small wife in the languor of his curiosity, slowly buttering another hot biscuit. He seems to meditate upon the catastrophe as he finishes his meal. Possibly he is discussing with himself as to whether he should have intervened or no, but all he says at last is, with little apparent relevance, "No, sir, not exactly."

Let it be added that the miasmatic apathy, which the party-giving could not break, was broken now! A revival of religion followed in my father's church, which lasted for months with large results.

CHAPTER XXIV.

As I said before, I can not specify the dates of events as the years rolled by, much less can I detail the innumerable conversations of the various persons of whom I have been speaking. Nor can I record, in fact, one in a million of the countless and ceaseless little events in virtue of which, as by the manifold drops of dew and rain and beams of light, and as by the veering, lulling, blowing of the breezes, our household harvest was being steadily ripened. Once or twice Archibald broke suddenly away from Mr. Clarkson's employ, to be brought back, sometimes by letter, often by my father or myself going after him: oftenest by his own weariness, in the far country into which he had gone, rather of the swine than of the husks which he shared with them. Through it all, so far as Archy was concerned, I persisted in the desperate hope that events would bring about a marriage between Miss Praxley and himself. I was aware that you would laugh at me, and have therefore hidden the truth from you, too, as, during all those years, I hid it from every body else. Nor can I detail how it came about. If all I did and said and managed with Miss Praxley on the one hand, and my brother on the other, toward this result were printed, it would exceed in volume, as it certainly would in delicacy of negotiation, the diplomacy of Talleyrand or any body else. Suffice it to say, that, unknown to a soul besides those two and myself, it was finally understood that, at the earliest opportunity, Archibald and Miss Praxley were to be married as in an instant. The lady was independent of the world in every sense, had met with a terrible disappointment in her life, was eccentric. To say it all in one word, she had finally fallen over the edge of the precipice, was deeply in love with my handsome brother, and that was settled. If it is demanded of me whether I did not help push her over, I decline to say. With Archy the matter was different. Terribly difficult, in fact, for me. I feared his usual unwillingness to do what every one desired him to do. I decline detailing matters, and my conscience perspires to this hour at the memory of all I did toward this result.

Cosma Adams lived so near that I could not help seeing her every day. She had improved in every sense. What is the use of saying that I was far more anxious to have her for my wife than Miss Praxley was, for that lady had really done most toward the education of one with whom I was desperately in love in the old-fashioned, wholesome, hearty way.

"Cosma is not at all smart, Mr. Bigboy," Miss Praxley would say when we tired of talking about that everlasting Archibald. "I know her well. She has not an original idea any more than you. Your genius of a brother, Habersham, would call her dull—a fool, possibly. And she will be as stout some day as Mrs. Governor Hone. She is very comely, and she will make you a domestic wife—"

"Why don't she say so, then?" I demand. "She won't say no, but just as she is about to say yes and be done with it, she gets one of those long, rhapsodical letters from Habby, full of aspirations and sublimities. I can tell she has had a letter the instant I see her."

"One sight of the poor little wretch will cure her," Miss Praxley said. "He will be here next June. He a minister! Your father will have to put a goods box behind his desk for him to stand on, if his face is to be seen above the cushion. Hold your tongue, Mr. Nonsense! It will all be right. Do you know that Miss Mabel's affianced, Mr. Alonzo M'Callum, is coming on to marry her about that time?"

It was absurd the pain her words inflicted. Mr. Patterson and I had gotten on together wonderfully. We did not pretend to the slightest liking for each other, except that we perfectly understood and relied, the one on the other, in business. Our coal speculation was a success in a sober, steady fashion, but by no means up to my wild expectations, for we had heavy losses in connection with it as well as gains. Purely upon business principles, which means that I had told Mr. Patterson I would not stay with him on any other basis, I was junior partner with him now, and, one year with another, we were doing the best business in our line in the city. But he was as unreconciled to my father as ever, and I was no more at his house than was demanded by the proprieties. But I did like Mabel. She was a beautiful brunette, and had been much in society abroad as well as at St. Charles. Very naturally she distrusted her mob of admirers, well aware that they knew her as an heiress. She had read many books; and was vastly superior to her poor mother in the elegance of her housekeeping, I dare say. By force of her determination—for Miss Praxley said she had no marked talent in that line—she had made herself an accomplished musician. I do believe her very experience of her father softened, if it did not conquer, her singular resemblance to him. The gold of the man was extracted in her case from its rough quartz; all there was in him of genuine diamond refined and fittingly set in herself. We had a thousand talks, Mabel and myself, which I have no intention of transcribing. She was all one could desire in a lady friend, but there always was an impediment between us. She was so cultured and refined and well read, and I did not need Miss Praxley, or my sisters, to inform me that I was a very plain fellow, unread, with no opportunity of cultivating my manners—a hard-working, square-dealing commission merchant. She could not but feel her superiority, and, in the kindness of her heart, that prevented her, I suppose, from being wholly at ease with me.

"Ah, Mr. Jesuit, I have seen you and Mabel together," Miss Praxley would say; "first she blushes and then you turn red, and so you are both glad enough to get away from each other. That makes it so comfortable for you and Cosma. She has nothing whatever to say, and so she sits looking down at her hands folded together in her lap, while you are looking at her, devouring her rather, with your eyes; and a pretty hearty meal she makes, Mr. Cannibal, for there is a quantity of her." For Miss Praxley did rattle on, it must be confessed, but she was of such sterling excellence that we made allowance for her.

"And people say that Dr. Grex and Miss Virginia are engaged, heh?" Miss Praxley continued, imitating the abrupt interrogatory exclamation with which that medical man closed every assertion.

"You must ask her," I replied.

"I did," said Miss Praxley, "and she only drew herself up in her queenly way, like Mrs. President, you know, and then ruined it all by coloring slowly and completely from, I suppose, head to foot. So I had to ask Dr. Grex. 'A pretty thing it is,' I said to him, 'for you to be falling in love with the daughter of our pastor—an infidel like you.' He is so independent with others that it is well for him to meet some one as independent as he is. Would you like to know what he said?"

"Why, yes," I replied, with considerable curiosity, for matters had drifted on so steadily, yet imperceptibly, that none of us understood exactly how they had reached the pass they had.

"It was when Mrs. Hone's last baby was threatened with convulsions, and Dr. Grex and myself were waiting down in the parlor for the water to get hot, to bathe it, you know. He said," Miss Praxley continued, "'You are an exceedingly smart lady, Miss Praxley. But did you know every thing from the moment you left school, heh?' 'What do you mean,' said I, getting angry. 'Mean, heh?' he answered; 'look here, Miss Praxley, there isn't a week that I, as a surgeon and physician, don't learn something about the human body that I didn't know before. That is what we call science. Every year or so we come to know something wonderful in this great universe no one ever before dreamed of.' 'But I don't see,' I said, 'what that has to do with your being engaged to Miss Quarterman.' 'Can't you hold on a moment, heh?' he answered. 'Now,' he went on, 'I don't say there is a soul any more than I say there is a God and a Christ; but I do say I've come to see that there is some evidence in that direction, heh? Do you suppose I am such a fool as to think I know every thing, heh?' 'Very good, doctor,' I said, 'and I am glad to hear it; but your first step in science in this direction, depend on it, is your coming to know a woman beyond any thing you had ever met among women before. Instead of one of his angels, God might have used one of his devils, doctor; remember the case of Job.' But he only understood the first part of what I said, and they told him the hot water was ready just then. I have no fear about Dr. Grex," Miss Praxley added; "he is as sincere as he is strong. Besides, he isn't a particle of a coward, and isn't afraid to change his views, whatever people may say—that is, if he *does* change them. He is like me. But it is a shame for your sister to have treated poor

Mr. Clarkson so. It was the very way she treated General M'Neil in his day—he such an orator, too. What are you smiling at?"

But I did not tell Miss Praxley. It was a household instinct with all of our family, that we never talked of home affairs to any one: we had no friend outside quite intimate enough for that. I could not help thinking, as Miss Praxley spoke, of the sudden gust which had caused Georgia to accept, as in the twinkling of an eye, the attentions of good, round, fat, easy Mr. Clarkson. It was partly in recoil from elocutional General M'Neil, largely because she had grown so used to seeing Mr. Clarkson in our parlor, that he was to her somewhat as was Squashy Hone; a somebody she could expend her overflowing energy upon, tease, command to go, as well as come; a soft and compliant body whom she could whirl about as a gust does a leaf, as a kitten does a ball—could amuse herself with and get heartily tired of, and return to again to caress or to scold, as she happened to be in the mood. However, although Mr. Clarkson never beamed out, amazed at his good fortune, quite so brightly before in his life, he did so with secret apprehension. Well did he know how uncertain a mistress he had; no telling what the event would be. I ought to add that I have not, I believe, recorded a syllable said by Mr. Clarkson; but it is because I can not, for my life, remember one to record. He was like Cosma in that; but, then, Cosma was so beautiful and child-like, simple and—and— Never mind.

With June, Habersham came home. He had made rapid work with his studies, and was actually a minister duly licensed. They all told him at home that he had grown; but I could not see it. Except that he had a more scholarly appearance, and that there was the promise of a beard upon his face. I saw but little change. He had taken the highest grade since Aaron Burr, sure enough, and there was an aspect in him of authority, of distinction, as well as of reserve by reason of having a good deal *in* reserve. He came about the middle of the week. We were all proud of his reputation, his very diminutiveness making his genius more wonderful, and I was eager to have him go out into St. Charles with me. But no, he wouldn't and didn't. He excused himself when they called, even to Cosma Adams and Miss Praxley. It was plain that his morbidly unsocial nature had intensified with the monastic course he had gone through in college. I would have felt badly about it; but then, you know, it was Habby, and we had classed him off to himself from his birth.

Sabbath came. I never saw my father and mother in such a state of nervous anxiety in my life before; Virginia, too. As to Georgia, she refused to go to church, and staid at home to weep, from sheer excitement; Habersham, as steely cold and set in his aspect as if carved of marble, for, by appointment, he was to preach for my father. I do believe my father would have broken down during the preliminary services in his emotion, but that he was afraid of throwing Habersham out. The edifice was crowded, and Habby had told us, in answer to inquiries, and somewhat curtly, that he should take no MS. whatever into the pulpit. Heaven alone knows the anguish of anxiety we all endured when he stood, at last, behind the cushion of the pulpit and announced his text. He was so small, so deadly pale, that failure, and ridiculous failure, seemed a certainty; and my anxiety was suddenly transferred to my mother as I sat beside her.

I can not understand, and therefore can not describe, the sermon; in this sense I mean, that it was upon one of the most abstruse points in theology. "What in the name of Heaven *can* you do with that subject?" I thought, as he began. Oh, Habby, Habby, you are so small, and it is so great. And there he stood, no Bible even before him upon the cushion, the audience, as on a jury, in front of him, for both the Legislature and the Supreme Court were in session, and the picked men from each were present. The face of my brother, pale, stern, set, resolved as for battle, is before me now. In low tones he stated his proposition, his voice growing clearer, his face more luminous as he proceeded. His sermon was thought—pure, clear, irresistible thought—from beginning to end. Deep, closely packed, profound, yet transparently evident thought; yes, the only word is "thought." You could not help listening. There was the hard stretch of intellect aroused, and compelled by its own

laws to follow—to follow with such a sense of satisfaction as only the intellect can enjoy when it is both aroused and required to exert itself, and satisfied to the utmost. I glanced at my mother, and saw how entirely she had ceased from all anxiety, and was reposing as upon the breathless satisfaction of all around her. It was like listening to a mathematical demonstration; a feeling in all that the speaker could no more fail than a stone hurled from the hand can fail from its due curve, or a planet from its orbit. There was the flash of illustration fast and faster toward the close; but any description of the sermon is impossible. The deep breath drawn by all as he stood aside for my father to close with prayer was of satisfaction — there is no other word — as after a deep draught to the thirsty, except that here it was the intellect that had been satisfied. How they gathered around my father and mother in congratulation as soon as the benediction was pronounced!—judges, legislators—even the dullest knowing that the sermon was wonderful beyond their comprehension. My father disengaged himself abruptly, and hurried to his study without a word when we got home, and so did Habersham to his room. There are things which silence alone can express; and how miserably selfish I was! I feel constrained to put it on record. In the midst of my pride in Habby there ran the under-tone, "Yes, he is a genius; but you are an ass, a lout, a clown, an unlettered, uneducated drudge, always and forever a dunce." The one whisper of consolation was, "Well, thank God if, by being a dunce, I have been able to help educate Habby."

The church had been crowded in the morning; it was packed at night on the mere hope that my brother would preach, for no notice had been given. I know you think I exaggerate, and therefore I will not describe the effort at night. It related to a more practical and emotional aspect of religion. The line of thought was as clear as in the morning; but now it was but as the thread upon which were strung jewels of fancy too, words that touched the fountain of tears, and of all Christian hope and gladness. It was eloquence. I do not comprehend wherein lay the electric condition of the audience — a condition created by the very presence of the speaker, a condition of highly charged expectation which confidently anticipated as well as responded instantly to the words of my brother, his most beautiful and touching sentences coming to the ear as if that very idea had been the instant before thought of by the hearer himself. If I were to indite many pages, I could merely say that it was so much beyond the common, that I had a feeling almost of fear for my father himself when his sermons of next Sunday should be contrasted with it. But I do not attempt to describe Habby's sermons. I will stop, or I will never stop! But I call Heaven to witness that I surrendered her on the instant! Heaven knows I did love her in my slow, old-fashioned way, and heartily. And I had dreaded it all along. She did not understand Habby's letters, but they had the nameless power over her which his words from the pulpit had over even the dullest. I saw her listening with a perplexed yet intense interest during the morning, admiring and trying to follow. At night she could and did understand. Governor Houe's pew was next to ours, and there she sat, her head thrown back, her color coming and going, her large eyes fastened upon the speaker. I smiled bitterly, and thought of pictures I had seen of an innocent rabbit under the fascination of a serpent. He went home with her from church. I understood it perfectly. She was his adoring slave, the very simplicity of her character causing her merely to adore the more she could not understand. I knew her too well not to feel that. No need of my waiting to know what her answer would be when he should ask her to be his wife.

"My dear boy," my mother said to me that night in my room, "I am sorry for you; but it is better as it is. We all love you, oh, how much! Your brother is a genius; but I fear he will be a morbid, nervous, unhappy man as long as he lives."

"An angel in the pulpit, and an oyster out of it," I replied, "he will be the most unsocial of men. The fire flashes out so intensely in the pulpit that it leaves him like a heap of ashes afterward;" for I did feel bitterly. "Do you know," I added, "that his sermon is never written out at all until after it is preached? He told me so himself, and he gives half the week following to it. A beautiful pastor he will make!" But, for all that, I did love my brother, and was proud of his great intellect.

"Cosma," my mother continued, "is the very opposite of Habersham, strong and simple. She will worship him. And he has a thousand times more need of her than she has of him. It is always so with those talented men. Look at Governor Houe. The more brilliant a man is, the more necessary it is that he should have a fool for a wife!"

I loudly and properly resented this, and my mother was compelled to say what she otherwise would not have said.

"Carter," she added, at last, "you have been doing a wrong, a cruel wrong, to Mabel Patterson. No, sir, I *will* speak;" my mother interrupted me in my outcries, so to speak, with her old authority. "Mabel began to like you in a foolish school-girl fashion from the time you were children together. How wonderfully she is like her father! When an idea once enters her mind, a liking or an aversion, it becomes part of her nature. She might have outgrown her liking for you had you not come back from school, and been hurt in shielding her from harm that day. And your long stay there, when hurt, increased her interest. She knows, too, all your self-sacrifice in educating Habersham. Not a word; we all know about that. She has refused many excellent offers, although she knows of your foolish fancy for Cosma Adams. She loves you, Carter; she loves you with the silent, determined affection of a woman of her character. None of us liked Mabel. But her love for you is very deep. It is victorious even over your indifference to her; which could be the case with no woman not constituted as she is. No wonder, then, that her love is victorious over herself. That is, it has broken down, conquered, changed in her all that was hateful in her, inherited from her father before her. It has made her humble and patient and gentle. What a wonderful way God has of working!" my dear mother added, with tears in her eyes.

"Habersham got his eloquence from you," I said, somewhat savagely—"his imagination and all;" for there was a power, through my self-conceit of course, in what my mother had said.

"The most powerful eloquence," my mother replied, "lies in saying what is true. Cosma is beautiful; but oh, Carter! she is very stupid. Pardon me, dear; but that makes her the very wife for Habby. And Mabel is very clever—"

"Which makes her the very wife for me!" I interrupted.

"Yes, Carter," my mother said, gently. "You have a common sense which is more valuable than talent. Habersham's talent is largely the result of his suffering, of the intense purpose aroused in him to make up in that way for his deformity; and it is through her mortification in regard to you, Carter, that Mabel has grown to be as gentle and good as she is refined and cultivated. She is vastly superior, Carter, to Cosma; superior in every way."

"It shows how little you know, my dear mother," I said, at last. "Mabel Patterson cares not a cent for me. She never has any thing to say to me. Besides, I happen to know that she is engaged to be married to that detestable M'Callum, of whom I can not speak to you, except that he is the filthiest human being, through and through his very intellect and soul, too, that you can imagine!"

We had a good deal more conversation that night, and, strange to say, my father never called from his room once entreating my mother to come. But I understood why.

The next two Sabbaths, Habby was preaching in a country town fifty miles away, with a view to a settlement. The third Sabbath he preached for us at night, the house crowded to its utmost. By this time he had become somewhat at home with the building and the audience, and his discourse was a success surpassing any thing before. But, alas!—there is sure to be a "but," sooner or later. In this case it happened on this wise, by the interposition of Major Hampton.

I fully intended to say a good deal more about the major; but he has been shamefully crowded out of my narrative, beyond the smallest mention now and then. A more devoted Christian never lived, only he *would* talk in prayer-meeting. The sermons of the Sabbath before were always the theme of his remark, and the major, a tall, thin, red-featured man, passed, when once on his feet in meeting, and under the impulse of the subject in hand, altogether beyond the verge of good taste, both in the warmth and length of his remarks. It was a dreadful trial to my father, and I believe it often restrained him in the pulpit, lest the major should get too much impulse for next Wednesday night's prayer-meeting. "And he is such a good man—he means so well," my father said.

This explains the catastrophe the night my brother preached. Under his impassioned eloquence the congregation listened and thrilled as it never had before. There were tears, and breath deeply drawn; the people leaning forward to catch the lowest tones of the speaker, who was so completely master of them, because, with not a scrap of paper before him, he was master of himself. Climax followed upon climax, until, in fullest culmination of his appeal, my brother stood in the pulpit as if he had grown into a giant, one hand held aloft during the deep pause. In that critical instant Major Hampton, swept beyond his own control under the stress of the theme, suddenly arose from his pew under the pulpit, saying:

"Yes, dear brother, yes, yes! It is indeed so! And"—facing toward the congregation, lifting both hands above his head—"I can no longer sit still. I must add my testimony. Our dear brother is right! Oh, let me entreat you—" As he said it, there was a change, as sudden as it was complete, from the sublime to the ridiculous, from pathos to the deepest bathos. An instant of amazement, and then the heads of the people went down, like a wheat-field before a gust of wind, upon the pews before them as they sat in amusement, the more violent because it was suppressed. The older members of the church, the officers and the like, were an exception: they proved themselves to be the pillars of the church by sitting bolt upright, white and rigid with indignation. Major Hampton said very little at last. He became confused, and then subsided into his seat as by the giving-way of the congregation from under him. "I was as much astonished," he vehemently explained afterward, "to find myself speaking as any body there. It was very wrong. Don't you suppose I know that as well as you? but I was swept away! I had no more *intention*—"

My father was equal to the occasion. As Habby sunk back into his seat, he arose and continued the line of the preacher's remarks —but to God, not man—in a prayer which silenced all mirth, and, except in the cases of a tittering few in the congregation, deepened as well as closed all that my brother had intended to say.

I glanced at Cosma Adams in the supreme absurdity of the reaction which ensued upon the major's getting up. Her eyes were fastened upon poor Habby as he stood, his hand still lifted up, ghastly pale. The admiration in her child-like face had changed into the adoration of pitying love!

CHAPTER XXV.

EVEN the century-plant flowers at last, and so the long-continued and, in a sense, laborious affair between Archibald and Miss Praxley culminated finally one Friday night in the early fall. I think my mother had vague suspicions all along in reference to it, but she said nothing; the whole thing was too absurd. Certainly, no person in the world beyond the parties concerned and myself knew any thing about it. We were so well acquainted with my brother's perversity of character that, unless we could be sure of the violent opposition of all to the match, we dared not let it be known. The least concurrence on the part of others would be certain to shake, at least, the wavering purpose of the lover. It was the only Jesuitical scheming I was ever engaged in, so far as I remember, during my life, and I can say unhesitatingly that it was admirably arranged.

Miss Praxley had been spending some weeks at her plantation, a dozen miles out of St. Charles, with the widowed aunt who lived there, and who was mistress thereof, in the owner's absence. The old minister employed by Miss Praxley to preach to her negroes, and who would be on the spot to marry the couple, lived near by, and was never away from home. Therefore, at six o'clock P.M. exactly, I was at our own door in my buggy to drive Archy out, and by eight o'clock that night the couple would be married, and off the next morning on a bridal trip until St. Charles could have exhausted its astonishment. A more excellent match could not be made. Miss Praxley was very little the senior of my brother, was comely enough for any body, and would make a devoted wife of herself, and a substantial and settled husband of him.

"My finding that coal-mine is not to be compared to it," I said to myself as I tied my horse, and went in. "That was mere accident, while this is wisdom and skillful diplomacy."

My mother met me in the hall. In all my life I had never done, said, thought, felt even the least thing that this mother of mine had not found out. I began to whistle as I went upstairs; but she looked at me as I passed, merely looked! Beyond what is herein recorded, no conversation had ever passed between her and myself on this subject. The deadliest poisons have, Dr. Grex says, the most powerful smell, and I ceased whistling as I neared Archy's door. It seemed as if there exhaled an aroma, a pervasive poison, from something in his room before I turned the knob of the door. There was no Archibald in the room, and the accursed source of the disheartening influence which I had felt vaguely as I drove up to the house, in fact, lay upon his table in a note addressed to me. How very little poison it takes to kill! Merely these words, in Archy's beautiful hand, dated that noon:

"DEAR CARTER,—I am sorry to disappoint you, especially as you, and, I suppose, all the family, are so *exceedingly* eager for it. Hand the inclosed letter to the lady. But I can not, and I will not! And I am gone. Your affectionate brother, ARCHIBALD."

My mother was still in the hall as I stumbled down-stairs, but neither of us said one word. I found myself driving out of St. Charles, and up and down the red and gullied road leading to Miss Praxley's planta-tion, in a mechanical way. I do not know what I thought or felt, except that my first and most painful reflection, of course, was for the lady. Next to that, I said to myself, "What an excellent thing it would be, Master Carter, if some stout overseer or other could take a rawhide to you for an hour or two!" Strangely enough, I could not think about Archibald at all; he hardly entered my mind. The fault was mine in supposing that he would ever act in any other way than he had always acted, and always would act: it was his nature. I was at Miss Praxley's place before I knew it.

With the energy of one who, having a desperate thing to do, does it as rapidly as possible, I fastened my horse, and went in. Now, I can take oath that Miss Praxley could not have known, it was so dark when I drove up, that I was alone; yet, as I was keeping off the yelping dogs in the front yard, with my whip, a bright little yellow boy ran out of the house and, coming close up to me, said in the parrot-like way in which those smart shavers are taught to repeat things, "She says, no—she can't see you, and she won't do it. Please go."

I did go. I have no memory of any incident of my miserable drive back through the night, except of my tearing up the two notes left by my brother, the one to me and the other to the lady, and scattering them in the mire. Really, it was my own brother whom I thus tore to atoms, and cast away from me. I remember this more especially as I had a little fear afterward lest her woman's quick eye should recognize the fragments, and was so glad, when it set in to rain, as I rode, that the bits of paper would thus be more certainly grimed into the mire.

Miss Praxley went off upon a visit to some friend of her school-days soon after; and they do say, since her return, that she is to be married to General M'Neil. Certainly, the general is paying the most elaborate and oratorical addresses to her. He will make a better husband by far than Archibald Quarterman could ever have been.

Let me merely add that I had sense enough not to get out a license in advance, knowing I could stretch the law enough to get it after the ceremony had been perform-ed, so that the matter was not made public. Yet this one thing I do know, that, had my brother been with me that night, they would surely have been married! As to Archibald, we did not hear from him until long after; but it is a thoroughly disagreeable subject to me, and I will say no more about it. Perhaps I should have left this brother of mine out of my story altogether.

It is a great relief to turn away from him to Virginia. It pleased our Maker to allow Eve to be the means of vast mischief, in a spiritual sense, as well in many an other sense, to Adam; but I shrink from attempting to detail the way, even if I could, in which this daughter of Eve was allowed to influence Dr. Grex for good. A man of strong, independent, somewhat violent character, thoroughly intrenched in his opinions, his affection for Jenny was much more sudden and energetic by far than was the alteration of his views. She was undoubtedly the means. It pleases Heaven to win some hearts by the power of a simple hymn sweetly sung, though it be by a child; and why not by my sister in the instance of this man whom nothing else, apparently, would ever otherwise have influenced? It was not by her reasoning, nor chiefly by her beautiful life, so evidently made beautiful by her Christian training and character. There was a power in her beyond even that.

"I do not pretend to be a Christian, you know," the doctor explained to my father and mother, when matters were finally arranged. "I hope I may be some day. I don't know. You will not understand me, Dr. Quarterman, for neither of us has time to go into it; but what scientific men are in search of to-day is not structure-organization. By the help of the microscope we have pretty much got through with all that. It is what is behind organization—it is Life, Force—that we want to get at now, heh? If any man has tried to ferret out matters, I have, in my way, you see. Well, we outsiders have plenty of the life and force which lie in doubting. We are tremendously strong in denying. Now, God and the soul do, as science says, belong to the realm of the unknown and the unknowable. What we can not discover, bless you, we can not comprehend. If there be a universe outside the small circle in range of our senses, it must be grasped by faith, heh? I am compelled to acknowledge that those who refuse belief, in some form, to the supernatural, are an almost inappreciable few. Now, I find that you people have a faith which is even more positive, vigorous, certain, than are to us hearing and sight, let alone reasoning. There is a larger measure of force, of life —do you understand?—in your assertion than there is in our denial. We are like night and winter: the absence merely, these are, you know, of day and summer. Darkness and falsehood are merely the absences of light and truth—are negations, nothings. Now, we non-believers do belong to that party in this, at least, that, so far as the supernatural is concerned, we do nothing on earth beyond saying No! The devil, you have read, is the spirit that denies, heh? Very well. Now, we infidels are like a swamp full of frogs. We all croak eternally the same monotonous and never-ending No, no, no! We haven't a syllable to sing or say beyond that; we use up our energies in that line. I do not know that you believers are right, mind! But there is the positive energy of nature on your side, anyhow. You have force with you as in the chemical combinations; life, as in the trees; and animals, and men, and women. You are in closer keeping with nature, heh? Yes, and in greatest identity with nature exactly where I, for one, have given up trying to find it out, at the precise focus where its glory, and beauty, and power, *and* mystery are—I mean at its life. There is an amazing amount of hypocrisy and rascality among Christians; yet, upon the whole, the largest amount of light and heat is on your side; that is, you are more certain than we are, are warmer in your belief—more life and force, more *nature*, heh?"

"I do see," my father said, with his usual enthusiasm. "Life and force, in their largest manifestations, are with the Church of God. Why, sir, we are doing the work of the world. We are another and higher nature to men in the mere matters of love and labor and light. The power, as of gravitation, the blooming of flowers, the blowing of winds, the ripening of harvests, is with us—yes, and the thunder of storms, too; for

I believe in fear in religion as well as love. It is because the God of nature is also the God of revelation. Thank you for your suggestions. I will prepare a sermon this very week on it," said my father. "Yes," he added, "and I've got my text: 'I am come that ye might have life, and that ye might have it more abundantly.' It is all in Christ, Dr. Grex; in HIM is life." And, forgetting all about Virginia, my father easily and joyfully went off into that theme which was the thought of his existence—Jesus Christ; his person, power, and victorious love.

Human love and religion are intermingled everywhere, as in this instance; and why not so record them? Virginia won the rude surgeon at once to herself, and to her belief, by being simply the most beautiful part of nature he had ever known. He had to believe in her and in her belief as he did in a rose, or a bird, or a star. In her serene way, she loved the doctor, strong and abrupt as he was, very sincerely. I am obliged to add here that she was scandalized at the way Georgia went on in reference to good Mr. Clarkson.

"It is disgraceful," she said to us one night, in that last loitering moment after company was gone, and before we went off, unwillingly, to bed, "positively disgraceful, the way in which Georgia acts. Last week she refused to walk with Mr. Clarkson; turned her back upon him when he tried to speak to her at the piano; played loud and louder; and sung on without stopping when he bid her good-evening. And here to-night—why, even Dr. Grex was astonished. She rumpled Mr. Clarkson's hair, put his new hat on the sofa so that he sat down with all his weight on it, laughed at him, whirled him about! It is shameful. You are too old, Georgia, and too large. Next, I suppose," said Virginia, "you will be throwing your arms around him in the parlor, and saying, 'Oh, you dear, darling dumpling!' as you do, in your paroxysms, to Squashy. And, instead of resenting it, as a man ought, there he sat, his hair and cravat all awry, his face glowing like a new moon, one smile all over. Shame, Georgia! The next time I will get up and leave the room. That you should be my twin sister, too!"

"I am sure I'm an angel, compared to

Cosma Adams," insisted Georgia. "Look at the way she has treated Carter, here. If he were not so old, and solid, and grave, he would have done something desperate. But, oh, wouldn't it be the funniest sight?—I mean, to see Habby over there this moment, at Governor Hone's. As sure as you live, Cosma takes him on her knee, and trots him up and down. No; she is too much afraid of him. He may be talented in some things, but he isn't very bright in others, to fall in love with a girl like her! It's like the halo about the pictures of saints, all the nonsense they think of each other. To her, Habby is a giant ten feet high, and he thinks, because she listens so to him, that she is the most intelligent as well as beautiful woman living. Did you know, Carter," Georgia rattled on, "that Mabel is to be married soon? I saw her lover at church. You remember, we met him that Sunday at your school. How very handsome he is!" But, while my sister went into a description of his curly hair and regular features and beautiful eyes, I was thinking of where and how I had met him last!

Dr. Grex is right. There is omnipotent force in religion—and force in religion precisely where we are most interested in force personally, in Providence, for instance. Alonzo M'Callum professed to have become a Christian. To speak sincerely, a saintlier youth than he, in outer appearance, never existed.

Now, I had not known, all these years of my infatuation in regard to Cosma Adams, how sincere and strong had been my estimation, my friendship, for Mabel Patterson—not love, friendship. To speak the simple fact, I suppose it is a necessity to some of us that we must love somebody. Sore as I was from my loss of Cosma, although my heart slowly turned toward Mabel more than to any other of her sex, I am satisfied it was the singular Providence of which I am about to speak that alone brought about the result. Nothing could seem slighter or more accidental.

I had a bad habit of walking a good deal of nights, after that matter in reference to Cosma, and of walking long and fast. I am ashamed to say it, but I had to tire myself out in order to get any sleep just then. The habit remained, even after I was beginning to get over my loss. One very dark night, when I was tearing along the sidewalk, I ran violently against a man. Strange to say, it was at the very spot where I had thrown the legislator into the gutter when he attempted to kiss little Mabel Patterson so long ago. It was too dark for the man to know me, especially as I said nothing. But he did speak with a vengeance. As I struck him he broke into a fury of cursing, not ordinary swearing. It was as if I had touched a vessel of foulest contents, and which was brimmed to overflowing, there were such readiness, fullness, force, in the profanity—so much of moral meaning and deepest intention in the damnation which he invoked upon me. I had heard the tones, and the very formula of words, too often before; and in the pitchy darkness of that moment I saw that Alonzo M'Callum was the same man, only grown older in vileness that he was when I knew him before. I had just then to hate some one, and it couldn't well be Habersham, since he was my brother, and was so small; and I do suppose that I was glad to have this object to loathe, especially as it had been the habit of years, where he was concerned. And how I hated him—a leper, and a leper so attractive in outer appearance, and making himself even more as an angel of light in assuming the garb of religion! I did, and do, abhor him with all the energy I possess.

There was but one thing to do after that discovery of mine. The deliberate consideration of a week left me more resolved to do what my first impulse had prompted. In most matters first, and not second, thoughts are best. One Thursday evening, I am not ashamed to say, I committed myself to the hands of a certain negro barber of my acquaintance, with grave charges as to my hair and beard. He felt that I intrusted myself seriously into his possession, and assumed the trust as a surgeon would have done that of a patient whose case was very grave indeed. He kept me under his careful manipulation for an hour. I did not examine the result in his offered mirror, but took his word for it, and turned my steps to Mr. Patterson's house. Mabel was at home, and received me as usual. I remember a peculiar kind of collar she wore, as well as a species of apron, impressing somehow upon my mind how wifely she seemed; but she was very grave, and had so little to say that I was thrown dreadfully upon myself. With Cosma Adams I always had been; but when with her I had always an abundance to say, with plenty of jest and laughter. I sat looking at Mabel, her eyes resting upon the chess-board, for we played chess as from sheer necessity whenever I called; and, miserable player that I was, to-night she was even worse. She seemed to me to be pale, dispirited, her eyes very rarely lifted to mine—such determined eyes, too. The air felt dreadfully close. I thought I should suffocate. I had not said a word beyond ordinary conversation, but she seemed to draw her breath as with difficulty, and I fancied she grew paler every moment. I understand nothing about sentiment; what I do understand is business—the direct way, I mean, in which two people talk or write when it is a question of how many cents it is that are to be given or taken on a consignment, say, of cotton.

"Miss Mabel," I said. Nothing but that, yet she looked up, startled and coloring.

"Miss Mabel," I said, "you know what a plain sort of a fellow I am. I do not understand how to talk. You know all about Cosma Adams and myself, and you know us both better than two such people as Cosma and I know ourselves."

"What do you mean, Mr. Quarterman?" she replied, with a sort of patient weariness in her eyes as she looked timidly at me, and then let them fall again on the board.

There was an indescribable something in her at the moment that reminded me of my mother, that made her seem so much older than myself, although I knew her to be so much younger; a something that made me feel how much deeper, truer, and superior in every sense she was to me.

"Miss Mabel," I began again, "I wanted to tell you that I did have what I thought was a genuine affection for Cosma. She was so much like me, you know; we were both so stupid and comfortable together. But—" and, to my own astonishment, I was seized with a trembling from head to foot as if I had the ague. I must have blushed and turned pale, and seemed the most pitiable fool living. What a pity it was that this determined lady could not have been cool and steady and strong as a woman so much my superior in culture and refinement, society, music, education, and every thing else should have been! But she was nothing of what the crisis demanded at all. She looked up like a frightened animal, then looked down, then she tried to rise.

I do not understand it any more than I do any of the other mysteries, but I know that the chess-table was upset, and we stood side by side, her head upon my shoulder, weeping violently, and as if she would never cease, while, with my arm around her, I was telling her, over and over again, that I loved her as I had never before dreamed that a man could love. It was like the sudden bursting forth of a fountain of which she had dreamed as little as I had myself. I never was more sincere in my life, but I was almost as much astonished as Mabel. As to my affection for Cosma, it seemed an infantile nonsense which had happened five hundred years before. How superior Mabel was to her! But not more so than was my love now to any thing I had ever before known, and I felt as if it had lasted a thousand years, yet was only beginning.

We had the happiest hour, after Mabel had returned to the room from bathing her face, re-arranging her hair and herself generally, that the man, at least, who writes these lines ever imagined. We both talked at once, and we both said a vast deal, having so many centuries of arrears to talk up. Yet, strange to say, I was glad when the door-bell rang. I had been eager from the first moment to go home and tell my mother.

As I went out I met Alonzo M'Callum in the hall. As I have said before, he certainly was the saintliest-looking as well as the handsomest of men. With a meanness which was part of my insanity, I shook him cordially by the hand as I went out—I was so glad he was going in, so glad and proud to know that Mabel had ample strength for the interview with him that was to follow. Let me add that the man of whom I speak abandoned, soon after, all pretense of religion, and became— But I prefer to say no more about him.

My walk home was as if into higher and rarer and more intoxicating realms of the atmosphere at every step. Nicer people take things more quietly; but when a rough, somewhat commonplace person like myself becomes deranged as I did, it is with a crash terrible to see on the side of the spectators, but not more so than it was terrible to feel on my part. I was alarmed at my own ex-citement. Before seeing my mother even, I hastened to Habersham's room, and found him sleeping profoundly. After thoroughly waking him, I explained to him, most heartily, in the midst of his dreadful irritation thereat, that I only did it to assure him how proud I was, how proud we all were, of him, but that I myself loved him—which was the fact—more than he was or could be loved by any other of the family. I never knew him to be quite so cross, nor quite so energetic in his irritation. But what did I care? As I got to my room, I heard my mother saying, as she came to me—and her voice never sounded so sweetly to me before—

"Why, Carter, what is the matter?"

There was no preface to this book: and why, when you know as well as I do what followed, should there be any formal conclusion? During the tremendous preparations which took place for the weddings at our house, how deeply did we miss good Mrs. Brown! There was a general feeling, which, however, no one but Georgia would have expressed.

"I do believe," that young lady said, as she stood, with garments tucked up, in the kitchen, beating eggs with energy for the icing of the cakes, "that Mrs. Brown would leave heaven, and take back all her terrible pain she bore so long, to be with us to-day, and help about the cakes. What a bother it is! I will be so glad, for one, when the fuss is all over. Look at the way Carter is carrying on! and he used to be so sober, too. If there is a thing I do hate, it is whirlwind and confusion."

"Habersham insists," Virginia (who was helping the black cook with the fruit-cake) remarked, "upon having his wedding over and done with first; but how the guests are to eat one supper over there at Governor Hone's, and then come over here and eat another the same night after we are married, I do not see."

"We can rely on Mr. Clemming to do his full duty on both occasions," Georgia suggested. "Is it not good in poor Carter to consent to put off his wedding until the week after?" she added.

May I add here that it was not so good in me at all? My experience is that the surest as well as the sweetest service one can do himself is found in serving others. Really, I only began my life where this book ends, as I trust to show hereafter. Yet if it must be converged up to this point into a moral, let it lie in that.

"Anyway," Georgia continued, I'm glad Habby takes Cosma off to the country church that called him. It is a shame to say it, but they are such a funny couple: he ought never to come down out of the pulpit—never. But I am so glad Mabel is to be our sister. I can remember, Virginia, when you did not like her. But she is so changed. gave her such a good hugging and kissing yesterday that Carter had to beg me to let her alone, if I was to leave any of her for him. I do wonder," she added, "what text father will preach from on that Sunday between the weddings? The marriage in Cana, I suppose."

My mother came in at this moment, and all knew by the sadness of her eyes that she was thinking about Archibald, who had not written since he had left.

"I wish I had your father's faith, children," she said; "about Archibald, I mean. He says that the same heavenly Hand which guides the planets in their regular orbits will take care of the comets also. He leaves your poor brother in God's keeping, and is happy. You were talking about his sermon? No, it is not about Cana at all; your father told me about it last night, and I never knew him to be more interested in a sermon. The text is, 'He hath done all things well.'"

THE END.

www.ingramcontent.com/pod-product-compliance
Lightning Source LLC
Chambersburg PA
CBHW021127020726
47500CB00003B/961